FLAWED

FLAWED

CECELIA AHERN

FEIWEL AND FRIENDS
NEW YORK

A FEIWEL AND FRIENDS BOOK
An Imprint of Macmillan

Library of Congress Cataloging-in-Publication Data
Ahern, Cecelia, 1981–
  Flawed / Cecelia Ahern.—First edition.
    pages cm
  Summary: "In a future society where 'flawed' people who have committed crimes are branded with an F, a young girl takes a stand"—Provided by publisher.
   ISBN 978-1-250-07411-9 (hardback)—ISBN 978-1-250-08024-0 (e-book)
  [1. Science fiction. 2. Prejudices—Fiction.   3. Governnment, Resistance to—Fiction.] I. Title.
  PZ7.1.A33Fl 2016   [Fic]—dc23   2015013379

Our books may be purchased in bulk for promotional, educational, or business use. Please contact your local bookseller or the Macmillan Corporate and Premium Sales Department at (800) 221-7945 ext. 5442 or by e-mail at MacmillanSpecialMarkets@macmillan.com.

Book design by Liz Dresner

Feiwel and Friends logo designed by Filomena Tuosto

First Edition—2016

ISBN 978-1-250-07411-9 (Feiwel and Friends hardcover)
10 9 8 7 6 5 4 3 2 1

ISBN 978-1-250-09829-0 (international paperback)
10 9 8 7 6 5 4 3 2 1

fiercereads.com

For you, Dad

FLAWED: faulty, defective, imperfect, blemished, damaged, distorted, unsound, weak, deficient, incomplete, invalid; (of a person) having a weakness in character.

ONE

I AM A girl of definitions, of logic, of black and white.
Remember this.

TWO

NEVER TRUST A man who sits, uninvited, at the head of the table in another man's home.

Not my words. They were the words of my granddad, Cornelius, who, as a result of saying them, landed himself the farthest away from this table, and he won't be welcome back anytime soon. It's not necessarily what he said that was the problem; it was the person he said it about: Judge Crevan, one of the most powerful men in the country, who is once again, despite my granddad's comment last year, sitting at the head of our dining table for our annual Earth Day gathering.

Dad returned from the kitchen with a fresh bottle of red wine to find his usual place taken. I could see he was put out by it, but as it was Judge Crevan, Dad merely stalled in his tracks, jiggled the wine opener in his hand a bit while thinking about what to do, then worked his way around the table to sit beside Mom at the other end, where Judge Crevan should have sat. I can tell Mom is nervous. I can tell this because she is more perfect than ever. She doesn't have a hair out of place on her perfectly groomed head, her blond locks twisted elaborately into a chignon that only she could do herself, having had to dislocate both shoulders to reach around to the back of her head. Her skin is porcelain, as though she glows, as though she is the purest form of anything. Her makeup is immaculate, her cornflower-blue lace dress a perfect match for her blue eyes, her arms perfectly toned.

In truth, my mom looks this beautiful to most people every day as a model in high demand. Despite having the three of us, her body is as perfect as it always was, though I suspect—I know—like most people she has had help in maintaining this. The only way you can know that Mom is having a bad day or week is when she arrives home with plumper cheeks, fuller lips, a smoother forehead, or less tired-looking eyes. Altering her appearance is her pick-me-up. She's persnickety about looks. She judges people by them, sums them up in a sweeping once-over. She is uncomfortable when anything is less than perfect; a crooked tooth, a double chin, an oversized nose—it all makes her question people, distrust them in a way. She's not alone. Most people feel exactly as my mom does. She likens it to trying to sell a car without washing it first; it should be gleaming. The same goes for people. Laziness in maintaining their outside represents who they are on the inside. I'm a perfectionist, too, but it doesn't stretch to physical appearances, merely to language and behavior, which bugs the hell out of my sister, Juniper, who is the most unspecific person I know. Though she is specifically unspecific, I'll give her that.

I watch my nervous family's behavior with a sense of smugness because I don't feel an ounce of their tension right now. I'm actually amused. I know Judge Crevan as Bosco, dad to my boyfriend, Art. I'm in his house every day, have been on holidays with him, have been at private family functions, and know him better than my parents do, and most others at that. I've seen Bosco first thing in the morning, with his hair tousled and toothpaste stuck to his lip. I've seen him in the middle of the night, wandering sleepily in his boxers and socks—he always wears socks in bed—to the bathroom or to the kitchen for a glass of water. I've seen him drunk and passed out on the couch, mouth open, hand down the front of his trousers. I have poured popcorn down his shirt and dipped his fingers in warm water while he slept to make him pee. I've seen him drunk-dance on the dance floor and sing badly at karaoke. I've heard him vomit after a late night. I've heard him snore. I've smelled his farts and heard him cry. I can't be afraid of someone whose human side I see and know.

However, my family and the rest of the country see him as a terrifying character to fear and revere. I liken him to one of those talent show judges on TV, an overexaggerated cartoon character who gets a kick out of being booed. I enjoy mimicking him, much to Art's delight. He rolls around laughing while I march up and down being Bosco in judge mode, whooshing my homemade cape around my neck; making scrunched-up, scowling faces; and finger-pointing. Bosco loves a good finger-point whenever the camera is on. I'm convinced the scary-judge persona, while important for his job, is all an act; it's not his natural state of being. He also does a mean cannonball into the pool.

Bosco, known to everyone else but me and Art as Judge Crevan, is the head judge of a committee named the Guild. The Guild, originally set up as a temporary solution by the government as a public inquiry into wrongdoing, is now a permanent fixture that oversees the inquisition of individuals accused of being Flawed. The Flawed are regular citizens who have made moral or ethical mistakes in society.

I've never been to the court, but it is open to the public and available to watch on TV. It's a fair process because in addition to witnesses of the event in question, friends and family are called to testify on the accused's character. On Naming Day, the judges decide whether the accused are Flawed. If so, their flaws are publicly named and their skin is seared with the *F* brand in one of five places. The branding location depends on the error of their judgment.

For bad decisions, it's their temple.

For lying, it's their tongue.

For stealing from society, it's their right palm.

For disloyalty to the Guild, it's their chest, over their heart.

For stepping out of line with society, it's the sole of their right foot.

They also have to wear an armband on their sleeve with the red letter *F* at all times so they can always be identified by the public and set an example. They are not imprisoned; they haven't done anything illegal but have carried out acts that are seen as damaging to society. They still live among us but are ostracized by society, having to live under separate rules.

After our country slid down a slippery slope into great economic turmoil because of what was believed to be the bad decisions of our leaders, the Guild's main aim at its origin was to remove Flawed people from working in leadership roles. It now manages to oust people before they even get into those roles so damage can't be done. In the near future, the Guild boasts, we will have a morally, ethically flawless society. Judge Bosco Crevan is seen as a hero to many.

Art gets his good looks from his dad—blond hair, blue eyes—and with messy blond curls that can't be controlled and big blue eyes that twinkle like a naughty imp's, he always looks like he's up to mischief, because he usually is. He sits directly opposite me at the dining table, and I have to stop myself from watching him all the time, while inside I'm jumping up and down that he's mine. Thankfully, he doesn't share his dad's intensity. He knows how to have fun and let loose, always throwing in a funny comment when the conversation gets too serious. He has good timing. Even Bosco laughs. Art is like a light to me, illuminating the darkest corners of everything.

On this April day every year, we celebrate Earth Day with our neighbors the Crevans and the Tinders. Earth Day celebrations are something Juniper and I have always loved, counting down the days on our calendar, planning what we're going to wear, decorating the house, and setting the table. This year I am more excited than ever because it's the first year Art and I are officially together. Not that I plan on groping him under the table or anything, but having my boyfriend here makes it more exciting.

Dad is the head of a twenty-four-hour TV station, News 24, and our neighbor and other dinner guest Bob Tinder is the editor of the *Daily News* newspaper, which are both owned by Crevan Media, so the three of them mix business with pleasure. The Tinders are always late. I don't know how Bob manages to stick to publication deadlines when he can never make it to dinner on time. It's the same every year. We've had an hour of drinks already in the parlor and hope that moving to the dining room will somehow magically hurry them up. We're now sitting here with three empty chairs, their daughter, Colleen, who's in my class, being the third guest.

"We should start," Bosco says suddenly, looking up from his phone, ending the casual chat and sitting up more formally.

"The dinner is okay," Mom says, taking her newly filled glass of wine from Dad. "I allowed for a little delay." She smiles.

"We should start," Bosco says again.

"Are you in a rush?" Art asks, looking quizzically at Bosco, who suddenly seems fidgety. "The trouble with being punctual is that there's nobody there to see it," Art says, and everyone laughs. "As I should know, waiting for this girl all the time." He gives my foot a light tap under the table.

"No," I disagree. "Punctual is 'acting or arriving exactly at the time appointed.' You're not punctual; you're always ridiculously early."

"The early bird catches the worm," Art defends himself.

"But the second mouse gets the cheese," I reply, and Art sticks his tongue out at me.

My little brother, Ewan, giggles. Juniper rolls her eyes.

Bosco, seemingly frustrated by our conversation, interrupts and repeats, "Summer, Cutter, we should start the meal now."

The way he says it makes us all stop laughing immediately and turn to look at him. It was an order.

"Dad," Art says in surprise, with an awkward half laugh. "What are you, the food police?"

Bosco doesn't break his stare with Mom. This has an odd effect on everybody at the table, causes a tense atmosphere, the kind you sense in the air just before the thunder rolls. Heavy, humid, headache-inducing.

"You don't think we should wait for Bob and Angelina?" Dad asks.

"And Colleen," I add, and Juniper rolls her eyes again. She hates that I pick on every little detail, but I can't help it.

"No, I don't think so," he says simply, firmly, not adding any more.

"Okay," Mom says, standing and making her way to the kitchen, all calm and placid as if nothing happened at all, which tells me that, underneath, her legs are paddling wildly.

I look at Art in confusion and know that he feels the tension, too, because I can sense a new joke forming in his mouth, the thing that he does when he feels awkward or scared or uncomfortable. I see how his lip has started to curl at the thought of his punch line, but I never get to hear what he has to say because then we hear the sirens.

THREE

THE SIRENS RING out, long, low, warning. The sound makes me jump in my seat, startled, and it sends my heart beating wildly, every inch of me sensing danger. It is a sound I have known my entire life, a sound you never want directed at you. The Guild calls it the alert signal, three- to five-minute continuous sirens that ring out from the Guild vans, and though I never lived through any war, it gives me a sense of how people must have felt then before being attacked. In the middle of any normal moment, it can invade your happy thoughts. The sirens sound close to home and they feel sinister. We all momentarily freeze at the table, then Juniper, being Juniper, who speaks before thinking and is clumsy in her actions, jumps up first, bumps the table, and sends the glasses wobbling. Red wine splashes onto the white linen like blobs of blood. She doesn't bother to apologize or clean it, she just runs straight out of the room. Dad is close behind her.

Mom looks completely startled, frozen in time. Drained of all color, she looks at Bosco, and I think she's going to faint. She doesn't even try to stop Ewan from running out the door.

The sirens get louder; they're coming closer. Art jumps up, then so do I; and I follow him down the hall and outside to where they've all gathered in a tight huddle in the front yard. The same is happening in each yard around us. Old Mr. and Mrs. Miller in the yard to our right hold each other tightly, looking terrified, waiting to see whose house the sirens will stop outside of. Directly across the road, Bob Tinder opens his door and steps outside. He sees Dad, and they look at each other. There's something there, but I don't quite understand it. At first, I think Dad is angry with Bob, but then Bob's face holds the same stare. I can't read them. I don't know what's going on. It's a waiting game. Who will it be?

Art grips my hand tightly, squeezes it for reassurance, and tries to give me one of his winning smiles, but it's wobbly, and too quick, and only carries the opposite effect. The sirens are almost on top of us now, the sound in our ears, in our heads. The vans turn onto our road. Two black vans with bright red *F* symbols branding their sides, letting everybody know who they are. The Whistleblowers are the army of the Guild, sent out to protect society from the Flawed. They are not our official police; they are responsible for taking into custody those who are morally and ethically Flawed. Criminals go to prison; they have nothing to do with the Flawed court system.

The emergency lights on the roofs of the vans spin around, rotating their red lights, so bright they almost light up the dusk sky, sending out a warning beacon to all. Clusters of families celebrating Earth Day cling to one another, hoping it's not them, hoping one of theirs won't be plucked from them. Not their family, not their home, not tonight. The two vans stop in the middle of the road, directly outside our house, and I feel my body start to shake. The sirens stop.

"No," I whisper.

"They can't take us," Art whispers to me, and his face is so sure, so certain, that I believe him. Of course they can't take us, we have Judge Crevan sitting in our home for dinner. We are practically untouchable. This helps my fear somewhat, but then anxiety turns to the poor, unfortunate person they are targeting. This surprises me, because I've always believed that the Flawed are wrong, that the Whistleblowers are on my side, protecting me. But because it is happening on my street, at my front door, that changes. It makes me feel it's us against them. This illogical, dangerous thinking makes me shudder.

The van doors slide open, and the whistles sound as four uniformed Whistleblowers leap out, wearing their signature red vests over black combat boots and shirts. They blow their whistles as they move, which has the effect of numbing my mind and stopping me from being able to form a single thought. In my head is just panic. Perhaps that's the intention. The Whistleblowers run, and I stand frozen.

FOUR

BUT THEY DON'T run to us; they go in the opposite direction, to the Tinders' house.

"No, no, no," Dad says, and I can hear the surge of anger in his voice.

"Oh my God," Juniper whispers.

I look at Art in shock, waiting for his reaction, and he stares ahead intently, his jaw working overtime. And then I notice Mom and Bosco still haven't joined us outside.

I let go of Art's hand and rush back to the door. "Mom, Bosco, quick! It's the Tinders!"

As Mom races down the corridor, hair from her chignon comes loose and falls across her face. Dad acknowledges her and shares a look that means something to the two of them, his fists opening and closing by his side. There is no sign of Bosco joining us.

"I don't understand," I say, watching as they approach Bob Tinder. "What's going on?"

"Shh and watch," Juniper silences me.

Colleen Tinder is now in the front yard with her dad, Bob, and her two little brothers, Timothy and Jacob. Bob stands in front of his children, blocking them, protecting them, puffing his chest up and out against the Whistleblowers. Not his family, not his home, not tonight.

"They can't take the babies," Mom says, her voice sounding slow and faraway, so that I know she is right here and panicking.

"They won't," Dad says. "It's him. It must be him."

But the officers walk straight by Bob, ignoring him, ignoring the terrified children, who have started to cry, and waving a sheet of paper in his face, which he stalls to read. They enter the house. Suddenly realizing what is happening, he tosses the piece of paper in the air and chases after them. He shouts at Colleen to look after the boys, which is a hard task because they're starting to panic now, too.

"I'll help her," Juniper says, making a move, but Dad grips her arm tight. "Ow!" she yelps.

"Stay here," Dad says in a voice I've never heard him use before.

Suddenly there's screaming from inside the house. It's Angelina Tinder. Mom's hands fly to her face. A slip in her mask.

"No! No!" Angelina wails over and over again until, finally, we see her at the door, held at both sides by a Whistleblower. She is almost ready for our dinner, wearing a black satin dress, pearls around her neck. Her hair is in curlers. She is wearing jeweled sandals. She is dragged from her home. The boys start to scream as they watch their mother being taken away. They run to her and try to reach her, but the Whistleblowers hold them back.

"Get your hands off my sons!" Bob yells, attacking them, but he's pushed to the ground, pinned down by two large Whistleblowers as Angelina screams wildly with desperation not to be taken away from her babies. I have never heard a human cry out like that before, have never heard a sound like it before. She stumbles and the Whistleblowers catch her and she limps along, the heel of her shoe broken.

Bob shouts at them from the ground. "Let her have some *dignity*, goddammit."

She's taken inside the van. The door slides shut. The whistles stop.

I've never heard a man cry like Bob. The Whistleblowers holding him down speak to him in low, calm voices. He stops yelling, but his crying continues. They finally let him go and disappear into the second van. They drive away.

My heart is pounding, and I can barely breathe. I cannot believe what I'm seeing.

I wait for the outpouring of love from my neighbors. We are a tight, close-knit community; we have many community days; we support one another. I look around and wait. People watch Bob sit up in the grass, pulling his children close and crying. Nobody moves. I want to ask why no one is doing anything, but it seems stupid, because I'm not, either. I can't bring myself to. Even though being Flawed isn't a crime, aiding or assisting a Flawed carries the punishment of imprisonment. Bob isn't Flawed—his wife is accused—but still, everyone is afraid to get involved. Our neighbors Mr. and Mrs. Miller turn around and head back into their house, and most of the others follow suit. My mouth falls open, shocked.

"Damn you!" Bob shouts across the road. It is quiet at first, and I think he's saying it to himself, and then I think as he says it louder he's saying it to the vans that have disappeared, but as he gets even louder and the anger increases, I see he's directing it at us. What did we do?

"Stay here," Dad says to us, then he gives Mom a long look. "Everybody, back inside. Keep it calm, yes?"

Mom nods, and her face is serene as if nothing has happened; the mask is back on, the loose strands of hair already back in place, though I don't recall her fixing them.

As I turn around to look back into my house, I see Bosco standing inside at the window, arms crossed, watching the scene unfold. And I realize it's him that Bob is shouting at. Bosco, the head of the Guild, is the head of the organization that took Angelina away.

He can help; I know it. He's the head of the Flawed court. He will be able to help. It will be all okay. Normality can resume. The world will be turned the right way around again. Things will make sense. Knowing this, my breathing starts to return to normal again.

As Dad nears Bob, the shouting dies down, but the crying continues, a heartbreaking sound.

When you see something, it can't be unseen. When you hear a sound, it can never be unheard. I know, deep down, that this evening I have learned something that can never be unlearned. And the part of my world that is altered will never be the same.

FIVE

"LET'S ADDRESS THE elephant in the room," Bosco says suddenly, reaching for the red wine and filling his glass generously. He had insisted we all sit back down at the table, though there isn't anyone who feels hungry after what we've just witnessed. Dad is still with Bob. Mom is in the kitchen preparing the main course.

"I don't understand," I say to Bosco. "Angelina Tinder is accused of being Flawed?"

"Mm-hmm," he says good-naturedly, his blue eyes dancing as he looks at me. It's almost as if he is enjoying my reaction.

"But Angelina is—"

Mom drops a plate in the kitchen, and it smashes and it stops me in my tracks. Was that a warning from her? To tell me to stop talking?

"I'm okay!" she calls, too chirpily.

"What were you going to say about Angelina, Celestine?" Bosco eyes me carefully.

I swallow. I was going to say that she is nice, that she is kind, that she has young children and she's a great mom and that they need her, that she has never said or done anything wrong in all the moments I've spent time with her. That she's the most talented piano player I've ever heard, that I hoped I could play just like her when I'm older. But I don't because of the way Bosco is looking at me and because Mom never usually breaks anything. Instead I say, "But she teaches me piano."

Juniper tuts beside me in disgust. I can't even look at Art, I'm so disappointed in myself.

Bosco laughs. "We can find you a new teacher, dear Celestine. Though you raise a good point. Perhaps we should think about stopping her from playing piano. Instruments are a luxury the Flawed don't deserve." He tucks into his starter and takes a huge bite of carpaccio, the only person at the table even holding his cutlery. "Come to think of it, I hope that's all she was teaching you," Bosco says, his smiling eyes gone.

"Yes, of course," I say, frowning, confused that he would even question that of me. "What did she do wrong?"

"Taught you the piano," Art teases. "Her downfall, if anyone's heard you."

Ewan giggles. I smile at Art, thankful for the break in nervous tension in the room.

"It's not funny," Juniper says beside me, quietly but firmly.

Bosco's eyes move to her immediately. "You're correct, Juniper. It's not funny."

Juniper averts her eyes.

And the tension is back.

"No, it's not funny, *comical*, but it's funny, *peculiar*," I say, feeling slapped.

"Thank you, Thesaurus," Juniper says under her breath. It's what she and Ewan always call me when I get bogged down by definitions.

Bosco ignores me and continues to direct his gaze at my sister. "Did Angelina teach you, too, Juniper?"

Juniper looks him square in the eye. "Yes, she did. Best teacher I ever had."

16

There's a silence.

Mom enters the room. Perfect timing. "I must say, I was very fond of Angelina. I considered her a friend. I'm . . . shocked by this . . . event."

"I did, too, Summer, and believe me no one feels more pain than I do in this moment, seeing as I am the one who will have to tell her the verdict."

"You won't just *tell* her, though, will you?" Juniper says quietly. "It will be *your* verdict. *Your* decision."

I'm afraid of Juniper's tone. This is not the correct moment for one of her soapbox airings. I don't want her to annoy Bosco. He's someone who should be treated with respect. Juniper's language feels dangerous. I've never seen anyone speak to Bosco in this way.

"You just never know what those among us, whom we consider friends, are really like," Bosco says, eyes on Juniper. "What lurks beneath those you consider your equals. I see it every day."

"What did Angelina do?" I ask again.

"As you may well know, Angelina traveled outside this country with her mother a few months ago to perform euthanasia, which is illegal here."

"But she accompanied her mother on her mother's wishes, to another country where it was legal," Juniper says. "She didn't do anything illegal."

"Nor is the Guild a legal courtroom, merely an inquisition into her character, and we feel that in her doing so, making the decision to travel to another country to carry out the act, she is deemed to have a Flawed character. Had the government known her plans to carry this out, it would have had a case to stop her."

There's silence at the table while we take this in. I knew that Angelina's mother had been terribly sick for years; she had been suffering with a debilitating disease. I had not known how she had met the end of her days, but we had all been at the funeral.

"The Guild doesn't take any religious views into account, of course," he continues, perhaps sensing our doubts on his judgment. "We merely assess the character of a person. The Guild must observe the accepted teaching about the sanctity of life. In allowing Angelina Tinder to return to this country having done what she did and continuing on as she had, the Guild would be ignoring the teachings and instead would be sanctioning anguish and pain. Whether it was in a different country and whether it was legal are beside the point. It is her character that we must look at."

Juniper just snorts in response.

What is it with her? I hate this about my sister. In everybody else's opinion, we are identical. Though she is eleven months older than I am, we really could pass for twins. However, if you knew us, we would never get away with it, because Juniper gives herself away as soon as she opens her mouth. Like my granddad, she doesn't know when to shut up.

"Did you know that Angelina Tinder was planning on traveling to kill her mother?" Bosco asks, leaning forward, elbows on the table, focusing on Juniper.

"Of course she didn't know," Mom says, her voice coming out as a whisper, and I know that by her doing this, she wanted to shout.

Juniper stares down at her untouched starter, and I silently beg her to keep quiet. This isn't fun. A room full of people I love, and my heart is pounding as if something dangerous is happening.

"Will Angelina be branded?" I ask, still in shock that I could actually *know* a Flawed person, have one live right on this street.

"If found guilty on Naming Day, yes, she will be branded," Bosco says, then to Mom, "I'll do everything to keep it out of the press for Bob's sake, of course, which won't be difficult, as the Jimmy Child case is taking over all the airwaves. Nobody cares about a Flawed piano teacher right now."

Jimmy Child is a soccer hero who was caught cheating on his wife

18

with her sister for the past ten years and faces a Flawed verdict, which would be disastrous, as it would mean he couldn't travel overseas for matches. Among many of the punishments the Flawed face, they must give up their passports.

"I'm sure Bob will appreciate your discretion," Mom says, and it sounds so smooth and easy to her that I know she really feels awkward and it's stilted in her mind.

"I hope so," Bosco says, nodding. "I certainly hope so."

"Where will she be branded?" I ask, obsessed with this. I just can't seem to wrap my head around it and can't understand why nobody else is asking questions. Apart from Juniper, of course, but hers are more accusing than anything else.

"Celestine," Mom says harshly, "I don't think we need to discuss—"

"Her right hand," Bosco says.

"Theft from society," I say.

"Indeed. And every hand she goes to shake from now on will know just what she is."

"*If* she's found Flawed. Innocent until proved guilty," Juniper says, like she's reminding him.

But we all know Angelina Tinder has no chance. Everyone who goes through the Flawed court is found guilty; otherwise, they wouldn't be taken in the first place. Unlike Juniper, I understand rules. There is a line, a moral one, and Angelina crossed it, but I just can't believe that I could know someone who is Flawed, that I could sit in her house beside her at her piano, a piano she touched, then I touched with my fingers. I want to wash my hands immediately. I try to think back on our last conversation, on previous conversations, to see if she showed any hint of a dent in her character. I wonder about her daughter, Colleen. Can I still talk to her at school? Probably best not to. But that doesn't feel right, either. I'm conflicted.

"Where is Cutter?" Bosco suddenly says, looking at Mom angrily.

"He's with Bob. I'm sure he'll be back soon," she says politely.

"That doesn't look good," he says. "He should be here."

"I'm sure he'll be—"

"I hope she can still play piano," Juniper interrupts Mom, out of nowhere. "With her hand seared."

"Do you feel sorry for her?" Bosco asks, his irritation rising.

"Of course she doesn't," Art pipes up, mouth full of food, knife and fork squeezed between his huge man hands and pointing up at the ceiling like he's a caveman. He waves them around as he talks, food spraying off and flying onto the table. "We're all just shocked, Dad, that's all. I mean, come on, you could have given us a heads-up, that our expected dinner guests were about to be taken away? When that siren went off, poor Celestine looked like she thought she was about to get carted away to the madhouse, which between me and you is where she belongs, but she doesn't need to know that."

He says it so easily, so fresh, so, *well*, judged that it seems to remind Bosco of where he is: in his neighbor's dining room with his son, and not in his courtroom.

"Of course." Bosco looks confused for a moment, and then he looks at Ewan, who has been remarkably quiet at the table. He reaches out a hand and pats my hand warmly. "Sorry, dear Celestine, I didn't mean to scare you. Let's start again, shall we?" He picks up his glass of red wine and holds it in the air with a beaming smile. "Happy Earth Day."

SIX

WHEN I HEAR that the quiet murmuring, which was decidedly longer tonight than usual after the evening's events, has ended in my
parents' bedroom, and the house has settled for the night, I make my
way to the summit, where Art and I have been meeting most nights for
the past three months.

I have spent more time with the Crevans over the past few months
than with my own family, often wishing I could stay with them for
good. I feel like I fit in with them more, that everything with them is
logical and makes sense. I have always believed in the workings of
the Guild. I am one of Bosco's greatest supporters. I like to hear him
regale people with stories of the courthouse over dinner, how he
Ousted a charity board member for taking a golden payment pension
package, or branded a celebrity who'd made millions on the sale of
her fitness DVD but was discovered as having a secret tummy tuck.
Every day, he has interesting stories coming through his courtroom,
and I love sitting down and hearing about them. I understand what
he is doing. He is preventing people from being deceived. I know the
difference between right and wrong. I understand the rules. But today

I feel that the rules, of which I am a true supporter, have been blurred, because today they were literally on my front doorstep.

It is 11:00 PM. The summit overlooks the sleeping capital city. We live in a valley surrounded by mountains. Atop one of those mountains, Highland Castle dominates the city. Lit up by powerful red uplighters at night, it watches over us menacingly. In existence since AD 1100 and once the seat of the HighKings, Highland Castle is a fortress. It stands above us all, the tallest round tower in the world, its powerful eye seeing far and wide. The scene of centuries of invasions and massacres, it now houses state conferences and dinners, guided tours of its architecture, museums of its ancient artifacts, and, of course more famously now, the offices of the Guild. We sit on the summit opposite the castle; to the left of us, the lights of more cities dot the night and stretch on forever, the castle keeping its watchful eye on them all. To the right are farmland and industry, where my granddad lives. Humming is the largest and capital city of Highland, and it is rich in history and beauty. Tourists flock from all over the world to visit our city, our bridges, our fairy-tale castle and palace, our cobblestoned pathways, and our ornate town square. Most of its buildings have survived the violence and destruction of the twentieth century, and it is a hub for appreciators of our Romanesque, Gothic, and Renaissance architecture. Humming Bridge is one of the most famous bridges in the world. At thirty feet wide and over six hundred yards long and built in the fourteenth century, it crosses the river and leads to Highland Castle. It, too, is a beauty at night, lit up at its six arches, three bridge towers, and the statues from our history lining the bridge to protect it.

I like to travel the world on vacations, but I intend on continuing to live here after school. Art and I have talked about it. We want to go to the city university, me studying mathematics, him studying science. We have it all worked out. Juniper wants to leave as soon as she can, become a snowboard instructor in Switzerland by winter, a lifeguard in Portugal by summer, or something like that.

Art says he likes going to the summit because it gives him per-spective. He's had a tough year. His mother passed away, and I think this place helps him rise above the worries on the ground, to look at it from a height as if he is distanced from the problems, detached from his grief, which is lessening with the months. I, on the other hand, see it as a place where it is Art and me against the rest of the world. While the one million people sleep in the city below us, Art and I are together, and it makes our bond feel even stronger. It makes me feel invincible, alive. I know how the castle feels watching over everybody: untouchable.

It is only over the past six months that I have felt this way about Art. We have been friends since we were twelve, when we started school together. The teacher placed us beside each other on the first day. We hung out together with a group, me with the girls and he with the boys, yet we always found ourselves side by side. We would never have met up alone despite living across the road from each other. It was only a year ago, when his mom passed away, that Art suddenly began to seek me out, not caring about the perception of us to the others. We'd come here together and talk, him grieving and slowly coming to terms with his mom's death; he watched her slowly die of cancer. And then the grieving gradually flickered out, didn't become the main rea-son for our meeting, and it became something else.

That was when the something happened for me. The rush of butter-flies when I saw him, the silly smile that would appear on my face at the very thought of him, the nervous bubbles in my stomach, the jolt of electricity when his skin brushed mine. Suddenly I cared about what I wore, what I said, how I looked. This didn't go unnoticed, particularly by Juniper, who watched me each day as I obsessed over my reflection before I dashed out of the house. Art noticed, too, and then I stopped flustering over myself for a moment to notice it in him. We've been together for three months.

I finally reach the summit and seeing his shape lit by the moon turns me into jelly as usual. He is always early, always waiting for me, sitting on a blanket, his face a picture of perfect concentration as he gazes out on the sleeping city below. *Perfect* is a word I use a lot to describe Art or any moment with him.

"Hello, early bird," I say.

He looks up, the sadness replaced with a smile. And do I see relief?

"Hello, mouse. If you're looking for your cheese, I ate it."

"Worms and cheese," I say, sitting beside him on the blanket. "Yum."

We kiss.

"This is yum," he murmurs, pulling me closer for another, longer, more passionate kiss.

I feel there is something different about him tonight. I pull away slowly and study his face, his eyes.

"How about we make a deal to not talk about any events of tonight?"

"Good idea." I sigh. "I have a headache just thinking about it."

He kisses my forehead and leaves his lips there. We're both silent, lost in our thoughts, both obviously thinking about the sights and sounds of Angelina Tinder being dragged away. We can't stay quiet for long. Art pulls away.

"My dad tonight . . ." He trails off, looking out at the tips of roofs and chimneys, and I see his anguish over what happened tonight. Ever since his mom passed away, I've seen it as my role to make him feel better, to get rid of the sadness. And despite my conflicted feelings on this evening, I need to pull it together for him.

"Look, Juniper should not have spoken to him the way she did, but you know what Juniper is like. She needs to learn how to keep her trap shut. She's just like my granddad."

"Juniper was only saying what she thought," he says to my absolute surprise.

"She shouldn't be saying these things to him."

He smiles sadly. "Everything is so black and white to you, Celestine. We're neighbors; we were in your dining room celebrating Earth Day, not his courtroom. And he must have known that was going to happen to Angelina tonight. I mean, why wouldn't he at least tell her, if not us? They're friends. At least she could have been ready and not dragged out like that in front of her family, her kids. . . ."

I'm surprised to hear this from him. Art has never spoken out about his dad. They're buddies, a team, the only two left, a connection made stronger after his mom died. They're survivors, or at least that's how they act. The two who came out of her loss alive. I can see he is as confused about all this as I am.

"He was following the rules," I say simply, and I know it's not good enough. It doesn't feel good enough to me, but it's the truth. "What happened to Angelina was horrible, but I don't think you can blame your dad for that."

"No?" he asks, bitterness in his voice.

"It's his *job*. A Flawed being taken into custody happens almost every day somewhere in this country. Your dad is under pressure to maintain perfection. What would happen if he turned a blind eye to some and not to others?" I ask, airing some of my own thoughts. "I mean, what then? Judge Crevan on trial for being Flawed for missing a Flawed?"

Art looks at me. "I never thought about it like that."

"Well, you should. Because he's your dad. And he's powerful. And some people adore him, practically worship him. And that makes it harder for you to have a dad like that, but that's who you've got, and he loves you so much. *And* he's one half of what made you, and that makes him a genius."

He smiles, takes my face in his hands, makes a disgusted face. "I don't really want to think of his part in making me, thank you very much."

"Gross." I laugh.

"Black and white."

"All the way." I smile, but my smile feels a bit wobbly, my footing not as sure as it was before. Convincing Art is easier than convincing myself.

Art clears his throat. "I wasn't going to do this until your birthday, but after tonight . . . I think you deserve it now more than ever."

He lifts his left leg and moves it beside me, pulling me in closer to him so that I am trapped between his thighs. Suddenly my uncertainty disappears and I am right where I want to be.

"I got you this for your eighteenth birthday, but I want to give it to you now to let you know that despite everything else going on in the world, you are the one thing that makes sense to me. You are beautiful." He runs his finger down my cheek, across my nose, over my lips. "You are clever, you are loyal." He drops his hand and hands me a small velvet box.

My hands are shaking so much I'm embarrassed. I open it and lift out the delicate silver chain, so fine I'm afraid I'll break it. On the end is a symbol.

"And you are perfect," he whispers, and it sends a shiver running through me, and my skin breaks out in goose bumps.

I examine the symbol, unable to believe what I see.

"I had a man at Highland Castle make it for me specially. You know what it means?"

I nod. "Circles are regarded as a symbol of perfection. All the radii bear a ratio of one to one to each other, showing there are no partial differences between them. They are proved to be in a state of harmony. Geometric harmony."

"Perfection," he says again, softly. "It's hard to get one up on the mathematician, you know." He laughs. "I had to do a lot of research. I think my brain is still sore."

I laugh through my growing tears. "Thank you." My words come out as a whisper. I attempt to wrap it around my wrist, but he stops me.

"No. Here." He takes it from my trembling hands, and he uncrosses my ankles delicately. He moves back from me and straightens my leg, sliding my jeans up my leg slowly, his fingers warm on my skin. He fastens the chain around my ankle, and then he moves forward again, closer this time, wrapping my legs around him.

He lifts my chin and we are nose-to-nose, the moonlight between us. He tilts his head and kisses me softly, smoothly, sweetly. His lips are succulent, his tongue delicious, and I lift my hands through his hair and am lost in him, in this moment.

SEVEN

WHEN I THINK back to that moment, my heart soars as it did then, and everything is heightened, magical, musical, and mystical, almost too good to be true. I could live that moment forever, his lips on mine, our bodies pushed together, both of us hungry for more, our future as wide open as the vista before us, as bright as the moon. It was just us on top of the sleeping world, invincible, untouchable.

It was the most perfect moment in my life.

It was the last perfect moment in my life.

EIGHT

I WAKE UP, and the first thing I do is slide my leg out from under the duvet to check my ankle. Anklet still there. It was not a dream, not some juicy figment of my imagination that dissolves as soon as I wake. I snuggle down under the covers to relive it in my head and then realize that delaying this morning would delay spending time with Art. He will be waiting for me, as he always is, at the bus stop, where we will go on to school together.

Despite my joy, my sleep was fitful, with so much to absorb after the Angelina Tinder scene. I feel unsteady on my feet as I get dressed. Something has been shaken, stirred within me. My feeling of security has been tested, and perhaps my trust, though not with Art, whom I trust more than ever. Oddly, I think it is with my own self.

I don't need to think when I dress; I never do, not like Juniper, whom I hear swearing and sighing as she pulls yet another outfit over her head in frustration, never happy with how she looks. She gets up a half hour earlier than I do just to get dressed and still ends up being late every morning.

Most people who don't know our personalities can't distinguish between me and Juniper. With a black dad and a white mom, we have inherited Dad's skin. We also have Dad's brown eyes, his nose, and his hair coloring. We have Mom's cheekbones, her long limbs. She tried to get us into modeling when we were younger, and Juniper and I did a few shoots together, but neither of us could stay at it. Me because posing for a camera failed to intellectually stimulate me, Juniper because she was even more awkward and clumsy under people's gazes.

When it comes to how we act, how we dress, and everything else about us, though, we couldn't be further apart.

I put on a cream linen dress and baby-pink cashmere cardigan, with gold gladiator sandals that spiral up my legs. It's hot outside, and I always wear pastel colors. Mom likes to buy pastels for all the family. She thinks that we look more like a unit when we're dressed that way. I know of some families who hire stylists to help coordinate not just the clothes but their overall look as a family. None of us wants to look out of place or like we don't belong, though Juniper often likes to do her own thing, wearing something that's not a part of our family color palette. We let her do just that—her loss, though Mom worries that it makes us look fragmented. I think the only person who looks fragmented is Juniper.

As usual, I'm downstairs before my sister. Ewan is at the table eating breakfast. He's wearing cream linen trousers and a baby-pink T-shirt, and I feel happy we match. A good start to the day.

Mom is staring at the TV, not moving.

"Look what I got last night," I sing.

No one looks.

"Yoo-hoo." I circle my ankle in the air, graceful like a ballerina.

Ewan finally looks at me, then down at my ankle, which I'm dangling near his face.

"A bracelet," he says, bored.

"No. A bracelet is an ornamental band for the wrist, Ewan. This is an anklet."

"Whatever, Thesaurus." He rolls his eyes and continues watching TV.

"Art gave it to me," I sing loudly, floating by Mom to get milk for my cereal from the fridge.

"Wonderful, sweetheart," she says robotically, as though she hasn't heard at all.

I stop and stare at her. She is completely engrossed in the TV. I finally pay attention and see it's News 24, and Pia Wang is reporting live from Highland Castle. Pia Wang is the correspondent for the Guild. She covers every case in extreme detail, providing a profile of the Flawed, during the trial and after. It's never a favorable profile, either. She does a good job of burying whomever she wants, though, to her credit, she's covering Flawed cases, people who have made bad decisions, so she's not exactly trying to glamorize them.

I look out the window. Dad's car is gone. He must have been alerted to the story and had to take off early. That happens a lot.

"This case has garnered more attention than any other," Pia says, her face perfect with peach-blush cheeks. She is wearing peach, and she looks like you could eat her, a perfect china doll. Glossy black hair, a fringe framing her innocent-looking, petite face. So perfect. "Even gaining attention around the rest of the world, which is reflected here in the turnout outside the Guild court in Highland Castle, with record numbers of people turning out to support their soccer hero Jimmy Child, Humming City's best striker, who has led us to victory so many years. And today he is victorious again, as he left the court only moments ago having been deemed by Judge Crevan and his associates *not* to be Flawed. I repeat, breaking news to those who have just joined us: Jimmy Child is *not* Flawed."

I gasp.

"What?" I say. "Has that ever happened before?"

Mom finally breaks her stare from the TV. "I don't know. I don't think so. I . . . maybe once," she says vaguely.

"Not a surprising result when a Crevan owns a share in the soccer team," Juniper says suddenly from behind us. I turn to her.

Mom's face looks pained. "Juniper . . ." she says simply.

"Damon Crevan. Owns a fifty-five percent stake in Humming City, but I suppose everyone will tell me that's just coincidence. If you ask me, it was his wife they put on trial," Juniper says. "And that dirty man got away with it."

Nobody disagrees. Jimmy Child's glamorous wife had been on the front page of every newspaper for the past few weeks as her lifestyle was thrashed out for all to see. Every aspect of her, every inch of her body, was fodder for gossip sites and even news sites.

"Go to school," Mom says in a warning tone. "Any more talk like that and they'll come for you, missy." She clips Juniper's nose playfully.

She was almost right.

NINE

WHEN I STEP outside, I see Colleen standing at her family's car. The front door of her house is open, and she looks like she's waiting. I guess she won't be going to school today, probably going to the courthouse to her mom's trial. My heart beats wildly as I try to figure out what to do. If I say hello, I might get in trouble. Anybody could see me speaking to her from their home, and I could be reported. What if Bosco sees me from one of the windows of his monstrous mansion or as he leaves for work? Saying hi may be seen as disloyalty toward the Guild, as support for Colleen and her mom. Would that be seen as aiding and assisting a Flawed? I don't want to go to prison. But if I ignore her, it will be rude. It is Colleen's mother who's accused of being Flawed, not her. She looks over at me and I can't do it. I look away quickly.

Behind me I hear Juniper say "Good luck today" to Colleen. It annoys me how easily she says that and then puts on her headphones and ignores everyone.

Art is already at the bus stop waiting for me, as usual, looking delicious, as usual. I leap on him as soon as I get to him.

"Bird."

"Mouse."

He kisses me, but I pull away quickly, excited to discuss the news.

"Did you hear about Jimmy Child?" I expect Art to be elated. Jimmy Child is his hero, and up until a year ago he had his posters plastered all over his walls. Most boys did. During the trial, Art had the opportunity to meet him, though a quick meet and greet in a holding cell before court wasn't what he'd been dreaming of throughout his boyhood, and he hadn't wanted to discuss it much.

"Yeah," he says. "Dad left at the crack of dawn this morning. He wanted to push the verdict through first thing, in time for the morning news."

I think about how I should have said hello to Colleen; I should have known Bosco wasn't home to have seen me—he was at court early—and what harm would it have done anyway to simply say hello? I'm angry with myself.

"I can smell your brain burning. You okay?" He sticks his knuckle into my frown and screws it around.

I laugh. "Yeah, I was just thinking. I didn't know they had secret Naming Days. I thought it was always public. That's so sneaky."

"Not as sneaky as you and me," Art says, fingers creeping up my cardigan.

I laugh and stop his hand from traveling, something suddenly on my mind. I look over at Juniper, who is listening to her music so loudly I can hear every word from here.

I lower my voice. "Do you think Jimmy Child's wife was put on trial?"

"Serena Child?" he asks, surprised.

"Yeah. When you think about it"—because I had been thinking about it, ever since Juniper said it, and on the walk to the bus stop with my new wobbly legs that haven't been working since I stood up this morning—"every day it wasn't about him or about what he'd done, but about how she was so annoying and so fake and such a *woman*, how could he not cheat?"

34

Art laughs. "I don't think that's exactly what Pia said." He smiles at me fondly. " 'Reporting live,' " he says, imitating Pia. " 'Isn't Serena Child such a *woman*? How could he not cheat?' "

I laugh, realizing how stupid it sounds, then turn serious, wanting to be understood. "No, but the way they talked about her looks. The surgery. The clothes. Her past . . . her cellulite. She'd kissed a girl—so what? Her tan being too orange, her eating disorder when she was fifteen. She went to school with someone who ended up being a bank robber. She never cooked a meal for her husband. He had to keep going to that diner. We learned everything about her. Like she was the one who was Flawed. Not him."

Art laughs again, enjoying the ridiculousness of what I'm saying, or perhaps the fact that it's so surprisingly out of character for me to say it at all. "And why would they put her on trial?"

"So he gets away with not being Flawed. People say she wasn't a good wife, so how could he not have cheated? And the star player is still the star."

His smile instantly fades, and he looks at me like he doesn't know me. "Celestine, be careful."

I shrug like I don't care, but my heart is pounding by even saying this aloud. "I was just *saying*."

Juniper has gotten to me. I had been unsure already, and what she said this morning niggles at me more and has me considering the truth in her words. I think about Colleen on her way to the courthouse to see her mother, her mother about to be branded Flawed for traveling to another country to help carry out the wishes of her mother. Does that really make her Flawed? I'm not ready to park this thought yet. It's Art, the person I share every thought with. Surely I can share one more. He can help sort out these muddled thoughts.

Art reaches for my hand and I feel safe.

"Do you think it's bad what Angelina did?" I say quietly.

He looks at me.

"Because I've been thinking about it. All night. And I don't think it's *that* bad. Not if it's what her mom wanted. I mean, I can think of worse."

"Of course there's worse."

"So even though there's worse, everyone gets branded the same?"

"She will only get one brand. On her hand. Some people get two."

He's not thinking about this properly. I know he's not. I know him. His answers are too quick. He is defensive, though I'm not attacking him. This is how it gets when people have discussions about the Flawed. Everyone has such strong opinions it's almost like it's personal. Only it's even more so for Art because his dad is the senior judge of it all—his grandfather was the founding member of the Guild. I was always in awe of them for that. I still am. Aren't I?

TEN

ONCE ON THE bus and in our usual seats, I concentrate on the Flawed lady in the seat that only Flawed people are allowed to occupy. There are two seats for the Flawed on the bus, because rules state that three or more Flawed are not allowed to gather together at any one time. It's to prevent the riots that broke out when the Flawed punishments were introduced. However, I wonder for the first time why they didn't just put another two Flawed seats at the back of the bus or somewhere else away from them. Alternate Flawed and regular people's seats. So often there are Flawed standing when the bus is filled with empty seats, which never bothered me before in a moral way, but bothered me when I was getting off the bus and had to squeeze by them. I swear some of them don't move deliberately, making me squish up against their Flawed bodies to get past. The Flawed seats have bright red fabric and are at the front of the bus facing all the other passengers so that everybody on the bus can see that they are Flawed. I used to find it uncomfortable when I was a little girl, having to face them throughout the journey, but then, as I got used to it, I stopped seeing them.

I watch the Flawed woman sitting alone on the seat, her armband with the bloodred symbol identifying her.

I see the symbol on her temple, too, and wonder what bad judgment she made to land herself in this predicament. The scar on her temple is certainly not new. It doesn't have the red-hot, crusted look of newly seared flesh as some Flawed have. She has been Flawed for quite some time, and I wonder if this means she's worse now, if Flawed get more Flawed with age or if the branding, the acknowledgment of it, stops it from spreading and growing. She is texting; and when she rests the phone on her lap, I see the screen photo of her with children. For the first time I wonder what it's like for the Flawed to live life in the same world as everybody else whom they love, but under different rules. It has never occurred to me before. I think of Angelina and her children. Angelina will have job restrictions, curfews, travel restrictions. How can she mother her children if she is living under different rules? What if there is an emergency in the middle of the night? Can she break her curfew to bring her children to the hospital? What if the Tinders go on a family holiday abroad and Angelina can't go? What if Colleen decides to work and live abroad? Her mother won't be able to visit her. Ever. And why have I never thought of these things before?

Because I never cared, that's why. Because if people have done something wrong, then I always thought they deserved their punishment. They're not criminals, but they're just missing being physically behind bars. If Angelina, who I believed could never hurt a fly, can so easily be considered Flawed, then perhaps this woman before me is no worse, either. I have never spoken to one before. It's not that we're not allowed to, it's just that I wouldn't know what to say. I step around them when they're near me, I avoid their eye contact. I suppose I act like they don't exist. They're always in the Flawed section of the supermarket, the one that I pass through aisles to avoid, buying their grains and oats and whatever else they have to eat as part of their basic diet for their basic living. A life with no luxury is the punishment. I never thought it would be such a bad thing; it's not like they're behind bars. But then I never thought of having to live like that when your husband doesn't, or your kids don't, or the rest of society doesn't. And then they're not really allowed to socialize together. No more than with one other at a time. For every two Flawed, there needs to be a regular person just for numbers. I think of a Flawed wedding, a Flawed birthday party, and shudder. I wonder what they even talk about with one another. Do they swap stories of how Flawed they are? Show their brands and laugh with pride, or are they ashamed, as they should be?

I feel Art's lips on my earlobe. "If you don't stop thinking, your head will explode," he whispers. His breath is hot, and it makes the hairs on the back of my neck stand up. I want to stop thinking. I really do, but I can't. For once he doesn't have my full attention. He's trying to bring me back to him, but I can't go there. I'm caught in this thought, in this moment.

The bus stops and a woman with crutches gets on. The driver helps her and guides her to the Flawed seats, which have the most legroom. The seats are deliberately set farther away so people don't have to touch them or bump against them, reinforcing that distinction between us and them. She sits beside the Flawed woman, who smiles at her.

The other woman throws her such a look of disgust that I'm embarrassed for the Flawed woman, who looks away, hurt visible in her eyes. She senses that I'm looking at her, and our eyes meet for a minuscule moment before I look away, heart pounding from having made contact. I hope no one has seen. I hope it doesn't look like I'm on her side.

"What is going on with you today?" Art asks, a slightly bewildered and amused expression on his face.

"Oh, nothing," I say, trying to smile. "I'm just perfect. That's all."

He smiles and rubs the palm of my hand with his thumb, and I melt.

Juniper sits across the aisle from us, her body pushed so far up against the window she couldn't possibly get any farther away from me and Art, or anyone else on the bus for that matter.

I don't know when things became like this between me and Juniper. Photos and stories prove that we were extremely tight as children. Juniper is the big sister by a small amount, but she enjoyed mollycoddling me, taking on the role of nurturing big sister. But when we began junior high, things started to change between us. Though we were in the same year, we were in different classes and made our own friends for the first time, and the divide began. I excelled in school—I adore information and am always hungry to know more. I read books, I watch documentaries, my favorite subject is math, and I hope to study it at the city university when I finish school this year. My aim is to win the Fields Medal, the International Medal for Outstanding Discoveries in Mathematics, viewed as the greatest honor a mathematician can receive, like a math Nobel Prize. You have to be under forty to win it. I'm seventeen. There's time. Test results so far prove that I'm on course to get into my university program with ease. Juniper isn't the jealous type, but our differences in grades were the first thing to set us apart.

My scores were celebrated; hers weren't. They were never bad; they just weren't perfect. Everybody always wanted her to do better, to be better. And I understand the pressure she was under, but I could have been there to help her, not be the one she eventually blamed.

She thinks I'm a know-it-all, which she has told me plenty of times, and I try not to be one with her. I know I have a habit of correcting people's grammar or recounting dictionary definitions, but that's just me. Doing it does not make me feel I am better than the person I am saying it to. It is just an expression of who I am. I try to ask her questions, the meaning of things, pretend not to know something that I do know, but she finds this patronizing. She's right, but I don't know what else to do. My striving for perfection includes wanting to have the ideal relationship with my sister, like in the movies I see and the books I read, the stories that tell you that sisterhood is the one real true love and relationship you will have in your life.

Juniper is dyslexic. She sees this as another failure, another trait that has let her down, but I can see that it makes her view things in a different way. I'm a problem-solver. I read the signs, the proof that I see before me, and come to a conclusion. Juniper is cleverer than that. She has an alternate way of reading things. She reads people. I don't know how she does it, but she watches and listens and arrives at conclusions I could never imagine, and usually she's right. I look at things straight on; her perspective seems to curve around things, wind and twist, turn things upside down to reach the answer. I have never told her that I think this about her. I tell myself it's because I don't want to come across as patronizing, but really I know it's because I have a jealousy of my own.

I think about what Mom said earlier about Jimmy Child maybe not being the only person to have been found not Flawed.

"Did you know that there might be other people who went through the Flawed court and were found to be not Flawed?" I whisper to Art.

I feel his grip on my hand loosen as he turns to me. He's annoyed I won't let go of this. "No, I didn't know."

"I think there must be other people found innocent that we don't know about. Has your dad ever said anything?"

"Bloody hell, Celestine, drop it, will you?"

"I'm just asking."

"You're not really supposed to."

"Aren't I?"

"Not here, anyway," he says, looking around nervously.

I go quiet. I can only look ahead at the Flawed woman, head swirling with unfamiliar thoughts. Dangerous thoughts.

ELEVEN

AT THE NEXT stop, the Flawed woman gets off and a rather large lady gets on. She recognizes the woman with the crutches and sits down beside her, and they chat.

At the next stop, an old man gets on the bus, and I almost call out to him. He looks so much like my granddad that I'm convinced it's him, which doesn't make sense because my granddad lives on a farm in the country, but then I see the large *F* symbol on his armband and I shudder, annoyed with myself for ever thinking someone like him could possibly be related to me.

My prejudice strikes me. I had been repulsed by the reaction of the woman with the crutches to the Flawed woman smiling at her, but I hold equal views of my own without ever realizing it.

The man is in his seventies or eighties. I'm not sure. He's *old*, and he is dressed in a smart suit and polished shoes, as if he's on his way to work. From this angle, I can't see any signs of branding, though it could mean it is on his chest, tongue, or foot. He looks respectable, and again I study him, surprised by his appearance. I always thought of the Flawed as less than us, and I can't believe I have admitted that to myself. He is unable to sit, because the two Flawed seats are taken—by two women who are not Flawed but are so busy chatting that they don't notice him. He stands near them, holding on to the pole to stay upright.

I hope they notice him soon. He doesn't look like he will go very far standing.

A few minutes pass. He is still standing. I look around. There are at least a dozen free seats where he could sit, but he is not allowed to. I'm a logical person, and this does not prove logical to me.

I look across at Juniper, who has taken off her headphones and is sitting up, poker straight, alert, and looking at the same situation that I am. Juniper has always been more emotional than I am, and I can see her on the edge of her seat, ready to pounce. Instead of fearing she will do something stupid, for once I am glad she and I feel the same.

The old man starts coughing. And then he won't stop.

His breath is wheezy, barely still for a moment before he coughs again. He takes out a handkerchief and coughs into that, trying to block the germs and noise. His face goes from white to pink to purple, and I see Juniper move closer to the edge of her seat. She looks at the two women chatting, then back to the old man. Finally, he stops coughing.

Moments later he starts again, and all heads turn away from him and look out the window. The fat lady stops talking to look at him, and I'm relieved, knowing she will finally let him sit in the seat he is entitled to. Instead, she tuts as if he's bothering her and continues her conversation.

Now I straighten up in my seat.

The coughing *is* bothering her. It is bothering everyone on the bus. His loud gasps for breath can't be ignored, and yet they are. Rules state that if anyone aids a Flawed, they will be imprisoned, but not in this case, surely? Are we to watch him struggling right before us?

The coughing stops.

My heart is pounding.

I let go of Art's hand. It feels clammy.

"What's up?"

"Can't you hear that?"

"What?"

"The coughing."

He looks around. "There's no one coughing."

The coughing starts again, and Art doesn't bat an eyelash when he looks at me intimately and says, "You know I can't wait to be somewhere alone. Why don't we miss the first class?"

I can barely hear him over the coughing, over my pounding heart. Does nobody hear the old man? Does nobody see him? I look around, flustered. All eyes are staring out the window or on him in disgust, as if he's about to infect us all with his flaws.

Juniper's eyes are filled with tears. My own flesh and blood agreeing with me is validation enough. I make a move to stand up, and Art's hand suddenly clamps around my arm.

"Don't," he says firmly.

"Ow!" I try to move, but instead his grip feels like a red-hot iron. "You're hurting me."

"And do you think when they sear your skin it won't hurt more than this?" He squeezes tighter.

"Art, stop! Ouch!" I feel my skin burning.

He stops.

"How is this fair?" I hiss.

"He has done something wrong, Celestine."

"Like what? Something that's completely legal in another country but that people are prosecuted for here anyway?"

He looks as if I stung him.

"Don't do anything stupid, Celestine," he says, sensing he has lost the argument. "And don't help him," he adds quickly.

"I have no intention of helping him."

How I walk by this coughing, wheezing, struggling-to-breathe old man is beyond me, but I do, seeing the faint *F* scar on his temple as though it has been there a very long time, like it's as much a part of him as the freckles and hair alongside it. I walk straight to the two women in the Flawed seats. They are chatting about making jam, as if nothing is wrong.

"Excuse me," I say sweetly, offering them the most polite smile I can muster. They respond immediately with their own bright smiles. Two polite, friendly women from the suburbs willing to help me with anything. Almost anything.

"Yes, dear."

"I was wondering if you could help me."

"Of course, dear."

"Could one of you sit in any of the available seats here? Or I could offer you two seats together where my boyfriend and I are sitting so that you can continue your conversation?"

As I look up at Art, all I can see is terror on his face. Funny, I no longer feel it. I like solutions. The problem was disturbing me, and fixing it just made sense. I'm not doing anything wrong; I'm not breaking any laws or rules. I've always been complimented on my timing, my perfection. I come from a good home. I have a pleasant manner. The anklet of geometric harmony proves it.

"May I ask why?" the woman with the broken leg asks.

"Well, this man here"—I point to the old man—"is clearly Flawed, and you are in the Flawed seats. He can't sit down anywhere else. And he is struggling."

I notice a few faces turn to stare at me when I say that. I expect them to understand. I expect there to be no further conversation. I even expect the few who have overheard to step in and agree, make sense of the situation. But they don't. They look confused, some even scared. One man looks amused. This is illogical. This is Juniper's territory, not mine. I look at her. She has the same face of terror as Art does.

She is not moving. If I ever thought she was going to back me up, I know now that she won't.

"But we're talking," the other woman says.

"And he's choking," I say with the same smile on my face, which I know looks a little psychotic, because we are no longer being polite.

"Are you trying to help him?" the woman with the crutches asks.

"N-n-no," I stutter. "I'm not. I'm trying to help the situation. . . ." I flash her a brilliant smile, but she recoils from me.

"I want nothing to do with this," the other woman says loudly, attracting more attention.

"With what?" I laugh nervously. "Your leg is fine. Perhaps if *you* just move to another chair and your friend stays here . . ."

"I'm staying right where I am," she hollers.

Now we have the attention of the entire bus.

The old man, who is beside me, can barely stand. He is bent over coughing. He turns to me, face purple, and tries to talk, but he can't catch his breath.

I don't know what he's trying to say. I don't know what to do. I don't know what medical help to give him. Even if I knew what medical help to provide, I wouldn't be able to give it to him. *Think, think, Celestine. I can't help, but a doctor can.*

"Is there a doctor here?" I call down the bus, and I see Art put his face in his hands.

There's an audible gasp in the bus.

I look around at everyone, the judgmental faces of surprise. I feel dizzy and confused. This man is going to collapse, maybe die. My eyes start to fill.

"Are we going to just watch this?" I scream.

"Stop it, dear," a woman says to me in a hushed voice. She is clearly upset about it, too. It's not just me, but she's warning me. I'm going too far.

47

This is completely illogical. Have we no compassion for this human being, Flawed or not, that we won't help?

Heads look away. Eyes are averted.

"Okay, okay," I say to the old man, who by now is panicking severely. He continues to cough, and I can see the *F* on his tongue, which makes me recoil slightly. I can't imagine the pain of receiving it. "It's okay."

He punches his chest, starts to fall to his knees.

I pull him up under the arms, and I bring him to the nearest open seat.

"Stop the bus!" I yell.

The bus stops, and I assure the old man everything will be fine.

I look over at Juniper and see that she is crying.

"It's okay," I tell her and Art. "It's going to be fine." My heart is still pounding. "This has all been so very ridiculous." My voice is high-pitched and shrill; it doesn't sound like mine. And then I hear the siren, loud, close, intense, and threatening.

TWELVE

EVERYBODY STAYS STILL in their seats, waiting, my heart beating loudly over the silence. Two Whistleblowers climb aboard blowing silver whistles so loudly most people block their ears. They make their way toward me and the old man.

"See? I told you it will be fine," I tell the man over the noise. "They're here. Help is here."

He nods faintly, his eyes closed. I expect them to go to the old man, who has passed out on the seat, exhausted and taking short breaths, a fine layer of sweat covering his skin. But they don't go to him. They come for me.

And then they take me away.

Juniper screams at them to leave me alone, held back by Art, who doesn't look much better. As they hold me under the arms and drag me away by the elbow, Juniper screams, "My sister! My sister!" They lead me down the steps of the bus and into their van, the sound of the whistles ringing in my ears.

THIRTEEN

BEFORE I WAS born, there was a great recession in this country; banks folded, the government collapsed, the economy was ravaged, unemployment and emigration soared. People were blindsided by what happened, and the leaders were blamed. The leaders should have known; they should have seen it coming. It was their bad judgment, their bad decisions that led to the country's collapse. They were evil people; they had destroyed families and homes, and they were to suffer. They were the morally flawed people who had brought about our downfall.

As a result, anyone who made the smallest error in judgment was immediately punished. These people were publicly ridiculed, held up as examples of failure, and forced to resign. They were named and shamed. They weren't criminals, but they had made bad decisions. Society demanded leaders who would not learn from hindsight— leaders who would not make the mistakes in the first place. No second chances, no sympathy, no explanations allowed nor required. Anybody who had made mistakes in the past couldn't take leadership roles in the future. And as hundreds of thousands of people marched on the government, it was decided that any person who made any error in judgment was to be rooted out of society entirely. Hindsight would be a thing of the past. Everybody would always—always—look ahead before it was too late, no mistakes made.

Could perfection be bred? Many ways to achieve this were tried and tested, and what the government eventually settled on was Crevan's Guild and its Flawed brandings. No matter what you do in your life, your Flawed title can never be removed. You hold it till death. You suffer the consequences of your one mistake for the rest of your life. Your punishment serves as a reminder to others to think before they act.

I'm taken to a holding cell in the basement of Highland Castle and guided to a table upon which sits an information pack containing all the information about the Guild that I need to know. It has a chapter dedicated to the rules you must adhere to living as a Flawed. It even has a comprehensive section on the searing of the skin: the process and how to treat your brand afterward. I slam the pack closed and look around.

The holding cells are pleasant; they are newly renovated. There are four total, two on each side of the room, separated by a walkway in the center, each one enclosed by bulletproof and soundproof glass. According to the information pack, the glass represents the transparency of the system, but I feel it is to prepare us for the lack of dignity coming our way and invasion into our lives. Each cell contains a table with four chairs, a single bed, a bathroom with real walls, and some randomly placed chairs should the desire for a holding-cell party take me. Everything is earthy tones, to make us feel like this is the most natural place in the world.

Of the four cells, I am the only occupant. The two opposite me are empty; the one beside me had been occupied—I can tell from the clothes, the items of belongings scattered. I assume this person is in the courtroom now, awaiting his or her fate. The bathroom, thankfully, has solid walls, but it has been made so small that you can barely spend a minute in there before feeling suffocated. It is where I have run to cry, though I may as well have stayed here and done it in full view because my tearstained face and red eyes are a giveaway, and there's nobody here to see me anyway.

I have not had the opportunity to speak with anyone yet, to analyze, dissect, and discuss what has happened. I was registered at reception by a nice lady in a Whistleblower uniform, who introduced herself as Tina, and then I was brought to this room beneath the Clock Tower, where the Guild has its offices. I know from watching trials on television, seeing Pia on every live report following the accused from the Clock Tower, all the way across the cobblestoned courtyard, to the Guild court, heads down and being hurled abuse by the public, who come to boo and hiss and show their support for the Guild.

I am definitely in shock. I must be. I cannot fathom how *I* can be *here*, me who doesn't do anything wrong, who is a people-pleaser, whose every report card is filled with perfect As, whose boyfriend's dad is the head judge of the Guild.

I go through my actions on the bus again, over and over in my head. I go through them so much they start to blur, like an overplayed song. I think about what I did, what I should have done, what I could have done better. I become confused as to what actually happened. I watch it happen over and over in my head; it's like staring at somebody's face until that person eventually starts to look different. I sit on the bed, my back against the only solid wall of my cell, and push my head to my knees, hugging my legs. I don't know how long I sit like this; it could be minutes, it could be hours, but my heart flits from calm to panic as I reason with myself.

I can't be Flawed. I can't be Flawed.

I am perfect.

My parents say so, my teachers say so, my boyfriend and even my sister—who hates me—say so. My sister. I think of Juniper's screams of defense as I was taken away, and my eyes fill. My big sister, who

52

was flailing against the unmoving Art to get to me. I hope she's okay. I hope they didn't take her, too. She will be forced to say she didn't agree with my actions, and I worry instantly. I don't want to drag her into this. Who knows what Juniper will say? And what about Art? How is he feeling right now? Is he in trouble? Will his dad help me or never speak to me again? Will Art ever speak to me again? The thought of ever being without him makes me feel sick.

Around and around it all goes.

A door slams and I look up.

Tina and a male guard escort a boy who looks about my age, maybe a little older. They pass my cell and take him to the one beside mine. I can tell by his familiarity with the place that he isn't new here, unlike me—as I was being led in, I frantically looked around to examine my new surroundings. His T-shirt is covered in white powder, and so is his hair. There are splashes of it on Tina and the male guard, too, which confuses me. The boy is tall, broad. He has a bold, stubborn face, a guilty look. He's young like me, but his face looks older.

The fact that he is young makes me sit up. I want him to see me. I want to share a look, a glance, something to comfort him, and to comfort me. The guards aren't as polite and gentle with him as they were with me, and this, selfishly, gives me hope that this has all just been a great big misunderstanding and I'll be able to walk out of here as normal. I watch him, his mean, tough, bold face, and will him to look at me. I wonder what he has done. It can't be a criminal act or he wouldn't be here, but it must have been close. Whatever he has been accused of doing, I have no doubt that he has done it.

He looks up at me once he steps into his cell and sees me through the transparent wall we share. My heart flips. Contact with somebody, for the first time in hours. But as quickly as he sees me, he looks away again and strides with his long, lean legs and sits with his back flat against the transparent divide, so that all I can see are his back muscles, rippling through his soiled T-shirt.

Insulted, scared, and suddenly feeling even more alone, I sense the tears start again. They comfort me; they make me feel human and remind me that I am human, even in here, in this box within a series of boxes.

The guards lock his door and leave. They disappear out the main door and I'm alone again, but this time with a boy who won't look at me.

The main door opens, and I see Mom, her face worried and frantic, and my dad, stern, wide jaw working overtime to contain himself. As soon as Mom sets her eyes on me, she becomes composed again, like she's taking a walk in the park and enjoying her surroundings, so I know that it must be bad. When Dad sees me, his face collapses. He's never been one to hide his feelings. Tina unlocks my cell door, and as they enter I rush to hug them both.

"Oh, Celestine," she says, voice laden with grief, as she squeezes me tightly. "What on earth possessed you?"

"Summer," Dad says harshly, to which she reacts as if she has been slapped.

I feel stung, too. The first real contact I've had since this happened and I was hoping for defense, for backup, not for an attack, not for my own mother to agree with them and point the finger at me. I knew that I was in trouble, but now it is really setting in.

"Sorry," she says gently. "I didn't mean to, but it is just so out of character for you. Juniper told us what happened."

"It didn't make any sense," I say. "The whole thing defied logic."
Dad smiles sadly.

"The man was coughing. Wheezing. He was about to pass out, probably die, and the fat woman and the broken-leg woman just kept on ignoring him! They were in his seat!" I'm talking quickly, leaning forward, in their faces, trying to make them understand. I'm almost pleading with them to see my side of the story, telling them how disgusting and unfair the entire thing was. I get up and pace. I start the story from the start, elaborating, maybe exaggerating, maybe the fat woman was fatter, maybe the coughs were more life-threatening, I try to get them to see what I saw, to say that they understand, that if they were in my shoes, they would have done the same. To tell me I am not Flawed.

Dad is watching with tears in his eyes. He is struggling with all this. It is Mom who jumps up suddenly and grabs me by the shoulders. Surprised by her grip, I look around and notice that the guy in the cell beside me is no longer sitting with his back to me but is instead on his bed, where he can see us. I wonder if he has in some way understood what I said, if he read my lips, but Mom grips me tighter and turns my focus back to her.

"Listen up." Her voice is a low, urgent whisper. "We don't have time. Judge Crevan is coming to see you in a few minutes, and you have to use every charm you've got. Forget everything we taught you. Right now, forget about right and wrong. This is for your *life*, Celestine."

I have never seen or heard Mom like this, and she's scaring me. "Mom, it's just Bosco, he'll under—"

"You have to tell him you were wrong," she says urgently. "You have to tell him you know you made a mistake. Do you understand?"

I look from her to Dad in shock. Dad is covering his face with his hands.

"Dad?"

"Cutter, tell her," Mom says quickly.

He slowly lowers his hands and looks so sad, so broken. What have I done? I crumple into Mom's arms. She moves me to a chair at the table.

"But if I tell Bosco I was wrong, it will mean admitting I'm Flawed."

Dad finally speaks. "If he finds out that *you feel you were right* to do what you did, then he will brand you Flawed."

"Don't lie about what you did, but tell him you made a mistake. Trust me," Mom whispers, afraid of being overheard.

"But . . . the old man."

"Forget the old man," she says sternly, so coldly, so devoid of all the love that I know her to have, that I don't recognize her, and for that I don't recognize the world. They are my roots, my foundations, and they sit before me now uprooted and saying things I never thought they'd say. "You will not allow a Flawed to ruin your life," she says, and her voice cracks.

We sit in silence as Mom tries to compose herself, to put the mask back on. Dad rubs her back smoothly, rhythmically, and I sit there, stunned. My thoughts are barely thoughts at all as they hop unfinished from one to the other over what they have just told me.

They want me to lie. They want me to say that what I did was wrong. But to even tell a lie is to be Flawed. To gain my freedom, I must for the first time become Flawed. It doesn't make sense. It is illogical.

The main door opens, and Mom and Dad bristle. Judge Crevan is coming.

FOURTEEN

I NOTICE THE boy in the cell sit up, too. I see the flash of red before I see him. Judge Crevan is like a winged man with his floating bloodred cloak. I see his sparkling blue eyes and his blond hair, and I think of Art and I feel at home. He smiles at me through the glass, his eyes crinkling at the sides as they always do, and inside I relax. I feel safe.

"Celestine," he says as soon as Tina lets him into the cell. He flashes his perfect white teeth and spreads his arms, and as he does, he looks like he's lifting his wings, about to take off. I run straight into them, and he closes his arms, the red robe wrapped around me. I feel protected. In his cocoon. It will be all right. Bosco will take care of me. He won't let this go any further.

As he hugs me, my cheek is pushed up against the rough crest on his chest. I am face-to-face with the Guild's crest and motto, "Purveyors of Perfection."

He kisses the top of my head and releases me.

"Right, let's sit. We have a lot to discuss, Celestine." He fixes me with one of his infamous stern gazes, and just as I always felt before, it looks comical, cartoonish. This is not the man I'm used to seeing in his house.

I hide the nervous smile that is twitching at my lips. Laughing now would not be good.

"Things are going to be very difficult for you over the next few days, but we'll get you through them, okay?"

He glances at Dad, who suddenly looks completely exhausted, and I think for the first time what he's had to tell people at work. How can he run a news station when his own daughter is headline news?

I nod.

"You'll have to listen to me and do as I say."

I nod again, feverishly.

"She will," Mom says firmly, sitting poker straight in her chair.

Bosco looks at me to respond.

"I will."

"Good. Now." He takes out a tablet and taps and swipes his documents. "This nonsense on the bus this morning." He sighs and shakes his head. "Art told me all about it."

I'm not surprised by this. Art wouldn't have had a choice in the matter, and I am sorry again by how my actions have affected the people I love. I assume Art told him the truth. Art would never lie to his dad, but would he to protect me? I'm suddenly unsure of the story I am to tell, particularly after being told by my parents to lie.

"Unfortunately, already there are people using your connection to Art to take advantage and undermine the work of the Guild. The minority, of course. You may be used as a pawn in their game, Celestine." He looks at my parents and then back to me. "This is just extremely bad timing in light of the Jimmy Child verdict this morning, where people think I was too lenient. But, Celestine, you have always been one of my greatest supporters. You're going to be just fine."

I smile, relieved.

"I have my notes, but I want you to tell me what happened this morning."

I wonder what Art has said, but then I settle for the truth, hoping I'm not getting him into trouble. After all, there were thirty other people on the bus who will testify to seeing exactly the same thing. All I have to say is that I know I was wrong. That *should* be easy.

"There were two ladies sitting in the Flawed seats. One had broken her leg and sat there because there was room to extend her leg, and the other was her friend. An old Flawed man got on the bus. He had nowhere to sit. He started coughing. He could barely stand. He was getting worse and worse. I asked the lady who didn't have the broken leg—"

"Margaret," Bosco interrupts me, staring at me intently, his eyes moving from my eyes to my lips, narrowed in suspicion, analyzing my every word, every facial expression, every little movement. I concentrate on the story.

"Right. Margaret. I asked her if she would move so he could sit down."

"Why?"

"Because—"

"Because he was disturbing the passengers on the bus, that's why," he interrupts. "Because his Flawed, disgusting, infectious cough was infecting the good people in our society, and you were concerned about them and yourself."

I pause, mouth open, unsure of what to say. I look at Mom and Dad. Mom is nodding coolly, and Dad's bloodshot eyes are focused on the table, not giving anything away. I don't know what to say. This is not what I expected.

"Continue," Bosco says.

"So she wouldn't move, and eventually I called out for a doctor—"

"To stop his disgusting condition from spreading," he says. "You were thinking of the people on the bus. Protecting them from the dangers of the Flawed."

I pause.

"Continue."

"So then I called for the driver to stop the bus."

"Why?"

"To help—"

"To get him off the bus," he snaps. "To get rid of him. So that the air of your fellow passengers would be cleaner, wouldn't be polluted. You are, in fact, a hero. This is what the people outside believe now. This is the story that Pia has been telling for the past two hours. People are gathering outside to see you, the hero who stood up to the Flawed."

My mouth drops and I look across at Dad, now understanding why he looks so shattered. Has he spent the whole morning spinning this story?

"But there's a problem," Bosco says. "You helped him into a seat. A seat for the flawless. And that is where my colleagues and I cannot agree, and I have spent the past hour discussing it with them. We have failed to mention this part to Pia, but, of course, there are at least a dozen people on that bus who will come forward with the story. They probably even have video."

He looks at my dad again and my dad nods. He has received video already, something recorded on someone's phone on the bus and sent directly into the news station. He's probably spent the morning fighting for it not to be shown. He knows what will happen if it is.

"Rest assured, your dad will do everything in his power to make sure that video doesn't hit the airwaves." It sounds like a threat.

"I told you I'm doing everything that I can," Dad says, looking him firmly in the eye.

Bosco holds his stare; they look at each other coldly.

Mom clears her throat to snap them out of their stare.

"So," Bosco says, "after hearing that testimony, I would say this accusation is a grave injustice, as someone who was, in fact, *aiding the Guild* cannot be condemned to a life as Flawed. However, my fellow judges disagree. With me and with one another. Currently, Judge Jackson, who is normally a sound man, regards your act as a moral misjudgment and would like a Flawed verdict. Judge Sanchez sees your act as aiding and assisting a Flawed, which carries a punishment of imprisonment."

Mom gasps. I freeze. Dad doesn't do anything. He probably already knew this.

"As you know, the minimum prison term for aiding a Flawed is eighteen months, and considering this act was carried out so publicly, on public transport, in full sight of thirty people, it carries the highest offense. We have argued this back and forth." He sighs, and I hear the weariness, the genuine discontent, for what is happening. "And we have reached an agreement of three years. But you will be released in two years and two months."

FIFTEEN

"WHAT?" I SAY. *Two years in prison?* But it's like I'm not there; they're talking about me like I'm not there.

"It is unfortunate timing for Celestine to have . . . slipped up," he says to Mom and Dad. "The vultures out there are willing to make an example of Celestine. Pia can only hold her ground for so long. Cutter, you and your team, of course, are pulling your own weight and covering the story as you always should, but there is extreme opposition from the other side. This isn't so much about Celestine being on trial as the Guild being on trial, and we cannot allow that. We cannot allow that." He sits up, puffs out his chest. "Cutter, I'll need your team to step it up. Candy has commented on the fact there has been some recent . . . upheaval at the station. I think, for the sake of your daughter, the reporting should be in strict keeping with the style and philosophy of the network. No wandering off . . ."

Is that a threat? Did I just hear Bosco threaten Dad? Candy is Bosco's sister; she's in charge of the news network. My head snaps around to look at Dad, and it appears as though there's another version of him underneath his skin just trying to get out but is being contained, restrained with force.

"Candy has quite rightly given Bob Tinder some time off due to personal issues. With the atmosphere being as it is now, I need him to be on his toes, performing at a high level to keep the gossipmongers and the opportunists at bay. The naysayers assume that Celestine will get away with this, that the Flawed court isn't entirely fair. She is the girlfriend of the son of the judge; she will get special treatment. And that is really what I want to do, Celestine," he says sadly, genuinely sad. "You make Art happy, the only person who can do that since his mother passed, and I know that he thinks the world of you. But, unfortunately, my colleagues, my own people, also see you as a pawn. They see you as the perfect example to show our doubters how the system is fair. How even the seemingly perfect girlfriend of the son of the head judge can be deemed Flawed. I am fighting two sides, dear Celestine."

I swallow hard.

"And I agree that no one can be seen to be above the Guild. No one can be seen to escape the justice of the Guild."

I think of the definition of what the Guild is: It is not a function of the Guild to administer justice; its work is solely inquisitorial. I want to say it aloud, but I know I shouldn't. Now is not the time for my black-and-white logic, though shouldn't it be?

"Do you realize just how much trouble you are in, child?" Bosco asks.

"Child," I say suddenly. "They can't send me to prison. I'm not eighteen for another six months."

"Celestine," he says, "an individual over sixteen can be deemed Flawed, and for a punishment of imprisonment, we can delay the start date until the day of your eighteenth birthday."

Bosco had said I could have a party on his yacht for my eighteenth birthday. Instead, I could be spending my first night as an adult in prison. I don't deserve this. Do I? Does anybody? Angelina certainly didn't.

I look over at the boy in the next room, who is sitting on his bed with his head down. I wonder how long he has been here, I wonder what he did. Bosco follows my gaze. As if sensing our stares, the boy looks up and looks directly at Bosco with a cold, hard stare, eyes filled with hate. Bosco matches the boy's look but holds such disgust and contempt for him that I shrivel and almost want to apologize on his behalf.

"You shouldn't be in here with such scum," Bosco says simply, and I'm glad the boy can't hear.

"What did he do?"

"Him? He's Flawed to the bone," he says, disgusted. "Though he doesn't know it yet. I don't even need to listen to the facts of the case to know his type. I can see it in him. Not like you, Celestine. You are pure. You should not have the future that is destined for him."

"What do I need to do?" I ask, voice shaking.

"You repeat the story we just discussed, and when they ask you about helping the old man into a seat, you say that you did not, that he sat there himself."

My mouth falls open. "But the old man will be punished for that."

"Yes, he will. He's old and very sick. He'll probably die before Naming Day anyway."

The old man did not sit down. He did everything in his strength to stay standing. It was me who helped him to the seat.

"I can't—"

"You can't what?" Bosco looks at me.

"I can't *lie*."

"Of course you can't," he says, confused, looking at me as if he doesn't recognize me. "To lie would be to prove that you are Flawed. I would never ask you to *lie*," he says, as though insulted. "It is the only way you will go free, prevent being branded for life, prevent being

64

Ousted. It is the *only* way. What we discussed here now is what happened, and you will confirm that in court, you will say loud and clear for all to hear that society must seek out and oust the Flawed scum in our society. It is the Guild's work, and you, in full support of the Guild and its values, were working under its rules. You didn't aid a Flawed. What you did was aid the Guild and, in turn, aid society. That's what you will tell them. Are we agreed?"

I'm the poster girl. One side wants to use me to prove the Guild is biased; the Guild wants to use me to prove that it isn't. The perfect girl to prove its power. It wants me to feed the fear.

"Agreed," I say shakily.

SIXTEEN

MY HEARING IS this afternoon. The boy in the room beside me, whom I have nicknamed Soldier, has continued to ignore me. I'm sure that seeing me embrace Bosco didn't do much to sway his initial feelings about me. The word that Pia Wang has been pushing on behalf of Crevan is that I was trying to get rid of the Flawed man from the bus, not help him. If Soldier has seen these reports, which I'm sure he has because Flawed Court TV is the only station we can get on the tiny television in our cells, then that is why he isn't looking at me. I can only gather from this that he is not anti-Flawed, that he feels my actions were unfair. If only he knew the truth, then he would know he had an ally in the cells. I know this untruth will save my life, but I can't help but feel embarrassed that this is the perception out there of me. I feel Soldier's disgust through the wall, and I don't blame him, but I wonder, if he had the same chance to get out of this, would he take it?

Dad goes back to work and Mom stays with me. She has brought with her a suitcase of my clothes for the trial, and it looks like she went into a clothes store and grabbed every item from the racks. Soldier watches with a sarcastic look as Mom lays out the clothes on my bed, hangs them from every point of the cell she can. He shakes his head and starts pacing. I feel self-conscious about all the fuss in my cell when he has been alone all morning, but I try to put his presence out of my mind and concentrate on saving my own life.

"That's a lot of pink," I state as I run my eyes over the selection.

"We've got pale pink, baby pink, orchid pink, champagne pink, pink lace, cherry blossom pink, lavender pink, cotton candy, hot pink. . . ." Mom lists the shades as she moves along the line, already eliminating the ones she doesn't like and tossing them back into the suitcase. The hot pinks, candy pinks, and lace are removed. The suggestive tops with the low fronts are taken away. We settle on baby pink: skinny cropped trousers and a blouse so light pink it is almost white, buttoned up the center with ruffles, and a pair of ballet flats. A walk across the cobblestoned courtyard in heels is too much of a stage set for a tripping/heel-getting-caught disaster. Not a good look for the cameras and the hysterical public, which will be there to watch me. The flats are pink-and-tan leopard print.

"They're sweet, but they say 'don't mess with me,' too," Mom says. "Remember, in this world, image is everything."

Tina arrives with a male mannequin, then leaves.

"Sweetheart, this is Mr. Berry," Mom says. "He will be representing your case. Judge Crevan recommended him, says he's the best. He represented Jimmy Child."

The mannequin suddenly moves. He offers me a big smile, a smile I don't believe, a smile that is as fake as the smooth skin on his face. From the neck down he looks sixty; from the chin up he looks thirty. He wears a dapper suit—like he's just walked out of the airbrushed pages of a magazine—shiny shoes, a handkerchief perfectly positioned in his pocket, and gold cuff links to match his gold tie. His face shimmers where his cheekbones have been accentuated, and I definitely see powder on his skin. He's perfect, and yet I don't trust him. I look over at Soldier, who is glaring at my newly appointed representative with suspicion. I must say I agree, once again, with his instincts. Our eyes meet, and he shakes his head as though I am nothing and then walks to the far corner of his cell, as far away from me as he can physically get.

"Celestine," Mom says. She jerks her head in Mr. Berry's direction, and I realize I haven't acknowledged him yet.

"I'm sorry." I move forward hastily, as if I've been pushed.

"I understand," he says, devoid of all understanding and affection, through his big white teeth. "So let's get to it." He takes his seat and bangs his briefcase down on the table before him. Gold clasps spring open. "Today is just procedure. You won't be required to say or do anything at all apart from deny the Flawed claim. Then they'll set a time for your trial tomorrow and send you home."

I breathe a sigh of relief.

"Celestine," he says, noticing my nerves, "you just stick with me, kiddo, do as I say, and we'll both be fine. I've done this a million times."

The *both* is not lost on me.

"Of course, your situation is unique. I don't usually have every member of the press and MTV outside my door. Not even for Jimmy Child, but then young women in the media are always more interesting. We found that helped us in Jimmy's case. They were more interested in his wife and her sister than him."

"MTV?"

"You're a pretty seventeen-year-old girl from a good part of town, no serious problems, girlfriend of the son of Judge Crevan. What's not to love about this case? Plus they're looking for a new reality show, and it looks like you're their newest target. You represent a generation that will be obsessed with every detail of every aspect of this case, a generation that is pliable, moldable, and just so happens to have more disposable income than any other demographic. Whatever shoes you wear today, they'll want tomorrow. Whatever earrings you're wearing, they will sell out by the end of this week. Whatever perfume you wear, there will be a waiting list for it tomorrow. It will be the Celestine North effect. The fashion and sales industry will love you."

He speaks so fast I can barely keep up with him, and he talks through a smile, which makes it difficult to read his plumped-up lips, which rarely move.

"Every single medium is going to use you for its own motivations— you remember that. You're a poster girl for the Guild, you're a poster girl for Anti-Guild, you're a poster girl for the clothes you're about to wear and for the lip gloss they're going to wonder about. Does your daily eating plan include carbs, and how many ab crunches do you do a day? Who does your hair? How many boyfriends have you had? Have you had a boob job? Should you? Plastic surgeons are lined up and ready to talk about every aspect of you, Celestine North, and I care about all those aspects because they affect the outcome of the biggest question of all: Are you Flawed?"

I don't know if he's waiting for an answer or not. He is simply studying me, all of me, with his snakelike eyes, which stare at me from under his eyelid-lift, so I don't respond. I will not give him the bene-fit, and I wonder again where this stubbornness comes from.

"Everyone is ready and waiting to use you for their own good, just you remember that."

Everyone? "And what's your angle?" I ask.

"Celestine." Mom gasps. "I'm sorry, Mr. Berry, but Celestine has the tendency to be so literal about everything."

"Nothing wrong with that," Mr. Berry says, studying me with his big smile, looking and sounding like there is everything wrong with all of that. "Like I said, today is procedural. You'll deny the charge, then you'll go home, and you'll wait until trial tomorrow. It will be all over by the end of tomorrow. You need to think about character witnesses. Parents, siblings, best friends who'd die for you, that kind of thing."

"My boyfriend, Art, is my best friend. He'll speak for me."

"Sweet," he says, flicking through his documents, "but he won't."

"Why not?" I ask, surprised.

"Better if I ask the questions," he says. "But seeing as you asked, Judge Crevan has decided he's off-limits."

I can tell he's uncomfortable with this decision, and I understand why. Bosco could not ask his son to lie about my helping the old man to the seat. It makes sense to me, and yet I feel deeply disappointed not to have Art on my side. I need him, and I wonder how hard he fought to speak up for me, or if he fought at all.

"Anyway, it doesn't matter. Nobody needs to hear how your boyfriend thinks you're perfect. Every boyfriend either thinks that or will lie about it even if he doesn't. And he won't be called as a witness to the scene, because there are thirty other people who are leaping at the chance to do just that. In particular, Margaret and Fiona, the two ladies involved."

I silently fume, then think hard. "My sister, Juniper."

"No," Mom says. "Juniper won't be taking the stand," she says to Mr. Berry.

They look at each other for a while, speaking a silent language that I don't understand.

"Why not?" I ask.

"We'll talk about that later," she says, smiling, but her eyes are warning me to leave it alone.

So Juniper won't speak on my behalf. Paranoia tells me she is ashamed of me, she has turned her back on me. She won't lie for me, or my parents won't let her lie. They don't want me to drag her down with me. Why lose two daughters when you can just lose one? My bitterness takes me by surprise. Earlier I hadn't wanted her to get into trouble, and now when I'm sinking deeper into it, I'm angered by those who are stepping away.

"You have other friends, I assume, and not just your sister and your boyfriend. We only need one."

Art became my life after his mom passed away, and by spending so much time together, we managed to alienate our group, who, though they understood, also felt a little betrayed and left out. But I know Marlena, my closest friend since childhood, will support me, despite how left out she's felt lately.

"You'll be out of here by tonight," Mr. Berry says.

"They won't keep me here?"

"No, no. They only do that in special cases, for those who are a risk of running, like that young man beside you."

We all look at Soldier, and Mom visibly shudders. He looks so lost, so angry, he doesn't stand a chance.

"Who is representing him?"

"Him?" Mr. Berry snorts. "He has chosen to represent himself, and he is doing a very bad job. You would almost think he *wants* to be Flawed."

"Who would want that?" Mom asks, turning away from him.

I think of the Flawed I pass every day, the people I can't look in the eye, the people I take steps around to avoid even brushing against. Their scars as identifiers, their armbands, their limited possibilities, living in society but everything they want being just out of reach. You see them all standing at the curfew bus stops in town, to be home by 10:00 PM in winter, 11:00 PM in summer. In the same world but not living in it the same way. Do I want to be like them?

"What's his name?" I ask.

"I have no idea," Mr. Berry says, bored, wanting to move on.

I look at him alone in there, me here with my selection of clothes, my mom, my representation, the head judge himself. I have people. He must hate me, yet that's what I must do to get out of here with my life intact. A light goes on for me. I could be in a far worse position. I could be in *his* situation. All that separates me from him is a lie. I must become imperfect to prove that I am perfect. I have to do everything Mr. Berry tells me to do.

———

Tina brings me a tray of food before I cross the courtyard to the court, but I am too nervous to eat. In the next cell, Soldier gobbles every bite as though his life depends on it.

"What's his name?" I ask her.

"Him?" She gives him the same look as everyone else has, though she hasn't treated me like that from the moment I arrived.

"Carrick."

"Carrick," I say aloud. Finally, he has a name.

Tina looks at me, eyes narrow and suspicious. "You should stay away from that boy."

We both watch him, and then I feel the weight of her stare on me as I watch him.

I clear my throat, try to act like I don't care. "What did he do?"

She looks at him again. "He didn't need to do anything. Guys like him are just bad eggs." She looks at my tray. "You're not eating?"

I shake my head. I'd rather eat when I get home later.

"You'll be fine, Celestine," she says gently. "I have a daughter exactly the same age as you. Reminds me of you. You shouldn't be here. You'll be at home tonight, in your own bed, where you belong."

I smile at her in thanks.

"They've called me upstairs for a meeting." She makes a face. "First time that's happened. Wonder what I've done wrong." She makes another face, and then, on my reaction, she laughs. "I'll be coming back, don't worry. You're doing great, kiddo. We'll go across to the court in thirty minutes, so eat up."

A new guard, Funar, appears, opens Carrick's door, and says something to him. Whatever it is, Carrick is eager. He hops up and goes straight to the door. Funar comes to my cell next.

"You want to get some fresh air?"

I jump up. Absolutely. He unlocks my door and I walk behind Carrick, realizing, as I see him up close for the first time and not through the glass, how solid and large he is. The muscles in his upper back are expansive, his biceps and triceps permanently flexed. I think about Art and feel guilty for even looking. Funar tries the side door that leads outside, but it's locked.

"Damn it, I'll have to go back for the key," he says. "Sit there and don't move. I'll be back in a minute."

He points to a bench by the wall in a corridor, and we both comply, sitting down side by side.

Our skin isn't touching, but I can feel the heat from his body from where I sit. He's like a radiator. I'm not sure whether to say anything to him. I don't even know what to say. He's not the most approachable person I've ever met. Do I ask him about his case? It's impossible to shoot the breeze in this situation. I sit, frozen, trying to think of something to say, trying to look at him when he's not looking in my direction. I finally sense he's about to say something when six people suddenly turn the corner into our corridor. The women are crying and huddling into the men, who are also red-eyed. They walk by us as though they're in a funeral procession and enter through a door beside us. When it opens, I look in and see a small room with two rows of chairs. It's facing a floor-to-ceiling pane of glass, which looks into another room. In the center of the other room sits what looks like an oversized dentist's chair, and there is a wall of metal units. I see the guard, Bark, open one unit, and there is hot fire inside. Confused, I stare in, trying to figure it out.

Then a man, flanked by two guards, is brought down the corridor. He doesn't look at us. He looks scared, terrified, in fact. He appears to be in his thirties and is wearing what I'd consider a hospital gown, but it's bloodred, the color of the Flawed. The guards lead him through a separate door from the one the men and crying women entered, which I'm guessing leads to the room with the dentist's chair. The Branding Chamber.

Carrick and I both peer in. The door slams in our face. I jump, startled. Carrick sits back, folds his arms, and stares ahead intently with a mean look on his face. His look does not invite conversation, so I don't say anything at all, but I can't stop fidgeting, wondering what is going on inside that room. After a moment, our silence is broken with the terrifying, bloodcurdling scream of the man inside as his skin is seared by the hot iron bearing the Flawed brand.

I'm stunned at first, but then my body begins to shake. I look across at Carrick, who swallows nervously, his enormous Adam's apple moving in his thick neck.

Funar strolls up the corridor with a smug look on his face. "Found them," he sings, jingling the keys in his hand. "They were in my pocket the entire time." He smiles and unlocks the door, revealing a narrow stairway that leads outside.

Carrick stands up and storms out the door. Once outside, he looks back at me to join him.

Everything around me starts to move. The walls come closer, the floor rises up to meet me. Black spots blot my vision. I feel like I'm going to be sick. Carrick looks at me in concern. I pass out.

We never did speak.

SEVENTEEN

A HALF HOUR later, with quivering legs, I stand at the enormous wooden double doors, with their elaborately carved embellishments, that lead out to the infamous cobblestoned courtyard. I know it from the daily news, seeing people walk back and forth from the court to the Clock Tower, giving the public and the media an opportunity to see the accused and vent their feelings. Mom and Dad are on one side of me, Mom linking my arm, and Mr. Berry is on the other side. We are flanked by Tina and Bark.

Mr. Berry adjusts his tie. "Is this straight?" he asks Tina.

Tina nods and then throws Bark a look that is easily deciphered.

I take a deep breath as the doors open, and I am greeted with sights and sounds that I could never have prepared myself for. The first thing I see is a cabbage that flies directly at me and hits me square in the chest. Boos and hisses fill my ears and my head. Mr. Berry starts walking, taking me along with him. For a moment I can feel Mom's hesitancy, but then, as though she's on a catwalk, she gets into her stride and I follow her lead, lifting my chin, trying to avoid the flour, eggs, and spit that are flying from the public.

Mr. Berry is giving me orders through his big smile: *Smile, don't smile, chin up, don't look worried or guilty, don't react, ignore that man, watch out for that flying dog shit.* All this he says through a perfect smile. Dimples and all.

I link Mom even tighter, moving my body closer to hers, and take a quick look at her. She is holding Dad's hand, her head up, her face completely serene, and her hair in an elaborate chignon. I try to copy her, nothing out of place, composure, innocence, serenity, perfection.

The cameras are in my face; the flashes are blinding. I hear some questions, but others I can't.

"Are you Flawed, Celestine?"

"Who are you wearing?"

"Do you believe the Guild will give you a fair and balanced trial?"

"Are you hoping for the same outcome as Jimmy Child?"

"Who's your favorite music artist right now?"

"Is it true you got a nose job?"

"What is your opinion on the government and the Guild's current relationship?"

I think of the many people over the decades who have walked this walk, who walk over perfect and walk back Flawed through a courtyard of catcalling and convictions, over cobblestones of prejudice. I think of Carrick, who returned this morning with flour on his T-shirt. I understand why now. We are to be held up to the rest of the world as a mirror of their worst nightmares. Scapegoats for all that is wrong in their lives.

Cameras are in my face, and this feels like the longest walk ever. Microphones, jeering, catcalls, wolf whistles. I feel the muscles in my face tremble and wonder if it's noticeable. I quickly search the faces in the crowd. They are the faces of normal, everyday people, but filled with loathing. Some are merely interested to see what's going on; others throw themselves into it. One woman gives me a nod. It's respectful, and I'm thankful for that one effort.

And then we are inside.

"I see people need convincing of our story," Mr. Berry says, a little shaken as he brushes down his suit.

Three judges in bloodred robes sit at the head of the room, at a raised level. The majority of the room is laid out with rows of chairs. It is not a typical courtroom because it is in a ballroom of the old castle. There is not a free seat. At the back, people are crushed and standing. I assume they are the press, but on closer inspection, I see that they are all wearing armbands and that they are all Flawed. They stand in twos, broken up by a member of the media or a public spectator in accordance with the Flawed gathering rules.

I sit at my table at the head of all the seating, beside Mr. Berry.

Mom and Dad sit in the front row behind me. There is no sign of Juniper. I look around desperately for Art, hoping for the energy that simply seeing him will give me. No sign of him, which breaks my heart. I see my granddad and I almost weep. He tips his hat.

Bosco asks me to stand.

"Celestine North," he begins. "You stand before me charged with the offense of being a Flawed citizen of this country, for acting on an error of judgment, and as a result face ousting from regular society. Do you deny or accept this accusation?"

"Deny," I say, my voice tiny in the large room, and I'm glad it's over, that it's the only thing I have to say today, because I fear that my legs, which are shaking so much, will crumple beneath me.

"Very well. We hear your plea and will over the course of your trial hear from witnesses to both the event and your character. Based on that, we will announce our findings. You may leave now, go to your home, and return to us here tomorrow morning at—"

"Just a moment, Judge Crevan," Judge Sanchez interrupts. "I, and Judge Jackson, would like to put forward the motion that Ms. North remain in our holding cells until the trial is over."

Bosco looks surprised to hear this.

"We feel that due to the status of Ms. North, and the attention garnered, that her going back to her home, to her life, could give her opportunity or give others opportunity to use her and her situation to their advantage."

"This is the first I've heard of this," Bosco says angrily. "And I am opposed to the idea. We only detain the accused if they pose a risk of running, and Ms. North is not a threat. It would be impossible for her to disappear given the attention on her."

"Indeed, Judge Crevan, but given the attention on her, we would like to prevent a circus, a spectacle being made of such a serious case."

"But if she stays in her home, speaks to no one?"

"This was the same for Jimmy Child, and we know that the parameters put in place were breached."

Bosco bristles at this, as though it has been directed at him personally. "Ms. North is not Mr. Child."

"No, but we have learned from his trial. We feel that it is in the best interest of the Guild and the accused to confine this case within the walls of Highland Castle."

"We need to discuss this in my chamber. This is not something that can just be—"

"I propose it now," Judge Sanchez says coolly.

"And I favor it," Judge Jackson agrees.

"And I oppose it," Bosco says, bewildered. "She is just a child."

"She will be eighteen in six months, and she is being held away from the other detainees. Only one other accused is in the same chamber as her, an eighteen-year-old detainee, which is the best we can do given the circumstances."

Bosco is speechless.

"And so it is passed. Celestine North will return to her holding cell for the duration of her trial." Judge Sanchez bangs the gavel against the block and looks smug.

The room erupts.

Mr. Berry stares at Bosco in a stunned silence, while the rest of the room is in constant movement, spinning.

"How can this happen?" Mom is asking Mr. Berry, who is so still it is as though he can't hear her. She grabs the arm of his suit, which is pin-striped with pink fine lines. "How could you let this happen?"

"There's something going on," he says, more to himself, but I hear him.

He looks at me, and there is a crack in the smooth exterior. I see pity in his eyes, and that, from him, terrifies me. "I'm sorry, Ms. North. It appears even Judge Crevan's enemies have decided to use you as a pawn in their game, too."

EIGHTEEN

WHEN I RETURN to the holding cell, covered in I-don't-know-what thrown at me on the return journey, Carrick immediately jumps up. He is as surprised to see me as I am to be back here. I am dazed and confused. Tina guides me into the cell. I have already said good-bye to my parents. Carrick follows me all the way from the door to my bed, the entire length of the cell. For the first time since I got here, he demands my attention. Even though this is what I've wanted since I saw him, I can't look at him. He wants an explanation. Everybody thought I'd go home; everybody thought I'd get away with this. Carrick thought he knew the rules, but the rules changed. He needs to know what is going on more than anyone else. If I am doomed, then so is he.

I can't be bothered to give him an explanation. I don't have one. I feel completely numb. I sit on my bed, staring into space, still feeling his eyes on me. He stands at the glass, two hands pressed up against it, almost ordering me to look at him. I want Art. I need Art. Only he could make everything all right, right now. I lie down and turn my back to Carrick, and I don't move all night, because I don't want him or anyone else to see me cry.

NINETEEN

AFTER A NIGHT of nightmares, of hearing that man in the Branding Chamber screaming in anguish, of dreaming of bleeding tongues and of ghoulish Flawed reaching for me and grabbing at me from the barricades as I walk through the courtyard, I wake up feeling exhausted and scared, confused as to where I am. It is the day that I will testify on my own behalf. The day I tell Bosco's lie. It is Naming Day.

I'm awake at 5:00 AM, lie still until 5:30, and then get up, pacing like a caged animal waiting for everything to commence. Carrick wakes at six and lies in his bed, sleepily watching me from under his blankets. After a while, he sits up, back against the wall, knees raised, elbows resting on his knees, already familiar with this routine. This frustrates me even more. There is nowhere I can escape him, apart from the small toilet, but I can't spend any amount of time in there longer than necessary. I'm sure they've made it the size of a hole for a reason.

At 8:00 AM Tina and Funar come to our cells, and we are guided to the showers. I expect Carrick to ignore me as he did most of the day yesterday, but he gives me a light nod, and there's something softer behind his eyes. Perhaps I've gone up in his estimation in not being sent home yesterday, and I understand. I have always felt that he and I are in this together, ever since I saw him walk into the holding cells. For him, it took about eighteen hours later to agree. Even in all the times I woke up during the night, afraid and disoriented, I looked across at Carrick and immediately was oriented and calmer. He was the trigger to calm me, nothing else in the room. I don't know if having someone of his build on my side is simply wishful thinking. I know this connection seems so intense over such a short period, but I feel as though I'm in a pressure cooker, and he is the only person in it with me who could possibly understand. Experiencing it at the same age only adds to that connection.

I smile a good morning, and he holds out his hand to let me walk ahead of him. Funar whistles lightly, childishly, a *whit-whoo,* and Tina tells him to shut up. I smile and look behind me quickly to catch Carrick's reaction. Not so much a smile as a light behind his eyes. Maybe they're green. Our eyes meet to share the joy of Funar's embarrassment at being silenced, and then I quickly turn back to follow Tina. I feel self-conscious that Carrick's behind me, and I'm also hoping we're not being taken on another "lesson." I guess that we're not, seeing as Tina is here, and I wonder if I should tell her what happened yesterday when she was upstairs, or if I should suck it up as Carrick has done. Perhaps there are rules in bravery. If so, I will follow Carrick's lead.

He's taken left, I go right. After the shower, I dress in fresh clothes and I'm taken back to my cell. Carrick is already in his cell, sitting at a table with a dumpy man in a tattered suit. Carrick's hair has a shine to it, still wet, and he looks freshly shaven and is in a new sludgy-green T-shirt. I'm sure Mom would have chosen something else, something warmer, to bring out his eyes, whatever color they are, but I like it. It's like he's a soldier, because it strikes me that he's not looking for clemency, he's looking for a fight. I study him when he's not looking, to see what color his eyes are. I don't know why I'm obsessing over this. I suppose it's because Art's are so clearly blue. You see them before you see him. They're one of the things I love most about him, whereas with Carrick, his eyes seem black, but they can't possibly be. Perhaps his pupils are just constantly dilated from anger.

The dumpy man in Carrick's cell has a red, flustered face, and it looks like breathing is a difficult act for him. He rifles through papers. They're talking and it's intense, but I can't hear what they're saying. The man is explaining something. He is hot and bothered, and Carrick's face is angry already.

My door opens. It's Tina.

"Who's he?" I ask.

"His adviser."

I notice she never uses Carrick's name.

"But I thought he was representing himself."

"He is, but he still needs assistance. Paperwork to be filed, et cetera. Paddy is his mentor. You would be sent one, too, but you have Mr. Berry."

I look at Paddy, who looks like he's about to die of a coronary, and I'm once again grateful for Mr. Berry despite the fact that in any other situation, I wouldn't trust him. Just enough to trust him with my life.

"There's someone here to see you. In the cafeteria."

My heart flips. Art. I need him. I want to be back on the summit with my legs wrapped around him, feeling his heartbeat through his chest. I know that as soon as I see him, I will feel calm and human again, and not like this caged animal.

As we're walking by Carrick's cell, something, a flash of color, attracts my notice. I don't hear anything because the glass is sound-proof, but I see it in the corner of my eye. I stop walking and look to see a tray of food fall from the window to the ground, cups and saucers and food lying in tatters on the floor of his cell. Behind it is an angry Carrick, the one responsible for firing it directly at my head, his face twisted in anger and aggression.

I'm stunned. It was clearly aimed at me, but I can't figure out what I've done.

Tina surprises me by laughing. "So I guess he just found out."

"Found out what?"

"Bark! Funar!" she calls. "Bad egg."

Funar appears at the guards' office door and grunts.

She turns back to me, and we continue walking. "He's learned that his case is on hold until yours is finished," she replies. "That's the fourth time that happened. First, Dr. Blake, then Jimmy Child, and then Angelina Tinder."

"How long has he been here?"

"A few weeks."

"Weeks?" I ask, shocked. "And how much longer will he be here?"

"Whenever you're finished. He's a flight risk and has anger issues, obviously. Can't risk letting him go. Been trouble ever since he got here. Serves him right, to be honest. If he didn't act like such an animal, his case could have been pushed through by now. Now come along this way. You can get breakfast here, too." She takes me by the elbow and pulls me along.

I look back at Carrick. He stares at me with his cold, hard eyes, chin raised, chest heaving up and down at the exertion of his fit of rage. Tina called him an animal, but I don't blame him at all. A few weeks in this place and I'd start to behave like one, too. I try to give him a look of apology, but I'm not quite sure how to pull that off. I need words, and he and I have never shared any. I half-walk, half-run along as Tina pulls me. He stands still, hands on his hips, and watches me all the way out the door, probably wishing I'd never come back. Maybe his eyes really are black.

TWENTY

MY HEART IS pounding when I arrive at the cafeteria, and it is a remarkably different atmosphere from the one I just left. It feels like civilization, and I can hardly believe it was only yesterday morning that I, too, was walking around freely. People having breakfast meetings before work, lots of dark suits with heads close together, tablets out on every table. Free people who come and go when they want. And Art. Somewhere in this room is Art. My stomach flutters.

"He's over there." Tina points and backs away. "I'll come back in half an hour so you can get ready for your big moment."

I swallow hard at the thought of it.

I go in the direction Tina pointed me to, searching for Art, for his white-blond hair, for his turquoise-blue eyes, but I can't find him anywhere. I'm aware of all the eyes on me as I weave my way between the tables. When I get to the end of the room, I look around, confused, then I start walking back again.

I feel a hand, a rough grip, around my wrist.

"Ow," I say, pulling away. An old, wrinkled hand with protruding veins grips my arm. "Granddad!"

"Sit down," he says harshly, but his face is soft.

I embrace him quickly and then slide into the seat before him, happy to see him but trying to hide my devastation that Art hasn't come to see me. I wonder if it's because he's not allowed or because he doesn't want to.

I don't get to see Granddad as often as I used to after he and Mom had their falling-out last Earth Day. He's welcome in our home, but only when invited, and he isn't invited as much as he used to be. It is all on Mom's terms now. Grandma passed away eight years ago, and he lives alone, tending to his dairy farm.

He looks around conspiratorially, and for once he's not just being paranoid. Most of the people here are staring at us.

"We have to keep our voices down," he says, moving his head close to mine. "Did you see this?"

He reaches inside his jacket and retrieves a newspaper. It's folded lengthways, and he slides it across the table to me. "They won't want you to see this one, that's for sure."

I open the paper and am shocked by what I see. My photograph takes up practically the entire front page, with only a small space for a dramatic headline and the rest of the story inside. My mouth falls open. The headline shouts, THE FACE OF CHANGE?

He slides another across to me. It's a variation of the same photo, with the headline NORTH. NEW DIRECTION FOR FLAWED CAUSE.

"What? Which papers are these?" I ask, not recognizing them.

"You won't see these papers around here," he whispers. "They're not Crevan's. He doesn't own them all, you know."

"He doesn't own any of them, Granddad. They're his sister's, Candy's," I correct him, scanning the articles.

"In name only. You're about to learn Crevan's more involved with those papers than anybody else is. You're all over Crevan's papers, too. However, their slant is slightly different. All about the girl who protects society from the Flawed. You're a hero on both sides. Or a villain, depending on your opinion."

Which explains the reason for the level of anger outside in the courtyard. I've annoyed just about every side you can imagine. Nobody comes to watch a Flawed cross the courtyard to support them.

Granddad's conspiracy theories are what Mom fought with him about. It was fine and harmless for him to believe them on his own, on his farm, in the middle of nowhere, but when he kept bringing them to her doorstep, he was, as she said, bringing danger into our home. Particularly when he was sitting at the same table as Bosco. I thought it was funny at the time, the comments he used to make, but now I see why Mom was afraid.

The sight of me on the front pages is overwhelming, the things they are saying about me, how they are analyzing and dissecting my actions when I, who did what they're talking about, gave it much less thought. If I am who they say I am, which side am I to believe? I don't think either of them know me at all.

"Granddad, have you spoken to Juniper? Do you know anything? Is she okay? She won't be a character witness for me. Does she hate me?"

"I haven't seen her and I'm sure she doesn't hate you. Your mother won't let me into the house. I've tried, but she thinks I've lost my mind. It's just that I've got all this. This proof." He starts taking out scraps of paper from every pocket of his jacket, some cutouts, some with scribbles on them. "I've been collecting information. A lot of which I think will help you. Your mother won't listen, but you need to. There are two very important names to remember, Celestine: Dr. Blake and Raphael Angelo. Forget Mr. Berry. They can help you with your case. We need to find them—"

"Granddad, stop please," I say gently, closing my hands over his. "It's going to be okay," I say, sounding calmer than I feel. The Branding Chamber really shook me up yesterday, and I know it was a warning from someone. I'm not about to ignore that warning. "Bosco is helping me." I keep my voice down incredibly low. "We've talked already. I just need to do what he and Mr. Berry say, and it will be okay."

But the old man won't be okay, my conscience tells me. The old man whom I'm about to accuse of breaking the Flawed rules. The man who reminded me of my own granddad. How could I do it to him? I push it to the back of my mind, knowing I must stay in survival mode.

Granddad snorts. "Celestine, whatever that man has promised you, I would not rely on it. He was double-crossed yesterday by his own two judges. Sanchez and Jackson have had enough of him and his double standards, and it will happen again. They're not happy about his decisions lately. They feel he's using his ties to the people to push through whatever decisions he wants, trying to convince the media of his beliefs, not to mention what he did to that poor newspaper editor's wife. There's a war brewing, Celestine. Don't let them use you."

"Bosco wouldn't *use* me, Granddad."

He studies me. "Do you believe in what you did, love?"

I look down. Then back at him and nod.

"What are you afraid of then?"

"Being *Flawed*! The *pain*, the scars, the rules, the curfew, the life, the Whistleblowers, losing my friends, people laughing at me, staring at me. Being thought of as one of *them*. Yesterday they made me listen to a man in the chamber, Granddad. He screamed so loud I'll never forget it," I say, my eyes filling.

"Ah, love," he says, taking my hand. "They're playing tricks on you, you know that. It's all mind games. It's about power. Control. This society we live in."

He loses me with his conspiracy words again.

"Live with me," he says, suddenly full of enthusiasm. "It's a simple life, but you can live as you like, no one looking over your shoulder telling you what to do and who to love. I won't bother with the curfews, don't bother with the diet nonsense. You can go to bed when you like and get up when you like, eat what you like, go out with whatever fella you like. It's not like here in the city. You can be as free as you can be."

"They have Whistleblowers in the country, too, Granddad," I say gently, grateful for the thoughtful offer, but it's not something I could even contemplate. "I can't do it. I can't be Flawed. And I'd miss Art. Tell me, have you seen him? Has there been anything about him in the paper? I thought maybe he'd visit me or send me a message or something. . . ." I chew on my nail.

Granddad goes quiet and studies me, concern in his eyes.

"I just . . ." I pull my finger from my mouth. "It's not just a childish thing, you see, me and him, it's serious. We have plans. We've talked about everything we want to do after school, together. I really, you know, love him." I haven't even said this to Art myself yet, but I will. As soon as I get out of here, it will be the first thing I'll say as I feel it more now, away from him, than ever before.

Granddad looks sad. He reaches inside his pocket, and I wait to see another newspaper, but instead he slides an envelope across the table. "This is from him. I didn't want to give it to you. They're not your sort, Celestine, that family." He shakes his head. "You're better than them. But I can't play God in your life. You have to make your own decisions now. And you've some big ones to make."

I nod, barely hearing what he's saying. I'm so excited about the letter, wanting him to leave so I can rip it open straightaway and see Art's words.

"But just think about this, love: Do you think your friend Bosco will let you go near Art when you get out of here? Even if you're not Flawed? I'd think twice about that if I were you. Prepare yourself. Nothing will go back to being exactly as it was before."

I have thought about that, in the deepest, darkest corners of my mind, but as Art is the only thing keeping me going, thinking about losing him would tip me over the edge.

"You tell the truth in court today, Celestine. And if they tell you that you are Flawed, then you wear that like a badge of honor. Look at what these papers are saying! You are in a position to make change. You already felt that yourself. You went with your gut, with what felt right, and you have inspired people."

"Inspired?" Tears fill my eyes. "An old woman *spat* at me yesterday, Granddad. A nice, decent old woman."

"Well, then there was nothing decent about her. The people who want change are just begging you to be their girl. Don't let the Guild wrap you up in their bloody red wings and make you think you're one of them. You're not, and you never will be. Seize the moment, Celestine, and *say* it. Give a voice to those who are silenced."

His eyes are shining with excitement, filled with tears, filled with hope that his granddaughter can be this person he so wants me to be.

"I'm not like you and Juniper, Granddad," I say sadly, feeling defeated. "This isn't who I am. I follow rules, I like logic, I solve problems. I don't speak out of turn on things I know nothing about. I don't want to stand out. I want to fit in. I don't want to be a poster girl for anything."

"Oh, but you already are, Celestine. The tide is changing, and whether you wear the branding of the Flawed or you walk out of here a free woman, you'll never be the same girl you were. They'll be watching you, all of them, and who would you prefer they watch? *You* or the girl you're pretending to be?"

TWENTY-ONE

Hi, Perfect Girl,

I hope you're okay in there. I can't believe they didn't let you come home, but Dad says he's doing everything he can for you. I want to be there for you, but I'm not allowed. Too much press, etc. Hope you understand, but I'm watching you on TV all the time. You look hot. I hope you're wearing the anklet. You'll always be perfect to me. Do whatever Dad and Berry Boy say, and we'll be back on the summit before you know it.

   I'm on your side.

Love always,
Art
PS-What did the elephant say to the naked man? How do you breathe through something so small?

I giggle and fold the letter into a tiny square and tuck it into my pocket. *Love always! Love always!!* Okay, it wasn't *I love you,* but it's close, isn't it? Is it the same?

I don't look at Carrick in the next cell, who's lying on his bed with his back to everyone, no doubt hating me even more than he already did. Art's words have given me hope that when I get out of here, there is a future for me and him. I hold on to that thought. I feel lifted, like I've been connected to the real world and this whole Flawed thing is a misunderstanding easily fixed. I don't even notice Mom and Mr. Berry enter the cell; and when I look up, I realize it's time.

"Green," Mom says, displaying the most beautiful dress I have ever seen. "The color of nature, youth, spring, and hope."

The dress is not entirely green. It contains the most beautiful scene, a picture of green leaves, flowers, exotic birds, a canvas of nature, of natural beautiful things.

"It's also the color of envy," Mr. Berry says, adjusting his green silk tie. "And that's what we'll be of every Flawed person in the country," he says with a grin. "For today is the day, dear Celestine, that you will walk away from here exactly as you walked in."

I find it a bad analogy. I will never be the same again. But maybe he wasn't mistaken. I will be as judged when I leave as I was when I walked in. Granddad's right. It will never end.

Before I leave the cell, I look at Carrick for something, a response of any kind. He is up from his bed now and his eyes run over my dress. I feel naked under his stare, but I can't move.

He nods at me. A good-bye, a good luck, I don't know, but it's not angry. I nod back. I take a mental picture of him, knowing it's the last time I'll ever see him as our lives go in two very different directions.

Dad, Mom, me, and Mr. Berry, flanked on either side by Bark and Tina, stare at the closed double doors ahead of us. Something is going on, because Bark and Tina are holding riot shields, which seems to unsettle Mr. Berry. He checks his green tie at least five times. They all know something apart from me. As soon as the doors open, I see that the security and crowd have doubled since yesterday, as have the media. The crowds are being held back by barricades, and security wear helmets and hold bloodred riot shields in their leather-gloved hands. The sound from the crowd is unbearable. I can't make out anything anyone is saying, but if you could trap anger in a jar, this is what you would hear each time you twisted the lid.

A can of something goes flying before us and emits steam. Security bundle around it, and we all quicken our step. Mom shows no sign of wobbling today, her head and chin are up. And as much as I want to keep my eyes down, she forces me to follow suit. If I can't feel it inside, then I at least want to appear as strong as her. Today there are people shouting at me for being Flawed, and there are people shouting at me for hating the Flawed. The only thing in common between them is that they detest me and are here to see me branded Flawed and Ousted from society. Nobody comes here to offer support, it's merely to vent frustration, to use me as a punching bag. I don't know how Bosco and Pia's media campaign is going in persuading people to think I'm the Guild's hero, but judging by the reaction today, somebody is losing: me.

Despite my terror, I look around. Maybe if I can put faces to the sounds, it will make me feel better. I see Pia Wang reporting from her raised platform, in her perfect clothes, with her perfect hair, even more doll-like in reality. A familiar woman with a pixie cut nods at me again respectfully, just as she did yesterday. A strange-looking man at the barricades blows a kiss at me. There is something familiar about him, but I'm sure I have never seen him before. He has a beard and long hair, hippie-like, but he seems too youthful to have such growth on his face. He wears a childish, elephant-shaped woolen hat. The large, floppy, oversized elephant ears cover his ears, and a trunk protrudes from his head. It is a bizarre thing to see on a man his age, as well as at this time of year, when it's not cold. As I near him, I study him more, and he winks. It's the blue eyes that give him away. Art. I knew he'd find a way to come. I almost stall in my tracks, but Mom and Mr. Berry keep me moving. I think of the elephant joke in his note and know that the hat is a reference to that and that he's trying to cheer me up. It's not something that's going to make me laugh in this situation, but it lifts my spirits. I try hard not to smile, though.

"Celestine! Pia Wang from News 24," she calls. The camera is on me, the red light on. "We're live. Can you wave to the people at home?"

"Smile," Mr. Berry says through his teeth, and I lift my face to the camera on the raised platform and give a small wave with a tiny smile. I don't want to look like I'm enjoying this.

Like yesterday, there are plenty more flying objects, though the riot shields do a good job of blocking most of them. Still, some manage to splatter my dress, but Mom is prepared this time. As soon as we step inside, she whips out wipes and cleaning products, and I am once again immaculate. Once inside, it's clear that we are all shaken. Mr. Berry asks for a glass of water and takes a moment to compose himself. Mom rushes to the bathroom.

Dad takes me aside.

"No matter what happens today, sweetheart, you know I'm proud of you. No matter what, I will love you," he says with urgency.

"Thanks, Dad."

He looks around, seems strained, unsure of whether to say something or not.

"Dad, tell me," I say, voice low.

"I haven't said much during all this. Your mom said it was better I don't, but I think I need to. It's just that . . . I don't want you to think that because of what *I* do, it means that you can't . . . that *you* can't use your own voice. You understand?" He looks at me intensely. He looks exhausted, like he hasn't slept in days. His eyes are bloodshot. "Bob took a stand at work, he wanted to use his own voice and . . . well, he was punished for that. Angelina was punished because of him. It was a warning to us all. I will defend you no matter what, Celestine. I have no problem with that. I'll tell whatever news story Crevan tells me to do, because that's my job and I try to protect Summer, you, Juniper, and Ewan, but don't be me. *You* do what *you* have to do."

Now? He says this to me *now?* Angelina Tinder was branded because Bob wanted to speak out? And yet, as soon as he said it, I know that I knew it already, somewhere deep down, somewhere I was afraid to say it out loud.

I swallow hard and nod, almost afraid of the intensity of his look, by his grip on my arm. I know Dad is trying to be helpful, but I can't help but still feel confused as to what *he* thinks I should do. The plan was always to lie.

To *not* be deemed Flawed, I must betray the old man on the bus.

To be true to myself, I will be deemed Flawed.

TWENTY-TWO

I STAND IN the corridor, mind reeling. I am seventeen years old, and though I have fought with my parents about my being more responsible than they give me credit for, I am not ready for this decision. I enter the courtroom, my mind far from clear, my focused plan now a blur in my mind. I don't even know what the right thing is anymore. Me, who is always so sure. My black and white is now fuzzy and gray.

I scan the room for Art. Even though I know we have just left him in disguise outside, I still remain hopeful he has entered through the public entrance. When I look at the back of the courtroom, I can't believe what I see. Carrick is standing at the back of the courtroom, his cap on low over his face, arms folded, shoulders up as if he's a bodyguard watching the door. Our eyes meet, but neither of us reacts. He even stands with the Flawed at the back as though he already is one. I'm beyond moved by his presence, and my eyes fill. I wonder if he has chosen to watch my trial or if they are making him, just as they forced us to listen to that man being branded. And if they are making him, then a lesson is about to be taught in order for him to learn. Either he is supporting me or they want to scare him.

Granddad grins broadly at me and gives me a thumbs-up. Juniper sits beside him, looking tiny and terrified. She gives me a small smile. I'm glad she's here. My mind is at peace with her being ashamed of me at least.

The trial begins by listening to the first of my character witnesses, Marlena, my friend since I was eight years old. She is nervous, but she is loyal, telling stories of how I have always been mindful of correct behavior, even when around those who aren't. I think she sums me up well: logical, loyal, fun, but always staying within the rules. It is the first time in two days that I recognize myself in somebody else's description of me, and I'm glad of the general description of my being considered boring for a teenager.

"Ms. Ponta, is it your belief that Celestine North's character is Flawed?" Bosco asks.

She looks at me, and there are tears in her eyes, but she speaks firmly. "No, not at all."

"Thank you, Ms. Ponta."

Dad speaks on behalf of him and Mom. He talks about how he took me to work with him when I was younger, to the TV station, and how I had to be removed from the editing suite because I wanted everything to be perfect and I kept pointing out imperfections and continuity issues. "Celestine is a logical child. She is a mathematician; she scores top grades in her class; she wants to study at the School of Mathematics at the city university; and her December results show that she is on course to receive far and above the required points. She is a very bright young woman, a pleasure to have as a daughter. She likes things to be in their rightful place; she takes problems and, using theorems, solves them. She follows rules."

I smile at Dad. This is me.

Judge Sanchez looks at Dad, with her bright red lipstick visible from the moon, and smiles, a sneaky look on her face. "Indeed, Mr. North, but I'd like to quote Kaplansky when he talked about mathematics: 'The most interesting moments are not where something is proved but where a new concept is involved.' Mathematics takes basic concepts, but these varying applications have led to a number of abstract theories. Is this the kind of mind your daughter has, Mr. North? The mind that creates new theories, new concepts, takes risks, and goes against the grain?"

Dad thinks about this and looks at me. "No." He pauses. "I would never have said that Celestine was the type of person to go against the grain. Never."

I understand what he's saying. To go against the grain in this circumstance is to go against myself. I have never been the type of person not to do what I believe. He's telling me to follow my heart.

Judge Sanchez smiles and hears the same thing I heard. "And what about now, Mr. North?" she says in her honey, dulcet tones. "Our children have the ability to take us by surprise. They change when we haven't noticed."

Dad looks at me and almost views me as if seeing me for the first time. I wonder what on earth he is going to say.

Bosco interrupts, annoyed. "What Judge Sanchez is asking, Mr. North, is it your belief that your daughter Celestine North's character is Flawed?"

Dad turns back to face him. "No, sir. Under no circumstances is my daughter Flawed," he says, working hard to keep the anger out of his voice when I know he just wants to jump up and scream and shout and punch whoever is closest.

"Thank you, Mr. North."

Then Margaret and Fiona have their moment in their glory. When I hear their testimony, it sounds like they're talking about somebody else. That's not me. I was never that brave. But then I also hear a group of clowns speaking completely illogically. What they are saying about the rules of the Flawed and us no longer makes sense to me. They only confirm to me that I was right to do what I did on the bus, if not doing it would mean I was one of them.

Mr. Berry's act is not like a performance as I thought it would be, like in the movies, bringing on the razzle-dazzle, sashaying around the floor as though he's dancing. He is perfectly normal and straightforward, and for that he is even more credible. But he is quick, and he is sharp, and he picks up on tones and nuances and pauses quicker than I believe even Juniper would. The women are dubious of him but can't help liking him. He is charming and interested in them; he is not—yet—calling them liars. He shares with them the theory that Bosco created, that I was trying to protect the people on the bus from the Flawed man.

They mull it over.

The first lady, Margaret, concedes that it's possible; the second, Fiona, with the crutches, is adamant that it was not so.

"I don't care what story the defense are trying to push," Fiona says. "They can't brainwash me. I know what I saw. That girl"—she points her cane at me—"helped that Flawed man to his seat."

The public erupts at her accusation, and a few members of the media rush out to make their reports.

Bosco announces that the CCTV in use on the bus at the time of the event, when seized by the Guild, was, unfortunately, deemed ineffective and cannot be considered as proof. I have no doubt this is Bosco managing to twist things in my favor and hold back the proof that could destroy me. Bosco announces that we must take into account it is merely the view of the people on the bus and not something we can witness ourselves. I suppose being able to witness my act themselves would be more damaging to me—at least they can make their own decision on whether to believe the witnesses or not. I'm thankful for his deception.

It occurs to me, as everyone speaks of the old man, that I don't even know his name. I never asked and it has never been mentioned, like it isn't important. The case revolves around him, and yet he is brushed aside as though he is nothing. I don't want to ask Mr. Berry. I don't want it to seem like I'm pitying the man, like I have sympathy for a Flawed. I need Mr. Berry to believe in me more than anyone ever has.

As the proceedings finally break for lunch, I quickly turn to my granddad before I'm taken away. "Can you get information to me about the old man?" I whisper in his ear. He nods, face intense, and I know he won't let me down.

Everyone goes back to their lives after my entertainment, and the reporters continue their reports outside. I'm thankful we can wait in a room near the court so that I don't have to cross the courtyard again.

I sit with my parents, Juniper, and Mr. Berry in the waiting room, picking at charcuterie and crackers, feeling sick from the hunger and unable to eat at the same time. I appreciate everybody's company, but I don't speak. I am happy to be away from all the noise, away from the unwanted attention, without having to worry about every part of me being analyzed: my facial expressions, my reactions, how I sit, how I walk. I can just be.

Tina enters the room and hands me an envelope, and I know it's from Granddad. He hasn't let me down. Unaware of whom it's from, Mr. Berry and Mom eye it like it's a grenade. When I read its contents, I feel it might as well be.

TWENTY-THREE

WHAT I LEARN from Granddad's note is this: Clayton Byrne, the old man on the bus, was the CEO of Beacon Publishing. With a degree from the prestigious Humming University, he studied English literature. He met his wife in college and married her when they were twenty-six. They have four children. He became CEO of Beacon Publishing when he was forty-two years old and at the time was praised for his leadership skills, his ingenuity, and his ability to take the company forward. He took risks, all of which paid off apart from one. Because of his failure, due to risk-taking, he was forced to resign from his position and, as a signal to all future employees in the company, was brought to the Guild and found to be Flawed. For making bad judgments in business, he received a brand on his temple, and because he lied about it to his colleagues and tried to cover his tracks, his tongue was also seared. His wife passed away two years ago, and he is suffering from emphysema. He had left the house that day without his oxygen.

Finally, I take the stand. The room is bursting with people. I see Carrick standing at the back, arms folded, beside the woman with the pixie cut who nodded at me in the courtyard. Juniper is in the front row beside Granddad. Granddad looks at me, and I nod, letting him know I received his envelope. There is still no sign of Art, though thinking he could be outside, in disguise, is better than nothing.

"We know the story of what happened on the bus," Judge Sanchez says, beginning it all. "We've heard it repeated time and time again in this court over the past two days, and we could spend another two days listening to the testimonies of the other thirty people on the bus who witnessed the same thing. Your representative, Mr. Berry, has kindly told us that you have waived that and accepted what it is they saw, and the court appreciates your understanding and respect of our time, so we will not ask you to tell us again what happened. We also understand that the only difference between your story and theirs is that they say you were helping the old man, and you say you were trying to get rid of him. And where the majority saw you as helping the man to his seat, you say he sat himself? Is this true?"

I take a deep breath.

Suddenly there is an outbreak of noise and protest within the courtroom. Four people, two women and two men, are standing and shouting, punching their fists in the air, pointing their fingers at me. They shout a single word.

"Liar."

They shout it over and over again.

"Liar. Liar. Liar."

"Order." Bosco bangs the gavel. "Order."

"If you do not silence yourselves, you will be removed from the court," Judge Sanchez says, raising her voice.

Three of them stop shouting and sit, but one woman continues. "Our dad did nothing wrong! Our dad followed all the rules! You are a liar, Celestine North! You should be ashamed, you should be disgusted with yourself!"

The guards make their way over to her; and as soon as they lay their hands on her, the other three jump up to defend her, their sister. I'm so close to calling out *I'm so sorry* to Clayton Byrne's children, but my mouth goes dry and my heart beats maniacally.

"It is not right what you are doing," one son shouts, glaring at me.

"You will be reminded to stay quiet," Judge Sanchez says. "If you have one more outburst, you will be removed from the court."

The four of them go silent and sit down. One daughter starts crying and is comforted by the other.

My heart starts to palpitate; my breathing is irregular. All eyes are on me, judging me, thinking these things of me. All this to prove that I am not Flawed, and by doing so I feel less than perfect. It feels wrong.

"Okay, Celestine?" Mr. Berry watches me intently.

My eyes dart around the room as I tally the people I am letting down: Granddad; Juniper; Dad; even Carrick at the back, who must know by now I'm lying; and the woman with the pixie cut who nodded at me with respect both days. Art, who is waiting for me somewhere outside, who told me to do exactly what Mr. Berry said. Myself. The people I will actually let down if I admit to being Flawed is far fewer.

"Can my client have a drink of water?" Mr. Berry asks.

My mind races as I see him pouring a glass of water and bringing it to me. I take a sip, my mind still racing, and suddenly I notice that Mr. Berry is trying to get my attention. The judges are talking to me and I haven't been listening.

"I'm sorry, pardon?" I ask, coming back into the room.

"I said, what possessed you, Celestine? It's a simple question, isn't it?" Judge Sanchez is looking at me over the rim of her red-framed glasses, which match her lipstick.

It was the question my mom had asked, that countless others had asked. What possessed me? I never had an answer for them, but now I do. It's not the answer I rehearsed with Mr. Berry, but they are the only words my mouth will allow me to say.

"He reminded me of my granddad," I say, and it's as though there is no air in the room. Not a sound. I see Carrick prick up at the back, stand more alert. I can now see his eyes, which were hidden beneath the cap. He's looking right at me. Something about having his eyes on me makes me feel stronger.

"The old man, his name is Clayton Byrne," I say closely into the microphone, the first time his name has been said. "When Clayton got on the bus, I thought he was my granddad." I think about how I felt then as he started coughing. "He was coughing, and I thought he was going to die. I didn't care if he was Flawed, I just saw a person, a human being, who reminded me of my granddad, who no one was helping. So to answer your question, of what possessed me . . . the answer is, compassion. And logic. He didn't take a seat; I helped him into it. At the time," I address everybody now, willing them to understand, "it felt like the perfectly right thing to do."

Outrage. Mania. Noise. Bang, bang of the gavel.

TWENTY-FOUR

I LOOK AROUND the courtroom and see madness. The media are in a scuffle to get out the door to make their exclusive reports, members of the public are standing and throwing their arms at me in disgust. Those who supported me are feeling betrayed. I see my friend Marlena bury her face in her hands. She vouched for me, and I didn't back her up. The Flawed in the back row appear genuinely moved, some angry that I took it this far in the first place, that I even allowed a day to go by with Clayton Byrne's name being tainted. My mom is in tears and is being comforted by Dad, who has her head on his chest and is rocking back and forth at the same time as wrapping his arm around Juniper, who is staring at the ground in shock.

In the midst of all the madness, Granddad stands and claps with a proud smile on his face. I focus on that look, on that face, while inside my mind and body try to deal with what I have done.

The judges are banging their gavels, fighting to be heard over the public, fighting to be heard above one another.

The Flawed are emotional, as though it's a win for them. They embrace one another, careful not to gather together in more than twos.

The old man's children fall into a huddle, weeping and rejoicing at their father's cleared name. I don't expect them to show any gratitude for something that should have been said from the beginning.

I see Carrick in the back row. His hat is off and his chin is high. He's standing still and solid in all the mania around us, nodding at me in support, his eyes on mine, not moving. I focus on him. For once not judging me, for the first time not laughing at me. I didn't realize it was his respect that I wanted so much, but I know now that it was, that without our ever speaking I knew his thoughts on me and I agreed with him. I know this because, despite the terror that's inside me over what is about to come, I am satisfied.

I focus on Carrick, even as Tina and Bark come to take me away. I watch him, still, strong, and silent, like the rock he was named for.

TWENTY-FIVE

TINA AND BARK take me out of court and lead me back into the waiting room where I had lunch not long before. My head is still spinning from what has just happened. It's all a blur already, and I need someone to help bring it all back to me, to remind me of what has happened. What did I say?

I notice Tina's grip on my arm is tighter than usual, and so is her face.

"Tina?" I hear the terror in my voice. Gone is my earlier certainty and bravado, if that's what it is called. I've learned that to be courageous is to feel fear within, every step of the way. Courage does not take over, it fights and struggles through every word you say and every step you take. It's a battle or a dance as to whether to let it pervade. It takes courage to overcome, but it takes extreme fear to be courageous.

Tina ignores me, purposely turning her face away from me, but I can see the scowl. "Do you have any idea how stupid you've made me look? I believed you. I told everyone who listened that you were a good girl."

"Tina, I'm . . . I'm sorry. I don't know what . . ."

"It's done now," she snaps.

She leads me into the room, and I look around, suddenly very afraid, uncertain of what will happen with every new second. Bark closes the door behind them. I hear the lock and I'm alone.

I hear footsteps coming in my direction, down the hall. Loud, urgent steps. There is only one pair. I stand in the middle of the room and brace myself.

"Open it!" I hear Bosco shout, and I jump, startled.

The door flies open and I see the flash of a red cloak. It is Bosco, but it is not Bosco as I've ever seen him before. His face is like thunder, and red to match his robe.

"What the hell do you think you're playing at?" he yells, louder than I've ever been spoken to before, and I'm stunned.

Tina gives him, then me, a nervous look and swiftly, quietly closes the door, leaving me inside alone with him.

"Bosco, I'm—"

"*Judge Crevan!*" he yells. "You will address me as such at all times, do you understand?"

I nod manically.

He seems to notice the effect he is having on me, and he calms a little. He lowers his voice.

"Celestine. You gave me your word. We discussed what we would do. I put my word, my *career*, on the line for you, and you betrayed me."

"I didn't, I mean, I didn't think—" I stammer, but he cuts me off.

"No, you didn't bloody think at all, did you," he says, pacing, lost in thought, and I'm glad to be removed as his target of anger. "They're having a field day out there with this. My own press, and the public. Seventeen-year-old young woman, educated, the envy of other girls, they've built you up as, that *I've* built you up as"—he rolls his eyes— "speaks out in court, admits to and is *proud* to be Flawed. Do you have any idea what this can do? How dangerous it is? It could breed an entire generation of imperfection, of greed and errors." He stops pacing and comes close to my face, and I wonder how I ever found him handsome, because all the handsome is gone now. "Did you not understand, Celestine, that this is not about you? It is about our country's future, ensuring reliable, perfect, ethically sound, morally competent leaders who can make pure decisions and lead us to prosperous times. Did you not understand that?"

He is in my face, demanding answers and explanations, and I can barely think.

"I will not have *them* make a poster girl of you. I wanted you to be on our side."

"I am on your side, Bos—Judge Crevan," I quickly correct myself. "And I don't think you have anything to worry about with my effect on people. I am not a motivator. I couldn't lead anyone even if I tried. I just want to be normal. I want to fit in. I want to be with my friends, I want to go home. I don't want anybody to build me up as anything that I'm not," I say, tears in my eyes. "You know I love Art so much. I love being a part of your family. I would never do anything to deliberately hurt you both. I am sorry that I have embarrassed you, and I am sorry that I have put you in this position, but I just couldn't do it to the old man. I just couldn't let him be punished for something I did."

"Who?" he says, confused.

"Clayton Byrne. The Flawed man."

"But didn't anyone tell you? He died, Celestine. He died in the hospital last night. I told you that he wouldn't live to see punishment."

"Oh." I exhale shakily. Was it all in vain?

"His family shouldn't have been in court." He continues pacing. "I wouldn't have allowed it. It must have been Sanchez. She's playing a game, and Jackson is falling for it. She's been against me for some time, but I see she's upped it now. This is a whole new level."

Sweat breaks out on his brow. I have never seen that before, not even on the hottest day as he stood over his barbecue. His hair, which has come undone from its blow-dry, is starting to stick to the beads of sweat on his forehead. He stops pacing and looks at me, desperate, close to my face.

"Would you recant, Celestine?"

"What?"

"We can still swing this. It will be difficult, but Pia can do it. A reality show. She can follow you around, show the country how perfect you are. And the world. You know there are other countries contemplating adopting our system? They have been watching us for a while. I could be president of the Global Guild; I'm going to speak about it in Brussels this month. Celestine, this couldn't be worse timing." He looks at me again, wild, desperate, intense. Terrifying. Art is gone from any of this man. I no longer see the face I love in him. "Would you recant?"

"I . . . I . . . I can't." I can't go back in there and take back what I said. It would be completely illogical. Who would trust me?

I once took my lead from Bosco. I thought that he knew everything, that he was perfect, but I'm surprised by what I see right now, this panicking, conniving man, desperate to maintain his sliding power. He is clutching at straws that are so delicate they will disintegrate upon his touch, and he is using me in the center of all this. Granddad was right.

"I can't. I'm sorry," I say gently. "Could you please let me explain this to Art myself?"

His face hardens, and I brace myself for another shout, but instead he is so quiet I have to strain my ear to hear, which, of course, is worse. It's almost a hiss.

"If you think I will let my son go anywhere near you ever again, you are delusional. Whether this court had proved you Flawed or not, I had no intention of letting you ever set foot near him again, and particularly not now, now that you are Flawed, Celestine North, Flawed to the very bone."

And on that he turns and leaves, his red robe flicking up and swishing with him. He slams the door closed.

TWENTY-SIX

A FEW MINUTES later Tina opens the door, with a new female guard. "They're ready for you now." Perhaps thinking of her daughter then, she softens her tone. "This is June."

June speaks up. "Bark is heating up your iron, Flawed, gonna make it nice and hot for your pretty little skin."

I look at Tina in horror and notice she in turn is looking at June in anger. I stop walking, terrified to go any farther, but they pull me along.

"Come on, keep walking," Tina whispers.

I feel my legs weaken, I crumple, and Tina pulls me up.

"You're not being branded yet, Celestine. They have to name your flaws first."

I allow them to pull me through the maze of corridors. I move limply with them, like a rag doll. We stop at a new door. Perhaps they took me out through it before. I can't remember, I was so stunned.

Tina looks at me. "Ready?"

"No."

The door opens and the place explodes.

The first person I see is Carrick, who's standing in the same place at the back of the room. He stands up straighter when he sees me, turns his body in my direction, and almost follows me with it as I make my way to my seat. I sense his newfound respect for me; there will be no back to my cell wall tonight.

The room is hot and stuffy. I can smell sweat and excitement, my life the entertainment of others. I see one woman offer a bag of candy to the man beside her. They ram the sweets into their mouths as they watch me pass, eyeing me up and down as if I can't see them.

I take my seat beside Mr. Berry.

"What's happening?" I ask him, and he shrugs, looking just as confused as I am.

"Ms. Celestine North, please stand," Crevan says.

I stand, my legs shaky beneath me. My mom clings to my dad. My granddad's cap is in his hand as he clutches it tightly, his knuckles white.

I stand alone in the courtroom and realize this is how it will be for the rest of my life, standing alone, branded Flawed forever because of one act.

I hear doors burst open, and the three judges look up.

"Don't do this," a voice shouts from the door.

It's Art. I turn around. The disguise is gone.

"Art," I say to him, afraid, and hear the quiver in my voice.

"Order in the court," Judge Crevan says, banging his gravel.

"Don't do this to her!" he yells again.

"Restrain him," Crevan says, looking down, moving his paperwork around, nervously.

Two members of security grab his arms, and he yells and struggles as they pull him from the room. I look away, turn to the front, eyes back to the ground.

"Shall I continue?" Judge Sanchez asks Crevan in her smooth voice, all honey and calm.

"No!" he snaps. "Celestine North," he says, looking up at me, eyes wild and bloodshot. He means business now. "Your so-called bravery in court suggests you wish to be a poster girl, and we don't take poster girls lightly. Not when the message you portray is dangerous to society. We see you as a poison that is prepared to inflict itself on our good and proper society. So take this to the people, poster girl.

"It is rare for any accused to receive more than one branding, but if you are to be looked at and adored by some in society, then let them see your flaws wherever they look. We must also take into account the seriousness of your actions, that they were done publicly, with an audience. This was not a private event that hurt a few. It was public and has become even more so. You have attracted the world's attention, Ms. North, and for that we must send a message. I will now name your brands."

Brands.

He pauses, and the room is so silent I'm sure everyone can hear my heartbeat.

"For stealing from society, you will be branded on your right hand. Whenever you go to shake the hands of any decent people in society, they will know of your theft."

People start to talk, thinking he's finished, but as he continues, they silence themselves.

"For your bad judgment, your right temple."

Two brands. And he continues to gasps.

"For your collusion with the Flawed, for walking alongside them, and for stepping away from society, the sole of your right foot. Every time you connect with the earth, even it will know that you are Flawed to the very root of you."

As he continues with a fourth Flaw, the audience protests again. Three brandings so far and continuing, it is unheard of. Only one person has ever received three brandings in the history of the Guild.

"For your disloyalty to the Guild and all of society, your chest, so that if anyone should wish to trust or love you in the future, they will see the mark of your unyielding disloyalty over your heart.

"And, finally, for the very fact that you lied to this court about your actions, your tongue, so that anyone you speak to or kiss will know that your words fall from a branded tongue and cannot be trusted for the rest of your life."

Explosion in the courtroom. People are cheering, celebrating the justice that has been done, the scum that has once again been recognized in society. Others are shouting with anger at the judges for a great injustice. Even more than before now that they have heard the ruling. I have gained supporters, but not many, and what use is that to me now? It is too late. Naming Day has come, and I must face my worst fear: brandings, and not just one but *five*. It is unheard of.

My legs are shaking so much they buckle beneath me, and Mr. Berry makes a weak attempt to catch one arm, but his heart isn't in it. Tina rushes to my side immediately and catches me. June takes my other arm, and I'm taken out through the hysterical public in the courtroom, out the main door, and across the courtyard, where I am shouted at and spat on. Objects pelt me, extra security hold the crowds back as they pulsate at me, more journalists than any other day hold cameras in my face, and I can barely see past the flashbulbs. I briefly see a large screen on the wall of Highland Castle and realize that my case has been aired for the public to see outside, and a huge crowd gathers beyond the barricade, many sitting on deck chairs.

I arrive back at the holding cell, covered in whatever filth people have spat and thrown at me, my ears ringing from the name-calling, my eyes still seeing the camera flashes. I try to adjust to the new light but find it hard. I trip and stumble, but Tina keeps me up. I'm aware of Tina's and June's worried glances at each other. They sit with me; they're as jittery as I am.

I notice they're covered in the same stuff I am.

"Sorry," I say to both of them.

June looks surprised by my apology.

"We're used to it," Tina says, brushing off some egg yolk. "Just not this much. Look, this is new to all of us. How about tea for everyone?"

June nods and goes to the guards' kitchen.

"I'll get you some fresh clothes." Tina leaves me. "I have to advise you to read the folder over there."

The Flawed file, which prepares me for my new future.

As soon as she leaves, Carrick arrives back, accompanied by Funar, racing in at top speed, as though he can't get back fast enough. He looks at me with concern. Big black eyes, worried, lost. He enters his cell and goes straight to the wall that divides us. I remember the first day, when he turned his back on me. This time he places his left hand up to the glass.

I don't know what he's doing, but when he doesn't remove it, it suddenly makes sense. I join him at the window and raise my right hand up to the cool glass, pressing it flat against his. My hand looks like a doll's hand next to his, and I realize that the glass that I felt separated us is the only thing that connects us. I rest my forehead on the glass, and his hand goes to my face, then away again as it hits the glass.

I'm not sure how long we stay like that, but I start to cry. We never speak.

TWENTY-SEVEN

THE "FRESH CLOTHES" that Tina returns with turn out to be nothing more than a bloodred smock, like a hospital robe, tied at the back and with a V-neck in the front to make room for my chest brand. It is what I'm to wear in the Branding Chamber. I recognize it from the Flawed man whom Carrick and I were forced to listen to as he screamed while his skin was seared.

Carrick's jaw works overtime as he watches me take the gown, his black eyes deep pools of oil. He doesn't ignore me anymore. There are no more smart faces and sarcastic looks. I have his full attention now, his full respect. I can barely escape his looks. When I return from the changing area, I see that his cell has been utterly trashed and that he is being held down on the ground by Bark. He has not reacted well to my ruling. Perhaps this makes him more unsettled about his own. We don't get to say good-bye. I can't even see his face. It is beneath Bark's knee, cheek pushed to the ground, his face facing away from me. Our contact is to forever remain without words, not that we ever needed them anyway. I have no doubt that he will find himself wearing a similar smock and taking the same steps as I am doing now.

Before entering the Branding Chamber, I sit in a small holding room with Tina and June. They go through pamphlets of information with me about what is going to happen, what I will see, what I will feel, which is apparently nothing as they numb my skin, and how to treat my wounds afterward. They hand me so many leaflets for aftercare services, therapy sessions, emergency hotlines, all branded with the Flawed branding. I sign some paperwork—quick, short agreements accepting all responsibility for what is about to occur—agreeing the Guild will not be held accountable if any of the brandings go wrong or if ill effects result down the line. It is discussed clinically, calmly, as though I'm going for a nose job.

As I step out of the holding room and into the long, narrow corridor that leads to the Branding Chamber, I see Carrick sitting outside on the bench where we sat together, guarded by Funar. Funar has a sneer on his face, and I can tell he is happy about both my situation and the fact that Carrick will be forced to listen. Carrick will hear me scream. My family will hear me scream. *I* will scream.

No. I will not let that happen. I will not allow them to do that to me. I will not scream.

Feeling defiant, I believe this is the first time I have ever truly felt it. The first time on the bus was compassion, on the stand in court my admission was out of guilt and not bravery, but now I feel anger and I am defiant.

Our eyes meet. His are strong, and I feel the effect of his stare.

"I'll come find you," he says suddenly, his voice deep and strong, and I'm surprised to hear him speak.

I nod my thanks because I don't trust myself to speak. He fills me with the strength I need to enter the room without freaking out, mostly because I don't want to lose it in front of him. My parents and Granddad are already seated behind the glass, as though they're at the cinema waiting for the reel to begin, but their faces display the terror I feel. They do not want to view what they are about to see, but they are here so I don't go through it alone. On seeing them, I think I would rather be alone, an unfamiliar feeling for me, who only ever wants to be surrounded by family. The excommunication from society is taking effect already within me, feeling detached from my family already, a stranger who can only go it alone.

Mr. Berry is here, too, which makes me uncomfortable, though I'm sure he must be here for legal reasons, and past the open door, around the corner, I know is Carrick. That gives me strength.

Tina places me in the chair. It is like a dentist's chair, nothing unusual apart from the fact that my body is bound to the chair—at my ankles, wrists, head, and waist—so I can't kick and flail as I'm seared. They want to get a clear symbol on my flesh for all time, the irony of a perfect Flawed symbol not lost on me. Tina is tender as she buckles the straps. I even sense a halt in sarcasm from June. Now is not the time for that. I'm getting what I deserve, the punishment speaking for them all.

Bark is busy with the equipment, doing whatever he needs to do.

The motorized chair reclines. I wince against the brightness of the ceiling lights. My skin feels hot as they shine on me, in the spotlight and center stage for all to see. This is it.

"It's better not to look," Tina whispers into my ear as she fastens the strap across my forehead. I cannot look now anyway, I can't move.

They inject my right hand first with the anesthetic. It immediately numbs. Bark picks up the hot poker, and I see it, with its cast-iron *F* surrounded by a circle at the tip. My hand is flattened out and my fingers are strapped down, too, my hand forced open so that my palm is ready. It is done simply and quickly. No modern equipment, just a cast-iron poker and a count to three by Bark.

"One, two . . ." Sear.

I jump, but I can't feel the pain. A sensation at most. And the smell of burning flesh, which makes me nauseated. I don't scream. I won't scream.

"There's a bucket here if you need to," Tina says, by my side instantly like a midwife.

I shake my head. I can hear the internal whimpering inside, see the burn on my open hand. The raw wound in my smooth skin. Four more times. It is the tongue I fear the most. I know they will leave this until last, they have told me that already, because it must be the worst.

The skin on my right sole is injected with anesthetic, and I lose all feeling instantly.

Bark moves toward my foot. He looks at my ankle and frowns, seeing my anklet.

"Where did you get this?" he asks.

"Bark," Tina snaps. "I let her keep it on. Keep moving."

"No . . . I . . . I just . . . it's just that I made it. For a young man. For his girlfriend. He said she was perfect. . . ." He looks at me, realizing.

I recall Art's telling me when he gave me the anklet that a man at Highland Castle made it for him. Bark is the man who branded me perfect, and the same man who brands me Flawed. We share a long look.

"Bark," June says sternly.

Bark is momentarily human as his sad eyes pass over mine, and then he snaps out of it.

"Brace yourself," Tina says gently, hand supportively on my shoulder.

"One, two . . ." Sear.

I can see my mom crying into a pile of tissues, her composure completely and utterly cracked, smashed, and shattered. My dad is on his feet, pacing. A redheaded guard is near him, keeping a concerned eye on him, ready to step in if Dad crosses the mark. I can't hear them, but they can hear me. It's all part of the fear they place on the public. Let them hear my screams. Make a mistake, and you'll end up like her.

So far I haven't made a sound, and I won't.

Bark's hand comes into sight and injects my chest with the anesthetic. Again, I'm numb. The red-hot poker comes toward me again. I can feel its heat. I feel the familiar squeeze of Tina and realize it has nothing to do with support and is merely procedure. She's readying me, but by now I'm ready to pass out. The smell is unbearable. It is the smell of my own burning skin.

I feel a blast of air. June has opened a window or something, must be to get rid of the smell of burning flesh. They're not used to this. I can tell from the anxious looks on their faces. The average Flawed person receives one brand, rarely two. One man in the entire history received three, but never, ever five. I am the only person in the world to receive five. I feel dizzy, but I know I'm not moving. I close my eyes and squeeze tight.

"One, two . . ." Sear.

I feel like I can't breathe. I haven't felt the sting on my chest, but it's as though psychologically I do. Pressure on my chest so immense I want to escape the constraints. I battle against them, still not making a sound. I refuse. The floor is moving. It's rising upward. It's going to hit me in the face.

"Celestine? Celestine, are you okay?" I hear Tina, but I can't focus on her, her face keeps moving. She's saying something about the bucket, but I can't concentrate. I keep thinking of the tongue. I see Clayton Byrne's tongue as he coughs in my face. I don't want my tongue to be seared.

Tina tells me to take deep breaths.

"This is too much for her," Tina says worriedly to Bark, who surprisingly is viewing me with uncertainty, too. "We need to alert someone. Maybe take a break. Do the rest tomorrow."

"Guys, I know this is hard, but we have to do it," June says in a low voice. "The longer we chat, the harder it is for her. Let's not drag it out on her any more. The family is watching," she adds with a whisper. "Let's finish this for everybody's sake."

An injection in my temple. Quicker this time.

A squeeze on my shoulder. I know that for all time, if anyone squeezes me on the shoulder, it will be the trigger that brings me back to this.

"One, two . . ." Sear.

I gag. I retch. Smelling burning flesh. My own flesh.

Bark is mumbling something.

"Sweet Jesus," June says, suddenly changing her mind. "We should be tending to her wounds now. This is taking too long."

"You're doing great, Celestine," Tina says close to my ear. "A real little hero, almost there now, okay? Hang in there."

I half laugh and half cry.

I look up and see both of my parents and Granddad standing now, in a row at the window, lining up. Distraught, angry faces. Mr. Berry is not pleased. He is pacing. He is on the phone. Probably hearing the guards' concerns, he is trying to do something about it. Granddad is arguing with the security guard. I can feel the tension in that room from here. I take deep breaths. I will not scream.

"Here." Bark appears in my line of sight with a bottle of water and a straw. It's a trick, it must be a trick. Tina guides it into my mouth, and as I suck I think about my tongue being seared. It's next. I retch again. I can't hold down the water.

It is pandemonium in the viewing gallery. I can feel their energy, their erratic, angry movements. My eyes move from side to side. I try to focus, but I can't. I know why I'm here, and then I don't know why I'm here. I understand, and then I don't. I think it's fair, and then I don't. I wish I'd never done what I'd done, and then I'm glad I did. I want to scream, but I don't.

Suddenly my family members scatter like a flock of birds, as though something was thrown at them, and then I see Judge Crevan in my face, a smug sneer twisting his mouth. Mr. Berry must have gotten him, tried to stop the inhumanity. Too late, but now he's here in the Branding Chamber. He blocks my view of my family.

"Had enough, have we, Celestine?"

I groan. I will not cry. Not to him.

They say I'm numbed, but I'm feeling sensations on my wounded body. Tingling. If the anesthetic wears off, it will turn to stinging, then burning. I don't want it to wear off. Suddenly, this is my main fear. I wish I'd paid more attention to the information in my cell—how long does it take before the anesthetic wears off?

"I warned you. I told you this would happen, but you didn't listen."

Crevan's red robe is the same color as the scar on my hand, and I'm guessing as my foot, chest, and temple. My blood is on his robe. He did this to me. Him. I feel nothing but disgust for him. I used to think that I couldn't be afraid of someone so human. Now I realize it is his humanity that scares me most, because despite having all those traits, having shared the moments we've shared, he could still do this to me. Now I find him terrifying. I see the evil in him.

"Oh, Celestine, it hurts me for you to look at me like that. I'm not the winner, either, you know. Art says he'll never speak to me again. Heartbreaking for me, as you can imagine. First, I lost Annie, and now Art. And you caused that."

Don't speak, I tell myself. One more branding and it will all be over. It will all be over.

"I'm here to give you mercy, Celestine. Say you're sorry, admit you were wrong, that you are Flawed, and I will cancel the tongue. It's the worst one, that one. Everybody says so."

I try to shake my head. But I can't. I won't speak. Instead, I stick my tongue out, showing him that I'm ready for the branding.

I see the look of surprise on everyone's face. Granddad punches the air in defiance, not happy, but bursting with anger. He won't want me to give in. I've come this far; it would be illogical to stop now, I will have gained nothing. I feel tears dripping down the side of my face, but I'm not crying.

"Brand her tongue," he says coldly, then steps back.

TWENTY-EIGHT

I SEE MY family take a step back from the glass, Crevan's closeness too much for them.

My family does not sit still. Nor does Mr. Berry, who starts thumping on the window, trying to get Crevan's attention. My dad shoves the guard, trying to make him do something to stop this, and they end up having a physical fight in the viewing room. I have never seen my dad like this before. Crevan turns around and watches the pandemonium.

"Get the family out of there!" he shouts. Funar appears at the door, and he manages to pull Mom and Granddad from the room. Mr. Berry follows them out, ranting and raving at Funar. Dad is holding his own against the security guard, delivering a blow to his jaw, but suddenly Funar appears again, having taken my family somewhere, probably into the holding room or the nearby cells, and takes Dad by surprise. The two guards gain control and drag Dad out. The viewing room is now empty.

"Oh my God," June whispers over my shoulder.

"Do it," Crevan says.

I whimper slightly as they open my mouth and place the clamp in.

"It will be quick, dear," Tina says, urgency and panic in her voice.

"Step away from her," he demands angrily.

"If it's all the same to you, sir, I'd like to do my job and remain by her side," Tina says, a tremble in her voice.

"Very well."

An injection in my tongue. It instantly feels swollen and enormous in my mouth. I gag.

"One, two . . ." Sear.

I don't scream. I can't. I haven't the use of my tongue. I want to kick my legs, stamp my feet, and wave my arms, but I'm restrained and can do nothing. I can just feel my body push against the restraints and hear a sound that I don't realize until a moment later is coming from me. It is worse than a scream, it is an animal, guttural sound, a groan, a grunt, something so deep inside me, a pain that I have never experienced nor heard before. One I never want to hear again, but I will, over and over in my nightmares.

"Repent, Celestine!" Crevan shouts at me.

I'm unable to get the word out as my tongue is numb and feels swollen and oversized, but I can see that he is distressed now. He is not getting his way. I'm not following his plan. It was for me to say sorry and the branding would stop. I will never say sorry to him.

"Judge Crevan, we must get her to the ward. Her wounds need medical attention," Tina says, urgency in her voice. "We have never gone on for so long. We must see to her quickly."

I feel the strap around my head release, and I am able to lift my head from the headrest and look at him directly now.

"*Repent!*" he shouts at me, louder again.

I shake my head violently. I've come this far. It's finished. I'll never tell him I'm sorry even if right now it is the thing I am feeling most.

They free my hands and my ankles. They are moving quickly now, wanting to remove me, and probably themselves, from this situation. They start to help me up, Tina on one side, June on the other. Bark begins to clean and tidy away the equipment. They can't wait to get me out of here. I can't walk, my foot is completely numb and my legs are shaking so badly. A wheelchair has been placed beside me.

"Brand her spine," Judge Crevan says suddenly, chillingly.

Bark turns to face him slowly. "Pardon, sir?"

Tina and June freeze, look at each other wide-eyed.

"You heard me."

"Sir, she's just a child," Tina whispers, and I can hear the shake in her voice and sense the tears about to come.

"Do it."

"Sir, we have never seared a spine before," Bark says nervously.

"Because we have never seen anyone so Flawed to their very backbone like this lady. Brand. Her. Spine."

"I can't do it, sir. I'm afraid I'll have to check first with the—"

"I am the head of the Guild, and you will do what I say or you will find yourself in my courtroom first thing in the morning. Are you aiding a Flawed?"

Bark freezes.

"Are you?"

"No. No, sir."

"Then get to it. Brand her spine."

"But we don't have any more anesthetic."

"Do it without."

"Sir, the law states—"

"*I am the law. Do it!*" he yells. "By order of the Guild!"

"No!" I protest, but it doesn't come out like that. My tongue has swollen in my mouth, from injury and numbness. I can taste blood, feel it rolling down my throat. I start coughing. All I can do is whine, but I don't like the sound I make, so I stop. I see the evil in his eyes, the enjoyment he is getting from this. I won't let him get any further satisfaction.

It is going to happen, and I must be prepared. I must ignore the madness and the pandemonium that have just occurred in the viewing room, the injustice that is happening in the chamber right now. I must block out the fears I have for what is happening to my family now and find stillness within myself.

Tina and Bark open the ties at the back of my robe.

"Oh dear girl, I am so sorry," June says, taking hold of my shoulder. "Oh dear God."

"Stop talking," Judge Crevan snaps.

Tina takes my unseared left hand in hers tenderly, then holds on for dear life, with her back to Judge Crevan so that he can't see the tears streaming down her face.

Bark comes toward me with the red-hot poker, looking uncertain.

"Do it," Judge Crevan says again, then watches me. "Any time you want them to stop, all you have to do is say you're sorry."

"She can't speak, Judge," Tina says through her tears. "How can she stop it?"

"She can stop it if she wants to," he says slowly, quietly.

He wants me to call out, to repent. I don't.

Suddenly, Carrick appears in the viewing room. I can see tears in his black eyes, so I know that he has heard it all. He is panting hard, as though he has run a marathon. Sweat and blood are on his brow, and he has a cut lip. Blood drips down onto his T-shirt. Funar, with a busted nose, struggles in the doorframe behind him, doubled over. Mr. Berry rushes in behind Carrick into the room, his phone in his hand. The security guard who had been battling with my dad runs into the room and jumps at Carrick, but Carrick knocks him out with one fierce blow. The security guard falls to the ground, out cold. Completely outnumbered, Funar doesn't bother to fight any more and slithers from the room, hand over his pumping nose. Mr. Berry pushes the door closed, and I see his face, and he suddenly looks his age. He is holding his phone up in the air, recording. Crevan hasn't noticed the activity behind him. Neither Bark, June, nor Tina have alerted him to this.

126

"Do it," he says, urgency in his voice, sweat above his lip. "Brand her spine."

Carrick stands right at the window and looks at me intently, forcing me to hold his gaze. He holds one hand up to the glass, presses it flat. Instantly, I zone out of the madness in this chamber and in my head and focus on the stillness in Carrick's body. I focus on his hand. The hand of friendship he offered me earlier.

I'll find you.

At least I have one friend. I am exhausted. I am still. I am ready.

"One, two . . ." Tina counts me in. But nothing happens. I don't feel a thing.

"Judge, I can't do it," Bark says. "I just can't. This isn't right."

"Fine," Crevan snaps. "If you won't do it, I will." He grabs the iron from Bark's grasp, and he and Bark swap places, Bark standing where Crevan was, so that he blocks Crevan's view of Carrick. I can't take my eyes off Carrick; I won't take my eyes off Carrick. I take a deep breath.

And as the hot iron touches my spine, the noise I make is the loudest, most excruciating, agonizing, animal sound I have ever heard in my life, and it echoes through the corridors of Highland Castle for all to hear, so anyone and everyone knows Crevan's poster girl has been branded.

TWENTY-NINE

DAY ONE

I'm home, propped up in my bed by a dozen cushions, organized by Mom, who keeps stepping back to take a look at her work before fluffing and punching again, as if it were a piece of art. If she can't fix me, she can fix the image around me. This is all for the visit of Dr. Smith, our family GP. After inspecting my dressings, he sits in the chair by my bed and looks at Mom as he answers her questions.

"A burn of the tongue will look and feel different, depending on the degree of the burn. A first-degree burn injures the outermost layer of the tongue. This leads to pain and swelling. A second-degree burn is more painful because it injures the outermost and under layers of the tongue. Blisters may form, which is what has happened here, and the tongue, as in her case, appears swollen. A third-degree burn affects the deepest tissue of the tongue. The effect is white or blackened, burnt skin. Numbness or severe pain."

Or both.

Dr. Smith sighs, his friendly grandfather face clearly finding this difficult.

"She appears to have received the correct medical attention at the castle. Her tongue is not infected. The blistering will eventually go away. Her taste buds have been destroyed—"

"Not that she's eating anyway," Mom interrupts.

"That's to be expected. Celestine has been through an ordeal. Her appetite will eventually return, as will her taste buds, which regenerate every two weeks. The severe untreatable pain that she is experiencing now can sometimes lead to feelings of depression and anxiety."

You don't say.

Mom purses her lips and lifts her chin. I watch them talk to each other, over me, across my bed, as if I'm not here.

"Most burns heal within two weeks; however, some can last up to six weeks."

He looks at me sadly, as if remembering I'm here.

"There is one more thing," he adds. "There is a . . . sixth brand. . . ." He seems uncomfortable mentioning it.

Mom looks at him in panic. He leaves the sentence hanging.

"We've known each other a long time, Summer," he says gently. "I've seen Celestine and this family through measles and chicken pox, vaccines and whatever else. I can assure you, you have my utmost confidence."

She nods again, and I can see the fear in her. She wasn't in the chamber when the final two sears happened, none of my family was, and I don't want to talk about it. Ever. I don't even know if Mr. Berry shared it with her. But she's my mother, and she witnessed enough for her to guess what Crevan did in the state he was in, and she is respecting my silence, though I know Dad wants to know. The question is on the tip of his tongue every time he looks at me, but he holds back, probably holding himself responsible for encouraging me to speak up for myself and landing myself in this agony. I don't think either of them could imagine, even in their wildest nightmares, that it could be Crevan who delivered the sixth and final brand.

"I'll come back in a few days to review the dressings again, but if there's anything I can do before that, contact me directly."

I don't bother to nod.

Everyone speaks on my behalf now anyway. They speak about me like I'm not in the room.

I'm not here.

I close my eyes and allow the pills I've just taken to help me drift away again.

DAY TWO

Sleep. Nothing but sleep, and pain, and disturbed dreams.

DAY THREE

There's a knock on my door, and I close my eyes. Mom enters. I know it's her from the perfume scent and the effortless, perfect way she glides in and sits without disturbing a thing. After a while, she speaks.

"I know you're awake."

I keep my eyes closed.

"That was Tina at the door. Tina from Highland Castle. She was asking for you. It took a lot for her to come here, especially with, you know, them outside. She knew you wouldn't want to see her. She just wanted to give you these."

I open my eyes and see a box of pretty cupcakes. Pink, lilac, blue, and yellow, with glittery flowers on top.

"She said her daughter made them for you. You can eat one this week," she says, trying to make that sound fabulous.

One luxury a week is all a Flawed is allowed to have. It is part of the basic living we must abide by, so that we can purify ourselves. We must eat staple foods, nothing luxurious or fancy, nothing considered unnecessary for our bodies, for our life. Basics. Our intake is measured at the end of every day by a test I've yet to experience.

"And she brought you this, too." Mom hands me a bag.

It's a Highland Castle tourist shop paper bag, which I feel is highly inappropriate. If she thinks I want a trinket to remember the worst experience of my life, she is sorely mistaken.

Inside the bag is a box. I barely want to open it, but curiosity gets the better of me. Inside the box is a snow globe, enclosing a miniature Highland Castle. I shake it lightly, and the red glittering particles are churned around inside the glass. Extremely inappropriate. Even Mom views it with distaste. I'm surprised by Tina, but I'm sure she was trying to be kind, maybe even say sorry, or that's my own wishful thinking. I put the globe back in its box and straight into my bedside table. I don't want to ever see it again.

I close my eyes.

DAY FOUR

I have a visitor. Angelina Tinder sits beside my bed, dressed in head-to-toe black, which is a look I've never seen on her before. She looks like a lady from Victorian times grieving her dead husband. She is wearing fingerless leather gloves to hide the branding on her hand. Her long piano fingers are as pale as snow beneath the leather. She's not allowed to wear these when she's out in public, but she can hide it in her own home if she wishes. She is not in her own home. She is breaking a rule. Though it's not me she is hiding it from, it is herself. She sits upright in the chair, looking at me rarely, just enough to see if I'm listening now, and then she speaks.

Her eyes are rimmed with red, as if she hasn't stopped crying since she was branded. The tip of her nose is red, too. She is paler than I have ever seen her, as though she hasn't seen the sun in weeks.

"You'll have a Whistleblower appointed to you," she says. "They're giving you mine. She's senior. A horrible woman with nothing better to do with her time. She'd volunteer for the post even if she wasn't paid. Mary May is her name. Calls herself a Christian woman. She's the same kind of woman who was burning other women at the stake. She won't give you an inch, Celestine, you remember that." She quickly glances at me, then away again. "She's looking to catch you out. She thinks you're disgusting." She sniffs as if smelling a bad odor herself. "But they are. The Flawed. Absolutely disgusting. We are not one of them, Celestine, and don't ever let them think that of you. Though, what on earth were you thinking helping that Flawed man to his seat? Saying all that in the courtroom? It's everywhere, you know that. The footage of you on the bus has gone viral." She looks at me, her face twisted in confusion and disgust.

I don't answer. I can't answer. I wouldn't anyway.

"Be home by ten thirty. They say eleven, but she'll be waiting for you, and anything can happen. Allow for delays, mistakes, anything. They will probably even try to trip you up. They're always testing you. I missed the curfew once. I won't miss it again, I can assure you." She thinks for a moment. "She'll test you every evening to make sure you're sticking to your basic meals, and a lie detector test to ensure you're telling the truth about following all rules. They rely on these to work. They can't keep their eyes on you all the time, but God knows they'll create something soon enough in those laboratories. A camera sewn into our head or something, seeing everything we see, hearing everything we think. Because that's what they want to know, you know. It's like they want to crawl inside us, under our skin."

She sniffs again and scratches at her arms. I look at her fingers and see that they're trembling.

She sees me looking at them.

"They won't stop. I can't play anymore. It's like they're not mine anymore."

She leaves a silence, and I try to prepare for the next onslaught, which inevitably comes. "It's awful. A woman looked at me today as though I had murdered every one of her children. I would rather they had killed me instead of living like this."

I'm glad my tongue is so damaged that I can't speak. I wouldn't know what to say.

"Good luck, Celestine."

She stands and leaves the room.

Mom comes to my room later with a hopeful look on her face. "Did that help, sweetheart?"

I close my eyes and drift away.

DAY FIVE

I wake up. And just as I have done every day for the past three days since I've come home, I force myself to go back to sleep. I realize it was not all a nightmare. It is true. Sleep is my only friend these days, so I roll onto my side, for my back is in too much pain, move my head on the pillow so that my temple doesn't brush the fabric, try not to crease the skin on my chest so that it doesn't sting, and leave my right hand flat and open, the dressings preventing me from closing it anyway. This is the only way I can find respite, though for a girl of definitions, I use the term *respite* lightly.

I have not left my room for three days. I have left my bed only to go to the bathroom. Apart from Dr. Smith and Angelina Tinder, Mom, Dad, and Juniper have been the only others I've seen. They're shielding Ewan from me, and I agree. Mom has tended to me night and day, cleaning my wounds, changing my dressings, putting whatever potions and lotions on them to take away the pain, to fight off infection. I have woken some nights to find Juniper sitting in the chair beside my bed staring into space; and then when I wake again, she is gone, so I wonder if it was merely a dream. We spoke briefly when I returned from the castle, but it was awkward, stilted. Though I know she did not plan for any of this to happen to me and it's not her fault, something is bubbling beneath me, an anger over her part in it. She could have come to my aid on the bus, and she could have testified in court that I didn't help the old man to a seat. Why couldn't she have said it? I sensed her guilt as soon as I saw her when I came home, and it made me angry, it made me want to blame her. Anything so as not to blame myself.

I am plied with painkillers, and I like this. They give me a woozy, out-of-body experience that takes me away from reality, softens the blow. I am aware, at different stages, of a crowd outside our house, but I don't watch them and we don't talk about them. I know when Dad leaves and arrives home from work, not because of the sound of his car engine, but from the camera clicks, the jump to life by the pack, the shutter speeds, the shouted questions. Some are kind, some are disgusting, directed at him as he comes and goes. I never hear his responses, if there are any, but I, too, would like to know if he could still love the most Flawed person in the history of the state.

"Do you love your daughter, Mr. North?"

"How can you still love your daughter?" another shouts.

Still, I appreciate the latter's assumption that there is still love for me at all, despite the fact that they find the very notion bewildering. It would never happen to them, not to someone they love. Impossible. I am poison to some of these people, but I am merely entertainment to others. I learned that from the way I hear some laugh when he drives away and they get back to whatever they were doing, having found the entire thing fun. My life is drama at its mightiest.

I recognize some of their voices. They are the gossip reporters, the news anchors, the familiar voices of my past. And now they're talking about me. Only it doesn't sound like me, not that person, just this revved-up version that I don't recognize. They analyze and dissect my own behavior with more thought than I've ever given it myself. I'm too weak to care about it and too embarrassed to listen to it properly. It is wafting in my ears and mind, and quickly out again. I would rather sleep.

There is a television in my room, but I haven't turned it on, nor have I turned my phone on. It's for the part of me I lost, the invisible part of me that I never knew was essential. The part I gave away to become nothing.

So far, technically, being Flawed has not altered my life. I haven't been anywhere, haven't done anything. I have stayed in this bed, and yet I don't feel the same at all. Not because of the physical scars and ache, either, but I feel different to the bone. Just what Crevan had intended.

There's a knock on the door, and I know that it's Mom. I've developed a way of knowing who's there, of recognizing the different styles. Dad's is tentative, hesitant as though he's afraid of disturbing me; Mom's is all business, like she belongs in the room. She doesn't even wait for a reply and enters. I turn over on my back to face her, feeling the pain in my spine as I do so.

"Your dad has worked out a way for people to visit. He blacked out the windows of his Jeep. So he can meet visitors at the station, then drive them directly into our garage without anyone seeing.

The garage has direct access to the kitchen, so nobody has to set foot outside the door.

"So if there's anyone you want to see . . ."

"Art," I say simply. Probably the first word I've uttered in days. It would be romantic if it weren't for the circumstances.

She looks down at her hands, the dread clear on her face that I've asked about him. I thought he would have visited me by now. I've been waiting. Listening. Each time I hear the doorbell, I hope it's him, but it's not, it never has been.

"Nobody knows where he is," Mom says, finally. "After your verdict, he went home and packed his bags and took off."

"I bet Crevan knows where he is," I say groggily, my tongue still heavy in my mouth. My throat is dry, and the words don't come out easily. My tongue feels huge in my mouth. It is this that has been the most difficult sore to deal with as it blisters and scabs.

"No. He's pretty much going out of his mind trying to find him."

I smile. Good.

Mom hands me a glass of water with a straw.

"Are people ashamed to visit me? Is that why they're going through the garage?"

"No." She pauses. "It's for privacy. So *you* can come and go in privacy."

"I don't plan on going anywhere."

"School."

I look at her in surprise.

"Next week. When you're healed. You can't hide in here forever."

I strangely hope I'll never heal, so I never have to leave.

"Besides, they won't let you stay in any longer. You have to face the world, Celestine."

I wonder whether she will apply this to herself, too. She looks tired around her eyes. She hasn't left the house for as long as I have been home, no visits to her clinic for a pick-me-up, though she will probably want an entirely new face after the scrutiny she has come under. I wonder how all this will affect her work, if she has been dropped from any of her portfolios. It would be naive to think not. No one can be discriminated against for having a relationship with a Flawed family member. They are not responsible for the actions of their loved ones, but still, people always find a way to get around that. My mom's life is just another life I've ruined.

"Mary May is your Whistleblower. She has stopped by every day, she has been thorough in what we and you are allowed to do. She is . . . meticulous in her work," Mom says, and I detect nerves. This woman must be some force of nature. "She has insisted on seeing you every day, but I've held her off," Mom says with a determined look in her eye, and I know it couldn't have been an easy task. "You'll meet her in a few days. She'll run through the rules and then stay with us during dinnertime. She wants to *observe* that we are abiding by the rules for the first few days. And you will see her every day after that. Each evening she'll do two tests."

"Angelina told me," I interrupt her, not wanting to hear about the invasion again.

"She won't be in your life apart from that." She tries to make the daily invasion not sound as bad as it is. "You need to eat something," she says, looking at my tray filled with food. "You haven't eaten for days."

"I can't taste anything anyway."

"Dr. Smith says your taste buds will come back."

"I can taste blood, so I must be okay." Bad joke. And I'm not sure I can taste blood. My tongue is blistered and scabbed, and I just imagine it flowing down my throat whenever I swallow.

Mom winces.

"Maybe it's better if I never taste again anyway, given the food I have to eat every day of the week for the rest of my life."

"It's a healthy diet," Mom says perkily. "Probably one we should all be eating. And we would, but we're not allowed to join you, sorry."

"Are you going to defend everything they do?"

"I'm just trying to look on the bright side, Celestine."

"There is no fucking bright side."

"Language," she says, propping me up with pillows again, but she doesn't sound like she cares what I say.

"Are Flawed not allowed to swear, either?"

"I think more than anything, Flawed are entitled to swear," she says.

We smile.

"There she is," she whispers, tracing a line around my face with her finger. "My brave baby."

I look at her properly. "How are you, Mom? You look tired," I say tenderly.

"I'm fine." Her resolve weakens. "I've booked myself in for an eye lift," she says, and we both laugh. It's the first time she's ever admitted doing any work to her appearance.

"Where's Juniper?"

"She's out at the moment." She stiffens.

"She's being funny with me."

"She's afraid, darling. She thinks you're angry with her."

I think of the sad way she looks at me when she sees me, the gentle tone in her voice when she asks me what she can do for me, and it makes me bark back at her. I'd rather we return to the banter that we used to have. I'm more comfortable with her being irritated by me, but instead now I see her pity. I think of the fact that she didn't come to my aid on the bus and how she didn't testify in court. Mom is right; I feel nothing but anger at her. I know I'm wrong, but somehow it is burning inside me.

"Are you angry with Art?" Mom asks. I know the point she is making: How can I be angry with my own sister and not Art? But somewhere deep down, I keep wondering why he didn't try harder to make it stop. Why couldn't he convince his dad? But I understand. I once trusted Judge Crevan, and he wouldn't have expected his own dad to land me in so much trouble.

"Do you think he'll come to visit?"

She purses her lips and pauses, and I know it's a no. "I'm sure he just needs to think about a few things. Away from his father," she says, and I see the anger in her eyes. "But, Celestine"—she thinks about how to say it—"don't expect him to—"

"I don't," I interrupt. "I already know."

The realistic view would be to believe that Art will never come back to me. I know that. But it doesn't stop me from hoping. And it doesn't stop me from dreaming of the way things used to be.

"I know you don't want to talk about this, but we're thinking of contacting Mr. Berry to discuss the extra brand."

"No," I interrupt before she takes it any further.

"Listen, Celestine, it wasn't part of the original ruling. What happened is unheard of. We want to talk to him to see what your options are—"

"And what might they be?" I say angrily. "Are they going to make it disappear? Is Crevan going to say sorry? No. Just because it's unheard of doesn't mean it doesn't happen. It's Crevan. He does what he likes, and he can do whatever he likes to me again. Promise me you'll leave it alone."

She purses her lips and nods. "I understand, Celestine. Your dad wants to protect you. He wants to defend you. Fight for your name." She smiles softly, loving this part of him. "But I agree with you. I think we should stay silent about it. If we talk to Mr. Berry about it, then I'm afraid we'll bring more attention to it. I'm not sure if he's aware of it or not, but your file still says five brands. They haven't contacted us to update it, and it hasn't been in any of the media reports. They've only mentioned the five. Nobody in the media knows or is talking about a sixth brand."

Yet. The silent word hangs in the air. This news does offer me some relief. I am still the most branded Flawed person in the world, just not yet known to be the most ridiculously branded. I never thought getting away with five would be a bonus.

Mr. Berry knows about my sixth brand already. He saw it happen. I think about telling her, but I don't. I don't want to talk about what happened in the chamber. I want to forget. But I can't. Carrick knows, too.

I see his hand pushed up against the glass, and I hear his voice from the corridor. "I'll find you."

I don't know if I want him to find me like this.

And on that thought, I close my eyes and drift away.

DAY SIX

I have a nightmare. Juniper is sitting in the chair in my room beside my bed, just staring at me. Our eyes meet, and she smiles a wicked, satisfied smile. I wake up in a sweat, my sheets damp beneath me. Feeling dizzy, I look around. Juniper isn't here. The house is quiet. It's midnight. I was sure someone was in my room; I felt a presence. I get out of bed, open my door quietly, and pad down the hall, limping as I keep the weight off my branded foot. I listen at Juniper's door. It's quiet. I slowly, quietly, push it open. I need to see her there, in bed, fast asleep. Her bed is empty. It hasn't been slept in.

DAY SEVEN

I meet Mary May for the first time. I am expecting a tank of a woman, instead I see Mary Poppins. I have seen women dressed as her before but never understood who they were or what they did. She's wearing what looks like an ancient nanny uniform: a conservative black dress with a white shirt and black tie. The tie has an embroidered red *F*. She wears black tights and black brogues. Over her dress she wears a heavy black button-up coat with a wraparound collar and red velvet cuffs. She wears a black bowler hat with a red band and another *F* on the front. Her hair is pinned up neatly and sits in a bun below the back of her hat. Her face is makeup-free and stern. I'm not good at guessing ages, but she's in her forties or fifties and is a tiny, bird-like woman. She looks like she's dressed for the middle of winter. She stares at me as I walk in. She looks me up and down, as I have done with her.

"Hi," I say. I'm not sure whether to shake her hand. The heavy black leather gloves tell me not to attempt it.

"I'm Mary May, your Whistleblower for the foreseeable future. You are aware of the rules, or shall I go through them again?"

I shake my head.

"Verbal communication," she snaps.

"No, I mean, yes," I stammer. "I understand the rules." I'm nervous because I don't want to make a mistake, I don't want to be punished again. I don't know what's right and wrong, what's expected of me in this new world. I've read the rules, I've been told about them, but the reality is quite different. My family is all sitting at the table watching me with her. I can feel the tension in the room. I can't make a mistake. Not again.

She likes how she has unnerved me. I see the smile in her eyes.

I sit for dinner for the first time since I've returned. A regular family dinner. Mary May remains in the corner, hat, coat, and gloves still on, her presence as calming as the Grim Reaper's. Mom has turned music on to fill the uncomfortable silence. Juniper is at the table, eyes down that nervously flit to me when she thinks I'm not looking. The more scared of me she acts, the angrier she makes me feel. Ewan won't stop staring at me, as though I'm not here to see him.

"What's she eating?" he asks, looking at my plate of food with disgust.

"They're grains," Mom says. "They're pumpkin seeds. And that's salmon."

"It looks like dog food."

It smells like dog food.

The others are eating chicken and rice. The chicken looks dry and the rice pasty, and I wonder if it is deliberately so. Mom has also cooked cabbage, which she knows that I hate. I can see she is trying to help me, to make this easier for me. I know Mom has tried to keep it basic, but I still want to eat what they're eating. I don't want their food because it looks better than mine, or because I'm remotely hungry, because I'm not. I want it because it's what I should be having. I want it because I've been told I can't. I wonder, again, where this part of me has sprung from. I was the girl who followed rules, I was on their side. I never questioned anything; now I find myself on the wrong side of everything, questioning everything. This must be how Juniper felt every day. I look at her. She has her head down and is playing with her food. Once again it irritates me that she isn't eating it. She *can* eat it. She has the right and she's barely touching it. She looks up just then, sees the look on my face, swallows, and looks away again.

Ewan is staring at me. At the dressings on my hand, covering my temple. He eyes my chest curiously.

"Mom, Dad," he whines. "She keeps looking at me."

"Shut up, Ewan," Juniper spits.

"She's allowed to look at you," Dad snaps. "She's your sister."

Ewan continues eating, in a huff.

"You know you're allowed to speak directly to me, Ewan," I say softly, finding strength within me to be gentle. He's my little brother. I don't want him to be afraid of me.

He looks startled that I've addressed him.

"Could you pass me the salt, please?" I ask.

It's closest to Ewan. He freezes. "I'm not allowed to help you. Mom, Dad," he whines again, absolutely terrified. He looks to Mary May, who is sitting in the corner of the kitchen, observing with her notepad and pen.

My heart hammers in my chest, and I feel like I've been punched, as if the air has gone out of me. I have caused such terror on my own baby brother's face.

"Oh for christsake," Juniper yells at him, picks up the salt, and bangs it down in front of me. "You're allowed to pass her the salt."

They all continue eating in silence.

I watch them, like robots, heads down, shoveling food into their mouths. All except Juniper. I know none of them wants to eat. None apart from Ewan, anyway, but they are, and I know they're doing it for me. I wish Juniper would. I have a bizarre feeling of wanting to force-feed her that chicken. And then I can't take it anymore, the anger, the hatred that I'm feeling toward my own sister. It's not her fault, and yet I'm blaming her.

I stand up. I take my plate and carry it over to the bin, beside where Mary May sits. I press the pedal to open the bin, and I throw the entire plate inside. I hear it smash as it hits the bottom. She doesn't even flinch. I stick out my finger, ready for her test. I just want to get this over and done with and go back to bed. She pricks my finger, puts a drop of blood on a test strip, and places the strip into a meter that is strapped around her wrist like a watch, which displays my blood results. Instantly, the machine says, "Clear."

She then puts a contraption on my finger, similar to a pulse oximeter, which is attached by a wire to her wrist sensor, and she asks the question.

"Celestine North, have you followed all Flawed rules today?"

"Yes." My heart is beating wildly. I know that I have, but what if it says that I haven't? What if they try to trick me? How truthful are these tests? How can I trust them if they're controlled by the Guild—they can say I'm lying even if I'm not, and it's their word against mine.

The watch once again gives a brisk, "Clear," and she removes the device from my fingertip.

I don't even look back at my family. I feel too humiliated. I go upstairs. I want to sleep.

Sleep, however, doesn't come. My painkillers have lessened. I don't feel as distant anymore, not as groggy, and I long for that feeling to return. I hear Mary May leave, satisfied that I have obeyed the curfew. I sit at the window and look across the road at Art's house. It's large and imposing, the largest house on our cul-de-sac. I suppose you could call it a mansion. It is at the head of the street, looking down on everybody. Crevan's brother developed it, the one who has shares in the soccer club, and they wanted to keep those working in Crevan media on the same street. To control us. Why didn't I see it before? Bob, Dad, Judge Crevan all together on Earth Day. I thought it was so cozy and fun. Now I know it was all about control. The many windows in Art's house are all dark. There must not be anybody home. The only life I've seen come and go over the past few days is Hilary, their housekeeper. I understand that he can't visit, that there are too many journalists and photographers outside for him to be able to do that, especially if he is in hiding from his dad, but no real harm could come from visiting me.

It's not illegal. It would be a show of disrespect to his father, but isn't he doing that anyway? Or failing that, a phone call, a text, or a letter like the one he sent me when I was in the castle would show that he cares, that he's thinking of me. Just something. Anything.

I wouldn't think that a visit to the Flawed could be seen as aiding, though I know that one minute in his arms would save me completely. Even though I'd tell anyone who'd listen that I know there's no hope for me and Art now, deep down, it still makes sense to me. It could still happen. It would just mean his taking a stand against his father once and for all, and it could be me and him against most of the world.

I scroll to his name in my mobile phone and press call. I know what will happen, the same thing that has happened for the last couple of days. It goes straight to voice mail. But I listen to the sound of his voice, jovial and always close to laughter, a cheeky look on his face, and then I hang up.

Downstairs I hear Ewan get a firm talking-to, a going-over of the rules.

I pretend to sleep and feel both Mom and Dad kiss me good night. I hear them go to bed. Talking in low voices and then nothing.

And exactly what I was anticipating happens next. I hear Juniper sneaking out.

THIRTY

I STAND NAKED in front of the mirror, my dressings removed. I hate what I see. My tears fall as my eyes run over the scars on my skin. They have taken away ownership over myself, and they have made me theirs. I want to rip the brandings from my skin. I look away from the mirror. I will never look at myself again. I will never let anyone else see my naked body. Not friends. Not a man. No one.

School is many different things to different people. It makes Juniper nervous, I know that. School is something she worries about constantly from the minute she goes to bed at night to the moment she returns home. She feels uncomfortable, restricted, maybe out of her depth. She can't wait for it all to be over so she can get on with what she considers the more important parts of her life. She worries about homework, about getting answers wrong in class, about her exams, and about what to wear. Her worrying isn't because she's lazy and doesn't try or that she's not clever. She's smart. She is constantly working. She constantly talks about studying, trying on outfits, laying out clothes, starting again. She has one close friend, and they are glued to each other as they walk around the halls, heads together, sticking to themselves. They don't want anybody else, they don't need anybody else. They just want to get through it and be done with it.

For me, school is solid. I like going. I feel comfortable there. I look forward to each day. I don't have any fears about it. I work hard but not so hard that I get bogged down or overly stressed. My teachers like me, and I like them. I don't give them any trouble. I have a great group of friends. Six of us, three girls and three guys including me and Art, and one of which is Marlena, who spoke for me at the Guild. We have fun. We are neither nerdy nor jocks. We might be remembered, we might not. We just are.

But for the first time in my life, I am experiencing what Juniper must feel every morning. I debate long and hard over what to wear. Everything in my wardrobe represents carefree to me, bought and worn by someone who blended in and had nothing to hide. I am not that person anymore.

I stare at the three outfits Mom has helped me to assemble. None of them feels like a place for me to hide in.

According to the rules, outside my home, my temple and hand must not be concealed. I must not hide my Flaws. Nothing can obviously be done about the sole of my foot. But when I am home, I have a list of clothing preferences now. My braids must stay down to hide my branded right temple. My sleeves must be long enough for me to hide the brand on my right hand. The neckline must be high to hide my seared chest. The sole of my foot and my spine will be okay unless I'm on the beach or in swim class, and I cannot wear flip-flops. I have a checklist of places on my body that I want to hide. I hate my body.

I look across the hall at Juniper's room.

I knock on her door.

"Hi," she answers, surprised. She looks tired, and I wonder where she's been going at night. There has been a funny mood between us lately, and I don't feel close enough to ask her this. Mostly because I think she'd lie.

"I need something to wear," I say, conscious that when I talk, my tongue feels oversized in my mouth and I sound like my friend Lisa after she got her tongue pierced. Though my speech is a lot clearer than it was days ago, when I felt like it would barely move.

"You want *my* clothes?" she asks, confused.

"None of my stuff is right."

"Oh. Right. Sure. Um. Come in." She opens her door wider, and I see the bomb site, her clothes are scattered everywhere. "I couldn't decide, either."

I feel like snapping at her that, clearly, this is for very different reasons, but I don't. I swallow it. I swallow it all. My eyes survey the mess. I know what I'm looking for and see it immediately.

"Thanks," I say, backing out.

"Are you sure?" She eyes the items in my hands. "I've other stuff you might like."

"No, this is fine, thanks."

I go back to my room and try it on. When it's on, I look in the mirror and start to cry. Black long-sleeved cotton top, high neck. Black skinny jeans. Black boots. I look like Juniper.

But the outfit isn't complete.

I slide the red *F* armband up my arm, removing the sticky tape from one side to secure it tightly to the fabric. It's supposed to be tight.

Like a second skin.

THIRTY-ONE

PRINCIPAL HAMILTON'S ROMAN blinds are closed because not far from his office the media are camped at the entrance to Grace O'Malley secondary school. A staff member had tipped them off that today would be my first day back. They had pushed cameras up against the darkened glass of Dad's Jeep so hard that I thought they'd crack the panes. Dad had to crawl through them; he could barely see where he was driving. Inside, I felt terrified, claustrophobic, suffocated by so many eyes on me, wondering how my merely sitting there would be twisted and analyzed. Juniper had stared straight ahead, not flinching, not moving, as though she hadn't even noticed. And by the looks of it, they've also been making Principal Hamilton's life a living hell. His face has broken into a rash, running down his wobbly neck into his shirt. Broken capillaries are even more exaggerated on his bulbous nose.

I had never had a conversation with Principal Hamilton before, had never had any cause to, but today a meeting has been called to discuss me. Present are my mathematics teacher, Ms. Dockery, and my civics teacher, Mr. Browne. Ms. Dockery gives me a nervous smile when I sit down. Mr. Browne doesn't even look at me. I fight the urge to pounce on them and shout in a strange animal noise, pretending to put a Flawed curse on them all. That would really scare them.

Mr. Hamilton looks hassled as he tries to organize himself for the meeting and the phone rings yet again.

"Susan, I said hold the calls, please." He listens. "No, I will not be holding a press conference. No, I have already discussed this with the Parents Association and the board." He sighs. "I will not make a statement, either." He hangs up.

"Mr. Hamilton," my dad begins. "I understand you are under a great deal of pressure. We all are, and we want this to run as smoothly as possible for everybody involved. I believe there is another entrance to the school that Celestine could use. One that would allow her to come and go without receiving the treatment she received this morning. She is no longer in Highland Castle. The ruling is over. She shouldn't be subjected to this in her own school."

"I hear you, Mr. North, and, personally, I agree."

Mr. Browne objects, and Mr. Hamilton throws him a look. "I take the view that all students should be treated equally, and that is the philosophy I have handed down to all the teachers here."

Mr. Browne objects again, but Mr. Hamilton interrupts him.

"We'll get to that," Mr. Hamilton goes on. "Using the other entrance is also an idea I suggested myself, but I have a document here from a"—he checks the cover letter—"Mary May, your Whistleblower, which informs me of what I can and cannot do in my own school." He seems annoyed about this. "And, unfortunately, allowing Celestine to use another entrance to help ease her arrival and departure would be seen as *aiding*."

"She is one of your students, goddammit!" Dad thumps the table in anger.

Mr. Hamilton allows a moment for Dad to calm himself. "And I agree. However, I have been instructed, and I can't put my teachers, or my school, in any further turmoil."

"We can't drive and collect Celestine to and from school every day, Mr. Hamilton," Dad says more calmly. "She is in an unusual position in that she can't even take the bus herself. She's too exposed if she cycles, and she doesn't have her full driver's license yet. I'm nervous about her traveling alone; the way these photographers drive is dangerous. Special dispensation must be made for her situation. It is dangerous for her."

This shouldn't be a surprise to me, but it is. To hear Dad say it makes my silent fears real.

"I understand. Believe me." Mr. Hamilton looks at me nervously. "Perhaps we should discuss this further when Celestine has gone to class."

"It's about me. I want to hear," I say simply. That's not true. I don't want to hear it, I need to hear it.

"Very well. I wanted to raise the issue of homeschooling."

"What?" Dad asks, sounding disgusted.

"Celestine only has a few months left of school before final exams. It is not long. She is almost there. I am aware she is one of our top students, gradewise. I don't want to see her results suffer. There has been a lot of talk with the Parents Association. Some, not all, are concerned that having a Flawed at the school will have a negative effect on the reputation of the school."

"You can't discriminate against my daughter because she is Flawed. She has a right to be in this school."

"I know that. But already our enrollment numbers for September are down after this . . . outcome. Parents are worried. Students are worried that in bringing down the good name of the school, it will tarnish their reputations for college and job applications. I am just telling you what it is being discussed, Mr. North," he says before Dad explodes again. "I have the reputation of the school to consider."

"You have the goodwill of your students to consider."

"The unfortunate thing is that a number of teachers, represented here by Mr. Browne, have said they are not in favor of teaching Celestine any longer. Though that is their decision, not mine, I still have to support my teachers and put the facts to you," he says gruffly. "I'm sure you'll agree that homeschooling is better than expulsion."

This makes me feel sick, and I think about Carrick, not for the first time, but as I do every time I'm faced with the new reality of being a Flawed. I wonder how he is surviving. I don't know if not hearing from him is a good sign for him or bad.

"Ms. Dockery, Celestine's mathematics teacher, has kindly offered to homeschool her."

She straightens up as the attention turns to her. I look at her, surprised. I don't know whether to take it as a compliment or an insult. Either she doesn't want me in the school and she's helping to get rid of me, or she's helping me. Tears prick my eyes, and I sink lower. Each time I don't think that's possible, it happens again.

"I think you should strongly consider Celestine's being educated at home," she says. "There will be no distractions for her; she can concentrate on keeping those grades up. The sooner she begins at home, the better it is for her, for everyone all round."

The meeting is heated in parts and ends with an agreement to not agree. The situation will be assessed as it unfolds. Mr. Browne will not teach me, nor will my French and geography teachers, and so, until Mr. Hamilton can figure out what to do with me, I am to go to the library for those classes. The one thing that everyone does agree on is that the media will back off after a few days, when my story dies down, though everyone is surprised it hasn't already. It seems to be as strong as it was at the beginning, as they continue to find new angles. I'm not aware of anything that is being reported. I haven't been paying attention, and my parents haven't shared it with me. In fact, they won't let it into our home. My home is a cocoon, where the day-to-day of my reality is lived and dealt with, not of caring what other people think. I need it to be like this so I can survive, so I can deal with my own reality before hearing other people's twisted perceptions. However, it has been a week and a half, and it hasn't died down, which makes me, for the first time, intrigued to know what they're saying about me.

Because the meeting ran over, I am late to English class. When I enter, all heads turn to stare. My classmates look at me as if they don't know me, as if they're seeing me for the first time. Art's seat, beside mine, is empty. He still hasn't returned from wherever he is hiding. Tears prick at my eyes, and I quickly brush them away as all eyes follow me. I sit alone in that class and every class that follows. Marlena takes me aside where she's sure no one can see her talking to me to tearfully tell me how let down she feels, how she placed her neck on the line and I betrayed her. She tells me what has become of her life since she stepped up to the witness stand, how she finds each day unbearable, how she feels people are viewing her as though she aided a Flawed. She was followed by a photographer one day. She worries about her safety. She hopes she won't be in trouble for giving a positive report on my character. I try to console her as much as I can for her loss. We part with the understanding that she would like to steer clear of me forever. Not once does she ask how I'm doing.

Next class, my biology teacher refuses to teach me. As soon as I sit down, she glares at me and leaves the classroom and doesn't return until ten minutes later, flanked by Mr. Browne and an even more hassled-looking Principal Hamilton, who calls me out of the room.

"Celestine," he says, wiping his chubby, clammy hands on the ends of his suit jacket. "I'm going to send you to gym for this hour." He looks me in the eye. "Sorry."

That apology means more to me than he could ever know.

"I thought I was going to the library."

"You will be afterward. I can't have you sitting in the library all day."

Ah. So the teachers are dropping out like flies.

My eyes fill. "But I don't have my gym clothes."

"You can use the school gear. Don't look at me like that. Contrary to popular opinion, they've been cleaned. Tell Susan to give you the key to the locker."

Gym class consists of twenty minutes swimming and twenty minutes in the gymnasium. I will not put on my swimsuit. I haven't brought mine with me, and I refuse to wear the standard-issue school swimsuit. It is not, this time, because I don't like the cut of it, but because now in my real world, I do not want anybody to see my body at all. And I can't stand the thought of water hitting my scars. It has been only a week and a half, and my scars are healing well, but I am careful about plunging into hot or cold water. Realistically, I can bear the pain of my wounds, I just do not want anyone to see my body. The only people who have seen it are those who branded me, the medical team, my family, and, of course, Carrick. I won't allow any more to see me ever again, and I wonder about Art, if I will ever be able to let him see me and touch me.

I follow everyone out into the swimming pool area. They are all dressed for the pool. The boys and girls smirk at one another, the usual reaction to seeing one another's partly naked bodies. I intend to sit in the viewing gallery and watch.

"You there, what are you doing?" our gym teacher, Mr. Farrell, barks at me.

"I'm not swimming, sir."

"Why not?" He comes toward me, his many whistles rattling around his chest reminding me of the Whistleblowers. I hear the others snicker.

I keep my voice down. "My scars, sir, I can't get them in the water," I lie.

He suddenly realizes who I am, what I am, and takes a step back from me.

"She needs a doctor's note, sir," one girl, Natasha, calls. "If she doesn't have one, she has to get in." She flashes an innocent smile at the boy beside her, Logan. I recognize him, too, from my chemistry class, though we've never spoken.

"Have you a doctor's note?"

"No, sir."

"Then if you don't have one, get in."

"I didn't know I had a gym class today. I was supposed to be in biology."

"And why aren't you in biology?"

"Because Ms. Barnes doesn't want me in her class."

"Well, I don't want you in mine, either, if you don't get into the water."

"I can't get in, sir."

"Do you shower?"

"Yes."

"Then you can get in. Get in."

I land myself in Principal Hamilton's office mere hours after I told him I wouldn't cause him any trouble. Dr. Smith e-mails the necessary note to the school, explaining how it is best for my scars to stay out of the chlorine, but it's too late, the damage has already been done.

I feel sick with nerves as I enter the cafeteria at lunchtime and chatter dies down as all heads turn to stare at me and judge me. Colleen, Angelina Tinder's daughter, is sitting alone, and I build up the courage to make my way to her. I stand at her table, and she doesn't look up. I know that feeling. The feeling that whoever is there is about to say or do something heartbreaking, so best not to look while they do it.

"Hi," I say.

She looks up at me in surprise.

"How's your mom?" I ask.

She narrows her eyes, then laughs. "Wow."

"What?"

"Are you really this desperate? Where were you two weeks ago? Why didn't you ask me then? Of course, you were too selfish to even say hi to me then." The shy Colleen is gone, and in her place is this angry, spiteful young woman. I don't recognize her, not from the girl I spent Earth Day with each year, and family get-togethers, when both of us were carefree and a life like this wasn't even a thought in our heads. Of course she's right about me. I didn't greet her that morning after her mom was taken away. I was too afraid. And then I went on to make the biggest mistake of my life. I deserve what I got, in her opinion.

A few people come to the table and sit beside Colleen. Logan, the guy from swim class who has a rare friendly face; Natasha; and a guy named Gavin.

"Is she bothering you, Colleen?" Natasha says.

Colleen seems surprised at first, then looks at me smugly. I move away immediately, not wanting a scene, as the neighboring tables have gone silent to watch.

"Maybe there should be a special Flawed table in the cafeteria," Natasha says, with her dark, sly eyes.

I keep my head down as I leave the cafeteria. My eyes are hot, and, just as I felt in the Branding Chamber, I don't want anyone here to see me cry.

THIRTY-TWO

WHEN I ARRIVE home after that horrendous day of school, Mom greets me dressed head to toe in perfection: glowing, healthy blond hair down in loose waves, with a pleasant smile on her face. I smell cookies or something baking. She is like a 1950s housewife, and I immediately know something is wrong. She doesn't ask me about my day at all, which I'm glad of because I feel like I'd just burst into tears.

"Pia Wang is here to see you," she says.

Juniper looks at us in surprise, then realizes we want to speak in private. Feeling left out, she trudges upstairs to her room and bangs the door. My being Flawed, in a bizarre way, has brought me and Mom and Dad closer, given us more reason to talk privately, which I know is making her feel like she's being pushed out.

"She's here? In this house?" I whisper, looking around for Pia Wang.

Mom nods quickly, takes me aside, and whispers, "She's in the library."

"Did she just arrive uninvited?"

"Yes. Well, no. She's been ringing every day for an interview, and

I've been putting her off, telling her you were . . . healing, but now that you're back at school, I can't put her off anymore."

"I don't want to talk to her," I hiss.

"By order of the Guild," Mom says quietly. "Apparently, it's part of the package. Every Flawed must be available to speak with Pia after the trial. And if I didn't let her in . . ."

"You'd be seen as aiding a Flawed."

"You're my *daughter*," she says, her eyes filling.

"Mom, it's okay. I'll do it."

"What are you going to say?" she asks nervously. "Perhaps we should call Mr. Berry."

"I don't want to be coached. He'll just tell me to lie, and I can't do that."

It still hurts for me to put full weight on my foot, but I don't want Pia to see me limping. She's waiting for me in the library. I take a deep breath and enter. I tell Mom it's okay for us to be alone. I would prefer it, without having to look at her constantly and worry if what I'm saying is okay. I don't plan on saying much anyway. Monosyllabic answers would kill Pia, and that's what I intend on giving.

Pia is even tinier in the flesh than on TV. She's like a petite doll that looks like the wind could blow her over, though I know that is not the case. Even the wind would lose a battle with her. Her skin is soft and peachy, her clothes delicate and pretty, a silk ivory top with delicate organza flowers and a lace pencil skirt. She even smells of peaches. Everything about her is so fine and pretty, but then her eyes are hard. Not cold, but ready. All-seeing, aware of everything like two zoom lenses on a camera.

"Pia Wang," she says politely, holding out her hand.

I stall, unsure what to do. My seared hand is no longer bandaged; I had to remove the light gauze for school so I wouldn't be seen as hiding my flaws. I haven't had to shake hands with anyone yet. My hand hangs limply by my side. I leave her hand hanging midair. Her eyes drop to my hand, and then she smiles. "Oh, of course." She drops her hand. I'm certain she knew what she was doing.

I didn't trust her before, and I don't trust her even more now. If she tried to put me in my place, on the back foot, then she has failed. It is she who has fallen back first, because I won't make this easy for her.

"Nice to meet you," she says. "Shall we sit here?"

There are two armchairs by the bay window, which overlooks a small, pretty flower garden that Mom tends when she insists she's having a fat day. But the shutters are still closed to protect our privacy from the press.

She holds out her hand for me to sit, as though this is her home.

"I've been wanting to meet you for a long time," she says with a big grin. "You're big news, Celestine. Seventeen-year-old ex-girlfriend of Art Crevan, branded five times, turns out to be the most Flawed girl in history. Talking to you is the biggest scoop of the year."

"I find it intriguing that my life entertains you so much."

Her smile lessens a little. "I'm not alone in that, obviously." She refers to the press outside the house. "As you know, under the Guild rules, I have a sit-down with the Flawed, which will go out on our on-line news, TV, magazines."

"All the Crevan media."

She pauses. "Yes. I'd like us to do an interview first, and I propose something new. A series of televised interviews as we follow you around and film your life as it is now."

"A reality show?"

"If you want to call it that. I prefer documentary."

"Because you're a hard-hitting journalist and all."

She pauses to take the insult. "I'm interested in people. Intrigued by what makes them tick. Interestingly, with you"—her eyes run over me—"I can't quite figure that out. I'd like to find out."

"I don't want to be followed around by a camera. My dad is a TV editor. I know exactly how you can make me look: whatever way you

158

want. If I have to do the newspaper interview, then I'll do it, but that's all."

She's clearly disappointed by this, but there's nothing she can do about it. "Okay. It will be a series of meetings, not just one sitting. I want in-depth. I want to understand you, Celestine, really get to know you."

I half-laugh.

"I amuse you?"

"You work for Crevan. Do you think I'm stupid enough to think that you want to understand me? That anything you have to say about me will be favorable? That anything I actually say will make it into your articles?"

"You're an interesting case, Celestine."

"I'm a person. Not a case."

"Friend of Judge Crevan, honors A student, a perfect good girl. You're an unlikely candidate for this situation. People want to know about you."

"Me and Angelina Tinder. Funny, isn't it, two Flawed on one street within the span of two days? Such a coincidence."

Something flashes in her eyes. Something different. A doubt of some kind, but then she resumes normal play.

"Euthanasia is frowned upon by our society," she says, defending the Guild's ruling on Angelina Tinder.

"So is compassion. I helped an old man to a seat."

Then I realize I just gave her a headline. She's thrilled.

"You see, Celestine." She grins, moving forward in her chair. "It's comments like that that are making people pay extra attention to you. You're refreshing. For one so young."

"I'm not *trying* to be anything."

She looks momentarily confused and then looks around quickly before changing her tone, as though she shouldn't be telling me this. I'm on the edge, trying to analyze her tactics. "Enya Sleepwell was at your trial every day."

I look at her for more. I have no idea whom she's talking about.

"You do know who she is," she says patronizingly.

"No," I sigh. "I have no idea who that is. Was that the old woman who spat at me? Or the young woman who threw a cabbage at me? Or perhaps it was the lady in the third row who ate an entire bag of Pick n' Mix on my Naming Day."

She frowns. "She's in the news a lot these days. You haven't heard of her?"

"I don't watch the news."

"I find that hard to believe. You're in it every day."

"Well, then, why would I watch it? I know what I'm doing every day."

She gives me a small smile. "Your parents don't talk to you about what's happening? About what's being said out there?"

"It's not important what's being said about me. I don't need to hear it. I can't control it and I can't change it."

She looks confused, then checks the door to make sure it's closed. "I mean, you seriously . . . you don't know this? Enya Sleepwell is in the Vital Party. You must know who they are. They picked up a lot of seats in the last election. They're the fastest-growing party in Parliament."

I shake my head. "I don't follow politics. I'm seventeen. All of my friends couldn't care less about it, either. We're not even allowed to vote until we're eighteen."

She looks at me in surprise, studying me as if she can't believe a word I'm saying, trying to figure me out. "Well, politics is following you, Celestine."

I mock her by looking behind me to check. I realize I've replaced monosyllabic answers with sarcasm, but it's far more rewarding.

"So you didn't work with Enya Sleepwell? Meet with her? Before the incident on the bus?"

"What? No!" I reply.

"Some people think you were trying to be a hero," she says. "That you still see yourself as a hero, that you're perhaps above everybody else. That your apparent selfless act does not make you Flawed, or at least that it puts you on a different level from the other Flawed. I think you wanted to be different, stand out, were tired of being in the middle of the road, normal girl, boring girl, abider of rules."

I bite my lip to stop myself from snapping at her, which is what she wants.

"Do you think you're a hero, Celestine?"

I sigh. "If I was such a hero, that old man would be alive now. Nobody seems to be considering the fact that a man is dead. A man died because an entire bus full of people failed to help him. Do I think I'm a hero? No. I failed."

She frowns, slightly confused. "But you succeeded in raising your issue to a higher platform. Everybody is now talking about the 'aiding a Flawed' rule. An overwhelming number of people want it stricken from the rules."

I'm surprised to hear this. If it's gotten rid of, will that mean I'm not Flawed anymore? How can they undo my scars? They can't. Never.

She looks at her watch, then at me eagerly. "When can we meet again?"

I shrug. "I'm here every day after school. Don't plan on going anywhere."

"A popular girl like you? I'm sure you have plenty of offers. I heard you were offered a perfume deal."

I snort. "What, Eau de Flawed? Who would be bothered to buy that, and why on earth would I want that? You really don't know anything about me at all, do you?"

"I just wanted to introduce myself today. Let's meet again tomorrow," she says eagerly, picking up her briefcase. "If you're not the boring teenager who was fed up with her life and did something as a cry for attention, then I suggest you talk to me or that will be my story."

She holds out her left hand this time. I reluctantly reach out and shake it with my unbranded hand.

I stay in my seat, fuming, thinking back over our conversation. "By the way, I don't have five brands."

She freezes at the door, pivots ever so delicately on her peach pumps. "Pardon?"

"You said I am the most Flawed person in history, with five brands. Crevan gave me six."

THIRTY-THREE

PIA IS STILL staring at me. She hasn't blinked once. I know the press hasn't reported my sixth brand for some reason, which surprises me. I assumed Crevan would want the whole world to know. If she doesn't know, she can't print it. And while Pia's not knowing gives me comfort, I also want her to know that she doesn't know everything, that even her basic knowledge of me is wrong. She tried to put me out when I walked in. I'll put her out when she leaves. If Crevan has lied to her, her little, solid world will be rocked, and I want to see the look on her face for my own gratification. Saying it is worth it for the reaction.

"He what?" she says, shocked, her cool demeanor completely gone. "In court, he distinctly said five."

I make a decision whether to continue. It will probably come out sometime anyway, better that it's from me. And even if she prints it, it's true. Crevan can't blame me for that. My heart pounds as I say it aloud. "He came to me in the Branding Chamber. He asked me to repent. I wouldn't. So he ordered a sixth on my spine. Without anesthetic. Said I was Flawed to the very backbone." I decide not to mention that it was him who branded me. Best to save my revelations.

"He . . . what?" She can barely speak. "But that's not allow—I mean, it's never been . . ."

She knows she can't say much more about it. Question and doubt Judge Crevan? In the company of a Flawed? She's not that foolish.

"Talk to your buddy Crevan about it." I leave her standing in the doorway in shock.

It's the first time I smile in almost a week. When the lows are so immense, the victories are small. But they are there despite it. You just have to know them when you see them, little pockets of light and hope hidden away in the darkness.

When I return to my bedroom, I find Mary May has been rummaging through my table beside my bed. I look around my bedroom in surprise. My wardrobes are open, clothes have been pulled off the hangers and left on the floor, and my shelves have been rooted through and left untidy. She's sitting on my bed reading my journal, which is sitting on her lap, my private diary. I want to cry right there. I haven't written in it since before the trial, I haven't had the energy. It feels like a different life, but they are my private thoughts, silly things, embarrassing things, but things that were important to me at the time of writing them. My *secret* thoughts, and she's sitting right there stealing them.

I open my mouth to protest, but as if sensing it, she holds up her gloved hand to silence me. She turns the page. Finally, she snaps the journal shut and looks at me up and down as if seeing right through to my soul.

"Rules state you are to expect random searches of your private possessions. If you're going to continue writing this journal, for example, further thoughts on whether your thighs are fat and if you'll be any good at sex"—she sneers, and I feel my whole face heat up with embarrassment—"I expect you to hand it over to me every Friday so that I can read it for myself. Is that clear?"

I swallow. And nod.

"What did I say about verbal communication?"

"Yes," I say, and it comes out as a whisper. I clear my throat and repeat it, but she's pleased by the effect she's had on me.

She picks up the Highland Castle snow globe that she's found in my bedside table and gives it a shake.

"Always good to have a reminder, isn't it?" she says, dropping it into my hands as she passes, the red sparkling glitter falling down and coating the bottom like drops of blood. It feels like a warning.

I rush to the bed and throw the snow globe back into the drawer. I never want to see it again. I pick up the journal and start to rip the pages out, first one by one, then frantically as I start to sob. When I've torn all the pages out, they lie scattered on the floor.

Mom comes to the door and watches me, concerned.

"She was reading my journal," I splutter.

Mom joins me on the floor and looks around at the pages. Then she picks them up and starts to rip them into little pieces, her face not as cool as usual, her eyes filling up. This gesture means more to me than anything she could have said. I join her, and we rip the pages of my handwriting, excited exclamation marks, stars and hearts around Art's name, doodles and words that came from my heart, concerns I ached over, stories I giggled over, private thoughts that were once only mine. I watch the hearts be ripped to pieces.

Angelina Tinder was right. They want to be in our heads. I will never let them in my head again.

THIRTY-FOUR

JUNIPER AND I barely speak.

She feels guilty and left out. I feel angry and bitter, and I must admit I have found an odd sort of joy at taking my pain out on her. With too much time on my hands to think, analyze, and dissect, my mind always drifts back to the moment on the bus. I try to live it out differently in my head, as if doing so would change the outcome. But every time I relive the moment on the bus, I can't help but relive Juniper's silence. Juniper, who could never usually keep her trap shut, couldn't find one single word to leap to my side on the bus or to defend me in court, but most of all, watching her live her life as I want to live mine is hurting me the most.

I can tell she is maddened by my silence with her. I can sense her shouting at me that this wasn't her fault. She's telling me that she feels guilty enough without my having to make her feel any worse. And I respond to all that with silence. *I* was the one who would have done exactly what I was told, not her. For her to suddenly become me and for me to become her is the most bizarre twist of all. I am wearing her clothes, I am feeling her insecurities, and she is suddenly silent, biting her tongue that she could never silence before, sneaking out at night to meet who knows at a time I am no longer permitted to step foot outside my house. It is my fault that we are behaving like this with each other, but I can't stop feeling as I do.

Most of all, I miss Art. My heart is broken and I need him. I can't understand why he hasn't written to me, why he hasn't called me, why he hasn't reached out to me. If it's true that he has run away from home, then not being under the thumb of his dad gives him even more freedom to contact me. This is beginning to feel more like Art's decision to stay away from me and less his dad's. That hurts more than any branding.

After what happened with Colleen, I give up on the school cafeteria. Instead, I read books in the library, huddling on a beanbag in a corner and getting lost in somebody else's victories and troubles. I never had much time for fiction before. I preferred real life. Mathematics. Solutions. Things that actually have a bearing on my life. But I can understand now why people read, why they like to get lost in somebody else's life. Sometimes I'll read a sentence and it will make me sit up, jolt me, because it is something that I have recently felt but never said out loud. I want to reach into the page and tell the characters that I understand them, that they're not alone, that I'm not alone, that it's okay to feel like this. And then the lunch bell rings, the book closes, and I'm plunged back into reality.

Today I'm too tired to read. I haven't been sleeping well. I've been forcing myself to stay awake because my dreams keep turning into nightmares of the Branding Chamber. Lately they've focused on Carrick, and instead of it being me in the Branding Chamber, it's him and I'm watching him being seared. Where is he? He told me he'd find me. When? Has he decided not to, or does he need my help? I have thought of him often, so often that he has started to appear in my nightmares. Internet searches of *Carrick Flawed* do nothing to help me learn anything about him. I don't know his surname. I don't know anything about him. Where he's from, what he even did. I don't know if he was found to be Flawed, but a wild guess tells me that he was. I wonder about his punishment for being there for me in the Branding Chamber, and I hope someone was there for him, that someone offered him peace as he did for me. I have written his name on my notepad, gone back over the letters in red ink over and over. It starts to break through the page. It helps me think.

Suddenly I hear a noise in the library, and I jump as Logan appears.

"Hey," he calls cheerfully. "I've been looking for you."

"Me?" I say in surprise.

He jogs forward and hands me an envelope. He's always so confident, but right now, he seems shy. "Invitation to my eighteenth. This Friday."

"Thank you." I smile, my heart surging.

"The directions are inside. You'll come?" He holds my eye.

I hold the invitation in my hands, feeling stunned and unsure. "Um, why?"

He laughs. "Why what?"

"Why are you asking me?"

"The whole class is invited. Couldn't leave you out."

"I don't think they'd want me there, Logan."

"Well, I do," he says firmly. "Are you coming or not?"

"Okay. I mean, yes. Thanks." I feel my grin take over my whole face, and I just can't stop. As soon as he leaves, I squeal and stamp my feet excitedly. Maybe things won't be so bad after all. Maybe things can change.

I hear another sound in the library, and I call out. "Logan? Is that you?"

I walk to the end of the row of books and look left. I'm grabbed from the right and pulled around the corner to the next aisle. I'm about to shout when I'm faced with Art.

"Shhh," he says, holding his finger up to my lips, and leads me down to the far corner of the library, behind the shelves, in the darkest corner.

THIRTY-FIVE

MY HEART IS pounding. I can't believe it. I can't wipe the grin off my face.

We're so close I'm pressed up against the bookshelf. I feel a few books slide behind me as I push against them. Art looks tired, his hair not as bright, a bit grubby, his curls looking more like knots. There are dark circles around his eyes, like he hasn't slept for weeks, and the mischievous glint is gone from his eyes; they're flat. While I take him in, he does the same with me. He studies my temple, the one with the brand, and winces as if feeling my pain. His fingers come close to touching it, but they don't make contact, just hover above my skin. His finger runs down my cheek to my lip, and he looks at my mouth with intensity. I know he's thinking about my tongue brand.

"It's still me," I whisper.

"I know, I just . . ."

"It's okay."

There's a silence, and I suddenly don't know what to say. I've wanted to kiss him for so long, but now it doesn't feel right, it feels different, he seems different, and I have so many questions, like *where on earth has he been?*

"Who's Logan?" he asks before I get a chance to speak. "You called out his name."

"Oh, that's just nobody. It doesn't matter. Art, where have you *been?*"

"What's that?" He looks down at the invitation in my hands, reads it.

"Logan Trilby?" His face looks hard, angry.

"He was just being kind, Art," I say quietly. "How did you get in here?"

He lightens up a little, but he seems flat. "The number of times I had to sit in here for study, I eventually found a way out."

"I've been so worried about you. I didn't know what was going on. I don't know what *is* going on. Where have you been all this time? It's been a week and a half."

"I can't tell you where I've been."

"Why not?"

He looks around, paranoid. "Because they'll ask you where I am, and I don't want you to have to lie, to get into trouble again."

"I couldn't possibly be in any more trouble."

Neither of us laughs.

"Please tell me."

"I can't. They'll follow you to me. They're watching you all the time."

He leans in, and I think he's going to kiss me. I watch his lips and wait for them to kiss my lips, but he moves away again.

"I've needed you," he says.

"Me too." I feel tears prick, feeling sorry for myself. "I feel like you just left me alone. . . ."

"I'm sorry. I just had to get away from him," he says, stepping away, agitated. "I've been so confused, trying to figure it all out. I was so

170

angry with you, Celestine." He shakes his head. "Everything was perfect."

I'm in so much shock I can't speak. After what his dad did to me, he's angry with *me*?

"And I can't even look at him knowing what he did to you. Five brands? *Five?!* That wasn't just to hurt you, it was to hurt me, too."

He doesn't know about the sixth. I can't tell him, his rage is so intense. I want to reach out to touch him, but for some reason I can't.

"And I can't live with you, either, knowing that my dad did this to you," he says, taking a step back. "I'm in the middle of the both of you, and whatever I do, it will be wrong."

"Art, listen to me," I say, feeling the panic rising. I can't lose him. If I lose him, then I'll have nothing.

"No, you listen to me. What you did on the bus was right, but it was wrong for us. If you were selfish like me, you wouldn't have done it. If I was as strong as you, I would have defended you. I would have stood beside you on that bus. Instead, I watched you do it all, in silence. I let the person I loved get dragged away."

Loved? He loved me! Does he still? The celebration of that idea is killed by the uncertainty of whether it exists anymore.

"It's not your fault, Art. None of it is your fault. I can't lose you. What about school? What about university?" I plead with him. "We can do all the things we planned, and then you and I can go somewhere together, away from everyone else. We'll take our time, build a plan."

"Where, Celestine? Where exactly can you go?" he asks, and I detect anger at me again. "You can't leave the country. And you can't go anywhere without alerting the Whistleblowers. Every single Flawed person is accounted for at all times. You have to report your every move to them. If you move, you get a new Whistleblower. And if you do that, then *he'll* know, too. He'll always know where we are. We'll never be free of him. He'll make our lives hell."

"We could make it work," I say, holding on to him, trying to stop his pacing.

Just being with Art would be enough for me, even if I have to live under Flawed rules and Art doesn't. Crevan couldn't possibly make things any worse for us.

But there's something else he has said that has my mind in overdrive, about every Flawed person having a Whistleblower, every Flawed being documented, their whereabouts known. I'm trying to find Carrick. Carrick will have a Whistleblower, his whereabouts will be documented. My heart pounds with excitement. "Art, can you help me find someone?"

"Who?"

"A Flawed guy. His name is Carrick."

"Who?" His eyes narrow.

"Carrick. I don't know his surname. He was beside me in the cells. I really need to find him."

His jaw tightens. "Yeah? Become close, did you? Just like Logan?"

"Art!" I say, surprised.

"Forgive me, Celestine, if I don't know exactly who you are anymore, if I have to question you."

"You know *exactly* who I am." I swallow hard.

He examines me again. He sighs and closes his eyes, the stress clinging to him, weighing him down. I don't know where he's been staying, but there's an earthy smell to his clothes.

"Carrick was kind to me, Art. I was alone in there and so was he, and he looked out for me. I just want to say thank you to him. I just want to know . . . what it's like for him. If it's the same for him as it is for me. It would be nice to talk to someone who understands—"

"You think that I don't understand you? Forget it." He walks away. "Do you know how hard it was for me to come here today? Dad has people out looking for me everywhere. Do you know what I risked? What I've risked for you period? And in the middle of my trying to explain, you ask me to help you find some Flawed guy you met in a cell? You're going to parties like nothing's happened? Well, I'm delighted everything is fine for you," he says sarcastically, storming down the aisle.

I'm stunned at first but then chase him, realizing I'll lose him. By the time I reach the end, he is out of sight, completely gone. I check every aisle. He's gone. I've lost him. I run up and down each aisle, feeling dizzy, wondering how he disappeared, when I finally come upon a narrow metal door, like a service door. I pull at the handle, expecting it not to budge, but it opens and brings me to the service area where Mr. Murray, the groundskeeper, does his recycling and stores his tools and equipment. He is ripping up enormous cardboard boxes, flattening them and piling them on the ground.

He doesn't even look up. "Get back inside, girl."

"What? I'm looking for someone."

"I know who you're looking for. Get back inside." He looks up then, and I see warning in his eyes, so I slowly back away.

Then from behind one of the enormous recycling bins, a photographer jumps out and starts clicking, the flashes disorienting me.

Mr. Murray tells him to stop, starts citing laws and acts and rights, but the photographer doesn't listen, he continues snapping away. He lowers the camera at one point, and I see a wide grin on his face. I suppose he can't believe his luck that I'm so startled I can't move. But his grin urges me back into action, and I disappear back inside the library and slam the metal door shut. I'm back in the silent library, my heart pounding so hard I'm sure the books can hear me.

It's then that I wonder why the photographer was there. What did he see? Did he see Art go in and out that door? And then me appear at the door? I haven't broken any rules, but it makes me feel panicky because there is one person who wants to see Art almost as much as me, maybe more, and will do anything to find out where he is.

Crevan will come for me.

173

THIRTY-SIX

"TELL ME ABOUT the last time you saw Art Crevan," Pia says in the library of my house at the end of the horrible day that I lost Art. I'm drained and not in the mood to talk to her, but I have to be on guard, because of her questions and because I'm waiting for Crevan and his army to bang on the door and take me away to interrogate me about Art's whereabouts.

I'm exhausted from my parting with Art, from my lack of sleep, from imagining Carrick's searing over and over again. I'm afraid of being caught by the photographer. I'm just completely zapped. They've taken all the goodness from me. I am just a scarred shell. But this new question about Art makes me sit up. Pia notices my body tense, and I'm annoyed with myself for being so obvious.

"Everybody knows what happened on Naming Day. Art was at the courthouse, it was on TV. Anything you want to know about that you can watch for yourself."

"That's not what I asked you." I think she's like a cat, rubbing her shiny legs together in her too-tight pencil skirt. She leans forward, a sly smile on her lips. "I've caught you out on two lies, Celestine. One"—

she counts it off on her manicured, peach-colored fingernail—"you met Art at school today. I've seen the photographs of him entering the library, where I know you both met, and I will keep it between you and me if you cooperate with me fully and give me the interviews that I need."

My heart pounds.

"And two, you didn't receive a sixth brand. There is no proof, no documentation, no record whatsoever of that event taking place. I checked the files."

She sits back, obviously enjoying the stunned look on my face.

"You know, you scared me when you told me, Celestine, and I think that was your intention. Perhaps you wanted me to confront Judge Crevan about it, write an article, cause a stir. Talk like that can be very dangerous, Celestine. Those kinds of accusations could have the power to bring down Crevan and the Guild, not to mention myself, and I won't let you use me to do that."

I can tell that she's annoyed that she feels used, that I tried to trick her. She is using the Art photographs as retribution. A part of my mind that never thought like this before kicks into gear; it whirls into action, spinning, plotting, planning. I had no idea that Crevan's giving me a sixth brand would get him into so much trouble that it could bring down the Guild. How could it? If I'd known that, I would have thought about it more carefully. I wouldn't have just blurted it out to her. I have power?

"Is it your intention to bring Crevan down, Celestine? Are you trying to bring Art into your plan? Turn him against his own father? Is Enya Sleepwell in charge of an attempt to set up Judge Crevan? Just what on earth are you planning, Celestine? Because everybody knows you're planning something."

She is so pleased with herself, as if she's caught me out in my great big master plan. She waits for me to break down, to cry, to confess. Instead, I throw my head back and laugh. She has given me an idea.

Confused, she fidgets in her seat and readjusts her skirt, uncomfortable with my reaction.

"I bet you didn't ask Crevan about the sixth brand, did you?" I ask.

"Of course not," she says, slightly flustered.

"No, of course you didn't. Because you're afraid of him. Because you know he's unhinged."

"Judge Crevan is not unhinged," she says, clearly as if somebody else is listening, as if I'm setting her up. "And I'm not afraid of him. . . . I simply wouldn't ask him something so ridiculous. I would need proof first. I asked your mother about your sixth brand," she says with another sly smile. "Even she can't vouch for you. She wouldn't even admit you have a sixth brand. She wasn't even in the viewing room for your fifth brand, Celestine; none of them were. Your family was removed for unreasonable behavior. The reports say it all."

The reports have lied.

No wonder Mom seemed nervous when I returned home from school. I thought it was because of Pia's presence, but it was because she'd been asked about the sixth brand. She is afraid Pia will write about it, but what Mom doesn't understand is what I now understand. Pia will never write about it because Crevan will never allow her to, *because he shouldn't have done it.*

"Who wrote the reports?"

"The guards on duty."

Tina, June, Bark, Funar. They lied for Crevan.

"So basically my grand master plan won't work because there's no proof," I say.

"Not an iota." She grins.

I think about it. I relive the moment it happened, the pain I felt and the strength I had in not giving in to Crevan by refusing to repent. The most painful moment in my life also became the moment I showed the most strength and courage. And I think of Carrick, his hand pressed up against the glass. I also remember Mr. Berry, with his camera held up in the air, recording the event. I never knew it was important before, but we have all the proof I need, and I'm not going to reveal that to her. For some reason, Mr. Berry has not come forward with that information. I should have that video in my own possession. That video is power, and maybe that's why Mr. Berry is keeping it, for his own interests.

"I can show you proof right now, if you wish."

She looks around the room, possibly thinking somebody is going to jump out of a hiding place.

"Before I share it with you, you have to promise that you will fully cooperate with me," I say, turning the tables. "I know you're not going to write about my seeing Art today, and I know you won't publish the photographs. You're just using them to threaten me. I know that because, if Crevan finds out that you knew where his son was today and you never told him, you will be in a world of pain. You knew where his precious son was, and you let him get away? Do you know how long he's been searching for him? I could cross the road right now and tell him."

That has worked. She *is* afraid of him.

"Fine," she says, swallowing. "I'll bury it. So where's this proof?" She's trying to act like she doesn't believe me, but I can see her fear. She's afraid of the sixth brand being true, afraid that the head of the Guild is a fraud, that everything she believed in isn't true.

I stand up. I step closer to her, and she pushes her back firmly into the chair, hands on the armrests, and braces herself. I turn around and lift my T-shirt, lower the waist of my trousers so she can see the base of my spine. I can't see her face, but I can hear her intake of breath. The brand on my lower spine is that disgusting. I squirmed when Crevan seared me. I felt the pain without the anesthetic, and ironically the *F* is not perfect at all, just red bubbling skin. I lower my T-shirt but don't sit down again. Instead, I make my way to the door.

"Thank you, Pia. This interview has been highly informative."

Instead of catching me out, what she's done is given me an idea. If I have the power to bring down Crevan with my sixth brand, then I will do it. Then Art and I can be together. But to do that, I need more proof and I need help. I need Mr. Berry's video, and there's one more thing. I'm not waiting for him anymore. I need to find Carrick.

THIRTY-SEVEN

I HAVEN'T HEARD from Art since we parted in the library. I run through our conversation over and over in my head and try to convince myself I shouldn't have brought Carrick up. What an idiotic thing to do at such a time. If I hadn't, Art and I would still be okay. But in my heart, I know we wouldn't. I can't play along with his moods just to stay together. It wasn't the same between us in that library. Everything felt different. He couldn't even bring himself to kiss me. One thing I'm sure of, though, is that yesterday I wanted to find Carrick to thank him, today I need to find him because I need his help to activate my plan. If there's one person who would want to take down Crevan as much as I do, it's Carrick. I can't do this alone.

My last class of the day is French, but the teacher refuses to teach me, so I will be in the library by myself once again. It is the perfect opportunity to get some time on my own, to be somewhere without anybody knowing. I catch up with Juniper in the school corridor. Everybody makes a wide circle around us.

"Losers," Juniper mutters.

"Tell Mom I had to go somewhere this afternoon, tell her not to wait for me. You guys go home without me."

"What? She'll freak out. Where are you going?"

"Tell her I'm fine. I just want to be independent, get a grip on my new life by myself, blah, blah, blah. She'll go for that."

Her eyes narrow with suspicion. "What are you up to, Celestine?"

There's a standoff between us. Neither of us trusting the other.

"Tell Mom I'm meeting Pia Wang for an interview."

"Are you really?"

I roll my eyes and walk away. She's not the only one who can meet people in secret.

After Susan, the school secretary who has almost become my babysitter during classes where teachers refuse to teach me, has checked up on me, my plan is to escape out the door of the library. I push at it, but it's locked. I bang at it and kick it in frustration, absolutely *nothing* going my way.

I slither down to the floor to cry in frustration, and suddenly it opens and I fall backward outside. Mr. Murray is standing there.

I scramble to my feet.

"I didn't help you," he says simply, then turns his back and goes about his work.

I don't step outside. As much as I want to grab this opportunity to find Carrick, I don't want Mr. Murray to get into trouble. He's been the school's groundskeeper ever since I've started here and probably even before that.

"It's illegal for you to help me," I say, testing him, giving him one more chance to close the door on me.

"No, it's not," he says, still not looking at me, scraping his muddy boots on a rug. "There's a mark on the sole of my foot that says there's no law against a Flawed helping a Flawed."

"What?" I look down at his feet, but he continues rubbing the muck off.

"You'll just have to take my word for it."

"But . . . but you don't wear an armband."

"Exactly, so nobody knows. I'm off the radar." He finally looks at me.

"I've never heard of that before."

"There are cracks that you can fall through. Harder for you, of course, being a household name, but if you look for them, you can find them. They don't win all the time. Be careful."

I nod, stunned by this. "Thanks."

I hurry away from the school, managing to avoid the dwindling press numbers by cutting through the trees. I don't want to travel on a bus—I think that would attract too much attention—so instead I take a bike from the city's bike-sharing scheme. There are thirty stations around the city. You take a bike from one station, cycle it to wherever you need to go, and park it at the nearest station. Highland Castle is one of the busiest tourist spots in the city, as well as employing a huge number of people, so it has one of the largest bicycle stations outside. I cycle across Humming Bridge, weaving through the tourists. It's a struggle to cycle uphill, so I abandon cycling and push it instead up the ironically named High Road. I don't think there's such a thing as anybody actually taking the high road to Highland Castle. As I'm locking the bike, I hear the familiar sound of people calling and yelling in the courtyard. It takes me back to my own experience and terrifies me, stopping me in my tracks until I realize it's not aimed at me. Somebody else is walking to court.

Because that is taking everybody's attention, nobody notices me. I buy a cap from the tourist shop, making sure not to cover my temple in case I'm caught, and push my way to the front of the crowd. I get there in time to see a man and a woman, holding hands, making the walk from the Clock Tower to the court. The woman is crying uncontrollably, and they are clinging to each other. There are two guards on either side of them, but I don't recognize the guards at all. This is good. It means I can go to the Clock Tower while the court is in session and speak with Tina. Hopefully, after all I went through, she will give me Carrick's address.

The gathered crowd is nothing like the scene I had during my trial. I look up at Pia's filming location, and there she is, live on air sharing her prejudiced thoughts on more innocent victims.

"You're disgusting!" the woman beside me shouts as the couple passes, and she spits. Her phlegm flies through the air and lands on the woman's shoe. This makes me flinch, and the woman walking by cries even harder, tucking herself under her partner's arm even closer.

"Did you see her face?" The woman beside me laughs, as do a few other spectators.

"Should have aimed for her face," a man says angrily.

"What did they do?" I ask.

"Have you not been reading the news?" she asks, surprised. "They're all over it."

I shake my head, and I can tell she enjoys having the opportunity to tell me the story herself, as though her disgust with people is the only thing keeping her going.

"She and her husband took their dying son out of the hospital, without permission, because they didn't agree with his treatment. Flew him across the world, were on the run for weeks; poor fella could have died. They took him to Spain. To get another treatment." She rolls her eyes. "Sure, what's wrong with our hospitals? They just can't play God like that."

"But . . . did the treatment work?" I ask.

"They flew back this morning. The Whistleblowers got them before they even got off the plane. The little boy is back in the hospital. He's grand. They're going to let him continue the alternative treatment. The Spanish police interrogated them but let them go. Nothing illegal, apparently, but it's wrong. That boy could have died getting there."

I shake my head, and she's satisfied by my response, but I'm not in agreement with her. I know now that I am totally and utterly against any Guild decision. The woman looks down and sees the *F* on my sleeve. Her eyes widen and her mouth drops and her face twists in disgust. Before she alerts anyone, I push my way back out of the crowd and hurry to the Clock Tower.

The receptionist greets me.

"I'd like to speak with Tina, the guard," I tell the receptionist.

"I'm afraid that's not possible," she says.

I take off my cap to reveal my identity. "I know her. I was in custody here two weeks ago. I just wanted to ask her something."

"I know who you are," she says politely, unfazed by me, or my sleeve, as she sees it every day, "but Tina no longer works here."

"Oh." My heart drops, and I scramble for another plan. "What about Bark?"

"He's no longer here, either, unfortunately."

I have a sinking feeling. "What about June?"

She shakes her head.

"Funar?" I ask reluctantly. I don't expect I'll get anything out of him, but I have to at least try.

"He is no longer employed here, either."

"What? Well, um." I think hard. "There was another security guard. I don't know his name. Red hair. Um . . ."

"Tony," she says quietly. "He no longer works here, either."

I stare at her in shock, totally speechless.

I can see that she's uncomfortable. She looks up at the corner of the room, and I see the security camera. "Is there anything else I can help you with?" she asks gently.

"I need to see Mr. Berry," I say urgently. If the guards are all gone, who were my witnesses, and I can't contact Carrick to help me, then I realize I need to get to Mr. Berry myself. I need that video now.

She looks relieved that she can help me with something. "I haven't seen Mr. Berry for some time. I believe he took a vacation, but let me see if he's back." She dials his number, then, disappointed, hangs up.

"Unfortunately, he's out of the office. Would you like me to pass on a message?"

"Can you tell him to call me? It's urgent."

"Of course."

"Could I have Tina's contact details? A phone number? Or e-mail address? Anything. I just want to ask her something. I won't bother her in any way if that's what you're worried about."

She bites on her lip. "I'm not really supposed to . . ." but I can see doubt there somewhere. "Just one moment." She stands up and makes her way into the room behind her, and I wait, still in shock that they're all gone.

I drum my fingers on the countertop, watching the clock. Mom will be collecting Juniper soon. She'll flip when she finds out I'm not going home with them. I need to make this risk worth it. When the door opens, I expect to see the receptionist, but Crevan steps out. My heart hammers wildly. I haven't seen him since the Branding Chamber, and it brings it all back to me, the lunatic look on his face as he shouted at me to repent, as he ordered the unbelievable pain on my skin. He's wearing his red cloak, ready for court. My breathing becomes heavy. I'm afraid of him. I don't see Art's father anymore. It's another man, an evil man, and I understand how Art can't stand to be near him any-more. Neither can I, so my body shivers from head to toe.

The receptionist's face has turned scarlet behind him. She has a piece of paper in her hand, and I know it's Tina's contact details, and I want it so badly. If I don't get it now, she will never give it to me. But Crevan is looking from her to me, and if he snatches the note from her hand, then it's all over.

"Celestine," he says, nostrils flared, as though there were a bad smell in the room. He looks at me with more hatred than I've ever seen in anyone. "What are you doing here?"

THIRTY-EIGHT

"WHAT AM I doing here?" I ask, and I can hear the tremble in my voice.

My obvious fear only makes him stronger, gives him an amused, patronizing look.

"I'm . . . I'm . . ." I can't even think. I can't lie, and I can't come up with any reasonable explanation. I am so stupid for putting myself in this position. I feel light-headed. What would happen if I just ran? Would he chase me?

"There you are," Pia Wang says suddenly from behind me, all business. "I was looking for you. I'm ready now."

Just what I need, Pia and Crevan together at the same time.

She stops beside me and looks up at Crevan. "Oh, Judge Crevan, hello, how are you? Celestine and I were just about to begin the next part of our interview. Were you looking for me?" she asks me.

I look at her in surprise. She's helping me? I nod.

The receptionist crumples up the piece of paper in her hand, and my heart drops.

"Let's go. There's a café around the corner," she says. "Judge, nice to see you," she says confidently, and leads me away.

With wobbly legs, and not a second look at Crevan in case he calls me back, I go with her. There are many narrow alleyways and cobble-stoned pathways around and through the castle. Pia leads me down one and into a tiny café with five tables close together. She must have known it would be empty, and the spotty teenager behind the counter makes us our coffees and sits on a high stool and disappears into his phone. Even if he hears every word we say, I doubt he'll care in the slightest.

By the time we've sat down, I've managed to gather myself.

"What are you doing here?" Pia asks.

"Looking for you, obviously," I say, sarcastically. "And ta-da!"

She views me with suspicion, but if I don't go along with her idea, then she'll want to know why I'm really here, and I can't tell her anything about looking for Carrick.

"I thought about your proof," she says, looking at the teenager, then back at me.

"Right."

"And it doesn't hold up. You could have done that to yourself."

I almost choke on my coffee, and she at least does seem to feel a little stupid for saying it.

"Or somebody else could have done it. There's no proof that . . . *he* . . . did it."

"There is definitely something wrong with you if you think that I would sear my own skin with a burning-hot iron without an anesthetic," I say a little more loudly than I mean to, but she is making me so angry. We both look at the teenager, but he hasn't taken his eyes off his phone.

"There's just nobody who can back up your story," she says. "Your family and Mr. Berry were all taken out of the room for the fifth brand. Nobody was in the viewing room. There's nothing about it in the reports."

She really doesn't know about Carrick or Mr. Berry, and I'm sure Funar wouldn't have told anybody that they managed to rush into the room and witness it all, seeing as it was his mistake.

"Have you talked to the guards?" I ask.

"No. But I've read the reports. The guards write them."

"Yes. But did you *speak* to them?"

"No."

"Interesting." I finish the last of my coffee and stand up feeling more confident but hoping more than anything that I won't bump into Crevan again. It's clear that I'm putty in his hands now. "I have to get home, or my mom will be worried. You should talk to the guards. They might tell you something different. Tina, June, Bark, Funar, and Tony. You should ask for them at the front desk."

She scrambles for a pen and writes those names down. The speed of her reaction reveals her desperation for the truth. If I can't find them, she can do the work for me, though it doesn't mean I can trust her to write the truth if she learns it.

"Thanks for the coffee," I say. I put on my cap, adjust my *F* sleeve, and go back out into the world. I leave three voice mail messages on Mr. Berry's phone, urgently asking him to call me.

There's one more place I want to visit before I get home.

Part of the Flawed rules is that the Flawed aren't allowed to be buried with their families; there's a graveyard especially for them. The idea is that you can't force the regular moral and ethically abiding people of society to be buried in the ground for all time alongside the Flawed. I go to the only Flawed graveyard in the city, which is surrounded by bright red railings.

There is a list of occupants at the graveyard office along with a log of their misdemeanors, part of the philosophy of being branded Flawed. Even in death, there is no escaping it. I don't need to go to the desk to search through the logbook. It's easy to find Clayton Byrne's grave site. It looks like that of a celebrated martyr. There are dozens of fresh flowers and sweet-scented candles decorating one side of his grave, out of respect for a man who died so tragically. His grave site has become a place for the Flawed to come to, with hope that he is the symbol of change, that his situation will bring light to their plight. I know this because I read the dozens of notes and cards that have been left behind. Others who visit are those who feel his death is a symbol that we are all truly doomed, that there is no hope. This comes in the form of the black roses and black candles that line the other side of the grave. I look at the color and I look at the darkness, the hope and the despair, and I don't know which side I fall on.

I sit by his grave and light candles; one black, one white. And I cry, for his loss and for mine.

THIRTY-NINE

I OPEN THE front door of my home, and the media look at me in shock. One photographer actually freezes with his sandwich halfway to his mouth. It is the first time since the bus that I have left from my own front door, having always arrived by car and driven directly into the garage. Even after my solo visit to Clayton's grave, I'd called Mom to pick me up. After being beside herself with worry and anger, she was understanding when she collected me at the graveyard, knowing it was a good step for me to make in my life. I still will do anything to avoid the scrum outside our house. Driving into the garage doesn't stop the barrage of lenses against the window, but at least it stops the men with cameras trying to aim their lenses up my skirt as I get out of the car, which they have been doing with Mom and Juniper. The prospect of exposed leg or parting thighs is too exciting and appealing for them to miss.

Mom has appeared on online sites most days. She is more than pleasant to look at and refuses to have a bad day, so they keep coming back for more, her wardrobes being analyzed daily, with captions under the photos of how Summer North "shows off" her long legs, "displays" her slender body. I understand that, for the media, *shows off* and *displays* merely mean *has*. They also describe her clothes as "snug" and "tight-fitting," and if she ever wears a trouser suit, they say she is "covering up," like women who don't reveal their entire figures are trying to hide something.

There is a stunned pause as the press all look at me, and I take advantage of the element of surprise and take off down the driveway. Finally, they remember what it is they're doing camped out in front of our house and fumble for their cameras and microphones to chase me. I cross the street, but they catch up to me. Now I'm surrounded, finding it difficult to know where to walk as their flashes blind me and they block my path. Their cameras bump into me as they push and pull one another for the best shots. I have to push through them as though they're not there. Some are shouting, "Give her space!" while another man shouts at me to blow him a kiss. I try not to react. I know that's just what they're looking for. I keep my eyes down, focused on the ground that I can see, knowing that if the line in front of me trips, then I will trip. I pass the FOR SALE sign in the Tinders' yard, and the media must stay outside their grounds. I go straight up their driveway and ring the doorbell.

Bob Tinder answers. He looks much older than the last time I saw him a few weeks ago. Grayer. Exhausted. He looks past me and sees the media at his gate and lets me in immediately. I can almost hear their disappointed sighs as I close the door behind me.

"Celestine," he says, not looking too ecstatic to see me with what I've brought to his front door. "Colleen is out."

"I'm not here to see Colleen." The fact that she and I have never called each other has obviously not registered with him. "I'm here for my piano lesson."

He frowns.

"It's Thursday," I explain. "I always have piano lessons on Thursdays."

"She hasn't . . ." He swallows, his voice cracking. "She hasn't played since . . ."

"She should."

"She thinks it's damaged her hands. That she can't play anymore."

"Can you tell her I'm here?"

He thinks about it. "You can wait in the music room."

I walk down the corridor and turn left into the music room. I haven't been here since my life has changed. The room hasn't changed, and yet everything seems different. I go inside. I sit at the piano. I wait.

I lift the lid and run my fingers over the tops of the keys. I'm waiting a long time. I can hear the rise and fall of Bob's and Angelina's tones as they talk down the corridor. She doesn't want to come in. I will make her.

I begin by playing the most recent piece she taught me, and my favorite. "Nocturne Carceris," a haunting piece. I play it better than I've ever played it before. And I play it from memory. I never liked piano class. It was always something that stopped me from seeing my friends, and then practice was something that stopped me from watching TV or going out. It was always an obstruction. At gatherings, I was always asked to play for everyone, and that, too, used to bother me because I'm a perfectionist, or at least I was, and I wouldn't be able to relax the entire evening until my party piece was over. And if I made a mistake, it would play on my mind for a week. Piano always seemed to stress me out. I played it for other people. I played it for Angelina in class, I played it for my parents when I practiced, and I played it for guests at parties. I never played for myself. I never had the opportunity. But that all changes in this moment. I play for myself. I play better than I have ever played before, getting lost in my head as my fingers glide over the keys.

When I was a child, I always thought that to run away, you had to physically get up and run, as the kids did in the movies. A hateful shout, a slam of a door, then run. I've learned that lots of people run away without even going anywhere. I see it in Mom's newly polished face, I see it when Dad disappears into his head at the dinner table, I see it when Ewan gets down on the ground and really focuses on his cars and helicopters. Juniper does it when she puts on her headphones and blares her music with her back to the world. I've never known how to do it before. But now I do. I'm running and running and running in my mind, through endless nothing but feeling free. When I open my eyes, I see Angelina Tinder standing at the open door, her head-to-toe black a stark contrast to the fresh white walls. She stands at the door listening, so I continue to play. Then she slowly nears me. I feel her beside me, behind me, and then she sits beside me. I'm afraid to look at her in case I scare her away. Bob stands at the door with a smile on his face. Happy and sad at the same time. Then he closes the door gently on us both.

When I'm finished, I look at her, the room in total silence. Tears stream down her face.

"You play," I whisper.

She shakes her head.

I look down at her hands, once again covered by the black fingerless gloves. They are clasped tightly on her lap. I slowly reach down and take her hand in mine. She doesn't protest, but she is intrigued, as though she has no control over her hands. So I slowly bring her hand up to the piano keys and uncurl her fingers. I reach for her other hand and do the same, getting more confident as I lift it to the keys and un-curl her fingers again.

She sits there, perfect posture as she always used to, her in that position fitting better than any glove over a Flawed hand. Her fingers start to move slowly over the keys, not pressing them. No sound is being made, but she gets a feel for the keys again. She smiles.

"Go on," I whisper encouragingly.

She lifts her hands gracefully, and I'm waiting, holding my breath to see what she will play, and then she quickly slams her hands down again on the keys. Up and down, up and down, bang, bang, bang, like a toddler let loose on the instrument. I jump at first, then freeze as I watch her, waiting for her to stop this madness. And it is madness; I can see it in her face. There is anger and hate and pain all bursting through her, trying to get out, but her eyes are mad and wild. The sound of the keys is disturbing, the clash of the notes being hit over and over again.

I look around uncertainly, not sure what to do.

"Angelina," I say gently, but my voice can barely be heard over the notes. So I raise my voice. "Angelina, please stop."

She ignores me, continuing her attack on the piano, moving from the lower keys to the higher keys, making the most unusual, distorted sounds from something that she used to make sound so beautiful. I wonder if it sounds beautiful to her, now that her mind, too, has become so distorted. If she hears Mozart where I hear madness. She continues as if I'm not there, her elbow digging into me, almost pushing me off the bench. I stand up and move away from her, and I wonder if I should call for help, as she's having some kind of an episode.

The door is flung open.

"What on earth?" Bob says, stepping inside.

She ignores us, continuing to be lost in her music with a smile on her face. But there is no happiness in it, just a demented picture of contentment.

Bob stands there in shock, watching her, not recognizing her.

"What's *she* doing here?" Colleen asks suddenly, appearing at the door. "What's going on?" She looks inside and sees her mother. Her mouth falls open. "What did you do to her?" she shouts over the noise.

"Me?" I ask, shocked. "Nothing. I didn't do—"

"What did you do to my mom?" she yells, angrily, coming close to my face.

I back away. "Nothing. I didn't do . . ." but she's not listening.

"Get out of our house," Colleen shouts.

I look to Bob for some kind of normality, to bring logic to the situation, but he is distracted. He makes his way over to his wife, holding his hands near her, hovering around her body as if he's afraid to touch her.

Colleen puts her hands to her ears as though she just can't take this anymore, not just the sound of her mother but whatever else she is hearing in her head. Her own voice, her own cries, her own anguish.

"Get out," she says to me, disgust written all over her face.

I move closer to the door. I give one last look to Angelina, crazily banging down on the keys, an entirely different woman, maddened by the branding of her body and the treatment that comes with it. Suddenly she lifts one hand off the keys but continues banging with her right hand, and she reaches for the lid. I think she's about to stop playing just as Bob is asking her to, and then I see what's about to come.

"No, Angelina!" I shout, and they both look at me and miss her slamming the lid down on her right hand. The hand that is branded.

Once is not enough. She cries out in pain yet continues it over and over again.

"This is not my hand! These are not my fingers!"

It takes both Colleen and Bob to stop her, but by then I know the damage has already been done. She has broken her own fingers.

FORTY

STUNNED, I STUMBLE down the corridor to the front door. I open it and am faced with the media. They see the look on my face, which I have forgotten to adjust.

"What happened, Celestine?"

"Are you planning a coup?"

"Are you gathering a Flawed army?"

"Is Angelina Tinder part of your alliance?"

"Is it true you're setting up a Flawed political party?"

I push through them and stagger forward to my house.

Mary May waits for me at the front door. The press aren't allowed to photograph her, but I know they're loving this. They can sense that I've done something wrong, that I'm in trouble again. Big news day. Already upset by what has just happened in the Tinders' house, I don't think I can take any more. Mary May steps aside so that I can enter.

Juniper and Mom are standing nervously in the kitchen. Ewan runs upstairs and away from me as he always does, afraid to be in the same room as me.

"What did you do?" Mom asks quietly.

"Nothing," both Juniper and I reply at the same time, which makes us look at each other and smile for the first time in a long while.

Juniper throws me a worried look and whispers, "Did you do something yesterday?"

I swallow hard. I think of meeting Crevan and wonder if he discovered I was looking for the guards and Mr. Berry, and if so, what is my punishment. Mary May marches into the kitchen in her black-and-red coat and looks straight at me. I'm so afraid that it has something to do with my trip to Highland Castle and asking for the guards that when she produces a newspaper and slams it down on the kitchen counter, I'm relieved.

Now I know that I can't trust Pia. It's a ridiculous article about how I am getting preferential treatment at the school by missing classes and swimming, something I know was written purely to pressure the principal to make me leave the school. If he is seen as aiding a Flawed, or even making my life easier, then the parents will want his head on a plate. The picture that appears alongside it is a photo of me taken sneakily by someone at school. It's supposed to be a photo of me with my braids down, covering my temple, which is against Flawed rules.

"That's not me," I say instantly.

We all huddle in closer.

"That's me," Juniper says.

"You understand the rules, young lady," Mary May says to Juniper. "You cannot lie for your sister, or you will face punishment or incarceration or both."

"I'm not lying," Juniper says, and I can sense her getting a hot head. The old Juniper is back.

"The newspaper says it is Celestine," Mary May says, a little put out, folding the paper again. "This photograph is a clear breach of the rules, Celestine. You will receive a punishment."

"I'd like you to call the newspaper and get clarification," Mom says quickly. "A mistake has clearly been made here. I know my daughters, and that is not Celestine in the photograph."

Mary May is having none of it. "For a total of one week, starting Monday, you will be under house arrest. You cannot leave this house after school hours." She signs a form, leaves it on top of the newspaper, and leaves.

"I hate her," I say quietly, watching Mary May drive away.

Mom shushes me even though she's too far away to hear.

"She's just a stupid woman in a ridiculous costume," Juniper snaps.

"No, no, no." Mom grabs her by the shoulders and looks her straight in the eye. Juniper is startled by Mom's aggressiveness. Mom realizes what she's done, and she sighs. Then she leads us both to the kitchen table and we sit. "Girls, we have to be careful. You think she's a woman with a grudge, but Mary May is one of the most senior Whistleblowers, and do you know why?"

"Why?" Juniper asks.

"She reported her sister to the Guild as soon as the Flawed rules were introduced. And then when her family turned its back on her, she reported all of them. Her father, her sisters, and her brother, something to do with their family business. Everyone was taken away, branded, punished."

"What?" I gasp. "Her own family?"

"She might look like a woman in a stupid costume, but she's dangerous. Let's not find out how far she'll go."

I swallow and nod. I may have gotten away easily here. My week-long detention isn't the worst punishment in the world. It means that I can still go to Logan's party tomorrow night, which I've been excited and anxious about, but it will pause my Carrick-finding mission, and I need to find him before Crevan manages to make any more people disappear.

FORTY-ONE

"SO DID YOU speak with the guards?" I ask Pia, biting into my apple.

An urgent request to meet with me has brought Pia to my house extremely early Friday morning. I can hear everybody getting ready for school and work, but I'm in no rush because the principal just called to say that due to the reaction to Pia Wang's article, I can't attend school until we figure out other arrangements. They have finally gotten their way, and they're using the article to get at me, no doubt Crevan's idea. I'm gone, now Art can attend. He just needs to be found first.

Pia is in casual mode, jeans and pumps and a cotton T-shirt, which is unusual on her. She almost looks human.

"I asked for Tina, June, Bark, Funar, and Tony at reception, just as you told me to," she replies.

"Great," I say enthusiastically. "So they were all able to back me up, corroborate my story?"

"They weren't there," she says quietly. "They no longer work at Highland Castle. But you already know that. You were there looking for them yesterday."

I shrug and bite into my apple. "Maybe, maybe not. I'm gutted, as you can imagine. Now I have absolutely no proof whatsoever that Crevan gave me a sixth brand."

She flinches at me, saying it aloud.

"My family was thrown out of the room, the guards were fired, and Mr. Berry has taken a sudden and unplanned holiday. He hasn't worked on a Guild case for the past two weeks and isn't responding to any calls. Everyone is gone. It's almost like somebody didn't want anybody who was present at the branding to talk about what happened at all. Like a conspiracy! Oh, wait a minute!" I gasp sarcastically.

This is obviously deeply distressing to her, and she sits very still in the armchair, lost in thought. It is terribly distressing to me, too, in fact, though I'm trying to hide it. It means Crevan really is hiding what he has done to me, somehow getting rid of the witnesses, which makes me feel unsafe.

"There weren't any reports of incidences of the guards' bad conduct," Pia says. "There were no warnings before they were let go. No reported incidences. No budget cuts. No contracts that had come to an end. It was very sudden. All gone. On the same day. The day after the Branding Chamber. As far as I can see, they're not currently employed elsewhere. I rang Tina's house. There was no answer. She has a daughter, so she must know something. I think I'll take a drive out to her tomorrow."

"So you believe me," I say nervously.

"No, I'm not saying I believe you," she says quickly. "I mean, I don't know, but, maybe, I think that I have to cover all areas before . . . you know. It's a very serious thing, and if he did it, then . . ."

"Then what?"

"Then . . ." She sighs. "Then it calls a lot of things into question."

"It calls *the entire system* into question," I say.

"Unfair treatment in the Branding Chamber doesn't necessarily mean you're not Flawed, Celestine."

I roll my eyes. I can't win with her. "No, but it means *he* is. And what happens if you have a Flawed person at the head of a Flawed court?"

She goes quiet. "I heard the school won't let you attend."

I feel the anger rising within me. "Because of your article, with the photograph of my *sister*."

Her guilty look tells me all I need to know. But it also shows me that perhaps there's a conscience knocking around in there that I never knew existed.

"Isn't it better to be at home?" she asks. "So that you're not the only Flawed in the school. That can't be easy."

"Are you trying to convince yourself you've done me a favor? Because you haven't. I wanted to be at school. It's my right."

She looks confused and thinks about it. "What's it like to be Flawed at school? The *only* Flawed person."

I can't find any hidden agenda with this line of questioning, but she's never asked me questions like this, about how it *feels*, because the readership isn't supposed to care about how it feels for a Flawed, unless it's to scare them.

I sigh. "I don't know what it's like when you're older, but every teenager wants to be perfect. Nobody wants to stand out, at least I never did. And the people that do stand out, they're just being themselves. Everybody wants to look like they know what they're doing, when really most of the time nobody has a clue. Maybe it's different with adults."

Pia smiles. "Not really that different with adults at all. It's not easy being a journalist," she says, and I throw her a bored look. "No, seriously. Not everything we write is published the way we want it to be. We don't always have control over our voice."

She'll never apologize for the article that got me thrown out of school, but perhaps this is the closest she'll come to it. Today her article is about whether Angelina Tinder "coached" me to become Flawed and questions who else she taught piano to. She misquotes me a few times from previous interviews, twisting my words to fit into her context. There is a photograph of Angelina before the Ousting and a photograph of my startled face leaving her house. The headline is FLAWED PIANO TEACHER RECRUITS.

I study Pia, and I know what she's struggling with: tell the sixth-brand story or not. Bring down Crevan, or not.

"So tell them you want it to be said your way."

"It's not that easy."

"Yes, it is."

"They don't listen."

"Then leave. Go work somewhere else."

"The world doesn't work like that, Celestine."

I shrug.

"So if I left this extremely well-paid job, where I might not get to report everything in the way that I want, but I get to report it—I have my own show, my own column—who would feed my two children?"

"Lies wouldn't."

This strikes her, and she's silent some more.

"I've changed my mind. I'm going to call Tina's house today, ask some questions. Can we meet later tonight?"

"I won't be here." On her look, I give her more. "I'm going to a party. Someone from school."

"Good for you," Pia says.

If I didn't know better, I'd think she was almost happy for me. But I can't trust her fully. What if she is working with Crevan to find out what my plan is? What if she finds the guards and talks them out of telling the truth? Threatens them with a story or with accusing them of aiding a Flawed? And if I tell her about Mr. Berry's recording of the Branding Chamber, what if she destroys the video? No, I can't trust her. She is too close to Crevan, and she has done little so far to earn my trust. I can't tell her about Carrick or Mr. Berry's video.

I'll just have to get to them before she does.

FORTY-TWO

"SO WHOSE PARTY are you going to?" Juniper asks me at breakfast, after Pia is gone.

"Logan Trilby's."

She stops chewing her cereal, her sugary cereal that she continues to eat while I'm limited to oatmeal. "Logan is the biggest asshole going."

"He's been nice to me."

She frowns. "What's he celebrating?"

"His eighteenth."

"I'm pretty sure Logan is nineteen. He had to repeat his final year he's so dumb."

"No, he's not." I whip out the invitation.

She studies it with a frown. "Oh." She hands it back, and we sit in silence. "I didn't hear anything about it."

Despite the tension between us over the past couple of weeks, she is my sister and I do have the capacity to feel sympathy for her. I'm thankful for that. It reminds me I'm human.

"Well, I'm sure they were just being nice to me. I wouldn't feel bad about it," I say gently.

She starts laughing. "Do you think I'm jealous? No way. Believe me, I'm not. You can have your party. What I meant was, I never heard about a party, and I wouldn't trust them."

"Why? Because I'm Flawed?" I ask, my anger flaring up instantly, always there ready and waiting for me to use in my overflowing reservoir. "You think the only reason I could be invited anywhere is because it's a trick?"

"I'm not saying it's a *trick*," Juniper says weakly.

"So where are you going tonight?" I ask, the anger thumping inside me. "Are you going to disappear tonight like you do every night?"

Juniper looks at me in surprise, a mouth full of cereal. She chews slowly, and I can tell she's trying to think.

I know it's unfair of me to bring it up so loudly in front of everyone, but she is up to something and what she said about Logan has really hurt me. Finally, I'm making friends and she's taking away from the thrill I should be feeling. My heart is racing as I watch her eat her sugary cereal; it's making me angrier and angrier.

"What are you talking about?"

"For the past two weeks I've gone into your room at midnight most nights, and you haven't been there."

She laughs as if I'm ludicrous, which annoys me. I don't like people thinking I'm crazy. Not now. Not after seeing Angelina Tinder lose her mind. I don't want that to happen to me. Mary May looks up from her paperwork. Mom and Dad watch us with interest.

"Fight, fight, fight," Ewan chants, before Juniper kicks him under the table.

"Maybe I was in the bathroom."

"You weren't."

"How do you know?"

"I checked."

"Okay, stalker."

I don't like how she looks at me.

"Is this true, Juniper?" Dad asks, coming over to the table.

"You're going to give me shit when you know Celestine was leaving the house most nights to meet Art?"

Mom looks at Mary May in panic. "*Before* the branding. Juniper, please clarify," she says sharply.

"Before the branding," she says as though she's a scolded child.

"What you both used to be able to do before and what you can do now is different, Juniper. If people see you and think that you're Celestine, she will get into trouble. Like the hair," Dad says, looking at Mary May angrily.

"So I can't live my life because Celestine can't?"

"Celestine can live her life, so watch your mouth, young lady," Dad raises his voice, which startles us all.

"Anyway, I haven't been sneaking out," she says, eyes down, and I know she's lying.

"Are you calling me a liar?" I ask.

She glares at me. "I don't need to call you anything. Stick out your tongue, Celestine."

"You stupid, little . . ." I pick up my oatmeal and hurl it at her.

Mom and Dad dive on both of us, separating us. Juniper is sent upstairs to change her oatmeal-covered clothes.

"Go on, take another hour to get dressed like you always do," I shout after her.

"Celestine, stop," Mom admonishes me.

Mary May takes out her notebook.

"What?" I snap. "Fighting with siblings isn't allowed, either? What do I get as punishment, extra pumpkin seeds for dinner?" I stand up and make my way to the sink. As I reach past Mary May to get the cloth behind her to clean the oatmeal, she must think I'm going for her and brings her hand back and slaps me hard across the face with her leather glove. The pain stuns me as much as the shock of it.

"How dare you!" my dad yells, rushing over to her, but then he stops right in front of her as though there's a force field stopping him from getting close, which I guess is exactly what there is. She's untouchable. She is what I thought I used to be.

My eyes prick with tears, my face stinging, but I won't let Mary May see me cry.

Mom rushes to my side, "My baby, my poor baby." She hugs me while over her shoulder Mary May looks at me menacingly with cold blue eyes. Mom pulls away and takes the cloth it is now obvious that I was reaching for, though I don't see a hint of regret in Mary May's face. "I'll do this," she says, her voice trembling with anger. "A mother can help her daughter. Now, is there anything else I can do for you this morning, or is that all?"

Mary May seems to be unmoved by it all, maybe she's even enjoyed it. "I understand that Celestine has a party tonight. Curfew breaking is considered a very serious breach of the rules. Celestine would have to go before the Guild court to decide her punishment, but punishments usually bleed into the rest of your family. Simply put, if you break the rules, your family will be punished. Just ask your friend Angelina Tinder; ask her where her boys have been this week."

I think of the silence in their house when I visited, how there were no signs of their presence, no sounds of their playing. I swallow.

Mom looks at me; her fear is clear. "They were taken into temporary foster care for one week."

"I won't be late," I say quietly. I couldn't cope with Ewan being taken away from us.

Mary May gathers her things to leave. "By the way, Judge Crevan tells me we will soon be recruiting an old friend of yours. Art Crevan is to become a new member of the Whistleblowers, and I've been honored to be asked to personally train him myself." She gives me a look, a satisfied twinkle in her eye, before she closes the door behind her, leaving me shivering in fear.

"Art couldn't. He wouldn't. Working for the Guild is the last thing he'd ever do. He wants to go to university. I'm going to study mathematics; he's going to study science. That's what we planned."

Dad sits on my other side as Mom applies cream to my face to stop the bruising from coming up.

Dad sighs. "Oh, Celestine, I'm sorry." He kisses my forehead. "Try not to worry. Last I heard, they still don't even know where Art is. Crevan has put a lot of manpower into finding him, but there's been nothing yet."

"I hope he got away," I say, for the first time realizing Art might be right, maybe we can't make us work.

"Me too." Dad smiles sadly. "Now put it out of your mind. I know that's hard, but you have to look forward. Let's think of tonight. New beginnings. New friendships."

I nod, trying to ignore the throbbing in my cheek.

"What was all that noise?" Juniper says, entering the kitchen. "Dad, did you shout?"

She has taken far less time to dress than I expected, and as soon as I see her, I suck in air. She is wearing my clothes. Pink skinny jeans and a cream crop top that I threw out last night. I'd tried it on, but it revealed the *F* brand at the base of my spine. I can never wear it again. I threw all those clothes out so I'd never see them again, never be reminded of the life I had to leave behind, the person I used to be. And now she's wearing them. It all looks unusual on her, out of place.

"What?" She looks at me self-consciously, angry and embarrassed at the silence that has greeted her. Wearing it is retribution for my calling her out earlier, but it has backfired. Even Mom and Dad are uncomfortable with what they see. "You're wearing *my* clothes. What am I supposed to do?"

I watch Juniper walk across the kitchen confidently in my clothes, in the crop top that would reveal both my chest and spine brands, in flip-flops that would reveal my foot brand. Reminders, rubbing it in my face.

Today Juniper must get the bus to school. She was quite happy with the chauffeuring, but now that I can't attend any longer, she's back to getting the bus. I was worried for her, hoping she wouldn't get into any trouble on the bus, but now I couldn't care less.

"I need some air," I say quietly, feeling dizzy.

"Hold on." Mom holds me back at my shoulders as Juniper steps outside into the full glare of the media. There's a small, amused smile on her lips. "They'll think she's you."

I look outside to see Juniper being surrounded by the press. She can barely move forward they're so much in her face. I bite my lip to hide a smile, then slip outside. Perhaps Mr. Murray was correct about being able to slip into the cracks.

FORTY-THREE

LOGAN'S HOUSE IS on the other side of town, in an equally leafy neighborhood in a nice part of the suburbs. I blare the music and lower the window to feel the wind in my face. I sing loudly, feeling free. As long as I have friends who will support me and be friends with me for who I am, I can do this, I can live this life. It's not what I wanted, it's not what I planned for in my carefully thought-out plans of yesteryear, but it's the hand that I've been dealt, and I will make as much of it as I can. I sing along to the radio, feeling happy, feeling like maybe I don't even need to worry about outing Crevan's act in the chamber. I can live this life. I can be happy.

I'm nervous about arriving at a party with people I don't know, but it's more of an excitement. I'm ready to do something new. I'll be there by 8:00 PM. Two hours of being young again ahead of me, because I don't want to be home late. I want to be home well ahead of Mary May's arrival, so there's no doubt that I have not broken any rules. Two hours is perfect. New friends, new beginnings.

Despite my parents' nerves about my going, they are both delighted that I'm doing something that a seventeen-year-old should be doing.

That I'm not holed up in my bedroom crying as I have been the past few days. But mostly one of the reasons they were so open about my coming here was that they know Logan's parents. Not personally, but they know of them. Everybody does. They are both pastors, a husband-and-wife team. Because of this, they get a fair amount of media attention, and they have been upstanding citizens. I feel this is probably why Logan reached out with the olive branch. He lives in a house that encourages understanding and forgiveness. He knows what it's like to be perceived as being different, to be watched by others and analyzed and dissected until there's nothing left of you but to feel raw and naked.

We follow the directions in Logan's invitation to a modest white house with a pretty yard. They even have a picket fence. Mom and I embrace, and Mom holds on to me tight, too tight, afraid to let go, but she finally does, eyes teary.

"I'll be here at ten. Call me if you need me to be here earlier. Or call about anything. Even if it's small. If someone says something stupid or nasty or—"

"Mom!" I laugh. "I'll be fine!"

"Okay, okay." She grins, finally letting go.

She watches as I make my way to the front door, and it reminds me of when I first rode my bike without training wheels. I look at her in the car, terrified of letting me go, terrified I'm about to fall.

For a party, it is remarkably quiet, but perhaps that's how the son of pastors has to party. There is a car in the driveway, and I recognize it as being Natasha's car. This makes me nervous, and not in an excited way. I don't get along with Natasha, not that we've ever spoken, but she has been vocal about my presence in the school, particularly in swim class on the first day I went back. She won't be happy about my being here. I know Logan and she are close, so perhaps he can convince her to change her mind. It occurs to me that I may need to do more mind-changing tonight than I'd thought. Perhaps tonight won't be fun. It will be an icebreaker, and the next night can be fun. Baby steps . . . I walk up the driveway, my legs wobbly in my sky-high heels. I ring the doorbell and wait. I turn around to Mom and wave at her to go. She gives in and takes off down the road, leaving me alone finally.

There is silence inside, and when I look through the side panel of glass, I see a single simple wall-mounted Jesus on the crucifix. His head is dipped, covered in a crown of thorns, his hands and feet nailed to the cross. It is a most vivid piece, stronger than I have ever seen before, and the hairs go up on my arms. My antennae suddenly up, I take a step back—right into a person standing behind me.

I yelp with fright. And then a bag comes down over my head and I can't breathe.

FORTY-FOUR

"SOMEONE GET HER hands," I hear Logan hiss as my fists land another blow to his face. I know it's a face because I feel my finger poke an eyeball and land on a tongue to be quickly snapped at by teeth.

I don't need anyone to grab my hands. I am genuinely still after I hear the sound of his voice. In the few seconds that I have been struggling, battling against the arms trying to restrain me, I had this crazy thought that if I screamed loud enough, Logan and his friends would hear me and save me. It hits me now that this *is* the act of Logan and his friends. My blood turns cold. I lose something and can't figure out what it is until I realize my hands are tied tightly behind my back and pulled in one direction: It's my faith, in absolutely everything and everyone. Desire to pick up my life and try to live as normally as possible is punched out of me right there. I surrender to my Flawed life; they have won, and I have lost.

It's difficult to breathe in the bag over my head, which is tightened beneath my chin, around my neck. And panicking is sucking up all the oxygen I need, but I can't stop gulping in air and screaming for help. I stop allowing them to pull me along and fall to the ground in protest, banging my knees on hard concrete. I cry out.

"What the hell?" Logan snarls again. He's trying to keep his voice down; we're in his neighborhood. If anyone sees this, they'll know. I scream louder, wishing my mom had stayed, but a blow in the stomach knocks the wind out of me.

Somebody picks me up and carries me. I gasp for breath and can't struggle any more.

"You said you wouldn't hurt her." I hear a girl's voice, and it chills me.

Colleen.

In retaliation for what? For not saying hi? For what happened to her mom's fingers? Is that all my fault, too? A scapegoat for society and now a scapegoat for everyone else who knows me. All their problems are all my fault. Nothing to do with their own decisions, their own mistakes, their own doing. Sheep.

"What do you want me to do? She's screaming the place down," he says angrily, and I know now that Logan is the one carrying me.

I kick my legs as I'm carried along, and I hear laughter.

"She sounds like a pig." I hear Natasha's nasty laugh.

A car door opens. "Get her in, quick." Another male voice I don't recognize. How many of them are there? Fear engulfs me. What are they going to do to me?

"You didn't say anything about killing her!" Colleen says suddenly, and I whimper.

Logan swears.

"She will die in there. She won't be able to breathe."

"Fine," he snaps.

Colleen manages to talk Logan out of locking me in the trunk of the car. Not because she's so convincing but because he seems eager to get inside, and he's probably not sure it's a good idea anyway. I'm thankful when I'm set down and shoved into the car. I whack my forehead on the frame of the car and I'm dizzy instantly.

"Oops." Logan chuckles.

I fall in, and somebody helps me into place more gently. Colleen. She sits beside me. Logan crushes in on the other side. Natasha is driving. The fourth person sits in the front. I think it's Gavin, from my chemistry class. Never spoken to him in my life. I don't know anything about him, but here he is all the same, ruining my life for his own enjoyment.

"Watch it, man," Gavin says.

"Are you a killjoy, too?" Logan snaps.

"You can't humiliate her if she's knocked out," comes the response. "What's the point?"

Logan is quiet. My head pounds from where it hit the car, and it feels sticky. I'm hot under the bag, and as the sweat trickles, it stings my head. I think I must be cut. They want to humiliate me? My heart races.

"I can't breathe," I say, and it comes out a sob, a terrorized mumble beneath the sackcloth. The sweat tastes salty on my lips. My stomach aches from the punch or kick or whatever part of Logan's body he used to knock the wind out of me.

They tell me to shut up, but the sack is loosened around my neck, and I can see down to my lap. The air rushes in, and I gulp it down, trying to calm myself. They won't kill me; they can't kill me. It will be something else, but what? I see that my dress has risen, revealing my full thighs, and I want to pull it down, but I can't, my hands are tied behind me. This alone is humiliation enough for me. I don't know if they're looking at me right now, making faces, laughing, judging, who knows.

We drive for I don't know how long. My head is racing with what-if scenarios. Whatever they do to me, I just hope they do it so I can be home by eleven. That is my main concern right now. The car stops at a gas station, and Colleen and Gavin get out. I'm terrified at what Natasha and Logan will do to me, but they just talk about some other students at school, a bitchfest that I can't bear to listen to. I can smell smoke; they're both smoking, and it drifts up the sack into my airspace. I cough.

"Bothering you, Flawed?" Logan says, close to my ear.

He holds the cigarette under the opening in my sack, and the smoke drifts up. I move my head to get it away. He laughs. Then he taps his ash on my thigh. It has cooled by the time it hits my skin, so doesn't hurt, but the sight of it fills me with fear.

"This remind you of anything?" He brings the hot cigarette close to my thighs, and I'm taken back to the Branding Chamber.

It comes close to my skin, and tears are running down my face. I'm grateful when the doors open and Gavin and Colleen return.

"What did you do?" Colleen asks firmly.

"Honestly, you're going to find yourself out on your ass if you don't stop being such a killjoy," he says. "It's just ash. You get my beer?"

They busy themselves passing around drinks. I hear can rings open, the sounds of glugging. Logan is flying through them quicker than any of them.

I hear a burp close to my ear, and Gavin laughs. "Gross, man."

"Let's drive," Natasha says, starting up the engine.

And that's what we do. I sit in the middle of them all, the car filled with smoke and alcohol, music blaring so loud they can barely keep up a conversation. We go round and round roundabouts, we drive and drive for what feels like hours. I think they're trying to put me off the scent as to where we are, but little do they know I lost direction as soon as I got in the car. I wasn't clever enough to try to figure out where we were going. As I listen to them all, talking like I'm not here, I think back to how I felt a few hours ago, with my mom getting dressed, excited about the party, about my new beginnings. Now, as I see ash fall onto my thighs from Logan's cigarette, some of it too hot, some of it cooled, I feel at an all-time low.

I don't know what they have in store for me. If humiliation is their aim, then they have already succeeded. If there is more to come, if this is simply the precursor, then I know I won't last one minute more. My legs tremble. I wish I'd worn more sensible shoes, sneakers so I could run, and not these strappy heels I can barely balance in.

I can't help it, but I start to cry.

"Hold on," Logan says, stalling the conversation. "Turn the music down."

I go silent quickly.

"Are you crying in there, Flawed?"

He listens. I can feel his breath on my shoulder and neck.

They all start laughing.

"You didn't actually think I'd invite you to my birthday, did you?" he asks, the coldness coming from him. "I mean, I can't believe you fell for it. I'm nineteen, Flawed. I thought Pia almost ruined it for us when she printed that story about you partying, but she didn't name me; and if you ever tell anyone about tonight, they won't believe you. My dad's a priest; my mom is, too. They're talking about making her archbishop one day, maybe the first woman in this country. We're a respectable family," he says.

"Well, two of them are," Gavin says, and he and Natasha laugh.

"Maybe we should just call you Jesus from now on," Natasha says, and they laugh again.

I feel Logan stiffen beside me, and I dread to think what consequence his humiliation will bear on me. Colleen, beside me, is quiet the whole way. I'm grateful for her presence, which is more sensible than the others, but she is working her way through the cans. I know from the amount of times I've heard the can ring pulled. Liquid courage. But for what? That's my concern. And not for one moment because she persuaded him not to put me in the trunk does it mean that I don't hold her accountable for everything that is happening right now. I think about my handbag and wonder if they have it.

"Here, have a drink, Flawed," Logan says, and I see the can of beer appear under the hood.

"She's not allowed to drink alcohol," Colleen says sharply.

"And Gavin's parents would prefer he doesn't sleep with boys, but he still does," Logan says, and receives something from Gavin in return for the comment that sends the can spilling down my top and legs.

"Drink up, Flawed."

He lifts the hood enough so he can put the can to my lips. I look away and purse them closed tightly. He laughs, a high-pitched sound, and uses his other hand, fingers that smell like smoke, to hold my chin in place and part my lips. He pours the beer in, and it goes down the wrong way. I start coughing it up.

He laughs but lowers the hood and drinks the remainder of his can himself.

"Left here," Gavin says suddenly, and I know the precursor is over and whatever is about to begin is suddenly upon me.

I don't know where we are. It feels like we have been in the car almost two hours, possibly more, but it could be one hour for all I know. I have no concept of time. We are driving up a steep hill. Could we have driven out of town and to the mountains? Are they going to leave me here? How am I going to get home from here? I am going to miss my curfew. I am doomed. My family is doomed. I have let everyone down again. All of a sudden, I wonder whether I will make it out of here at all. Do they have it in them to kill me? They've been drinking a lot. Whatever they have planned could go wrong.

I think of Art suddenly and long to be with him. He's not like these guys; he was always my protector. Before . . . all this. I wish for him to rescue me right now, but on and on we drive, no one coming for me. Instead of staying and facing it with me, he ran away.

"Wake up." Logan kicks me in the shin, and I cry out and move my legs closer to my body, away from him and closer to Colleen. I feel her inch away from me.

The car finally stops and the doors open. Finally, fresh air. The smoke and alcohol diminish, and I can breathe again. Logan pulls me out of the car, and I think of my dress, my hemline so short it must be around my waist now. I try to shake it down. The ground beneath me is uneven, pebbled stones, and I can't keep up with them in my shoes. I go over on my ankle twice.

"Take the dumb things off," Natasha says.

I feel my shoes come off, and my feet are on pebbles now. My Flawed scar is rooted to the ground to remind me how Flawed I am.

"Suit me?" Natasha says, and Gavin whistles.

I'm pulled farther up the hill. I gasp and curse as the soles of my feet land on sharp stones. I can't see where I'm going through the sack, and even the light that shone through is now gone. It's dark. It's late. Mom was due to collect me from Logan's house at ten. Is it close to that time? Has it passed? I may even have already missed my curfew.

"I have a curfew," I finally say. "Please let me go home."

They're silent.

"What time is her curfew?" Natasha asks.

"Eleven," Colleen replies.

"It's ten fifteen now," Natasha says.

"So?" Logan says, panting as he pulls me along.

"So we better hurry this along."

"Or what?"

"Or . . . what happens, Colleen?" Natasha asks.

"Missing a curfew is a big deal. Anything could happen. She goes in front of the court again."

Logan laughs.

"No, but it's serious," Colleen says. "It's not just her that's punished.

It's her family. My brothers were taken away for a week." Her voice trembles.

"Never met her family," he says. "Don't care."

"Right here," Gavin says, and we all stop.

I hear them unlock a door.

"Step up," Colleen says quietly, and I step up, onto timber. Splinters immediately pierce my skin. I smell soil, moss. We're in a shed. Soil and dirt beneath my feet. We all pile in, and the door closes and locks. Logan pushes me suddenly, and I almost fall face-first but manage to keep my balance. I bump against a wall, and a spade or a rake digs into my arm.

"What was the Flawed's problem in swim class?" Logan asks.

"Afraid to show her body," Natasha says.

I shrink away from them. "No. Please, no," I say, terror in my voice.

FORTY-FIVE

SOMEBODY PUSHES ME away from the wall and unzips the back of my dress. I struggle but am held in place by Natasha. I feel her small hands around my arms. Her nails dig into me.

My dress falls to my feet, and I'm left standing in my bra and underwear in the shed. The only other item on my body is the anklet that Art gave me. Despite our uncertain future, I don't want to take it off. It reminds me of a time when things were perfect, that I'm not as Flawed as everyone says. I start crying again. There is nowhere to hide.

"Okay, you've done it," Colleen says quickly. "Let's go."

Someone whistles.

"Shut up, Gav, she's Flawed. She's scum."

"Looks like a girl in her underwear to me."

"Look at those scars," Natasha says, close to my face. She's examining the one on my chest. I swallow hard. I want to cross my legs, bring my arms around the front of my body to protect myself.

Gavin and Natasha talk about me like I'm not there. Logan doesn't say a word, which scares me all the more. They examine my scars. Lift my hand and my foot. They keep the hood over my head. It wouldn't help to see that the body has a head, has a heart.

"Not looking, Colleen?" Logan says. "Oh no, I forgot. You've seen them before."

"This is sick. I'm getting out of here," Colleen says. The door unlocks, and I smell fresh air and I hear her footsteps leave the shed.

I'm left alone with them. My body is trembling. I'm afraid and I'm cold.

There are a number of things I realized later that I could have and should have done. Lashed out, screamed, ran, but I am frozen to the spot. They picked the one thing that humiliated me most: my body. I never wanted anyone to see it, no one, and yet here I am standing near naked while three people who I thought wanted to be my friends are shining a flashlight on all the parts of me I can't even bear to look at myself. Through the sackcloth, I see the camera flashes as they take photographs of my scars and who knows what else. They talk among themselves, at how gross and disgusting my skin is. I know that by the time they leave here, these photographs will have worked their way around to every student in the school. Who knows, they could possibly be Pia's front page tomorrow.

I feel someone walk around me, light on the toes. Must be Natasha.

There's a gasp. "Oh. My. God," Natasha says suddenly behind me. "Look at her spine. Get over here."

They jostle around the back of me to take a look.

"Man," Gavin says. "Crap. That one must have hurt. It's not as neat as the others. But wait, how many is that?"

They go through them all, counting my sears, counting my flaws.

"Six?" Logan says, surprised. "The reports only said five."

"Five was the most ever," Gavin said.

"*Three* was the most ever," Natasha corrects him. "She's got six," she whispers. "I don't think we're supposed to know she's got six." Suddenly she sounds nervous.

Their energy has changed. I sense that they're not enjoying it as much as they thought they would. I've made them uncomfortable. The reality is not what they imagined it would be. My scars are scars caused by pain. Pain in theory and pain in the flesh are two different things. I think it has had a sobering effect on them. This, oddly, gives me strength. I have gone through what they seem to fear. They have brought me here because they are attracted to their fears. They want to analyze it. Understand it. Rise above it. Laugh at it. But I have lived it. It is my tragedy that they fear. And that gives me strength.

"What time is it?" I ask. There is still hope.

"You'll be home in time. Get over it," Natasha says, trying to sound tough, but I can hear her fear. "Right, my buzz is gone. I'm bored. Food, anyone?"

"Yeah," Gavin says, a little too quickly, and I almost smile beneath my sackcloth.

"You coming, Logan?" Natasha asks.

"I'll be right behind you."

I can sense the others' uncertainty and reluctance to leave.

"Go on if you're going," Logan says, eager to have me to himself.

"Just don't . . ."

"Don't what?"

Gavin pauses. "You won't, you know . . ."

"Gavin, don't offend me. She's Flawed scum. I wouldn't touch her with a barge pole."

"Don't flatter yourself," Gavin says, and he and Natasha laugh. "Okay, just don't leave this place in a mess. My granddad will kill me."

There's a long silence, and I hear Gavin's and Natasha's footsteps disappear. I'm all alone with Logan. Not a safe place to be.

"Please don't touch me." I tremble.

"I wouldn't lay a finger on you," he says close to my ear. "You're disgusting to me. Disgusting to any man. No one will ever want you."

221

He starts to circle me slowly. I'm relieved by what he's said but at the same time wonder what he wants to do with me.

"Do you know what the significance of sackcloth and ashes is?" he asks.

"No." I sniff.

"The others haven't a clue. Tonight has been a stupid joyride to them; they've no idea the significance of what I've done." He takes on an unusual voice. Like he's lecturing or preaching. "Sackcloth and ashes were used in the Old Testament times as a symbol of debasement, mourning, and repentance. Someone wanting to show their repentant heart would wear sackcloth, sit in ashes, and put ashes on their head. Ashes signify desolation and ruin."

I lower my head, the humiliation complete, but he continues talking and circling.

"When Jonah declared to the people of Nineveh that God was going to destroy them for their wickedness, everyone from the king on down responded with repentance, fasting, and ashes. They even put sackcloths on their animals. God saw genuine change, a humble change of heart, and it caused him to relent and not bring about his plan to destroy them. Sackcloth and ashes were used as a symbol of a change in heart, demonstrating that sincerity of repentance."

He stops talking, stops circling, and there's silence apart from my heavy breathing under the hot and stuffy sackcloth and my terrified heart banging.

"God is far greater than me, Flawed, but if you repent, I might relent. If you do not admit repentance, then I will lock you up here all night and no one will be able to find you. You will miss your curfew and your whole family can be seared for all I care."

I bite my lip as the tears stream. I think of little Ewan, how scared he would be, how I have brought such danger to my family.

"And I mean it, Flawed."

I know he does. He means every word. I feel like I'm back in the

Branding Chamber again, with Judge Crevan shouting "Repent!" in my face. I refused to do it then, thinking that I was finished, that things couldn't get worse. I couldn't admit I was wrong, not then, but the rules changed and things got worse. They got a whole lot worse. I don't have the energy anymore.

"Yes," I cry out suddenly.

He whips the sackcloth from my head, and I'm grateful for the air but terrified by the look in his eye.

"You repent?" he asks.

I nod.

"Answer." He raises his voice.

"Yes, I do." I sniff.

"Say you're sorry," he says, pushing it.

"I'm sorry."

"Say you were wrong," he says quickly, and I can tell he is getting far more of an adrenaline kick out of this than the alcohol or whatever it was they were smoking.

"I was wrong."

"Get down on your knees and beg me for forgiveness."

I stall.

"Do it."

I get down on my knees.

He stands behind me and finally removes the rope from my wrists. I immediately bring them to the front of my body and massage my wrists. They are cut, raw. I can't look him in the eye.

"Say it," he shouts.

"I don't know what to—"

"Beg for my forgiveness. Hands together, in prayer, like you're in a church. Do it."

"Please," I say, crying. "Please. I'm sorry, I was wrong. I repent. I just want to go home. I just need to get home."

He smiles, as if satisfied, and throws my dress at me.

I fumble with my dress, finally relieved that it's all over, wanting to hide my body from him as quickly as I can. He watches me from the open door. For someone who thinks I'm scum, he sure watches me long enough.

"By the way, Flawed, you have twenty minutes to curfew."

He slams the door to the shed. The bolt slides across, and the keys rattle as he locks me inside.

FORTY-SIX

I HEAR NATASHA'S car drive away, and I look around the dark room lit up in one corner by the moonlight, searching for a way out.

"No," I start to cry. For a moment, I give up. I completely give up. I huddle in the corner and cry. I am in a shed, on a mountain, who knows how far from my home. Even if I screamed, no one would hear me. But then I begin to think rationally. Natasha seemed to think I could be home in time, which means I'm near my home, and it clicks with me. We didn't go far away at all. We drove uphill for some time. I am in a shed, surrounded by gardening tools. I know where I am. I'm in the community gardens on the summit minutes from my house. Although I know the gardens are closed at this hour and there will be nobody around to hear me, I try it out and scream anyway. I scream until my throat is raw and my voice is hoarse. I try everything, but from inside it sounds muffled. No one will hear me. I am not here.

I break down and freak out. I pull and push at the door, but it's useless; it's locked from the outside. I bang the wood with a spade, but it has no effect; I'm exhausted and don't have the required strength.

There is a narrow window high up. I could squeeze out if lying flat, but to get up that high and get out at such an angle would be difficult. Then I would fall straight down on my head once out the other side. But it's the only option I have. I have to work with it.

I take the spade and smash the glass. I clear the edges of broken glass as much as I can. I stack a toolbox, boxes of plants, and compost bags on top of one another to try to reach the window. I work out the logic, painfully aware that my time is running out. I pull myself up, line the window ledge with the sackcloth so as to protect my skin from the broken glass, and push my head out, thankful for the fresh air. That is enough to invigorate me. I can do this. I pull myself out, scraping my belly over the cloth, sucking in air, and hissing from the pain. I reach for the fencing to the left of the shed and hold on as I pull the rest of my body out through the flat window. I cling to the fencing for dear life, hands, fingers raw from grasping the wood. I dangle from the fence momentarily and then fall, feeling the sting in my feet on the pebbles. I sit on the ground for a minute to wait for the pain to go. I look around to get my bearings. I'm familiar with this hill. It is where I used to meet Art, not here by the gardens, but nearby. Despite my time being precious, I feel drawn to the spot where we always met. I will never in my life be able to be here at this time again, ever, and it is so close. And something, an instinct, is telling me to go there.

It is a one-minute sprint away; and when I arrive there, I know that it was the right decision. Two figures are in the place where Art and I used to be. So quickly replaced. A spot that I thought we owned now belongs to another couple. It looks like me and Art.

Because it is Art. And the girl with him looks exactly like me.

Me as I used to be, happy, beaming, smiling, laughing, looking like there is nothing wrong in her world. But I know it's not me, because I am here. Barefoot, bleeding, bruised, and crying. Running for my life.

Fighting for my life, but I don't know why I'm bothering, because the last piece of hope and energy that I had for myself has been instantly drained from my heart, and I no longer care. My heart is empty; they can do what they like to me now.

The girl is my sister.

FORTY-SEVEN

ART IS THE first to look up.

I realize I'm crying.

His eyes, his eyes that I love, run over me in shock. For the first time since all this began, my heart breaks. I feel the pain in my chest instantly. I didn't cry out for five of my brandings, but I cry out now. This is a pain more intense than anything so far. More than the pain of the brandings, more than the humiliation in the shed. This tops them all.

Juniper twists around to look in the direction he's staring, and her face gives it away, too.

Caught. Immediately my tears stop and anger takes over.

"Celestine!" Art jumps up. "What happened? Are you okay?" He comes toward me, worried, panicking, but I know it's not about what I've just witnessed. He's worried about the state of me.

"Stop!" I yell, and he freezes.

"Oh my God, Celestine," Juniper whispers, looking at me, hands going to her face. "What happened?"

"Celestine," he says, taking steps near me again. I take steps back, which makes him halt again. "Are you bleeding? Where are your shoes? What happened? Who did this to you?" I hear the emotion in his voice, how it cracks with anger and pain.

Juniper joins him, and the two of them side by side again angers me intensely once more.

"Don't you come near me ever again. Either of you. You both betrayed me once. I should have known you'd do it again." I turn to Juniper. "You knew where he was hiding all this time?"

"Yes, but—"

"Up here?" I ask, shocked. I think of his hiding in one of the garden sheds and being cared for by Juniper, the very space I was imprisoned in and had to break free from. "I *knew* you were missing every night." And then I realize. "I *knew* this was happening, but I just didn't want to believe it. . . . You made me look like a liar." I know now why I was acting so cruelly toward her. I think I knew this but wouldn't admit it.

"No, Celestine, please, let me explain. I was just helping him!"

"Shut up! You're both liars!" I shout, and he backs down and looks away, not able to defend himself.

"This isn't what you think it is. She was just helping me hide out. We weren't, you know . . ." He runs his hands through his hair, in complete turmoil.

"You both looked very cozy to me," I say, looking from one to the other.

"It's not like that," he says. "I told you I can't go back to my dad. Not after what he did to you."

"What *he* did to me? Don't you think you two had a part in it as well?"

This brings tears to Juniper's eyes, and Art's jaw hardens. I know it was a cheap jab, but I am so angry I want to hurt them both more than they have ever known, so that they can feel at least some of what I'm feeling now. I've wanted him every day, and every day she's known where he is, doing who knows what. She could have told me, she could have got a message to him for me, she could have helped me, but instead she helped him.

"Well, isn't this nice for you." I look around. "Cozy. Guess what, Art? *I* don't have a hiding place. There is none in this world for me. I have to face it all, *every day* on my own. I don't have the luxury that you do, using people to make things better for you like you always do. But you can't stay here forever. Someday you will actually be a man and face it all." That seems to deeply hurt him, and I'm glad. "You always said you'd be there for me, but you're nothing but a coward. Both of you."

"Celestine," he says, his voice cracking as it nears a sob. "I miss you so much."

The emotion from him is real. It's raw. I might be stupid, but I believe him.

"Then why are you sitting here with my *sister*?"

"Let me explain," he says, angrily now, frustrated that I won't let him talk. He steps toward me, and I back away.

"I can't." I think of another face-to-face with Judge Crevan in his courtroom, and the fight within me returns. I'm not done yet. "I'm not going to let you two ruin my life again."

I have four minutes. I turn around and run.

The next few minutes are a blur of leaves, branches snapping in my face, stones on my feet, and twigs cutting my legs, my breath loud as I run the fastest down the hill that I have ever run before. I don't look at my watch; I don't have time. I sprint to my backyard wall. I climb it faster than I ever have and land on our grass, which feels like fur in comparison with what I've trodden over tonight. I can see Dad, Mom, and Mary May in the living room. They are looking at the clock on the wall. Dad is pacing. Mom's hands are clasped by her chest, begging, praying as I was earlier for a miracle to happen. I push open the back door and fling myself at their feet, on my knees, panting and crying, unable to breathe, unable to speak, unable to see, I am so dizzy.

I look up. The minute hand reads one minute past eleven.

I look at Mary May in desperation, unable to speak, still panting.

"One minute past eleven," she says.

Mom and Dad explode with anger at her, at the injustice.

Then suddenly the watch on her wrist starts beeping. Confused, she lifts it and studies it, and I realize our timings are different. Surely, I will be judged by the Whistleblower's time. Mom and Dad must realize the same thing and freeze as they look at her for confirmation.

I look up at her from the floor, and I have a sudden fit of giggles. I start laughing, and it hurts my ribs where Logan winded me, but the pain makes me laugh even more. The three of them watch me on the floor, lying down and holding my sides, my head bleeding, my legs and arms scraped and cut, laughing like a maniac.

I did it.

I beat them all.

FORTY-EIGHT

MY PHONE RINGS at 4:00 AM, waking me in the middle of a terrify-ing dream. I'm standing in the viewing room, hands up against the glass, and Carrick is in the Branding Chamber, tied to the chair. They have forgotten to give him the anesthetic, and he is screaming so loudly, his face contorted in pain, the veins bulging from his muscular neck. Instead of Tina, June, Bark, and Funar in the Branding Chamber, it's Logan, Natasha, Gavin, and Colleen.

"There's something you didn't tell me, isn't there?" Pia says on the other end of the phone. Her voice is low and urgent, not her usual perky TV voice, and it takes me a moment to register what's going on, to dif-ferentiate between being asleep and awake.

"What? About what?"

"In the Branding Chamber. Your family was all sent away before the fifth brand, but there was somebody else in there who saw what happened. Wasn't there?"

I'm suddenly wide awake. I sit up and feel the pain in my body from Logan's kicks. I groan.

"Are you okay?"

I close my eyes and take a deep breath, waiting for the dizziness to pass.

"Celestine?"

"I'm here."

"I know you were looking for Mr. Berry at the castle."

She knows something. "He's my solicitor. There were things I needed to discuss with him about my case."

"Why have you left seven urgent messages on his voice mail over the past few days?"

This stops me. How does she know that?

"Mr. Berry was in the Branding Chamber at the time of the sixth branding, wasn't he?" she says quickly, urgently. "He saw."

I freeze. I don't know if I can let her know this. I don't know if I can trust her.

"Who's there with you?"

"No one." It sounds like she's moving around. There's a clicking sound on the phone again. Her presence comes and goes. "I'm alone, I promise. Celestine, trust me."

Goose bumps rise on my skin. This is the moment. It's either make or break. If I trust her and she's lying, I'm putting Mr. Berry in grave danger. And after tonight, there is no one that I can trust. Then again, I'm alone in all this, whom else have I got to help me?

"Pia, this can't all be on your terms," I say. "I need to know why you're asking."

She says something I can't hear properly.

"What? Pia, where are you? This is a bad line."

"Doesn't matter. *Think*, Celestine. There's something you're not telling me and I need to know it."

I'm sick of all this, sick of everyone taking from me. "Why the hell should I tell you?" I hiss, not wanting to wake anyone in the house. "So you can twist it in Crevan's favor? He's not going to let you print any of this. If nobody knows about this now, it's for a reason. He's gotten rid of just about everybody who's a witness to it. In fact, he's probably listening to us *now*. How do I know you're not trying to set me up? How do I know you're not working with him to make sure there's nobody left who saw what happened?"

"He can't hear this conversation," she says through clicking noises, her voice coming and going. "And you can trust me. You have to trust me," she says, more clearly this time. "Who else have you got, Celestine? Who else do you know can find out information for you?"

I think fast. "What do I get in return?"

"Celestine," she almost shrieks, "I'm trying to help you here."

"You're trying to help yourself."

She sighs. "What do you want?"

"I want information on a person."

"Who?"

"Carrick." I don't even know his surname. "He was in the cell beside me in Highland Castle."

"The Flawed boy? Why?"

"No questions. It's my own business."

"Does he know something?"

"No!" I lie. "I just want to find him. Let's just say I'm running low on friends right now. I need someone who can understand what I'm going through."

"Fine. I'll get whatever details I can, but I never interviewed him. It wasn't a story we wanted."

This maddens me.

"I'll find out something and get back to you. Now you think for me, Celestine. I need something. I need more. Was Mr. Berry in the Branding Chamber? Did he see the sixth brand? The reports say he wasn't there after the fifth, that he was removed with your family. Are they wrong?"

A long pause.

"Yes, Mr. Berry saw the sixth brand," I finally reveal. She's right, I need her help.

I picture that day again, in the Branding Chamber. I have tried so hard to block it out, but I can't. It comes to me in my nightmares, at certain times of the day when I'm least expecting it, the pain, the smell, the horror of it, and I want to escape it. It happens when my dad comfortingly puts his hand on my shoulder and squeezes. He doesn't know it, but I tense up, immediately taken back to the chair, feeling Tina's touch before each branding. To willingly put myself back in that chamber, while in the comfort of my own bed, is against everything I have been trying so hard to do, especially after the events of tonight, when I'm scared and sore and want to forget it all. But I go there. The smells, the sound, the fear, my banging heart, the ache in my wrists and ankles. Crevan shouting at me in his bloodred cape, the angry spittle flying from his mouth.

"He wasn't thrown out with your parents?" she asks.

"He somehow made his way back in. He had a phone in his hand. He was recording."

No need to mention Carrick being in there, too. I need to keep something further for myself.

"Recording? There's video? Oh my God. Okay, thank you, Celestine. Thank you." She hangs up.

My heart is racing, anxious from reliving the moment, for revealing Mr. Berry's possible video, also for asking about Carrick. I don't want her to think that he has anything to do with this, and I don't want to get him into trouble, but I have no other way of finding him.

Now that I'm awake and have the Branding Chamber scenario firmly in my head, I can't go back to sleep. My head is pounding from hitting it earlier on the car, and I feel a large bump on my head. My mouth is dry, and I'm parched. I get out of bed, feeling shaky, and throw an oversized cardigan around my T-shirt.

I go downstairs to the kitchen, going straight to the fridge for water. As I open it, I sense a presence and turn around to see Mary May sitting in the corner of the room, in darkness, watching me. The overhead light of the oven fan is all she has to see by. She has a book, which she covers with her hands, the first time I've seen her flesh without the leather gloves. She smiles at my obvious fright, though she seems tired.

"What are you . . . I mean, why are you . . . you're staying the night?" I ask.

She takes me in, looks me up and down slowly, and it makes me wrap the cardigan around me tighter. This woman gives me the creeps.

"Bearing in mind the events of tonight, I thought it best I stay here. That's a fine bump on your head," she observes.

My hand goes to it, and I wince. It's pounding. I need water and headache pills. I help myself as she watches.

"You're worried I'll have a concussion?"

"No." She laughs, but it's not a joyous sound. It's cruel, like she's laughing at me, as though I'm the most stupid person she's ever met. "I wanted to make sure you stay where you should be. No rule break-ing. I know about events like these, what they do to a person."

"What do you mean?" I down the pills and water.

"Revenge," she says, and I see the coldness and the darkness in her eyes, and I think back to what she did to her sister, reporting her to the Guild, and then to her entire family when it turned its back on her.

"Is that why you did what you did to your family?" I ask. "Out of revenge?"

"No," she says, not blinking, not seeming bothered that I've asked a personal question. "I caught my sister with my boyfriend. Reporting her to the Guild was out of revenge."

The story is too close to home for me right now, and I wonder if she's testing me. Does she know about Art and Juniper? She couldn't. If she did, the Whistleblowers would have found him by now.

"My family . . ." She looks away a little, and I detect a hint of sadness that is quickly covered up. "That was just necessary."

I get the shivers from head to toe.

She looks me over again. "Dr. Smith says nothing's broken."

"No. If you don't count my heart, my pride, and my complete belief in humanity."

I hold her stare, her eyes black in the darkness, and I almost think she gets it.

"No," she says, simply, going back to her book. I see a Jane Austen cover. "I don't."

FORTY-NINE

THAT AFTERNOON PIA comes to the house. Apart from the dramatic trip to the police station with Dad, I have spent the day in bed curled up in a ball. Still aching from last night's attack, I drag myself out of bed, pull on some loose dark clothes, and meet her in the library. I expect her to be seated in one of her crisp peach chic pencil skirts and blouses, but, instead, she's pacing. Her shiny black hair is scraped back sharply, and she's wearing jeans, sneakers, and a hoodie.

I look at her in surprise.

She looks at me in surprise.

"What happened to you?" I ask.

"Never mind me, what happened to you?"

The bruise on my forehead has come up nicely, an enormous, cartoon-sized bump that today has turned a shade of yellow and black. My face is scraped from the twigs and branches that cut my skin as I ran blindly through the trees in the darkness.

I sit in the armchair and wince from the pain in my stomach. My ribs aren't cracked, but they may as well be.

"Celestine," she says with urgency in her voice and nothing but concern on her face. So I have to drop the act. "What happened?"

I sigh. "Turns out there wasn't a party. Not for me, anyway."

"You were set up?"

"Ambushed, I believe the word is." My eyes fill up at the memory of it, which is still raw in my mind and in my body. Each time I move, I feel the aches.

"That kid who invited you?"

"Logan Trilby. L-O-G-A-N," I say slowly, sarcastically. "T-R-I-L-B-Y. Aren't you going to write that down? Oh, no, of course not, nothing that might make people pity me."

Her eyes are angry, but not at me. "You don't want people's pity, Celestine."

"I actually do." I half-laugh. "I want everybody's pity, because then I will know that everyone is human, instead of whatever it is everybody is now."

She sits down in the armchair across from me, but not delicately and prissy as before. She's on the edge, feet parted, elbows on knees; she's getting down and dirty today.

"What did he do?"

"Not just him. He had a few friends. Their mission was to humiliate me."

"And did they?"

"Yes."

"Tell me." She's being soft and patient, but underneath it there's a sense of urgency about her today, nothing calm and calculated like our previous conversations. The first time we met, Pia was in "Pia TV Personality" mode, then I saw "Off-Duty Pia," but this woman is new, this is a side to her I've never seen. I have been gullible in the past, but I believe this person.

"They put a sackcloth bag over my head, tied me up, hit me, kicked me, dumped ashes on me, stripped me, and locked me in a shed. That about covers it."

I don't mention their forcing the alcohol into my mouth—that would get me into trouble, even though I had no option. I'm not going to take my chances, not even with Pia in this mood.

Her eyes turn cold. "Logan Trilby. And who were the others?"

I give her fuller details and she shows her disgust, discomfort, and empathy in all the right places and I believe that she cares.

"So what's happening?"

"Nothing. My dad arranged for everybody to be at the police station today. Principal Hamilton, Natasha, Logan, Gavin, Colleen. Their parents, apart from Angelina. Logan's parents have vouched for him, said he couldn't have had anything to do with it, because he was in Bible study."

"They don't believe he was lying?"

"*They're* lying. They say he was with *them* at Bible study."

Her mouth falls open. "What about the other kids?"

"Natasha and Gavin blamed Colleen, said she masterminded the entire thing, in retaliation for something that happened between me and her mom."

"What happened?" She naturally switches into her journalist mode.

"Can't tell you. Natasha's dad is some fancy lawyer, started jabbering on about human rights and his daughter protecting herself from a Flawed. The police aren't going to do anything about it. They let the school punish us. My dad went crazy. Gavin and Natasha were suspended for two days. Colleen is expelled, but it doesn't matter, because Bob Tinder was fired as editor of the newspaper—"

"Believe me, I know," she interrupts, and her eyes start racing again as I see her mind ticking.

"I forgot he was your boss. Anyway, they're moving. You probably know that, too, so it's hardly a punishment. Colleen will have to start at another school anyway."

She shakes her head, seemingly appalled.

"Pia, there's one other thing I'm worried about. Last night, when they stripped me"—I swallow hard, feeling the humiliation all over again—"they photographed me. They've seen the sixth brand and have proof of it."

Pia focuses hard while she thinks it through.

"The thing is, they were afraid of it, they backed away after that. So I think they know not to say something, but sooner or later it's going to come out. Natasha's bound to let it slip to someone. She couldn't keep a secret if you paid her."

"But they don't have the video," Pia says. "We need to get our hands on that video. And we need to move on this story fast." Pia starts pacing again. "We need to break it before they do. Before Crevan hears their rumors and has a chance to spin it, if he's not working on that already." She looks around the room to see if anyone can hear us. "This morning I learned that there's an inquiry into Crevan," she says, her voice a hush. "A private inquiry. The outcome of your case, Angelina Tinder, Jimmy Child, Dr. Blake, they've all got people talking."

"Who's Dr. Blake?" The name's familiar. Granddad mentioned him to me during the trial. He said I needed to find Dr. Blake and somebody else. It didn't seem important at the time. I was putting it down as his conspiracy ramblings, but I should have taken note.

"Dr. Blake is the woman who misdiagnosed Crevan's wife, Annie," she says. "Your granddad told me to look into her at your trial, and I fobbed him off as a crazy old man. I started looking into it, though, after meeting you. She didn't catch the cancer in time. Crevan found her Flawed just before Jimmy Child's case. She was found Flawed on another personal matter, much like Angelina Tinder was. The case had nothing to do with Crevan's wife. I would never have caught the link until your granddad tipped me off."

Good old Granddad, I think proudly. He was always on my side, but I, too, thought his views were extreme. If he got Dr. Blake right, perhaps he's right about it all.

"Crevan is using the Guild as his own private court," I say.

"I believe he was planning the Dr. Blake case for some time. The outcome gave him confidence to proceed with Angelina and Jimmy Child. He got away with them, but now people are questioning his decisions."

I roll my eyes. "A Guild into the Guild?"

She smiles weakly. "Kind of. A private inquiry into a public one."

"Well, let me guess the outcome. The Guild will find that the Guild acted perfectly and appropriately. Ta-da! Inquiry over."

"It's an investigation into Judge Crevan only. Members of the government feel he has been abusing his powers. Remember, this began as a temporary fix to look into wrongdoing. It has become far more than that and grown faster than the government has had time to control it. The lines are blurring between legality and Guild rules. The government wants to take back its power."

"People like Enya Sleepwell."

"Exactly. Because of pressure by her, a private commission has been set up to first investigate the cases privately."

"Privately," I sigh. "They hide well, these rational-thinking concerned people."

"Not everyone is as brave as you are."

I look for the sarcasm in her voice, but there isn't any.

"You know." She sits down. "A new journalist arrived on the online scene a few days ago. She's getting popular, very quickly."

"Jealous?"

"A bit." She smiles. "She's a fan of yours."

I'm surprised. "Who is she?"

She takes out her tablet to show me. "Her name is Lisa Life."

I snort.

"She's on your side. She's part of a new news site called X-It. They have millions of readers every day."

She flicks through her tablet to show me the article. The headline reads, IF I WAS SUCH A HERO, THAT OLD MAN WOULD BE ALIVE NOW. I FAILED. Underneath that is a pretty picture of me sitting by Clayton Byrne's grave site and lighting a candle, with the quote, "I helped an old man to a seat." I hadn't known I was being followed that day. I should have been more careful, especially after escaping school to visit the guards and Mr. Berry in Highland Castle. I read on.

The story is about how my actions on the bus have made the Flawed issue a human rights issue. Clayton Byrne's death is the first recorded death of a Flawed through negligence of society, a society that was following rules. Yet those rules led to the death of a man. There's a quote from Enya Sleepwell, "I'm not condoning what Celestine North did, but her actions, and recent comments, raise serious and valid points that must be questioned and answered by our government. If we are to question the rule of aiding a Flawed, then surely the entire system must be questioned."

I look closely at the photograph of Enya and recognize her as the woman with the pixie cut who nodded to me each day in the crowd as I was jeered and jostled on my walk across the courtyard at Highland Castle.

"Lisa Life published this today," she says, handing me a new article from a folder.

"Compassion and Logic: The Perfect Pairing. Our Perfect Leader?"

There is a photograph of me, looking strong and determined, standing in court. I don't remember ever feeling how I look in the photograph. It's a girl, no, a woman, whom I would trust, a woman I would think is strong and powerful. A woman who appears to know exactly what she's doing. How deceiving appearances can be.

Pia dumps article after article on top of my lap, one after another, so quickly that I have time only to take in the headlines and the photographs before another lands on my knees. She spreads them out on the coffee table. More and more. Images of me, page after page of stories and familiar quotes, so much that I don't recognize the person I'm seeing.

"This is all Lisa Life?" I feel embarrassed, feel my cheeks blush. It's overwhelming to see all this support.

"No, not all of them. I gathered as many supportive articles as I could. There are many more, Celestine."

I can't believe that people I have never met think so highly of me. If they had seen me on my knees, begging and cowering in the shed in front of Logan, taking back everything I had done . . . Pia interrupts my dark thoughts. "Do you see what's happening? The power you have and don't even know it?"

I laugh bitterly and feel the ache in my ribs and in my pounding, pulsating head. Earlier this week I thought I could take on Crevan; all day today I've curled up in a ball and cried, admitted defeat.

"Power? I got locked up in a shed by four people in my class, and the police and the school don't care. They can't help me. Two people I love most in the world betrayed me. I can't even stay out after eleven PM. I have no *power*, Pia."

"Yes, you do. You know you do. The power doesn't just lie in the sixth brand on your spine, but in the strength you've had in getting it. What you did on the bus, what you said at the trial, the way you faced Crevan. I've worked at the castle for ten years, and I've never seen anyone speak to him like that. Now use that power and hone it, because you're going to need it with what's to come." She sighs. "The thing is . . ."

My heart hammers, and I brace myself.

FIFTY

"I'VE BEEN TRYING to meet with Mr. Berry," continues Pia. "I've called his office, cell, home, every number I have for him, and there's no answer. I went to his home, and his husband doesn't know where he is. Says he's been gone for weeks and hasn't heard from him. None of Mr. Berry's clients have heard from him, nor his staff, though they think he's on a sudden holiday as he was inclined to do that, but I know that's not the case this time. Not with what we know, Celestine."

"Maybe his husband knows where he is and won't tell you. Everyone knows you're Crevan's media girl. Why would he trust you?"

"I told him I want to find the truth. He says he doesn't know where he is, and I believe him," she says firmly.

"Why doesn't he call the police?"

"He doesn't think the police can help him," she says quietly. "He's afraid."

I swallow hard. "Let me guess. Mr. Berry disappeared after Naming Day. Just like Tina, just like June, Bark, Funar, and Tony."

She nods.

"Do you think he's hiding or that he was taken away?"

"I don't know, I really don't know. I went to Tina's house yesterday. It's boarded up, all the furniture still inside, like they just upped and left. Her teenage daughter is gone, too. Her school hasn't heard from her. Tina's divorced and not close with her family, so they weren't surprised she hadn't been in touch the past few weeks. I've called Bark's, Funar's, June's, and Tony's houses, but their families won't talk to me. I haven't visited them yet. I think they're more likely to speak off the phone, but guessing from Mr. Berry and Tina, I'm expecting the same thing. They're all too afraid."

"So now there's no video of what happened in the chamber?" I say, my eyes filling up. "Everyone who saw is gone, and it's my word against Crevan's."

But that's not true, and I'm the only one who knows it. Carrick was there, Carrick saw what happened. Would anybody believe a Flawed witness? And has Crevan managed to get his hands on Carrick, too? Does Crevan even know he was there? Did he see him? Am I next? Should I be worried?

"I can't write the story without proof," Pia says. "I'm going to need more time."

"You still don't believe me, do you?" I ask angrily.

"Of course I believe you." She raises her voice and stands. "Do you have any idea how much I've risked already for you?"

"Sorry," I say quietly.

She rubs her hand over her face, and suddenly she looks tired. "No, don't apologize. I'm not doing you a favor; you deserve this. I covered the Guild court and wrote about the Flawed because I believed in it. The words weren't always mine, but I believed in the stories. I believed in outing those who were ruining our society, threatening to break us down. But . . . then there was Angelina Tinder and Jimmy Child, one right after the other, and then there was you, and now I know about Dr. Blake." She shakes her head. "Whatever I told myself about the others at the time, I can't tell myself that about you. Your case was flawed from the start," she says to my utter surprise. "First, I was told to report you as a hero. Then I was told to report you as the enemy. It didn't make sense. I believe Crevan is at a breaking point. My theory is he got a taste for revenge when he succeeded in finding Annie's doctor Flawed, because she missed the early signs, and he got confident and did it again with Angelina Tinder and Jimmy Child. These cases have shown he's starting to crack, and I believe he'll get far worse. He is under extreme pressure now. With Art missing, Crevan is beside himself with worry and anger at *you* for taking his son away and for putting the Guild in the spotlight in this way. He was supposed to prove to the rest of the world that the Guild is something every country should adopt. It would give him an international stage, and he won't want anything to jeopardize that. I heard that tomorrow he will announce that any journalist who writes a favorable article about a Flawed will be seen as aiding a Flawed."

"So much for Lisa Life." I feel my hope wither away. "There's not much power in a Flawed journalist writing favorably about a Flawed."

"He won't find her," she says, her jaw firm. "There will be trouble. Especially with my friends. Freedom of speech isn't something you can mess with with journalists. You try to silence them, they'll shout even louder. He's digging his own hole, Celestine. Support for you will rise soon. You don't need Lisa Life, Celestine, you are the bravest person I've ever met, and you've inspired me to find my own voice."

She takes my hands in hers and squeezes tightly; I'm reminded of our first meeting in this room together, the one where we shook left hands so that my branded skin wouldn't touch hers. Now she holds on tightly, my skin against hers. My wound pressed against her smooth skin. It's how it should be, but it moves me deeply. "You are what the movement needs, Celestine, but remember you don't need *them*. Don't let them use you."

There is so much urgency in her words. I'm so surprised by her change in personality, in her tone with me, that I can barely take it all in, yet I know she is telling me that what she is saying is important, so I try to treat it as such. She removes a file from her backpack and places it down on the strewn articles on the table.

"I appreciate your telling me about Mr. Berry's video. I appreciate your trust. I know, after everything you've been through, it's a difficult thing to do, and you probably don't even trust me completely."

I look away, feeling guilty.

"It's okay, I understand. I just need to prove it to you. Here's the information you requested." She grabs her backpack, looking like she's off on an adventure. "I'll be in touch as soon as I can."

"Are your kids going with you?" I ask.

Her eyes glisten, the hardness cracks. "They're safer with their dad for now. Good luck, Celestine."

I look at all the Lisa Life articles she has left behind on the table for me and my eyes scan the quotes, exact quotes that I have said, for the first time nothing twisted or out of context. I realize as I read them all that I have only ever said these words to one person and that's to Pia.

Pia *is* Lisa Life.

"I thought that you hated me," I say.

She smiles, sadness in her eyes. "I did."

I respect her honesty, and I want her to know that I know the full extent of what she's doing for me. I feel a lump forming in my throat as we say good-bye, and I hope that the next time we see each other, this will all be behind us and Crevan will be gone. "If you meet Lisa Life along the way, tell her I said thank you, from my heart."

She smiles, knowing that I know, tears in her eyes. And she leaves.

FIFTY-ONE

"IS PIA ILL today?" Mom asks as I pass by her open bedroom door. "She didn't seem her usual self. She was wearing jeans and not a hint of peach to be seen."

"Yeah," I reply, distracted, hugging the file about Carrick close to my chest. My heart is pumping. Just by having this information, I feel so close to him already.

I lean against the doorframe as Mom lifts a sweater over her head and throws it down on the bed. Her bed is covered in what looks like the contents of her entire wardrobe, only they're not. They're clothes I don't recognize, and each one still has a tag on it.

"What are you doing?"

"Trying on clothes."

"You went shopping?"

"Got a delivery while you were at the police station."

I enter the room and start picking up some items. I'm intrigued because something doesn't seem right, and I'm confused because I can't figure out what it is, but then I realize what it is that's jarring with the picture. The clothes are the wrong color, they're the wrong shapes, they're not meant for her.

"What are you doing?" I ask again. "Really."

Mom sighs and pulls a red T-shirt down over her toned stomach. "I'm trying a different look."

My mouth falls open. Sure, Mom does this every day for a living. As a fashion model, she has to try different looks, but at home, in her personal life, Mom has a very specific look that she sticks to. A look that has been studied and honed to within an inch of its life, a look that tells the world exactly the kind of person she is. She is the leader of this type of dressing. Her looks are flawless, seamless, figure-hugging, shape-flattering, coordinated with that of her family's, safe when they want to be, daring when they need to be. Appropriate for all occasions.

She pulls on a pair of ripped denim jeans and a pair of scuffed-up boots that she has bought brand-new. They're cool, but they don't match. Not one thing goes with any other item she is wearing; she is clown-like. She looks in the mirror, studies her reflection with an intensity that concerns me.

It's not just Pia who is different today. Mom still looks perfect, flawless makeup, not a hair on her head out of place, but . . . I study her. There is vehemence in her eyes, a determined line to her jaw, the finest of creases in her brow. Am I seeing a crack in the surface?

"Did Mr. Berry get in contact with you lately?" I ask.

She looks up and tries to read me. When she can't, because I fix her with my best impression of her own unreadable face, she replies, "Not since Naming Day. We never got in touch with him about the sixth brand, if that's what you're wondering."

Not what I was wondering, but good to know. "Did he give you anything? Send anything?"

"A bill," she snorts. "But I'm sure that's not what you mean."

"A bill?"

"Turns out if the Guild finds you Flawed, you have to pay for your representation. Bills that they rack up. Judge Crevan just so happened to hire us the most expensive representation going."

"Oh. I'm sorry."

"Sorry. I didn't mean to . . . We'll sort it out." She sighs, throwing an oversized purple cardigan over the red T-shirt.

"Your Beauty Box contract can cover it for now, though, can't it?" I ask. "I mean, I want to pay you back, eventually, but I can't right now."

"Celestine"—she comes toward me and gently wraps a braid behind my ear—"you're so kind, but we're covering the cost. Beauty Box has a new ambassador for the foreseeable future."

My heart falls. Beauty Box was Mom's cash cow, a cosmetic company whose famous tagline was "Flawless on the outside, Flawless on the inside." Mom had been saying those words for almost a decade. She is synonymous with those words. When people think of Beauty Box, they think of Mom; she is the face and voice of it.

"I can't believe they fired you," I say, shocked.

"Oh, they didn't fire me," she says, lifting a loose dress out of another bag. She always said unstructured clothes were a no-no, that people must always be able to see her figure. "I just couldn't bring myself to say those words. *Flawless on the outside . . .*" She trails off, unable to finish. "What does that even *mean*? Why does anyone even *want* that? Whoever said that is what we *should* be?" She looks confused. Conflicted. Tortured even. Then it disappears again.

I look around at her bedroom covered in multicolored clothes—she has emptied her old, muted, pastel-colored clothes onto the floor beside the bed. I watch her for a while. She hasn't left the house in as long as I have, but while I've been to school, she hasn't been at work. I realize now the extent of our problems, of what I've caused. Her walk-in wardrobe, which is usually color-coded and immaculate but now quite the opposite, is eerie.

She undoes her hairpins, and her long hair falls down in beautiful curls around her shoulders. She starts to mess it up.

"What do you think?" she asks of her overall look.

I have never seen anything so mismatched in my life. I don't want to insult her. I'm afraid she'll crack, if that's not what she's doing already. "It's really cool."

She frowns and looks confused. "Oh."

"Didn't you want it to be cool?"

"No," she says, distracted, picking up a zebra-print pair of trousers. "No, I did not." She smiles sweetly at me. "We've been invited across the road to the housewarming of Candy Crevan."

"Candy Crevan is moving into the Tinders'?"

"Right beside her brother, to keep an eye on him through his difficult time," Mom says, without a note of sarcasm, though I know it's intended. "So I will go to her party, for your father's sake, because she always likes to have the presence of an international model at her parties," she says through gritted teeth. "And I will sashay up and down for all her party guests in my beautiful outfit. Give them all something to look at," she grumbles. "I'll tell them it's the new season's look. And then, hopefully, they'll all rush out and all be looking like clowns by next week. I'll show them what Flawless is all about."

She pulls off the cardigan, aggressively, and fires the T-shirt to the far corner of the room and starts again, rooting through more boxes. Her toned arms and fists rid her of her tension, while her face still manages to look calm and serene. I'm still standing there looking at her, feeling shock by what she has said. Candy Crevan is Judge Crevan's sister, who owns News 24, the news station my dad works for, and the *Daily News*, the newspaper Bob Tinder was famously recently fired from and that Pia works for. To have her directly across the road would be a disaster, *is* a disaster. They're closing in on us. Them versus us.

I exit the bedroom and leave Mom to herself to figure it out, how best to continue her silent protest at the treatment of her daughter. I'm worried, but the overriding feeling is pride that she is trying to find her own way to rebel. There's a first time for everything.

In the home study downstairs, I search through the filing cabinet for Mr. Berry's invoice. I don't know what I'm looking for, but I need to see if there's any hint, any code that would tell me where the video is, if he's hidden it, or even better a copy of the video itself. I find the letter and take it out, my heart pumping.

The invoice is still in the envelope. I slide it out and study the pages. A cover letter explaining the breakdown of charges, a second page, which is the invoice, and a business card. I turn the business card over and find a phone number scribbled on the back. I pocket the card. No clues, no private messages, no hints as to where the video could be. It isn't even signed by him, but by his secretary on his behalf. I look inside the envelope. It's empty. I hold the pages up to the light, wondering if anything will reveal itself, but I've watched way too many mysteries. There's nothing to be found. It's just a regular bill.

I sit at the desk and open Carrick's file.

There's a photograph of him from the day he was taken into the Guild's custody, and my stomach flips at the sight of him. His entire demeanor has succeeded in being captured in the photograph, those black eyes, broad shoulders, pumped arms, and chiseled jaw. He's like a soldier. I run my finger across his face. I'm surprised by my physical reaction to seeing him. I only knew him for two days and we never really spoke, yet . . . I feel such a connection to him.

My ghost is about to have a name, age, and address.

But the file is as enigmatic as the man. All the file reveals to me is that my ghost is eighteen-year-old Carrick Vane and his status is F.A.B., which I've no idea what that means. I take a guess that it's similar to AWOL, because despite being found guilty of being Flawed, and branded on his chest for disloyalty to society, and being appointed a Whistle-blower, he failed to appear for any of his tests and is AWOL.

I hope Crevan didn't find Carrick, but that Carrick found a crack.

FIFTY-TWO

NINE AM ON Monday morning, my teacher, Ms. Dockery, arrives for our first day of homeschooling. I can't say she and I had a particularly close student-teacher relationship, but she taught me math, so there was mutual respect in that she left me alone to figure most things out for myself while she gave more attention to those struggling. She had been at the forefront of pushing the homeschooling idea at school, and I assumed she was among the group of teachers that didn't approve of my presence. She didn't ignore me in class as some did, but she didn't take me aside to offer a cuddle, either. Not that anybody did, for that matter.

I've learned that people aren't cruel. Most people aren't, anyway, apart from the Logans, the Colleens, the Gavins, and the Natashas of the world, but people are strong on self-preservation. And if something doesn't directly affect them, they don't get involved. I should know; I was like that up until last month. Those who do get involved usually have an agenda. Like Pia, like Mr. Berry, like Colleen. And now I wonder why Ms. Dockery has volunteered to face the onslaught of media camped outside my home, every day, to enter the house of a Flawed.

My mom is in the fashion industry, and this is not a lesson she has newly learned. She has always believed that everybody has an agenda, so we sit at the kitchen table with Ms. Dockery before I go to the library to begin.

"Celestine is the best student in my class by far, Ms. North," Ms. Dockery says, in response to Mom's rather forward question as to why she's here.

"Call me Summer, please, and as you can see, and as you know, my daughter has been through a lot. Too much. I need to make sure that you have her best interests at heart, that you will not abuse her or treat her unkindly, and that you will give her every chance that she deserves to succeed."

I look at Mom in surprise.

"Summer," Ms. Dockery says, smiling, "I appreciate everything you have said, but I am merely here to teach. Anything else that has happened has no bearing on what will happen in our classes together. Celestine's grasp of complex theorems is remarkable. She seems to understand and remember them almost instantly. She has a wonderful mind. I simply want to make sure my A student does not misrepresent me. Call it selfish, if you will"—she blushes—"but I believe my students represent me, my value as a teacher. For Celestine not to reach her full potential would be a personal failure to me."

I've learned by now that I haven't been a good judge of character. I always knew that Juniper was but never knew that I was so bad. I seem to have gotten it wrong each and every time, and I need Juniper's strength of understanding and reading people to help me through. Though the irony is that I even misjudged my own sister. I think of Carrick and how he read every situation. A roll of the eyes; a square, untrusting jaw; black eyes that never moved when he found a target, that had the ability to sear the surface off everything, as though he were trying to analyze a person and cut right to the heart of the truth with one long look.

I am not in the mood for today's schooling. I'm exhausted. I've lost all hope. Heartbroken by what Art and Juniper did to me, still sore from Friday's beating, frustrated by Mr. Berry's and the guards' being gone, and now Carrick, the one I thought could help me, is impossible to find, managing to avoid even the Whistleblowers. No wonder he hasn't come to find me. It's too dangerous.

Mom seems satisfied by my teacher's responses. I, on the other hand, am not so sure. Ms. Dockery and I go into the library.

"First things first," she says in a no-nonsense tone, quite different from the one she used in the kitchen. "Call me Alpha, not Ms. Dockery. If I'm to be in your house, then we're on the same level."

I nod.

She retrieves papers from her bag and sits down opposite me. "Second, here's our schedule of work, cleared by the school and the Guild," she says in a bored tone. "I had to go through it with them so clearly and slowly that I should have charged them a teaching fee."

I laugh in surprise at her sudden change in personality.

"Should anyone ask, and they most likely will, this is what we're doing. But between you and me, we'll be working on so much more." She rolls up her sleeves. "And third, I should inform you of this." She stands up and pulls her blouse out of the waistband of her trousers.

I look away, embarrassed by my teacher's sudden show of flesh, her stomach so close to my face. But when I can see from the corner of my eye that she won't cover herself up until I've looked, I slowly turn to face her. And there on her lower abdomen is a red *F* contained by a red circle. Not a scar, but a tattoo.

FIFTY-THREE

I GASP. "WHO put that there?"

"I did."

"But I would do anything to get mine *off* and you put it there *yourself*?"

"It's different when the power is taken away from you," she says gently. "And there are many more people with these tattoos. We see being Flawed as a strength, Celestine. If you make a mistake, you learn from it. If you never make a mistake, you're never the wiser. These so-called perfect leaders we have now have never made a mistake. How can they have learned what's right and wrong, how could they have learned anything about themselves? About what they feel comfortable doing, about what they feel is beyond the scope of their character? The more mistakes you have made, the more you have learned."

I try to let this sink in, but I just can't wrap my head around it. "Then I must be pretty wise," I joke.

"The wisest," she says seriously. "That's my point. The Flawed court is Flawed in itself, Celestine. This doesn't just represent that I feel we're all flawed, it's a *symbol*, showing that I support your cause."

And I know that it has begun. This secret movement that Pia had warned me about, that Lisa Life is writing about. I am face-to-face with someone who is a part of it.

"When you get it right, Celestine North, boy, do you get it right. Your actions on the bus aside"—she waves her hand dismissively as if that was no big deal—"because we all have at least one random act of kindness in us, even the bad guys. But your quotes have been nothing short of perfect. Bang on the money." She bangs her fist on the table, and I jump.

"Pia Wang's articles have been distortions of the truth."

"I'm not talking about Pia Wang. I'm talking about her alter ego, Lisa Life."

"You know about that?"

"I recognize her signature style. Not too skilled a writer, if I'm honest, but she somehow has a knack for getting the stories, getting people to speak. She writes better as Lisa Life. The name makes me smile," she says, not smiling. "You obviously struck a chord with her. Tell me, has she been behaving differently, or is she still a pent-up shark in a box? A puppet shark, mind you, for all the freedom Crevan gives her writing. Freedom of speech, my eye," she snorts. "And as of this morning, that is set to change. Only minutes ago he announced—"

"That writing favorably about the Flawed will be seen as aiding a Flawed." I stand up and start pacing, the adrenaline surging. It's happening. Crevan is unraveling just as Pia said. Who knows what he'll do to me now. I'll have to think of a way to act, fast.

"Correct," she says. "So you do read the papers. Usually kids your age need a bomb up their backsides, but it's good to see you've got your wits about you. Frankly, I would have liked to have started this last Monday, but you were insistent on staying in school. Perhaps I should have taken you aside and talked to you in school, but I didn't think you were ready. In a way, Logan Trilby did me a favor. Though don't get me wrong, I hope all four of them rot in hell for what they did to you, and thanks to Lisa Life, her article today tells the world just what they did. She doesn't name names, of course, but she hints just enough for people to be able to guess. People are complaining about your treatment already. The police have a lot of questions to answer for not bringing them to justice. Crevan's going to want Lisa Life's blood."

And mine.

I'm not happy that people know what I experienced Friday night. I don't want it to give others any ideas, but I'm glad that Logan and the gang have been implicated.

"Before we begin, do you have *any* questions? Any questions at all."

The way she's looking at me I know I have to sit up and listen. I know it has begun. It's time to take control of myself now.

"Tell me about Enya Sleepwell."

She smiles for the first time. "Excellent question, kiddo. You're going to be an A student, I can tell. Tell me what you know about her."

"She's a politician. She has a pixie cut. She came to my trial every day. I remember seeing her. She always stood in the back, near the Flawed. She's a member of the Vital Party. She's on my side."

"Two corrections." She holds her fingers up. "She's now *leader* of the Vital Party. She managed to stage a coup against the party leader. He was sweet but stupid. Enya played him, his own fault, really. He should have watched his back as soon as that girl was voted in. She was voted in as leader just last week, and she has you to thank for that.

"Second correction, she's not *necessarily* on your side. She's a politician, a fast riser at that. I believe she cares, and she cares hard, but she leans whichever way the wind is blowing, and she's noticing that the Flawed problem is a rising concern with people, some people anyway. But there's enough growth in that area to get behind it, so she can surf the wave to victory."

As she tells me about her, she flicks through dozens of photos of

Enya, many of her caught by cameras standing among the crowds at my trial.

"If you make one mistake, she'll drop you like a hot potato, but so far she sees you as her poster girl, her shortcut, freeway to leadership. Power. It's all about that, don't you forget. People want money or power. Which do you want?"

I frown. "Neither."

Alpha frowns as she studies me.

"Wait." I try to think clearly. "But Enya is already leader. What more does she want?"

"She's leader of her party, sweetheart. She's gunning for leadership of the *country*."

"She thinks that *I* can help with that?"

Alpha smiles again, liking my naïveté, but I'm learning fast. "No, she'll use you to get that; and if you fail, she'll find something else to get behind, like package holidays to Mars."

"So I shouldn't trust her."

"That's not what I said. You can trust her as long as you're aware of where she stands. She's using you, you use her right back. I'm surprised she hasn't made contact yet." It's a statement, but I know she's questioning me.

I shake my head.

"Soon, I imagine."

The idea of this scares me.

"Don't worry, I'll coach you. Anything you need to know, you ask me, okay?"

I nod, but I'm unsure. At this point, I don't feel like I can trust anybody. Alpha is no different, and she senses this.

"Yes, I'm using you, too," she admits. "I've an agenda, too. I've opinions and beliefs that I want to see come through. You're the girl of the moment. With a bit of guidance, you're the one who can make it happen."

"Why do you believe in this so strongly?"

"My husband is Flawed. His temple and tongue."

Bad judgment and a liar.

"He made an ethical mistake at work. Got caught. He was a rising man in the ranks, with great prospects and a bright future, so they put a stop to that and made an example of him."

"Why was the Guild so threatened by him?"

"Interesting, Celestine. You asked why the Guild was so *threatened*. . . . You recognize that's what's happening. That's good. Let's continue."

She continues showing me the landscape, which she believes has been opened up because of my actions on the bus and my responses on the stand.

"Compassion and logic. I *loved* that," she says, banging her hand down on the table and grinning. "Did it take you long to come up with that, or did someone else write it for you? Was it that Mr. Berry? Some believe that, but I don't. It's not his style." She moves in, hanging on my every word to come. "Who wrote that line?"

I frown. "No one wrote anything. It just came out."

She shakes her head, incredulously. "Marvelous. We need more of that. You know word is that Enya is going to use that as the Vital Party's campaign logo. *Compassion and Logic: The Perfect Partnership. Vote Vital Party.*"

I shake my head in disbelief.

"I know. It's a lot to take in, but we need more of that stuff; and if you think of any more like that, just write it down. I can find a way to use it. So what else . . . you're looking a little dazed, maybe I'll move on to math, something you're familiar with. For now, anyway . . ." She rummages around for the schedule. "We better do something on this list today, to help you out with dear sweet Mary May's lie detector test."

"You know her?"

"She was responsible for my sister-in-law and her husband going to prison for aiding my husband. They helped him break a couple of rules, and they're locked up for four years each. I wouldn't mess with her. She looks like a bird, but she bites like a lion. They mean business when they place her with you. She's the most senior in her position. She eats, sleeps, lives being a Whistleblower. Knows more than any of them put together, which isn't a lot, but she's the control center."

This is the first I've heard of people going to prison for aiding. Before this, it was just a threat. And it was a very real threat to me. Two years for aiding Clayton Byrne to his seat, or Flawed. "I'm sorry to hear about your family."

She waves her hand dismissively again and doesn't even look up from the paperwork.

"Is there a reason why you tattooed your stomach?"

This unsettles her a bit, but she rises to the challenge. "I've had six miscarriages in four years. My womb won't carry a baby, not full term anyway. Believe me, we've tried. And don't say sorry again, it's not your fault." She looks at the schedule again and then drops it and slows down. I know she's going to open up. "The tattoo is there not because I believe there is something *wrong* with me. It's there to remind me that our flaws are our strengths. It was this that made me start my foundation. Not being able to conceive my own, I looked into adoption. Specifically, I've tried to adopt an F.A.B. child over the years, but I have been unsuccessful. But I'm not telling you anything you don't know," she says. "You know all about this from your Flawed At Birth friend, I'm sure. Carrick, isn't that his name?"

Now she has my attention.

FIFTY-FOUR

"HOW DO YOU know about Carrick?" I ask, suddenly suspicious.

I begin to question my instincts again. Is this a setup to try to find Carrick? Crevan has managed to somehow make Mr. Berry and the guards disappear, and now he's searching for Carrick? Are they using Alpha to find out the information from me? I can't trust her. This all could be a trick, a trick to catch Carrick, to catch me. I'm not as gullible as I once was. If anything, that attribute was my main flaw. My eyes are open now, wide open to everyone around me, but I also know I need to be smart and try to learn as much about Carrick from her as I can.

"You're right to be suspicious," she says. "That's good. You're wondering how I know all this. Carrick didn't receive much, if any, coverage in the wake of you, Angelina Tinder, and Jimmy Child, and it's safe to say the Guild doesn't like stories of Flawed At Birth children searching for their Flawed parents."

Flawed At Birth children? I try not to react to this news, when inside my mind is whirling, my stomach churning.

"I'm sure you know the children are not allowed to search for their biological parents. First, they're taken away from their Flawed parents and locked up in an institution for eighteen years to 'teach' the Flawed out of them. As soon as they reach eighteen years of age, they are released. If they search for their parents, even so much as *think* about it, they're branded Flawed. Loyalty to their own flesh and blood is seen as disloyalty to society." She shakes her head, the anger causing the veins in her neck to pulsate. Despite my fear that this is a setup to locate Carrick, Alpha's anger on this subject is certainly not fabricated.

I think of Carrick's file and remember the F.A.B. beside his name. *Flawed At Birth*. The file also said Carrick received a brand to his chest for disloyalty. This would add up if what she's saying is true. I decide to believe her, but I'm still not sure if I can trust her.

"Carrick should have waited a few months," she says angrily, almost as if she's directing it at me and it was my fault he did this. "They always keep a close eye on their students for the first few months to make sure they don't search for their biological parents, but he searched for them too soon, almost like he *wanted* to be caught. . . ." She trails off, eyes studying me for my reaction. I don't respond to her. I'm too stunned by what I hear, too moved, feel too sad for Carrick. I want to find him and hug him right now. I wish I'd known this when I was in there, when we were sleeping side by side in our glass cages. I thought he was a soldier, somebody who had done the worst possible act, but really all he had done was the gentlest. The caged animal who paced and fought and looked like he wanted to fight the world had merely tried to find his parents, who were forced to give him up as a child because they were Flawed. Does knowing that Carrick is the son of Flawed parents change my opinion of him?

Yes, it does.

He'd spent years being endlessly brainwashed, being told that his parents were worthless, that he was better than them, only to search for them too soon after his release. His love couldn't be broken; he won. He is even braver than I'd thought. He *is* the soldier I believed he was.

The comments Tina made about him in the cells now make sense to me, that he was a "bad egg," and Judge Crevan's flippant comment about his being "Flawed to the bone." It's true. He never even had a chance. His trial must have been a joke. He was branded as soon as he was born. He was never going to lose that. Maybe Alpha's suspicions are right, maybe he did deliberately want to become Flawed. Maybe he wanted to be who he really was for better or for worse, and not somebody the Guild had reared him to be. The more I think about him, the more he goes up in my estimation.

Alpha slowly breathes out, trying to calm herself. "Carrick's was an unfortunate case."

My heart is broken for him. "Yes," I say sadly. "Yes, it was."

She views me again in her studious way, as if realizing what I am slowly learning myself. "You two were close?"

I feel my cheeks go hot and I look away. I've felt a connection to Carrick ever since he walked into that cell and turned his back on me. I felt it every second that he was beside me and every moment he was behind me in the courtroom. It seems ludicrous to feel like this about someone I didn't know, but we experienced something so intense and were the only two people at any time, in any room, who knew how each other felt.

"Tell me about the institutions. He didn't talk about them very much."

"I'm not surprised," she says. "Though they're not horrible places. In fact, they're probably quite the opposite, state-of-the-art facilities, greater luxuries than most people ever know. The state supports these institutions because most of our greatest athletes have come from them, some of our greatest recent scholars were educated in these places. Despite that, there is no hiding from the fact that all these children have been taken from their parents from birth, never allowed to see them or hear from them again. That is cruel, that is *wrong*. Carrick's situation is slightly different, though," she says. "As you know."

"How is it different?" I ask, confused.

"Well, because of the age he was taken. It probably explains why the brainwashing didn't work so well on him. He had memories of them, which couldn't be taken away. Carrick was taken as a young boy, at the age of five. His parents had managed to hide out when they had him, but he was found, unfortunately," she says sadly.

"I don't know which is worse," I say, thinking of him as a young boy knowing what was happening as he was taken away, torn from people who loved him.

"So"—she straightens up—"that is why I have tried so hard to fight for adoption rights for F.A.B. children."

"F.A.B. children can't be adopted?"

"Of course not. It interrupts the brainwashing process, and, anyway, the Flawed community isn't allowed to adopt at all," she says. "My husband even suggested divorcing me just so I could adopt a baby, because he knows how much I want it. Only on paper, of course. He wasn't intending on leaving me. Where's the logic in that, Celestine, you tell me that? Modern laws tell me I could adopt a child on my own but not with my Flawed husband." She sighs. "Sorry. It's just a subject that angers me."

"I can see that," I say softly, relieved to finally hear somebody speaking out against the Guild. "How do you know so much about Carrick?" I ask, still not completely trusting her rage against the Guild. "His file didn't reveal very much about him."

"So you saw his file," she says, amused. "My, my, Celestine, you have more access than I thought."

I don't respond to that. It takes great nerve to hold my tongue.

She continues.

"All Flawed files are a matter of public record, available through citizen information, because everybody is entitled to know if they are living near a Flawed person, unless of course you are a Flawed person and you, therefore, have no access to these files."

I swallow hard, caught out.

"However, to receive the files, you must submit a form to the Guild requesting access, and this raises alarm bells. *And* on top of that, Carrick's files aren't as readily available as yours are. The Guild doesn't like to admit that the system has failed, or at least that the brainwashing has missed a brain or two. So to answer your question of how do I know so much about Carrick? I have a large organization. When a case like Carrick's reaches the courts, people tell me. I went to his trial."

I'm immediately envious of her. I wanted to be at his trial. I wanted to stand in the back and be his pillar of support as he was for me. I wonder if he had anyone, or if he went through it all alone. I feel more urgency to find him.

"How . . . how was he?" I ask, feeling my body starting to tremble.

"Remarkably strong," she says with a fond smile on her lips.

"Did you go to the Branding Chamber?" I ask.

She nods. "Because of my charity foundation, I was allowed. The Guild understands that it's important for me to witness events such as those to help the families and Flawed community in counseling."

I think of him in the Branding Chamber, remember how hot it felt with the bright ceiling lights on me in the chair, picture him in the red gown feeling the same thing as I felt. My eyes fill with tears. "How was he?"

She takes my hands, and I feel the tears slip down my cheeks.

"Celestine, you'll be proud to know, he was remarkably quiet. I've never attended a branding where there was such . . . silence."

Inside, I feel broken, but I also feel like dancing. He did what I did. He followed my lead. He wouldn't let them hear him cry.

"Have you seen him lately?" she asks as I wipe away my tears.

I smile, a knowing smile, like I know where he is but won't say. "Do *you* know where he is?"

She laughs. "Actually, no. He's doing a good job of hiding. To escape undetected from the Whistleblowers is a rare and difficult thing."

I nod in agreement.

"He must have help."

I know she wants to say more on that, but she doesn't. Instead, she changes tack, and I now know why she's really here. "When you next see him, please tell him that his support would be greatly appreciated. The organization needs as many Flawed who are willing to share their stories with us and speak out. Doing it alone doesn't give us the weight we need to make a difference. To have a child of two Flawed parents, who was raised at an F.A.B. institution, who *wanted* to find his parents, whose only flaw was to break F.A.B. rules and try to find his parents, would be a real bonus for my campaign for F.A.B. Adoption. You'll tell him that, won't you?"

I nod. Whenever I see him again. If I ever see him again.

"I'm holding an event tonight. A small gathering for those who need support. It's at five PM. You'll have time to get there and back for your curfew. Here's the directions," she says urgently, pushing a folded piece of paper into my hands. "Come speak for us tonight. I know you will inspire the people. Move them to action."

"Action?"

"I call it a support group." She raises an eyebrow. "But really what I'm trying to do is make something happen. Bring an end to the Guild. What the Guild knows is that I work with the Flawed, with their families, providing a counseling service for those affected by it. I arrange fund-raisers for families. The F.A.B. Adoption campaign is supported by many in the government and the Guild. These institutions are costly, and adoption would help their budgets greatly. They always have their eye on the bottom line, of course. So I have many of them on my side. That's how I can make this work. And not just the adoption campaign. They know that my counseling work with the Flawed and their families is vital in maintaining calm in society."

Even hearing that she is supported by the Guild makes me distrust her again, despite what she's saying. "Alpha." I barely look at the crumpled paper in my hand. "I appreciate your support, but I'm not a speaker. I don't even know what I would say."

Her eyes linger over me for a moment as though she's trying to figure me out. "I often think you're more clever than you let on, and other times I think you're a child who has found herself in a situation that is so much bigger than she and has no idea what to do."

I don't answer her. It's not for me to help her analysis of me. Understanding myself doesn't keep me awake at night, but I'm still not used to people airing their opinions of me so boldly like that. Any thoughts I have of her I have politely kept to myself, though some people, like her and Pia, have found that it is their right to express their opinion of me freely, as though it can't hurt or alter me. It's the branding that does that, and I know it. It dehumanizes me in a way to others. I'm to be stared at and talked about as if I'm not here.

"My work began as a charity, counseling, and fund-raising, but since your case, the numbers have grown. I see a rise in our donations. Privately, of course, but there are some big names. I feel a change coming, and you have started that change. Of course, much of it is political. My organization can do so much more. It's time. Try to bring your friend Carrick if you can. It's time to urge the people into action."

FIFTY-FIVE

THAT AFTERNOON, KNOWING that I have a week of confinement to the house ahead of me, I pace my room like the caged lion Carrick always seemed. Even if I could speak at Alpha's gathering, which I wouldn't, I can't leave the house. How empowering is that to people?

Home from school, Juniper walks by my open door. She looks lost and as though she has been crying. I'm glad. She stops and looks at me. She's back in her own clothes, head to toe in black. Apart from my brandings, there's not much to tell us apart.

"Nothing ever happened with me and Art if that's what you're worried about." She sniffs. "All we ever did was talk about you."

I want to slap her hard I feel so angry, but instead I calmly raise my hand out and push the door closed in her face. It is a gratifying feeling, but it doesn't do anything to fill the emptiness inside me. I know she hasn't left the house at night since I stumbled across them together. I know because I lie awake in bed, unable to sleep, and listen for her. I think of all those nights she went to meet him on the summit while I was trapped inside on curfew, in agony, healing, and my heart pumps with rage. I don't know what I think about something happening between them. When I found them, they were sitting side by side and laughing. If it hadn't happened already, it might have. It is the sound of their laughter that haunts me, particularly as I was running for my life. I will never forgive them. But it doesn't mean I can stop myself from caring about him. I wonder who is helping Art now that Juniper isn't. I wonder if he has run away for good, if he has had the courage to leave Humming, even Highland altogether, and live somewhere far from the reach of his dad. I wonder if I'll ever see him again. I shouldn't care about him and I shouldn't worry about him. But I do.

I'm summoned to the kitchen because Mary May has paid me a surprise visit and apparently has an announcement. I'm immediately terrified. I'm guessing it has something to do with the alcohol test I took Friday night that tested positive. Despite Colleen, Gavin, and Natasha being unable to escape the situation as Logan had, the three of them had categorically denied drinking any alcohol, which made it look like it was an act I had done on my own, which is against Flawed rules. Though how I, tied up and locked in a shed, had happened upon alcohol all by myself is too stupid for even the Guild to pin on me. Though I'm sure they spent the weekend trying.

Mary May produces some documents from her satchel. Looking at her, I feel the sting of her leather glove on my cheek and I see the woman who reported her entire family to the Guild and watched them one after another be branded for life. Who knows what else she's capable of, and my life is in her hands.

"Your detention this week has been withdrawn," she says in a clipped voice, and I can tell she hates delivering this news. I can tell she hates even opening her mouth wide enough in this house to breathe in the Flawed air. She's appalled by it, yet she's drawn to it. "An anonymous source submitted the photograph in its entirety to the Guild. The Guild had it tested for Photoshopping or meddling of any kind and is satisfied with the claim that it is original and is the image of Juniper North in her art class. On your separate charge, the Guild has also ruled to drop the alcohol charges. Colleen Tinder's testimony matches with the amount of alcohol found in your bloodstream, which was minimal."

To my utter surprise, Mom, who is wearing dungarees and a plaid shirt, punches the air close to Mary May's face and hisses, "Yes!" Then she throws her arms around me in a tight embrace so that I can't see Mary May's reaction. Mom warned me only days ago not to test Mary May, but she is playing a dangerous game herself. I hear the door slam as Mary May leaves.

Feeling victorious from my double win, I feel like I can take on the world, that I can go further to righting more wrongs. Now I am free to investigate as I planned. Leaving everybody to celebrate without me, including Juniper, who looked genuinely pleased for me but knew not to come near me, I go to my bedroom. I take out Mr. Berry's business card from my pocket and dial the number written on the back.

"Hello?" a quiet voice answers.

"Hello, is that . . . Mr. Berry's husband?"

"Who's this?" he says, even quieter, so that I have to strain my ear to hear.

"My name is Celestine North. He represented me in—"

"I know who you are," he interrupts quickly, but not rudely. "You shouldn't be calling here."

It sounds like he's moving around. Distracted. Something brushes against the phone.

"I'm sorry, it's just that Mr. Berry provided me with this phone number in the invoice, and I thought that he wanted me to call here. Can I speak to him, please?"

Silence. At first, I think he's gone, but I can hear him breathing.

"Hello?"

"Yes," he says quickly again, so quietly it's as though it's a bad line and he's a million miles away. "He's not here," he says, and my heart falls. "She already called looking for him."

I'm confused at first, unsure of whom he's talking about, but then I remember Pia and note that he doesn't want to mention her name. He thinks people are listening.

"You don't need to worry about . . . her," I say. "She says she's trying to help me." He must be afraid she's going to write an article about Mr. Berry. Of course he would tell her he's not there. They're all afraid of Pia. Who would speak to her? I would insist on her honesty, but I can't do that when I'm not completely sure myself.

"He can trust me," I say.

"He's not here, I told you," he says, more impatient and a little louder. Then quietly again he adds, "He had to go away. He didn't tell me where. He was in a hurry. He knew about the others."

That startles me. So Mr. Berry wasn't taken by Crevan. He is in hiding after what happened to the guards.

"Okay . . ." I think quickly. He doesn't want to give names away, any information away. How can I say what I want to say? "I'm looking for something—do you know what it is?"

"Yes," he practically whispers.

He knows about the sixth brand.

"Did you see it?" I ask, not wanting to mention the video directly. If Crevan's people are listening, I don't want to make it too easy for them.

There's a long silence again, and I know my patience is being tested. This is like pulling teeth, but I must stick it out. I know he won't answer the phone to me again. It's now or never.

"Yes," he says, finally, so faintly. "I saw it. I'm sorry about what happened to you."

I try hard not to cry. "Do you have it? Do you know where it is?"

"No," he says. "I told the other woman already. I don't have it."

I collapse back on my bed, so disappointed, so angry, my eyes fill up.

"But I didn't tell her this," he adds quickly. "You have it. He told me *you* have it." He hangs up.

FIFTY-SIX

I SPRING UP to a seated position on my bed and stare at the phone in shock, goose bumps all over my body.

I have Mr. Berry's video?

I redial his number. It rings and rings, no answer.

I have it? *Mr. Berry* says I have the video? How? When? Where? I look around my room, my head spinning, trying to think where it could be, how he could have given it to me, trying to remember those final moments when I was removed from the chamber and taken to the ward. Did I see him then? Did he slip his phone to me? But I was just wearing a gown. Where would I have put it? Did he visit me afterward? I was so heavily drugged, and in such shock, I remember very little. I remember Tina. Tina cared for me mostly while the nurse tended to me. But I don't remember anyone else. Mary May already thoroughly searched my room. Was that what she was looking for? If she was, did she find it? I doubt it. I believe she thinks I have only five brands—she has referred to that fact enough. I don't think she has any idea of what happened in that chamber, and I won't make the same mistake I made with Pia, blurting it out just to show I have the upper hand. I know now that this information is highly sensitive.

And then I realize. Carrick is the only other person who was in that room with him. Carrick must have it.

I need help. Pia is gone on her mission and will report back to me who knows when, and the only other person who has been able to give me any information whatsoever on Carrick is Alpha. I decide I'm going to Alpha's meeting, but I'm not going alone. I dial another number.

"Hello?"

"Granddad, I need your help." I was never ready before, I never believed him before, I thought that he was a conspiracy theorist and that he was too irrational, but I know now that he was right about everything. I am ready now.

"Ah, she finally calls," he says, a cheery sound. "And so it begins."

———————

The positive outcome from the week's house arrest is that the press have disappeared from outside of the house, and they haven't yet learned that the punishment has been withdrawn. If I'm not coming or going, there's nothing for them to report, so I successfully manage to get to the local ice-cream parlor, my meeting point with Granddad, because that's where he always used to take me and Juniper after Ewan was born to give Mom a break from us. Granddad is waiting in his dusty pickup truck with two ice creams.

"Showtime," he says when I sit inside, and it's the best I've felt for weeks.

After driving for almost an hour, during which I've filled him in on everything that has happened to me since we last met, including Alpha and her charity for the Flawed, the guards' going missing, Pia's helping me search for them, and my mission to find Carrick, especially now after Mr. Berry's husband has told me that I have the video. Grand-dad listens intently as we drive, sometimes pulling over and asking me to repeat what I've said, listening to every word and, most important, *believing* me.

"What makes you think this lad Carrick has the video?" he asks.

"Well, it just makes sense," I reply.

"But Berry's husband said that *you* have it. Not anybody else. That *you* have it."

I nod, hearing him but thinking it couldn't possibly be true. I would have remembered being given it.

"Did Berry send you anything since you've been home? Think about it, Celestine."

"Granddad," I say, holding my hands up to my pounding head. "I haven't been able to do anything but think about it. But there's nothing. Apart from an envelope with an invoice, there was nothing. He left his home number for me, and I called his husband. That's the only message he left for me."

He goes silent. "Don't worry, we'll figure it out."

"Thanks for your help, Granddad. I appreciate it. I don't want to get you into trouble, though."

"Trouble?" he barks. "I've been trouble since the day I was born. You're not cutting me out of this excitement."

I smile, feeling grateful.

We turn off a country road onto an even smaller track, and Granddad slows.

"This can't be right," he says, confused, squinting out the windows at the view of fields around us. We're surrounded by thousands of acres of wind turbines, and a liquid-air storage plant rises from the horizon, enormous though it's miles away. "Let me see the directions again."

I hand him the crumpled slip of paper with Alpha's handwriting. It's a messy scrawl, something I think she did deliberately so nobody else could decipher it.

"Hmm," he says, face screwed up in concentration as he reads. Then he looks up and around. "Looks like we're going the right way," he says, but he sounds uncertain. "This woman, do you trust her?"

I look at him. "I don't trust anyone anymore."

"That's my girl." He chuckles. "Well, we'll soon find out."

He continues driving down the narrow road, on the hunt for Gateway Lodge. I'm expecting a hotel of some sort, a conference room with a dozen or so people all talking about their experiences, but this doesn't seem like the place anybody would come to to stay in a hotel. It's too remote. My stomach tenses. Becoming lost is a concern of mine now, as is running out of gas. I worry about a random event occurring that will stop me from returning home in time for my curfew. Even worse, I'm afraid Mary May will orchestrate something to deliberately get me into trouble. She can't be happy with the outcome of the photograph and alcohol charge, and I'm expecting trouble. I must beat this fear. I thought the Guild couldn't do anything to hurt me anymore, but I was wrong—targeting my family would be an unbearable pain, a guilt I don't think I could live with, and it's the fear that they instill in us that is the continuous punishment for what we've done. I trust Granddad. I trust he will make sure I get home. But he's old. What if he has a heart attack, what if he passes out . . . ?

The road gets increasingly narrow as we delve deeper. The branches of the trees are now brushing up against our windows. Just when I think we'll be crushed by branches and overgrowth, a gate appears after the next bend in the road. The gate is enormous and towers over us with multiple security cameras covering all angles. A twenty-foot wall hides whatever is behind it. The plaque on the wall announces it is Gateway Lodge.

We've arrived.

FIFTY-SEVEN

WE LEAN FORWARD and strain our necks to look up at the height of the walls.

Before Granddad even has a chance to reach out the window of the truck to press the buzzer, as if hearing our conversation, the gates suddenly open. Granddad moves the truck forward, and after following a mile of driveway, surrounded by perfectly manicured lawns and sloping hills, which block what's coming up next, as though driving through a golf course, finally, we are faced with an enormous mansion. "Lodge" did not accurately describe it. There are dozens of cars parked in front of the house and a series of minibuses that must have had a hard time squeezing their way down the country roads. As we park, the front door of the mansion opens.

"That's not her," I say, walking toward our greeter.

Granddad immediately speeds up and almost blocks me, reaching the woman first.

"You made it," a timid, but polite, woman says excitedly. It's pulsating from her, her smile so enormous it is contagious. "I'm Lulu," she says, her voice high-pitched, but soft, like a cartoon character. "Alpha's assistant. I've held you a seat. Two, just in case." She smiles and gives Granddad the quick once-over.

Granddad always receives these looks from people. For someone with a soft heart, he does a good job of scaring everyone off with his deeply lined, scrunched-up, grumpy face.

"This is my granddad."

"Oh my," Lulu says, her voice going up an octave as she gets excited. "It's an honor to meet your family." Lulu pumps his hand up and down enthusiastically. Then she turns to me. It hasn't been long, but I instinctively know not to offer my branded right hand to her to shake. She reaches for it instead herself and holds on for dear life, looking at me expectantly. I'm not sure what she's waiting for. I look to Granddad uncomfortably.

"Okay, okay," Granddad barks, and she jumps a little.

I finally free my hand from hers, which seems to break her from whatever spell she's under.

"I'm sorry." She blushes. "It's just so nice to see you in the flesh. I'm a big, big fan of yours."

"We all are," Granddad says proudly.

"Follow me," Lulu says, and we make our way through endless halls and corridors. "All of us are thrilled you're coming today. It will mean so much to everyone. A boost. These are such hard times, and you mean so much to them." She stops walking and clasps her hands together at her chest and gazes at me.

"She's not that special," Granddad snaps, which makes me giggle. "Now, let's keeping moving. We're late."

"Indeed," she says, continuing. "Though all our first-timers are always late. It's not the most obvious of places. Most people turn back at the main road. Exactly as Alpha intended."

Granddad looks around. "Does her husband live here, too?"

I'm about to interrupt, with embarrassment that this isn't her home, when Lulu replies.

She looks at him uncertainly and gives him a brusque, "Yes."

We follow her to an elevator and go to the basement. We step out of the elevator into a large lobby. There are double doors ahead of us, plush carpets with elaborate designs. It feels like the Four Seasons, not somebody's home.

She stops before the double doors and turns to me, eyes wide and filling with tears. "I can't tell you how excited everybody is about hearing you speak. You speak what they think, if you understand. You represent a voice that has been silenced for decades, and all of a sudden you're here. The person we've been waiting for."

"Lulu, I'm not speaking today." I don't have Juniper's paralyzing fear of public speaking, but I'm not ready to say anything to anyone. I don't have anything prepared, nor do I really know what I'm getting myself involved in. I just wanted to be a spectator, see what it's about, ask Granddad his opinion on whether we can trust Alpha or not, as that's something I'm uncertain of.

"Oh." Her face falls, and then she's confused. "But everybody is here to hear you."

I fume at the mistake that's been made; it's strike one against Alpha. Before I get a chance to object or run away, Granddad pushes open the double doors.

Faces turn to stare as we walk in. The room is enormous, like a ballroom, with a chandelier dripping from the center of the ceiling. A woman is speaking at a lectern onstage, so most eyes are on her. Only a few people at the back of the hall turn to look at us when we enter. Each time one sees me, the person in the next seat gets an elbow or a nudge, and the other turns around. Lulu walks right up the center aisle to the front row, expecting Granddad and me to follow her, but Granddad grabs my hand and pulls me into the back row. We slip into two seats and watch as Lulu turns around first with pride, then confusion as no one is behind her. Her face turns puce, and she hurries from the front row and back through the double doors in search of us.

The man I sit beside shakes his head and motions for me and Granddad to swap places. At first, I think it's because he doesn't want to sit beside a Flawed, but then I realize we're at a Flawed gathering; he has an *F* on his temple, an armband on his sleeve, and only two Flawed people can sit together. I am making it three. So Granddad sits between us, and I notice that this has been the case in every row, just as it was in the courtroom. Despite the fact that there are at least one hundred people in the room, every two Flawed have been separated by a regular, unflawed person. This is not the small counseling group that I had been imagining. A banner on the stage reads BRING BACK OUR BABIES.

Granddad notices it, too, and whispers to me. "She's on dangerous ground here."

"She says the Guild and the government are on her side. They want to end the institutions because they cost too much, but instead allow specially trained families to take in F.A.B. children and continue the Guild's teachings." I picture someone like Mary May only too glad to help brainwash young children and shudder at the thought.

Granddad nudges me and points to the far side of the room. I follow his gaze and see what he's looking at. Leaning against the wall is a Whistleblower, a man, dressed in his black gear and red vest, keeping an eye on everything.

The old familiar feeling of doubt creeps in. What if the Guild is in on all this? What if it's Judge Crevan's way of catching Carrick so that he can take him away and silence him as he has silenced the guards? What if this is an elaborate setup? I look around, nervously checking the room for more Whistleblowers, waiting for them to all surround me like I'm in a trap. Though if they're here, they're not in their uniforms.

A woman stands at the lectern, addressing the audience. Alpha sits beside three others on the panel on the stage. She sees me and sits up straighter. She nods at me, her eyes sparkling with delight. She looks to see who is beside me, sees Granddad, notes that it's not Carrick, and gives me a small smile, not doing anything to hide her disappointment. Her acknowledgment of me garners more stares, nudges, and whispers in my direction. I can hear the hiss of my name on strangers' lips. I try to block them out and, instead, concentrate on the woman speaking.

She is talking about her baby, who was taken from her at the hospital, all because she and her husband are Flawed. She had refused termination. Her daughter, two years old, is still in one of the five institutions in the country that house and rear Flawed babies. She doesn't know which institution, she doesn't know how she is, and she receives no communication from them whatsoever. She has lost all rights to her child. The speaker can no longer continue at this point and breaks down. There is an uncomfortable silence as she cries alone onstage, her visible pain making my heart ache. I feel Alpha leaves it a little too long before coming to her aid, as though she wants to rub it in all our faces.

"Loves the drama, this one," Granddad says in my ear, and I nod in agreement.

Alpha joins the woman at the lectern, wraps her arm around her, and looks right down to the back of the room when she speaks. At me.

"We appreciate how difficult it was for Elizabeth to come here today and share her story with us. But Elizabeth's reliving her story, sharing how shattering it has been for her and her husband, is not in vain. We can learn from this. It hurts us and it moves us, but we can take this with us and use it to spur us on to make change. Change doesn't just happen. We all know that. We have to force it. Let us use Elizabeth's story to help us to force change."

There are nods of approval all around us, and applause breaks out.

Elizabeth, still crying, shows her appreciation as best she can. Alpha faces the audience as she embraces her, and we see her eyes closed intensely as though this is the biggest hug she has ever given in her life. It's a little too orchestrated for me.

Alpha's back at the mike stand. "Of course, Elizabeth's not alone in her pain. All of us here today have our own stories, our own heartache. Our next speaker is Tom Hancock, and he is here to share his story with us. Please welcome him."

For the next twenty minutes, we listen to Flawed Tom explain how, after his Flawed wife died, he spent ten years trying to find their son, a journey we hear in all its tortuous detail, only to find that on discovering him, and his grandchildren that he didn't know anything about, that his son didn't want to know him. His son had been so brainwashed by the institution that Flawed Tom had to beg his own son not to report him to the Whistleblowers.

After we hear Tom, we listen to a woman who used to work in the F.A.B. institutions and doesn't believe in, or agree with, them. She gives us a rundown of their daily schedules, the lives the children lead. As she does this, I think of Carrick and what he has lived with for the past eighteen years of his life. These institutions are pumped up with government money, the facilities second to none. The government and the Guild pride themselves on creating such successes and say it is because the Flawed can be successfully cleansed at birth. For people like me, it's too late, we cannot be healed.

"I suggested to a colleague," the woman says, "that perhaps the reason these children are so well-rounded, so fully functional and successful, is because of the very fact that they have both genes of the Flawed and that in itself is a strength and breeds perfection."

Everybody looks at one another in shock that this woman, an employee of the Guild, would have suggested such a thing. I watch the Whistleblower in the corner of the room, surprised that she is able to say this in his presence, but he doesn't react. He looks bored, as though he's heard it all before.

"Of course, that's how I lost my job," she says. "But I enjoyed the looks on their faces when the board called me in to explain what I'd said."

There is light laughter.

I think of Carrick, of his build, the extensive training the F.A.B. children endure, and the education. He must be fast and strong. And clever. To have beaten the endless brainwashing he received daily makes him mentally strong, too. Perhaps he is perfect, as she says. Yet everybody in the Guild was so dismissive of him. I want him, I need him. I don't think I will ever rest for the remainder of my life if I don't find him again. Art and I talked every day, nonstop. Even when we got home from meeting on the summit, we would talk into the early hours over the phone about nothing and everything. Yet Carrick and I never had one conversation, and I feel we've shared more than anyone else I know.

My heart is pounding as I feel like just taking off right there and then on a mission to find him, but Granddad's elbowing me in the already sore ribs brings me back into the room.

Alpha is at the lectern; she has been speaking, though I haven't been listening.

I understand now why Granddad has elbowed me. People are staring at me. Alpha is looking at me, pretending as though she can't see me. "Where is she?" she asks. "Celestine, are you still here?"

My heart pounds.

"Be careful," Granddad whispers. "I'm not sure, Celestine, I'm not sure. . . ." He looks around as if looking for an exit.

I nod and stand up. I hear the gasps of surprise, and I am stunned that all these people recognize me. It does not thrill me. All I can think is that all these people know that I'm not perfect. All these people know what I did. They know what I am. There is nowhere for me to hide. I can't even pretend, not as most people can do when they walk into a room.

I can't help but shake my head and laugh nervously at the applause. I worked so hard to be perfect, to achieve plaudits, not admiration, but to be normal, not to stand out. My grades were excellent, I had enough friends so that I wasn't a weirdo, but not too many so that I was popular. I was average. I worked so hard to be so average. But I made a mistake, the worst thing I could do, and in a room full of Flawed, I am celebrated. I'm embarrassed. I think they must be mistaken. I am not who they think I am.

They applaud, an enormous applause that grows and grows. Alpha beckons me up to the stage to her. I shake my head, but those around me urge me. Despite his reservations, Granddad looks proud. He starts to clap, too. They call me to the stage, and I have no choice. As I make my way out of the back row, people start to stand. It spreads as I walk up the center aisle, everybody standing and applauding me. The Whistleblower steps away from the wall, alert, not looking so bored now. His eyes on me make me nervous. I climb the steps to the stage and join Alpha, who is spurring them on to cheer. When I near her, she reaches out and takes my hand. She raises it in the air with her own in triumph. Then, suddenly, the cheers die down, so does the applause, and then everybody takes a seat. The rumble dies down, and soon the room is so quiet, my heart beating wildly from the adrenaline of what has just happened and now from the fear. They all look at me, so many faces, looking for me to say something hopeful, something meaningful, *something* that they can take home with them. Alpha steps away from me, gives me the stage. I can't. I shake my head, but they encourage me.

"Say what you feel," someone in the front row urges.

I try to think of how I feel, but all I feel is that this is wrong. I shouldn't be here in front of all these people. I am not who they think I am. I helped an old man, and I want to bring Crevan down, but I am no leader. I can't even say that because of the Whistleblower's presence. I can't inspire these men and women before me. The silence continues. I can hear my breath through the microphone. I take a step back, look down at my shoes. I have nothing to say. I look back at Alpha; I have to get off this stage. She looks a little angry, not the face I wanted to see. I was hoping for comfort. I'm not getting it from her. I look down the room to Granddad for his support, for his guidance, but he's gone. I look around in surprise, trying to find him, locate him among the crowd, but there's no sign of him.

Confused, I search the room. This feels all wrong. Warning bells are ringing. This is not me. Pia Wang, Lisa Life, Alpha Dockery, and Enya Sleepwell can take their mandates and their causes and forget me. I'm not who they think I am. I turn to look at the Whistleblower, but he, too, is gone.

I know it's going to happen before it happens. The double doors are pushed open. Lulu stands in the doorway.

"The Whistleblowers are here," she shouts, panicked.

Then, as the sirens take over, there is no more silence.

FIFTY-EIGHT

ALPHA GRABS ME. I feel her nails dig deep into my skin.

"Come with me," she says firmly.

"My granddad," I say to her, feeling breathless already. "I have to get my granddad."

"He'll be fine," she says dismissively, leading me down from the stage.

"No. He comes, too." I stop walking.

She tries to tug me again but can see I'm not moving until we sort this out.

"All right. I'll tell Lulu to bring him to us." She quickly barks orders at Lulu, who looks on the verge of collapse, but instead pushes her way through the panicking crowd to get to Granddad, whom I still can't see. I don't have much faith in Lulu at this point. I think she will be more concerned about saving her own skin than my granddad's. I can see his cap in the moving crowd. Everyone is trying to make a way to the door, trying to escape.

"Granddad!" I call. He doesn't hear me.

I start to panic. I pick up the microphone that only moments ago I couldn't think of a word to say into and shout into it, but it has already been turned off.

"I have to find him."

"Lulu will get him." Alpha grabs me by the arm and pulls.

"Forgive me if I don't have much faith in Lulu," I snap. "Did you tell the Whistleblowers I was here?" I shout. "Was this a trap to catch Carrick?"

"What?! Why would I do that?" she asks, so alarmed and disgusted that I believe her.

"Lulu thought I was speaking here today. Did you advertise this?"

She looks guilty. "I might have mentioned it to a few people, but I certainly didn't advertise it."

"Damn it!" I shout, pulling my arm away from her. "You used me!"

"Let me explain," she says, changing her body language. She appears panicky. "Come with me and I'll explain."

"Where are we going?"

She doesn't answer—she just moves more quickly. The room is in utter chaos. There are those who want to leave, and those who are strong and firm in their stance and stay where they're seated, arms folded in defiance.

The speaker from the F.A.B. institution tries to get Alpha's attention. She runs along the side of the stage, chasing after us. "You said I would be protected!" she says, panicking, as Alpha ignores her and pulls me away with her.

As we reach the back of the room, I hear the whistles, and my heart pounds with the memory of Angelina Tinder and my own experience ringing in my ears. It makes me freeze on the spot, and it has that effect on most people. Caught. The room starts to go silent at the sound. Freeze. Panic. Alpha gets me moving again, pulling me in the opposite direction.

"Granddad," I say, a sob catching in my throat. I see the red vests swarming into the room, I see a baton swing in the air, and I hear people scream. Alpha pulls me through another door, and we leave the mayhem behind.

"Jesus." Alpha pants as we start to run now. "Jesus, Jesus, Jesus."

We run faster. She leads me down a corridor and into an elevator. We go down another floor. When we come out, the ceilings are low, the hallways narrow. This part of the house is not so plush. It's more like a bunker.

"This way." We can no longer walk side by side in the narrow hallway, so I follow her, her looking back regularly to make sure I'm still there.

"The Guild likes to keep an eye on us, and, more important, lets us know that it's keeping an eye on us. It sends one or two Whistleblowers. They sit in the back row, listen, and keep an eye on things. This isn't an illegal gathering. They know about my cause. Usually there's nothing to worry about," she says.

"Usually," I say bitterly. "But you told people I was coming. That I was speaking. And I'll bet Crevan has introduced a new law against this. He's going to say you were holding a rally. That I was speaking at a rally."

She looks at me and swallows. Her look of fear doesn't do anything to comfort me. "But we're not doing anything wrong. We're just sharing our stories. We're allowed to do that."

That wasn't the vibe that I was picking up on as I was encouraged to walk to the stage. It changed from story sharing to a different kind of energy. "The rules have changed," I say. "Crevan is changing everything now."

Crevan is scared. He feels his power slipping away. Perhaps he's heard about the secret committee investigating him, perhaps not, but either way there is enough rising opposition to the Guild among the public and now among the government to make him panic. And on top of that, if I'm right, he's going to extreme measures to silence the Guild guards and Mr. Berry, if he gets his hands on him. He is panicking.

Alpha stops in the middle of a hallway and lifts a section of the dado rail and inserts a PIN code. "I can assure you, Celestine, that I did not alert them to your presence. I may have told a few people that you'd be here, but I'm not ready to announce you as a friend of the foundation yet."

"Good," I snap. "Because, right at this moment, I certainly am not a friend of the foundation; and if you think you'll be allowed to home-school me from now on, you better think again. I'm sure this is the last time you and I will ever be allowed in the same room together. I'm surprised they let you in the first place."

"Like I said, the Guild encourages counseling of the Flawed. They felt that I would be a positive force in your life. That I could stop you from speaking out against them."

I snort.

"I'll tell them you were going to share your sob story and persuade them not to make mistakes, that life as a Flawed is miserable, that you weren't going to glamorize it."

"I wasn't going to glamorize it."

She looks at me in surprise. There's a beep, and a door that I hadn't noticed before suddenly opens.

"A secret door?"

"Not secret, just not as clearly marked," she says defensively, with a sly smile.

Once inside, I find myself in an office. Walnut desk, shelves filled to the brim with books. Leather chairs with gold buttons. Photographs in gold frames covering every inch of the wall. "You'll be safe here. They don't know about this room," she says quickly. "I have to go back and talk to the Whistleblowers, sort this mess out, but I'll be back with your granddad. Stay here till I return."

The door closes behind her, and I'm left in the room alone.

FIFTY-NINE

I BEGIN BY looking at the photographs. The same man is in all of them with different people. All formal business photographs of hand-shakes. Alpha is in some, standing alongside him, and I don't know who any of the people in the photographs are. I see Alpha and this man in a frame on the desk, and I guess it's her husband. I don't know any-body else, but then the more I study the people in the photos, the more I recognize them as being with world leaders. Important men and women whom I see on the news on the rare times I watch the news. And I do recognize one man: Judge Crevan.

Alpha, her husband, Judge Crevan, and his wife. At a garden party, the ladies in summer floral dresses, all with a glass of champagne in their hands, all four of them looking like they're in the middle of a big laugh, as though somebody had just said something funny. The best of friends. Again, I question Alpha's motivations. Have I allowed her to sweep me away from the Whistleblowers, thinking she was helping me, and am now a sitting duck?

Another wall reveals a series of framed qualifications and acco-lades for a Professor Lambert. I hear a cough behind me and I turn around. Expecting to see a Whistleblower, instead I find a man in a crumpled shirt and jeans standing at yet another door that appeared from nowhere.

"Yes, yes, another secret door. She's got quite the little rat maze going on down here." He chuckles. "Bill," he says, holding out his hand.

He wavers a little as he does this, loses his balance.

As I step closer, I can smell alcohol on his breath. He has gray stubble on his face and looks as though he's gone a few days sleeping in the same clothes.

"You're Alpha's husband," I say, recognizing him from the photographs.

He chuckles again. "Do you know, there was once a time when she was my wife? Anyway. There was once a time when lots of things were a lot of things. So you're the one. The One." He widens his eyes in mock-worship. "She's been talking about you a great deal." He studies me and then goes around to his desk and searches through the drawers. It takes him some time, enough for me to study him and the room he has come from. It looks like a kitchen, which no doubt has another door into another room. Why would they have another home buried beneath? In the last drawer he checks, I hear the clink of bottles.

He looks at me in mock-surprise. "Fancy that. Want a drink?"

"We're not allowed to drink," I say firmly, noting the branding on his temple.

"Ah, yes." He chuckles again, and then he whispers, "Don't worry, I won't tell if you don't."

"The Whistleblowers are upstairs," I say, astonished by his behavior.

"Oh, yes, the scary whistlers." He whistles, imitating their sound, and chuckles. "I'm not afraid of them. Are you?" He pours the whiskey into a glass tumbler on a silver tray by the desk and sits down in the leather chair behind the desk. He sinks low.

"I'm afraid of what they'll do to my granddad."

"Don't worry about your granddad. He's a pro. He's currently hiding in our morning parlor." He presses a button under the desk, and the framed photographs disappear to reveal a dozen screens of CCTV images. "Fourth one down, third one in."

I move closer to the screens and find the room he's talking about.

"I don't see anything."

"See? Told you he was a pro. That bookcase opens; a small, little room; hope he's not claustrophobic. But he'll be safe. They won't find him in there."

I look at the other screens and see mayhem. People have been lined up; others who rose up against the Whistleblowers are on the ground and have been wounded. Some are being marched out of the building and into vans outside. On one screen I see Alpha standing aside and giving a Whistleblower in charge a firm talking-to.

"Most of them won't be charged with anything," he says calmly. "It's just to scare you all, break it up. And it worked."

I nod, relieved that Granddad is okay but hoping he'll be able to hold on until they're gone.

"What about your tests?" I ask him, curious to know how he gets away with being in his state when he's Flawed. "Won't your Whistleblower find traces of alcohol?"

"Us geniuses always pass with flying colors, isn't that so?" He smiles. "Mathematics is your thing, isn't it?"

"I hope so." I don't know what my job possibilities will be now, now that I'm Flawed. I will never be allowed to rise to any position of power, most likely not as manager, and definitely never any higher.

"You *hope.*" He makes a face. "No, don't use hope. Use your mathematics to get out of this so-called problem."

I frown. He has definitely drunk too much. "I don't think math can solve any of my problems now."

"One of my favorite quotes is from Albert Einstein: 'We cannot solve our problems with the same thinking we used when we created them.'" He looks at me, eyes bright. The quote does more for him than it does for me obviously.

I shrug. "I guess."

"You guess? Mathematicians don't guess!" he says dramatically, sitting up. "They make an orderly list, they eliminate possibilities, they use direct reasoning. Never guess, my dear. Are you familiar with George Pólya?"

"Of course."

"I bought a book of his once. I liked his philosophies. You know he said there are four principles to solving a problem. First, you have to understand the problem. After understanding it, you make a plan, then you carry out the plan, then you look back on your work. If this technique fails, which, of course, it often does, Pólya advised, if you can't solve a problem, then there is an easier problem you can solve: Find it."

I smile.

"Thought you'd like that one."

"You're a friend of Judge Crevan's," I say.

"I am?" he says, surprised. "Where did you hear that nasty rumor from?"

"The photographs."

"Oh that." He waves his hand dismissively. "I can safely say I see none of those people anymore. Apart from her, of course." He looks at the photo of him and Alpha on the beach, both sun-kissed, him cleanly shaven, looking years younger. "And she probably wishes she was one of them. Does Judge Crevan even have friends, might I ask?"

I like him. "Did you work for the Guild?"

"The Guild? No." He shakes his head. "The government? Yes. Which the Guild works for, too, I might add, though I think they both forget that fact." He smiles at me. "She says you don't ask enough questions. I see you're getting over that part of it. But be careful, sometimes it's best not to know, because even when you know, it doesn't matter anyway.

Ignorance is bliss. Knowledge is often a responsibility nobody wants." He closes his eyes and lazily leans back in the chair, which tilts under his weight and looks like he'll fall backward. "She and I don't agree on that point, of course. Obviously. She always wants to be in the know. She's got this crusade. I don't know. Keeps her busy."

"You don't believe in her foundation?"

"Foundations are rather wobbly, wouldn't you agree?" He opens one eye and raises an eyebrow. "If you and I are down here and the rest of them are scrambling around upstairs." He buries his face in the tumbler again, and the caramel liquid disappears. I actually wish I could join him, from the look of serenity that washes over his face when he's swallowed it all, but then I think of how Logan forced the beer down my throat and I'm quickly over it.

"He tried to take my house and fortune, you know," he says. "Crevan. He's trying to find a way to freeze the assets of the Flawed, take them to fund the Guild. Like they do with criminals. Only we're not criminals, are we, Celestine?"

I shake my head.

"Good. You remember that. It's easy to forget sometimes. Though criminals get better treatment than us. As soon as they serve their time, they're out. We're like this forever." This he says without humor. "Did you know Crevan has been paid over one hundred million since the beginning of the Guild? Taxpayers' money, too. If the public knew that, I think it would be Crevan they boo and hiss in the courtyard and not us. Now, that's a crime."

I shake my head, shocked at his earnings.

We leave a silence. I think of the holiday home I stayed in, the yacht we partied on, the elaborate parties, the endless food and drink. I feel sick that it was funded by his crusade to better his own life. Has it been for justice, as he says, or for money?

"So what is she having you do, then?"

I note that he never says Alpha's name. "I don't know. She wanted me to come here. She was about to make me speak, but then the Whistle-blowers arrived. Thankfully. Didn't think I'd ever hear myself say that."

"Not a fan of speeches?"

"Not when I don't know what I'm talking about."

"They're the very people who usually love them," he says, and we laugh again. "Actions speak louder than words, remember that. Not everyone is made for podiums and microphones. I suggest you find a partner, a Flawed one, that's best, easier, yes. You can live by the same rules, nice and balanced, two Flawed make perfect. Fall in love. Settle down. Make babies. Cherish them. Live your life."

"I can't have a family with a Flawed person."

"Of course you *can*; they just say that you *may not*."

"That doesn't sound like an easy life. I thought you said not to cause trouble."

"Did I say that?" He looks at me again.

I think about it, and then I shake my head.

"No. Indeed. I said actions speak louder than words. Don't talk about it. Do it. All of them upstairs, her included, though I love her, all they do is talk. You *do*. That's why they found you. Will cling to you. Will make *you* do for *them*. No. You do for you." He stands up and comes around the desk to me. He takes my hand and bows theatrically. "Ms. North, a pleasure. You are even more beautiful in the flesh than they describe in the daily rags."

I smile. "Take care of yourself," I say gently. "They'll test you tonight."

"Indeed, they always do, but there are ways around them. You'll find that out. Who's your Whistleblower?"

"Mary May."

"Oooh." He winces. "Can't say I envy you. No way around her. My life shuddered forward again the day she left here. Rattling along like a rusted ghost train, but at least it's moving. Like I say, look to your strengths, look to your heroes for guidance. I'm a scientist. That helps me." He salutes and makes his way back to the hidden door. "Don't tell her that you saw me."

"Why?"

"Just don't. It will worry her. She never knows what I'm going to say. Good luck." He opens the door and, as if remembering something, turns around. I try to see past him into the other room, and when I look in, I freeze in terror.

There's a Whistleblower.

SIXTY

BILL NOTICES THE look on my face and turns to the Whistle-blower, who is standing in the doorway and doesn't see me—for now, anyway.

"Marcus," he says, his tone friendlier than I expected. "What's going on up there?"

Marcus the Whistleblower shakes his head and runs his hands through his hair. "Crevan has them all panicking. Everyone's turning on one another. Flawed, unflawed. Whistleblowers, with each other. It's a mess." He suddenly sees me and stops talking. He turns and walks away, out of view.

"Marcus is shy," Bill whispers loudly to me.

I am so stunned by how he and the Whistleblower have just conversed. The Whistleblower is on our side?

Bill comes back over to me. "She told me about your search, you know," he says. "I'd like to see him again, too. I liked him."

I'm unable to keep up. Liked *whom*?

"Almost as much as she did. We never had children, she and I. I suspect she's told you that already. He was the first one they allowed to live here after years of her begging. It was difficult for her because of me, of course, but she proved herself over the years. They told her a year in advance that he'd be coming here. They like to vet the families, you see, prepare them, make sure they'll follow on in their teachings. She visited him a few times in there, struck up a friendship, and she counted down the days to his graduation, even watched him graduate. We thought he'd like it here; he seemed to like it here. But then he just upped and left, never said good-bye. I think that's what hurt her the most. She could have helped him, but he didn't give her the chance. He never learned what she was capable of or what she was planning. He might have stayed if he'd known. She very quickly grew attached to him. So did I, but mostly because I just liked seeing her so happy." His eyes fill. "If you see Carrick, tell him to visit us again. Tell him I'm sorry it ended like it did."

SIXTY-ONE

GRANDDAD AND I travel home in the truck in silence. It took two hours in hiding before the Whistleblowers left the house and we felt it was safe to leave. Professor Lambert was wrong about nobody being taken into custody. If it had started out as scaremongering, it didn't end that way. The Whistleblowers didn't expect a small percentage of the gathering to defend themselves, to simply not heel to the Whistleblowers' requests, something I'm sure that I will be blamed for despite the fact that I never even opened my mouth. I believe this is the first time people have risen against them; nobody would dare before. A threat to a Whistleblower is seen as a threat to the Guild's rules, which in turn is seen as aiding the Flawed cause, therefore, aiding a Flawed. It's a stretch, but that's how they justify protection of Whistleblowers.

Six people were taken away in the vans. Four were Flawed who would be punished in accordance with Guild punishments, two may be facing imprisonment for aiding a Flawed. Four more were taken to a hospital for wounds caused at the hands of the Whistleblowers' batons.

Some of Alpha's greatest "perfect" supporters had turned on her instantly, telling the Guild absolutely anything it wanted to hear to save their own skins. Overall, Alpha's peaceful "counseling" session had been a disaster. She herself is safe, but only by a breath, and I imagine she is on the watch list. She was shaken when I saw her. She had had a long session with the Whistleblowers, trying to understand what had gone wrong.

Bill's Whistleblower, Marcus, located Granddad and brought him to me, and I was surprised to learn that he was the person who took Granddad to the bunker in the first place. Granddad and I learned that Marcus was married to a Whistleblower, Cathy, and that they were both on the side of the Flawed campaign. He told me that there were many more of these people and that the numbers were growing, but the numbers in opposition to the Flawed were rising, too. Cathy and he felt things were unsettled even among the Whistleblowers. They were turning on one another, and those who were deemed traitors would be made examples of. Marcus was naturally worried.

I'm angry and still don't trust Alpha for so many reasons, but on the other hand, the protection of my granddad and the revelation that she and her husband once looked after Carrick in their own home give me reasons to stay on her good side. Her desperation to find him and be reunited with him tells me that she genuinely doesn't know where he is. I wanted to ask Marcus, the Whistleblower, to help me out, but I couldn't bring myself to do it. If this is a trap, I don't want to fall into it. I can't let Crevan know that I'm searching for Carrick. I can't let him ever know that Carrick was a witness to the sixth brand. That power belongs to Carrick and me alone.

After being briefed on everything, Granddad and I finally leave Alpha's home and get back on the road. I'm anxious to get home well before my curfew.

"That was Professor Bill Lambert," Granddad says, checking the mirrors constantly. "I remember him being in the news. He had a contract with the government. He was an old friend of Crevan's. Reading between the lines, I think Crevan set him up to get rid of him. Crevan's cousin took over the job. More Crevans everywhere. I think half the reason Alpha gets away with her campaigns is because Crevan feels guilty, if he knows what such a feeling is."

"I don't get it. Alpha said she wasn't using me, but if she wasn't trying to set me up with the Guild, she was using me to bring Carrick to her. That must have been why she told people I was speaking. If he heard, maybe she thought he'd come."

"Do you think Carrick would have gone if he'd known you were there?"

"I don't know."

"It's just that, he knows where you are, Celestine. Everyone does. All you have to do is open a newspaper or turn on the TV to see reporters standing outside your house. If he wanted to find you, he would."

I feel hot as tears spring in my eyes. That has upset me. "Okay, fine," I snap, "he doesn't want to find me."

"No. What I mean is, I hope Crevan hasn't got to him already, Celestine."

That's my fear, too. We continue the journey in silence. But I don't think Crevan has found him; otherwise, why would he be panicking? I'm the only person left who knows what he did, and he has full control over my every move. I think of what I know of Carrick, of what I've learned about him. He's clever, he's smart. He must be biding his time.

"I don't think that you should go home," Granddad says.

"Why not?"

"The Whistleblowers were looking for you in there. I've no doubt about that. They wanted to catch you speaking, stirring up anti-Guild feelings. They didn't. But they know you were there. Some traitors would have made up anything just to save their skin. It's true the Flawed cause is gaining more support, but like we've seen tonight, it can just as quickly scare people away. People like to support the underdog, but not when it gets dangerous. Dangerous times, Celestine."

"But where will I go if I don't go home?"

"Stay with me. I told you I'll keep you safe on the farm, away from Crevan. You think Marcus and his wife are the only Whistleblowers on your side? There are plenty more where they came from."

"But, Granddad, if I don't get home for the curfew, everyone will be punished. Mom, Dad, Juniper, Ewan. I can't do that to them! I have to go home and face whatever it is."

Granddad nods solemnly.

"Anyway, I didn't do anything wrong," I say, my anger rising again. "I was invited, by my teacher, to go to a counseling session. What happened was her fault. Not mine. They'll listen to Marcus. He saw the whole thing."

"That's the spirit." He smiles sadly, because we both know nobody will listen to my version of events.

"They'll have seen your truck there," I say, finally. No point hiding it. The Whistleblowers would have taken note of everybody's vehicle in the parking lot.

"The truck isn't registered to me," he says.

I look at him in surprise. "Who's it registered to?"

He chuckles. "Never you mind. I'll have to dump it, though."

I shake my head in disbelief at him.

"Well, that took me back, all that ducking and diving."

I twist my body around to face him. "What is it exactly that it took you back to?"

"Ducking and diving." He winks.

"Granddad," I say suddenly, fearfully, seeing a drop of blood appear at the line of his cap. It slowly trickles down his face and cheek. "Stop the car! You're bleeding!"

"I'm fine." He wipes it away quickly and concentrates on the road. "I just banged it dodging one of those Whistleblowers before Marcus found me and took me to the hiding place. My own fault."

I lift his cap and see he's received a blow to the head.

He flinches as I go near it. "I think you need stitches."

"I'm not getting stitches."

"Granddad!"

"I'll have someone look at it at home, someone who won't ask questions, thank you very much."

"But it will take you hours to get home. We have to put something on it."

He doesn't disagree.

"Stop at the supermarket. It's two minutes away. Let me just clean you up a bit, stop it from getting infected."

"I'll do it after I drop you home safely."

But neither of us knows that we don't know what will await me when I get home. We need to give him medical attention now.

"Okay." He pulls over gruffly, at the back of the supermarket, near the loading area, so that the truck isn't on the main road. "I'll be right back."

"No way. You stay here, I'm going in. You've lost a lot of blood already." I look at his saturated cap.

"They might be looking for you," he says.

"Where? Here? At a random supermarket? And anyway, we're just jumping to conclusions. What happened at Alpha's might have nothing to do with me at all. Alpha is stirring up something dangerous, an opposition to the Guild. Maybe they know. Maybe they're pretending to play along, but really they're waiting to catch her out."

He nods in agreement. "When did you get so sensible?"

I laugh and kiss him on his forehead.

"Go in and straight back out again," he says. "Don't get into any trouble."

I get out of the car and lean in through the open door. "I've been trouble since the day I was born," I echo his phrase from earlier, and he laughs.

SIXTY-TWO

I ENTER THE supermarket. It is nine PM. I have two hours until the curfew, and we're ten minutes from my home. I have plenty of time. I can do this. I think of Granddad's gash and I quicken my pace. My heart is pounding as I walk through the store by myself, with all eyes on me. Women pull their children out of my way when I'm near; teenagers stare, call out insulting things to me. Those who recognize me take photographs. One man even follows me for way too long holding his phone up in the air and recording me. Another makes kissing noises near my ear. I keep my head down, I watch the floor, and I stay close to the shelves. So much for going in and out unnoticed. I want to be invisible, but the bright red patch on my arm marks me, as does the scar on my temple. I see another Flawed woman making her way along the supermarket. She is holding hands with a little girl. Somebody kicks the bag from her hand, and the group starts laughing. The woman stops, keeping her child close to her as she bends to put everything back in her bag. The group taunts her. The child stares at them with big sad eyes, while her mother is on her hands and knees picking up rolling fruit.

I hug the walls, keep my chin down. I need to get out of here drama-free. I can't afford the extra attention. I feel like a rat scuttling along the gutter, getting under everybody's feet, in everybody's way. My eyes fill, and I let my tears fall, but nobody asks me if I'm okay, because nobody cares, which hurts even more.

I make my way to the cash register. I keep my eyes down. I hear my name on some passerby's lips. I don't look up. I don't want any trouble.

"Hey!" I hear a man call angrily. I keep my head down. It can't be directed at me; I have done nothing wrong.

I study the cotton pads, antiseptic, and bandages and focus on the branding: the swirl of the writing; the happy little cotton ball characters on the packet, with arms and legs and smiling faces. Everything has been given a soul in advertising. Yet the soul is being taken from people. Humanizing objects, dehumanizing people.

"I said, hey!" he yells again.

My heartbeat speeds up. This does not sound good. Slowly, I look up. He's staring at me. As are others. I wonder why the woman at the cash register has slowed down. Why can't she just hurry up so I can get out of here? But I look to her seat and realize she's gone. She is standing away from us. Just as everybody else is doing. Everyone is moving away. A man on my left remains, and so does a man on my right. They are taller than me—I barely reach up to their shoulders—but as I look at them, I understand immediately what the problem is. The flash of red on their armbands is like a warning light right in my face. They are Flawed. Both of them. As am I. Three of us stand together. This is not allowed.

My first reaction is to step away. I have recognized the problem, and now I know the solution. If I step away, then there will be only two. But that is a bad move.

"Stop! Stay right where you are!" The man shouting at me is a policeman.

I step back into line.

"Don't move, Celestine," the man on my right says gently. "It will be okay."

"You know me?"

"We all know you." He smiles.

"Don't talk!" the policeman yells again.

"We've got a wild one," the man on my left mutters to us both.

"Back away from the desk, the three of you," he says, panicking. "I need to see you." He is getting himself worked up over nothing. He is young. He is alone. He is making a stupid mistake.

Despite the fact that we are Flawed, and I am in the middle of them, I feel somewhat safe between the two men. I feel protected. They are young, in their thirties, and they are well built. Strong. One has an *F* on his temple, the other I can't see; it could be his chest, hand, foot, or tongue. Perhaps their age and strength are what panics the police officer all the more. They look like they could do some damage. Wide jaws, broad shoulders, big hands. They remind me of Carrick. Soldiers. I have never stood between two Flawed before, and now I know why we are not allowed. It gives us strength. Security in numbers. They don't want us to feel safe. They don't want us to have power.

"We were just standing in a line," I finally say, annoyed by the crowd that has gathered to watch this. I feel like an animal in a zoo. I need to get back to Granddad, who is waiting for me in the car, bleeding. "I'm buying cotton balls." I lift the package up to the police officer. "Nothing dangerous is happening here."

A few people snigger at my joke.

The police officer's face reddens. "There are three of you standing together. This is against the law."

"It's not a law," I say, and the two Flawed men look at me in surprise.

I'm more surprised that the police officer doesn't know this.

"It's just a rule that an organization enforces with punishment. It's not *law*. You can't put me in prison for standing beside these two men. You are a police officer, not a Whistleblower. Your job is to work with communities to protect and serve."

"Yeah, protecting us from you," a man shouts out from the crowd.

"No," I disagree. "Your job is to protect and serve *me*," I say to the policeman. "I am a part of this community."

"I won't serve you, *Flawed*," he snarls, like I'm diseased.

He is a police officer—a member of a force I once trusted, admired, felt protected by. I think of the people who have hissed at me on my walk here today, the children who have been pulled out of my path. I think of the lack of eye contact. The anger rises. Nothing makes sense.

I am a girl of definitions, of logic, of black and white.

"HARP!" I shout at the police officer, feeling the anger fully within me now. I learned this at school. I learned all this. Why doesn't he know these basic principles that I was taught, that he was surely taught, too? Why doesn't anybody in the real world do what we're taught? *"H is for honesty,"* I say, hearing the tremble in my voice, not from fear but from anger. I try to control it. "Being honest and ethical and adhering to the principles of fairness and justice. That's what a police officer must do. *A* is for accountability. Accepting individual responsibility and ensuring public accountability."

There is a rumble in the crowd. I continue, not moving my eyes from his.

"*R* is for respect! Having respect for people, their human rights and their needs."

Members of the crowd start to mumble in agreement. The police officer steps closer to me. He lifts his receiver to his mouth and calls for backup.

"Watch it now," the man to my left says quietly.

The police officer is standing right before me now with a sneer on his face.

"Let them go," somebody calls from the crowd.

"Yeah, they're not doing any harm. They're just shopping."

People begin calling out their opinions, which I see panics him some more. Beads of sweat break out on his forehead. He is beginning to lose control. He is badly outnumbered.

"She's the girl from the TV, the famous one," someone calls out. "You can't arrest her."

"The girl who has five brands."

The police officer narrows his eyes as they wander over me, and it registers with him who I am. He looks afraid of me.

"She's the most Flawed of all," someone else shouts, and others call for him to shut up. The people in the crowd are beginning to argue among themselves.

The police officer lifts the baton from his hip belt.

"Whoa, now," the man to my right says. "What are you going to do with that?"

"You keep quiet," he says, sweat on his upper lip now.

"She's just a child," a woman calls out. "For the love of God, would you all leave her alone."

Her desperate cry introduces a whole new wave of emotion.

"And you"—he looks at me menacingly—"need to keep your mouth shut. Understand?"

I take a deep breath. I'm not finished. It would be logical to at least finish what I was saying before the inevitable happens. Granddad will know something has happened if I'm not back outside in three minutes. He will know to start the engine and get out of here. Whatever he did in the past will give him that gut instinct.

"Professionalism," I say, finally, gently, just to the police officer. "Providing a professional policing service to *all* communities."

He looks over my shoulder, and I twist my body around to see what he's looking at, but there's nothing behind me. By the time I realize he was trying to trick me, he brings the baton down and hits me across the back of my legs. I crumple and go down. The antiseptic bottle smashes as it hits the ground.

It's almost as if there is a second when everybody takes a moment to make a decision, to pick a side, to figure out who it is one really is. And then the riot begins.

SIXTY-THREE

THE FEET I see standing around us, once observers, are now in on the act. They suddenly take flight, and they are everywhere. Some are on me, trampling me, some are doing their best to block for me, but every time I try to get up, I am swiftly brought back down to earth again. With a bang, with a knock, winded, I lie on the ground, hands covering my head, waiting for the black spots in my vision to clear. I feel hands trying to pull me up, hands trying to push me down. I can barely breathe. Then I hear the whistles. The Whistleblowers have arrived, and I see black leather boots descending on the scene. Some people run away, more people hear about what's happening and join in. I see fists flying, blood spraying. I don't even know who is on whose side anymore. At one point, when I manage to see straight, I think I see Enya Sleepwell standing at the door of the supermarket, watching. But I have been knocked on the head too many times, and I know I'm seeing things. I give up trying to fight, trying to stand, and, instead, I lie down as I feel another blow to my head as a boot steps backward, not knowing I'm there, and I feel the leather on my cheek. Then it's all a blur.

I hear noises and then I hear nothing. A buzzing in my ear seems to block out most of the sound. I'm on the ground, and then I'm floating, and I wonder if I'm dead, if this is what it's like to rise toward the light. But the light is only the strip lighting of the supermarket, and I realize I'm alive, but I'm flying. Then I feel hands around my body, large, comforting, safe. Those hands place my arms around his neck. I feel flesh. My head rests on a chest. I feel flesh on my cheek. I focus on the chest and see an *F*, just like mine, below the clavicle, where a T-shirt has been ripped in the fight. A Flawed man is carrying me. He smells good, of clean sweat and something else I can't place, but I feel safe. He carries me like I'm a baby, and I cling to him, turning my head to his chest, my head resting beneath his chin to block out the light that hurts my eyes. As we move, I run my fingertip over the *F* on his chest, which makes us stop moving. I have never felt anybody else's scar. It feels like mine. Five of mine, but not like the final one on my spine. The one that was done without any anesthetic, which made me jump and the sear moved, smudged. I see his large Adam's apple move as he gulps at my touch. I allow my finger to rest there on his chest. Even though he's a stranger, the feel of the brand is comforting, like my own skin.

I know immediately who this is. I move my head away from his chest and look upward and see that he's looking down at me.

Carrick.

With his intense eyes, worried and concerned as I smile at him. Carrick, who I only ever really saw through glass. There's no glass now. Despite the madness around us, he returns my smile.

"I told you I'd find you."

And we float away, away from the light, away from the sound.

SIXTY-FOUR

I WAKE UP with a groan, feeling raw from head to toe. I'm in my bed, in my house. It is dark apart from the light from the landing shining through the gap in the door. It takes a moment for my eyes to adjust to the gloom, but soon I can make everything out. There is no one in the chair beside my bed. I am still wearing the clothes I was wearing earlier. It is night outside, which means only a few hours have passed since I remember being awake. The events in the supermarket come back to me in a rush, and I think of Granddad, of his waiting outside for me and of his bleeding wound. I need to get my phone to call him, to make sure he escaped safely, but voices downstairs stop that thought.

The voices are low and urgent. Then I hear Mom's voice, quick and pleading, higher and faster than usual, and it is quickly talked over by someone else. I recognize the voice, but it can't be. *Crevan, downstairs!* I must be dreaming. He wouldn't be here, in this house. I try to sit up but groan again. My stomach is sore; my ribs must be broken, at least one of them. My hand goes to my stomach and I feel a bandage wrapped around me. I swing my legs out of bed. I'm dizzy. I wait with closed eyes for the floor to stop spinning, for the nausea to pass.

I see water beside my bed and gulp it down. I manage to stand, feeling an ache everywhere, in every muscle. I don't remember getting home, though I remember the floating sensation in the supermarket, being held by Carrick, feeling so comfortable and safe in his arms. His smiling at me, my resting my head against his chest and closing my eyes. After that, my memory is gone, and I wonder, did I imagine him? Was he real?

My door opens, and Juniper steps inside. There is panic on her face, and I know something is very wrong. "Celestine, you're awake."

"What's wrong?" I think of Granddad being left behind and prepare for the worst.

Her breathing is fast. "Crevan is here. Downstairs. He's threatening Mom and Dad. He says Dad will lose his job and they will be imprisoned if they don't hand you over right now."

My mouth falls open.

"He's going to call the Whistleblowers to take you away if they don't bring you downstairs themselves, but I don't believe him. He would have called them by now himself. He's up to something. I think he just wants to take you somewhere himself. What does he want to do with you, Celestine? Do you know? Is it about Art? He asked them where the video is. They don't know what he's talking about. Do you? He says you have it and he needs it."

I look at her, feeling dizzy, confused. He knows about Mr. Berry's video. *How?* He thinks *I* have it. I need to speak with Pia. She's the only person who knew about it other than Mr. Berry and Carrick. She was the one searching for it. Suddenly I'm worried for her. I haven't heard from her in days. Then I remember my phone call with Mr. Berry's husband. Crevan must have been listening in. My phone was bugged.

"Mom and Dad are trying to talk him out of taking you. He says you were at a Flawed rally this evening. And then caused a riot at the supermarket. Two people died. The police fired tear gas. It's all over the news. There are riots on the streets. The media are blaming you.

314

Somebody filmed it, but Celestine, my God, Celestine." Her eyes fill up, and she starts crying. "I watched it, and I am so proud of you. I could never have said what you said, could never have done what you've done. The court, the chamber, the supermarket . . . I don't know how you've done it, but you're amazing, and I'm so proud of you. He says he'll drop the charges if you give him the video."

I shake my head, confused by all this, still dizzy, head pounding.

Juniper tries to compose herself, realizing now is not a time for her emotions, the urgency back. "I've packed you a bag. Crevan is in the library with Mom and Dad. You can slip out the back door. The man who carried you home left this for you." She pushes a note into my hand. "Don't lose it, Celestine. He wanted to help you. He knows people who can help you. Find him, okay? Promise me you'll find him. Then I know you'll be okay." She runs her hand over my face and cries again. "My brave little sister, I've missed you. I will miss you."

My mind is racing with all that she has said. I have to go away? I have to leave my family to protect them. Crevan knows about the video of the sixth branding in the chamber. He thinks that I have it—he *knows* that I have it—only I have no idea where it is, but he will never believe that. He will not give up until he finds it, and I must move to safety until I can figure out my next move.

"The curfew," I say.

"Mary May has been already. It's after eleven. If Mom and Dad can keep Crevan at bay, you have until morning before anyone realizes. Celestine, I love you." Juniper is crying. "I'm so sorry for how everything has turned out between us."

I make a move to walk away. I can't hear this now.

She reaches out and holds my arm tight. "Please listen to me. I need to explain. I need you to know what's been going on."

I slowly turn around, ready to hear the worst, prepared to hear about her and Art. My worse fears realized.

"Nothing happened with Art," she says, tears rolling down her face.

"He contacted me for help. He needed someone to help him hide out in the sheds, bring him food. He didn't want you knowing because he didn't want you to get into any trouble. He knew his dad would hurt you to find out where he was, and he knew you were being watched. He made me promise not to tell you, but some days, I swear, Celestine, I was so close to telling you. I should have. He was locked up most days, hiding in the Tinders' shed, and so at night we met to talk about you. About how we both felt we'd let you down. Neither of us could live with it. He was the only person who could understand how I felt. That's all it was, honestly. I was trying to help him, keep him safe for you." She sniffs. "I'm so sorry."

I breathe a sigh of relief that there was nothing more between them, that they were genuinely trying to protect me, even if it still feels like a betrayal. We hug tightly, as if we never will again.

"I've always been so jealous of you, always," she continues. "You were always so perfect. You always did everything right, said everything right. Everybody liked you. I was jealous of your perfection. And now I'm jealous that you're Flawed. It should have been me who did what you did on the bus. I wanted to. I thought about it all the time. But even when it came to it, I wasn't brave enough, another thing I couldn't do. I'm so sorry."

"You can't blame yourself for what happened on the bus," I say, and I mean it. "It was all my own doing. None of this is your fault. I never asked for either of you to save me. You couldn't have. The three of us would be in the same situation that I'm in right now. You didn't do anything wrong." I don't want to dwell on the Art issue now. I need time to find the right words.

"No," she interrupts me, firmly. "I chickened out. I relive it every second of every day. I should have backed you up on the bus." She wipes her cheeks, an air of bravery in it, the little soldier. "But now I'm doing the right thing. The brave thing. You have to go, Celestine, or else Crevan will take you away, and I don't know where that will be."

"Thank you," I whisper, squeezing her hands in mine. "The man who brought me here. Do you know his name?"

"Carrick Vane."

I smile. I didn't imagine him, I didn't dream him.

"Does he mean something to you?"

I nod and remember the feel of his seared chest beneath my finger as he carried me away from danger, see his Adam's apple at the tip of my nose.

"Will you find him?"

"Yes," I say, full of confidence now, not able to think about the fact that I am leaving my family, going into the unknown alone. I think of how Professor Lambert quoted Pólya, "If you can't solve a problem, then there is an easier problem you can solve: Find it." I can't take down Crevan all by myself, not now, but I will have to find Carrick Vane. It is all I have now.

SIXTY-FIVE

I TIPTOE DOWN the stairs as quietly as I can, knowing one false move will be the end of me. Once downstairs, I hear the raised voices of my dad and Crevan, Dad going at him full throttle. I want to burst in there and stop Dad, afraid that he'll be next in the firing line for protecting me, but I know I can't. It won't help anything in the long term. My only way to end this is to reveal Crevan to the world.

"Go," Juniper whispers loudly, and I feel her pushing me.

I stare at the door to the library, unable to leave Mom and Dad in this situation, feeling frozen on the spot. If I leave, they could be punished, accused of aiding me. If I give in and stay, they will be safe. The door suddenly opens and Juniper grabs my hand. Both of us freeze. It's all over.

Instead of Crevan, Mom steps outside, face pale but angry. She has a new undercut hairstyle, one side of her hair has been shaved close to her head, the other side still a reminder of her long, beautiful waves. She looks like a warrior. She sees me with the packed bag, ready to leave, and she closes the library door firmly behind her. I know she won't let me leave and I will have to try to convince her. She rushes to me, throws her arms around me, and covers me in kisses. She whispers one word close to my ear that leaves no question in my mind and goose bumps on my skin.

"Run."

With tears almost blinding me, I leave her side, feeling torn from her, ripped at the seams. I clamber over our backyard wall. I stay low and run to reach the lane, which will lead me up the hill to the summit hidden from view.

A car appears from around the corner, lights on full, and heads toward me. It stops me in my path. I'm not sure whether it's going to stop; and with its headlights on, I can't see who's driving. But I fear whoever it could be intends on running me over. I don't recognize the car, though it is brand-new, expensive. It stops inches from me. The headlights are still so bright I can't see who's behind the wheel. I think about turning around and running, but I know Crevan is in the other direction. I am so close to the lane that will hopefully take me to freedom, the lane I used to take to see Art on the summit, when life was simpler.

The driver's door opens, and Judge Sanchez gets out. My heart races.

"Nice evening for an escape, Ms. North," she says, coolly.

"What do you want?"

"I want what you want," she says. "We have something in common."

"I doubt that," I say, bitterly.

"To bring Crevan down."

I'm shocked by that admittance, but, of course, I shouldn't be. She was trying throughout my entire case to undermine him. She was just using me to do it.

"I hear you know something about him that could be beneficial to both of us. Something that's making him awfully nervous, sending out groups of Whistleblowers here, there, and everywhere. I don't know what it is, but I'm hoping you can tell me."

"What makes you think I can trust you?" I'm panicking. I need to get away from this. I need to escape. My family can't hold Crevan back from searching the house for me for much longer, and if it's true that I'm being held responsible for both the rally and the riot in the supermarket, then the Whistleblowers and the police will be here to take me away. I hope the police find me first, but Crevan won't let me get away from him that easily.

"You can trust me. I'm going to let you go," she says, and I am totally confused. "You're not much use to me in Crevan's control. I can see the damage you can do when you're free. You've really shaken him up, and he's making more mistakes than usual. Do you know what it is you have over him?" she asks, curiously. I can tell that it's killing her, not knowing what it is that I know.

I swallow hard, thinking about it, and then finally nod.

She smiles, a small, sly smile. "Who'd have thought it would be you." She looks me up and down. "You know, I believe in the Guild, a public inquiry, inquiring into matters of urgent public importance, but I don't believe in how it's being used now," she says, eyes hard and focused on mine. "I was trying to help you in the court case, Celestine. You should have taken the prison sentence. Did you like the little show I arranged for you to hear at the castle? I thought witnessing a branding would scare you out of going through with it, that you'd just admit to aiding a Flawed."

It was *she* who arranged for Tina to have a meeting so that Funar could force me and Carrick to sit outside the Branding Chamber.

"If you help me, I can do something about that band around your arm." She roots in her pocket with black leather gloves and produces a card. "I'll let you run away, Celestine, but contact me when you're ready, and we can help each other."

It's almost too good to be true, but I slowly reach for the card, take it hesitantly, and inch away from her, waiting for someone to jump out from hiding and grab me, but nobody does. I keep moving, quickening my pace. She watches me and then gets back into her car. She starts up the engine and reverses.

I follow my mother's advice.

I run.

ACKNOWLEDGMENTS

FOR THE PAST twelve years, I've been writing one novel every year, which is a difficult-enough pace to keep up with. But in the summer of 2014, when I had finished editing *The Year I Met You* and should have been recharging my brain for my next novel, *The Marble Collector*, the premise for *Flawed* arrived in my mind and wouldn't go away. Celestine North arrived in my life and wouldn't go away. I have never experienced such a rush of adrenaline, have never written with my heart so much in my throat, with such a trembling hand, and have never written a novel so quickly. I had to get this story out of me, whether people wanted to read it or not. Six weeks later, *Flawed* was finished. For that, I thank David, Robin, and Sonny for your love and patience while I wrote, and my mom, dad, sister, and brother-in-law for your encouragement in my writing about this subject matter. Thank you, Marianne Gunn O'Connor and Vicki Satlow for your guidance and encouragement and for believing this isn't just a story for myself, but one that could be shared.

I wrote *Flawed* in six weeks, and there was inevitably a lot of editing required. A *lot* more than six weeks' work. The story would not be what it is now if it weren't for the clever insights and support of Jean Feiwel, Anna Roberto, and Will Schwalbe at Macmillan. Your input raised this story to a new level, making it faster, bigger, better, deeper.

I wrote this story with anger, with love, with passion; every word and sentiment came from the heart. If there's one message that I hope this book portrays, it's this: None of us are perfect. Let us not pretend that we are. Let us not be afraid that we're not. Let us not label others and pretend we are not the same. Let us all know that to be human *is* to be flawed, and let us learn from every mistake made so we don't make them again.

Thank you for reading this FEIWEL AND FRIENDS book.

The friends who made

possible are:

JEAN FEIWEL, Publisher

LIZ SZABLA, Editor in Chief

RICH DEAS, Senior Creative Director

HOLLY WEST, Associate Editor

DAVE BARRETT, Executive Managing Editor

NICOLE LIEBOWITZ MOULAISON, Senior Production Manager

ANNA ROBERTO, Associate Editor

CHRISTINE BARCELLONA, Associate Editor

EMILY SETTLE, Administrative Assistant

ANNA POON, Editorial Assistant

Follow us on Facebook or visit us online at mackids.com.

OUR BOOKS ARE FRIENDS FOR LIFE.